SLEEPERNET

MIKE MCCOOL

All characters appearing in this work are fictitious. Any resemblance to real persons, living or dead, is purely coincidental.

PROLOGUE

Really, what we want now, is not laws against crime, but a law against insanity.

--Mark Twain

Chapter 1

July 2084 - One and a half years ago

The decrepit medical frigate materialized in the fog, its running lights reflecting red and green in the misty air. A pulsing signal lamp flashed weakly from the conn tower. The water around it glowed a sickly yellow, waving lazily in the current. The warped deck sprouted frayed cables, adding to the sense of decay.

I rolled the Cavallino to one side, circling the refurbished vessel just outside their sensor range. The car responded nimbly to my touch, slicing through the cloudy air. I concentrated on the visual boosters in my grav suit to get a better look. The sensor-enhanced image clarified as I ramped up my focus, narrowing in on the target.

The ship had started its existence as a military grade stealth cruiser. Dual hulls plowed through the water in front, rising into an octagonal deck designed for medevac landings. The trapezoidal bridge hunkered low behind the deck. The hooded conn lights and main gun resembled a sniper waiting in cover. Bulbous aftermarket weapon pods blistered around the deck's rim, clashing with the otherwise angular design.

Although the fusion reactor and desalination plants would last for decades, the rest of the ship was in terrible disrepair. The black and gray camouflage wore thin where it hadn't been scraped off entirely. Some armor panels were simply missing. Carnivorous barnacles packed themselves shell to shell on the hulls, their barbed tongues dragging the water in a luminescent halo around the edges of the ship. They looked like long hair flowing around a swimming head.

I focused the sensors to see through the landing pad, using a combination of field effects to examine the hospital section below. Around thirty people occupied the medical bay in various states of distress. A supervisor sat in an office nearby, reclining in a sleepernet chair. She lost herself in a virtual concert, eyes closed and body relaxed. Her feet twitched as she danced in the mental simulation. A medical bot monitored the patient beds, tending to their various needs as they occurred.

Inside the bridge, the boss conducted business on one holographic display while watching something depraved on the other. I had trouble locking onto his sleepernet connection. I tried to pull more resolution from the business display, but couldn't get a good signal. Still too far away.

Back in the car, Sleeper Titan appeared in the holographic projector between the seats. He wore his usual tuxedo, hands clasped behind his back. He inclined his diamond-like head in my direction. "Congratulations, sir. You have found the target."

I let go of my concentration. The boosters bled heat into an exhaust system behind the seats. "It only took, what, eight months?"

"Important things take time, of course."

I shrugged. “If it was easy, everyone would be doing it, I suppose.”

I pulled back on the wheel, flooring the accelerator. The nose pitched up. The fusor snarled with a harmonic roar, pushing me back into the seat as I accelerated away.

Titan projected a course map in front of me. “I would suggest coming in from the following heading at the indicated speed. Once you drop from the vehicle, you should fall in an unpowered dive with only minor visibility risk. Your landing will take you directly behind this missile cluster. There is an access tunnel that leads to the lower deck from there.”

I looked over his plan, running it forward and backward to study the details. I rotated the model absentmindedly. “Are they running active detection equipment?”

“Their stealth, what remains of it, dictates a need to use passive sensors only. On inspection, I am uncertain that their active equipment is functional in any meaningful capacity.”

I scanned the data inside the ship, looking for defense machines or guards. There were a few derelict bots scattered about. “Seems poorly protected on the inside.”

“Given how long it has taken us to discover the ship’s location, protection from boarders might be considered an expensive redundancy.”

I examined the medical charts of the various patients, clenching my fist unconsciously at their various states of decay. One was almost certainly near death. Another struggled weakly, apparently freshly captured. Serum filled the storage vats behind them to half capacity, enough to supply a dozen users for several years.

The office supervisor continued twitching in her sleepernet trance, fully immersed in the world of the concert. It contrasted strangely with the unimaginable suffering she oversaw in the next room.

I pitched the car to the approach vector, setting the desired speed. "Guess I'd better be going then."

Titan straightened in the display. "Good hunting, sir."

"That's the plan."

I grabbed the handles in the ceiling, pressing the switch to open the hatch underneath the seat. The chair folded away gracefully. The floor irised open, filling the cockpit with the sound of rushing air. I took the weaponizer staff off my back with one hand, letting it drop out the hole.

Taking a deep breath, I let go of the handles, falling into the wind like a human projectile. The force of the air spun me into a headfirst dive. I caught the staff, forming a shield bubble at the tip. I dropped toward the ocean. I concentrated on the visual boosters again, seeing the trawling ship burbling along obliviously. I shifted my body and the staff to refine my trajectory.

Sooner than I would have thought possible, the rotting ship rushed up to meet me. I rotated to a feet-first approach, briefly scanning the defenses. It looked like Titan had spoofed them all.

I flared the grav boosters on landing, slamming into the hull in a preprogrammed crash. Bright orange light exploded from the boosters, reflecting sharply in the foggy air before darkening again. I ended up kneeling in a small dented crater behind the missile cluster, leaning on my staff. After checking to make sure I'd landed undetected, I vented heat from the suit. Dense cold air blasted across the heat sinks, turning into a noisy rush of steam behind me. The overwhelming roar of the barnacles churning the sea muffled the sound.

I switched to flashing with Titan, allowing us to trade thoughts silently.

"I'm in."

Titan flashed a sense of accomplishment. *"Well done, sir. The hatch is approximately three meters to your left."*

Not surprisingly, years of built-up cruft had rusted the hatch shut. I formed a plasma scythe on the tip of the staff. I could focus the blade into any shape, fitting the contours of a cut down to the millimeter range. I carefully sliced off only the crusty parts of the hatch. It cracked open with an audible pop.

The access tube inside had once been pristine white with brushed luminum trim. The style was fashionable twenty years ago but looked dated now. This particular example of the trend hadn't aged well. Mold and filth grew on the surfaces. The old luminum glowed an anemic orange instead of the bright blue it once produced. I felt dirty just looking at it.

I dropped down the tube, landing on the deck below with a soft thump. The hallways were narrow, in roughly the same shape as the access tunnel. I wondered if the ship had spent some time as a yacht before it fell into criminal hands. The layout was relatively simple, with a circular hallway leading around the rim of the sick bay. It was easy to find the forward entrance to the chamber.

I hugged the wall next to the double sliding doors, reaching into my visual boosters. I spent some time looking through the doors into the room itself. Everything looked clear. The office was in the back, its occupant still enjoying her concert.

I eased the doors open, slipping inside. Here, the walls were clean and white. The fresh luminum trim glowed a pleasing white-blue. It still looked dated, but at least it wasn't disgusting.

The rows of beds were filled to capacity. The hair-sized carbon microtubes attached to all thirty occupants throbbed slightly with the fluid they harvested. Bile rose in the back of my throat. The living patients shivered sporadically on the beds, more so if they hadn't been here as long. Their eyes were open but vacant, showing a state of semi-consciousness.

The idea that they might be aware in any way while their brain tissue dissolved sickened me. Did they feel the absence as memories of life and loved ones were stripped away one at a time? Could they sense the difference in their emotions as the facets of their personality disappeared piece by piece? How long until they faded into nothingness, all so that some ghoulish old freak could spend one more year cheating death?

Physically, the distillation process caused their hair and fingernails to grow at a phenomenal rate. It also siphoned the muscles and pigment from their bodies, turning the longer-term victims white and skeletal. You could see the progression in their hair, which was colored at the tips but slowly turned chalky the closer it got to their head. Their irises faded to red as swollen blood vessels overwhelmed the disappearing pigment. Combined with the muscle loss and pale skin, it made them look like terrified skeletons.

I gripped my staff angrily, making my way between the beds. The medical bot turned from tending the agitators in the serum vats. I slammed a shutdown hack on its brain with a forceful thought, resisting the urge to destroy it completely. It made a startled yelp, gibbering a bit before crashing into a jumbled pile.

I stepped into the office, towering over the supervisor in her sleepernet trance. She looked young, although that could be deceiving. Her blonde hair flopped jauntily in pigtails on either side of her head. Her lab coat was open to the waist, maximizing the view of the animated tattoo between her breasts. The expensive color-shifting ink displayed a stylized beating heart pulsing through a riot of colors. Her nail polish thrummed along with it.

Her virtual concert reached its climax. I couldn't help myself. I knew how this particular simulation ended, so I grabbed her debugging stream. I eased into her feed, making some alterations.

The concert featured a boy band called the People's Republic of Cowboys. The five members, each chosen to represent a particular caricature of personality, strutted around onstage wearing ruby cowboy hats and golden dragons. The leader, whose name I couldn't remember and couldn't be bothered to look up, raised the microphone.

"Tonight we have a very special guest." His accent was a fascinating mix of Mandarin and Southern drawl, mesmerizing in how naturally they flowed together. "I think she knows who we're talking about. Tasha, come up on stage!"

The spotlights focused on the young office manager in the crowd. Tasha clasped her hands to the animated heart on her chest. "Me?" She looked around incredulously, unable to believe they had chosen her. The crowd lifted her, carrying her to the stage while she squealed with delight. They deposited her in the middle of the band. The singers circled her, turning her to face the audience.

"Yes, tonight, folks, we have a genuine mass murderer in our midst!"

The crowd went bananas. It took her a moment to parse what he'd said.

Her face fell. "Wait. What?"

He looked at her quizzically. “Perhaps you’d rather be known for your work torturing their minds beforehand?”

The cheers from the audience deafened everyone once again. The band surrounded her more tightly, as if trapping a startled animal.

She tried to squirm out of their grasp. “What are you talking about? What’s going on?”

The leader tipped his hat at her. “Why, the vampire juice, of course! Should we call it Lazarus serum? Perhaps you prefer life extension treatments.”

The band all smiled at her at once, displaying the characteristic dripping misshapen teeth of long-time serum users. “Give yourself a hand.”

Tasha startled herself out of the simulation, bolting awake on the chair. She found me leaning over her in my shrouding cloak, plasma scythe crackling with energy.

I let her get a good look at the skull-like mask under my hood. “Morning.”

Chapter 2

Tasha had just enough time to scream before I hit her with a neuromagnetic pulse. The nemp blast knocked her out cleanly for up to six hours.

I made my way out of the office, waking up the medical bot. It wobbled uncertainly to its feet, rubbing its head.

I pointed my staff at it. "You."

It beeped its confusion at me.

"Yes, you. Put her in that open bed and keep her sedated."

The bot buzzed inquisitively.

"She's not your supervisor. I am until further notice. Disconnect these other patients from the serum tubes and keep them comfortable. Do you understand?"

It swayed uncertainly, so I punched it in the head with more programming. "I said, do you understand?"

It perked up noticeably, nodding and tipping a nonexistent hat at me. It trundled to the office to bundle up Tasha and put her to bed.

I strode to the aft doors, heading to the elevator. I sent a flash to check in with Titan. *"Has the big guy noticed I'm here yet?"*

Titan paused before answering. *"Not at present. He appears to be quite distracted by his displays. I have programmed the elevators for silent running. I have also prevented him from disconnecting from his credentials. Once you make physical contact, I will be able to extract the information from his datastream."*

I stepped into the elevator, pressing the button for the bridge. The doors closed with a quiet bong. As always, I felt mildly ridiculous doing something as mundane as riding an elevator in a combat grav suit.

The doors opened on the command deck. In contrast with the rest of the ship, opulent dark brown butterwood paneling covered the walls. Dark red drapes covered the bridge windows. Various shiftsilver sculptures rested on pedestals, displaying stylized antique nautical instruments.

Behind the luxurious crystalwood desk, my old informant Donnie looked up, startled to see me. He desperately tried to shut down his suddenly unresponsive displays.

I wasn't entirely surprised to see him behind this particular operation, but it was a new low. He stood up, knocking his chair back into the wall. His voice grated on my nerves, sounding like an anthropomorphic rodent.

"Hey! You. Uh. Hi! Wow! What a pleasant surprise. Ha, ha. Wasn't expecting to see you here!" He ran his hands through his greasy black hair, nervously glancing at the data still scrolling past on his display.

I reached out with my grav boosters, clenching an invisible fist around his collar. I yanked him across the room, holding him up to inspect his face. My eyes flashed bright orange on my mask.

His bloodshot eyes darted around wildly. He licked his lips with a wet wriggling noise. "Looking good, there, pal! Is the eye flash new? Got to say, very intimidating. From one professional to another, that's really well done. Fits with this whole grim reaper thing you got goin' on."

I used the tip of my staff to open his mouth and inspect his teeth. Sure enough, his upper teeth were misshapen pointed lumps in his mouth, dripping downward like stalactites. Lowering his collar, I found the characteristic red scars on his neck from the serum injection sites. Vampire juice.

I pulled his face close. He might have wet himself in fear. It was hard to tell, what with the rest of the body odor. "I come in here to find you not just using but selling? I'm disappointed in you, Donnie. I thought we had an agreement."

His black eyes darted around my face. "Oh, oh, you mean this? Oh, this is all just a misunderstanding. Ha, what a terrible misunderstanding! No, I'm just watching this place for a friend."

I hurled Donnie back across his desk. He crashed into his chair, landing with a startled gasp. He scrambled to get back to his feet.

With a flick of a grav booster, I shoved him down again. "You lie to my face when you know I can see the truth right there in your datastream? I'm even more disappointed now, which hardly seems possible."

"Look, well, okay, maybe I kind of took it from someone who wasn't really a friend. And maybe, just maybe, I might've gotten a little carried away. But we're buddies, right? Old partner? Friend? I can feed you information, right? Just like the old days!"

I towered over his desk. "Start talking and we'll see how charitable I'm feeling."

"Okay. Okay. Well." He licked his lips, looking away briefly. "You're not gonna like this, but word on the street is that your boss is dirty."

"The street, you say."

He perked up when he realized I hadn't immediately shut him down. "Yeah. Yeah, man. Your old pal and Sleepernet Chief Executive Hero Reggie Talbot's been doin' illegal stuff with the government, man. Ain't you never wondered why you vigilantes are allowed to run free while the military wonders what it'd be like to get their hands on a sleeper supercomputer?"

"That's his job. To keep the government out of private matters."

His gaze flicked to the side of my head and back again. "Yeah, man, but don'cha think he's a little too good at it?"

Titan flashed a warning. *"On your left, sir."*

I sensed the micromissile bot hovering behind me, firing its missiles. Booster-assisted reflexes took me out of the way of a dozen intelligent warheads. They streaked through the space previously occupied by my head. The warhead systems were simple enough to reprogram. I let six of them brush their exhaust across the left half of Donnie's face on the way past. The other six lightly burned the right half of his face.

I sent them back to the robot that fired them without bothering to turn around. The drone made a startled shriek, turning to flee before exploding into a clattering heap behind me.

Donnie screamed, clutching his cheeks. He looked down at his hands in terror. "My face! You burned my face!"

I reached across the desk with my staff, pushing his head back up by his chin. The burn marks looked like whiskers. "Quit wasting my time. I come in here looking for useful information and you try to sell me some half-baked garbage about a guy I've known for a decade and a half? Thought you were smarter than that."

"Hey man, I ain't the one with the truth fetish here. I'm in it for the money. If it was true, wouldn'cha wanna know about it?"

"Try harder. And if you try to kill me again, I cannot overstate how catastrophically disappointed I will be."

He rubbed his face uncomfortably. "Well, okay then, how 'bout my customer list? Bet you wanna know who's illegally extending their life, am I right?"

"Again, I need to remind you that I can see your datastream."

"Yeah, man, but ain't no personal information in there. Bad for business, you know? All done anonymously through agents. But hey, I tell you what. Let you in on a pretty big secret. One of the guys that buys from me, he's some big huge government honcho. That's right, real mover and shaker. Any time I got me some legal complications, he makes 'em disappear. Almost like he orders the military around, ya know what I'm sayin'?"

"Consider me shocked. Who could have guessed those sorts of people might want to live forever. I don't suppose you have a name? Or an office?"

"Naw, man, ain't like that. Could be the president for all I know. I bet he's at least a member of the Cabinet."

"More rumors without evidence. One more chance."

"Uh. Well. Oh! Hey. How 'bout this. You tap my ship. Classic crime deal, am I right? I sell out to you. You get the big fish, you let me go free. It's one of those win-win sort of deals, ain't it? Don't see those come along too often. No sir."

"Tell me. The thirty people downstairs. How'd they get here?"

He shifted nervously again. "Those chumps? They, uh, volunteered."

"Volunteered."

"That's right. Wanted to kill themselves. We pay off their families or their debt or whatever. They all got their reasons."

"And if they change their minds?"

He guffawed. “Well we ain’t gonna give the money back, that’s for sure.”

I stayed silent long enough for it to become uncomfortable. “So. They volunteer. Come to the ship, get hooked up to the machines. Takes six weeks to finish them?”

“Huh? Naw, man, maybe thirty years ago. Takes about two weeks now. And we ain’t takin’ no babies or children no more neither. Turns out mid-twenties to mid-thirties are best. Only problem is they gotta sorta be awake the whole time.”

“Do they?”

Donnie leaned back, relaxing a bit to talk shop. “Yeah man. All those years of education and experience. You can’t just up and replicate all the energy that went into makin’ that brain, you know? The way I see it, we’re just takin’ all that an’ makin’ sure it don’t go to waste if someone don’t like their life all that much. ‘Sides, you seen the population count lately? Ain’t like we got some kinda people shortage.”

I leaned forward on his desk. A flash of fear returned to his eyes. “Let me get this straight. You want me to put a bug in your shop and watch you torture people to death over a period of no less than fourteen days. Let’s say two months and multiple patients to get any interesting data. Then I get to spend my time trying to trace back through the layers of obfuscation to figure out who the customers might possibly have been, all while these people continue dying. Is that what you’re proposing?”

“Uh. Well, yeah.” He licked his lips again. I wanted to

knock them off his face. “You know. For the greater good.”

I reached out with my boosters, grabbing him by the collar. I yanked him across the desk, dropping him on the floor.

I dragged him toward the elevator. He struggled in my boosted grip. “Hey! Let’s not be hasty here. What’re you doin’?”

“Thinking I might go tie you to the deck.”

He yelped as I hurled him into the elevator, pinning him to the back wall. I stepped inside, turning my back on him. I pressed the button for the landing pad. I briefly savored the ridiculousness of not just riding the elevator in my grav suit, but feeling Donnie squirming on the wall behind me.

He clutched at his collar, trying to loosen the invisible grip. “Wait, wait. What’cha gonna do with the serum? That’s top quality stuff, man, you could make a fortune!”

“Thinking I might feed it to the barnacles.”

His breath exploded out in an expression that was hard to pin down. “The barnacles? What would ya do that for?”

I looked over my shoulder at him, letting my eyes flash. “Hoping they might reach up and eat you off the deck.”

He began struggling in earnest. “That’s it? You’re just gonna leave us to die out here? You can’t do that, man! You ain’t no killer! I know you, you ain’t no killer!”

I leaned in close, trying not to flinch at the smell. “Thought you weren’t a killer either. But here we are. You’re right, though. I don’t think the barnacles will kill you. I’m going to set this ship on autopilot to the biggest media event I can find. Splash it on the news so hard that even your high-powered government buddy can't cover you up. Then I'm going to use your datastream to go after your competitors."

His shocked look proved that I'd hit the mark. I smiled at him. "That's right. I bet there are all kinds of reasons you don't keep customer information around. But competitive analysis? That's another story. Probably enough data in there to find a couple more producers before they wise up. Kind of curious, though. Why didn't you try to sell them out?"

His eyes went so wide I thought they might bulge out of his head. "Are you kidding? Those guys are animals. You got any idea what they'd do to me?"

PART ONE:

ORIGIN

Barring that natural expression of villainy which we all have, the man looked honest enough.

--Mark Twain

Chapter 3

July 2068 - 17 years ago

Kara touched the inducer terminal on her temple to check the time again. "He's late."

I took a sip of my drink. "I can see that, thanks."

"It better be worth it." She stabbed a chunk of buffalump with a pick, dipping it in ranch cheese. A new one appeared from underneath the table as she ate. "Did you have to pick a place that plays nothing but skiphop?"

"We're here because there's a gap in overhead reconnaissance until midnight. Personally I'm more annoyed by the retinal projectors."

Tiny projector beads embedded around the room beamed signals directly into our eyes, augmenting the reality around us. The booth seat in front of us appeared to be bouncing to the beat. Dimples in the red velvet formed smiles as they compressed. The rest of the room danced similarly, giving everything a scent of madness. The walls throbbed in time with the thundering bass.

The other customers appeared to be smiling, having the time of their lives. It was like being inside a threedee commercial. Product logos faced your eyes at all times. Conversation engaged your entire body. Laughter engulfed the table in explosive blasts. Even taking a bite of salad produced a leafy orgasm in your mouth.

The technology had become cheap, which meant that it was springing up everywhere. The safety was questionable at best. For our purposes, it neatly concealed our identities from the other patrons.

Kara put her finger over a tiny spot on my side of the table. The circuit pads on her fingertips glowed as she accessed the network. A short time later, the artificial reality faded in intensity, revealing that the bar and its occupants were just as exhausted and miserable as the rest of us.

A tall man at another table eyed us before turning back to his female companion, who was lost in her own world. It looked like she was playing a game on her inducer terminal. She swiped her fingers in the air, eyes tracking something no one else could see. The man swirled his drink in the glass before tossing it back in one gulp. He sighed at length.

Kara took her hand back. “There. Is that better?”

“Much. Thank you.”

She brushed a lock of blue hair out of her eye. It shimmered gold where she touched it. After her finger passed through, a golden wave crested across her head, turning her hair pink in its wake. The tips that flared out behind her ears sparkled with particular drama.

We spent some time looking around at the mismatch between the haggard expressions of the staff and their manufactured enthusiasm. The next song started, expressing a desperate need for a new kind of cola.

The door opened, letting dirty street light in from the outside. Our guest appeared, stepping into the gloom with a relaxed expression. He had dark hair and intense black eyes. He was shorter than I expected. One of those people that looks larger than life in pictures.

He gave our table code to the hostess. In reality, she gestured in our direction with her nicostick without looking up. In the retinal feed, she gave him directions with eager perkiness.

The man turned, looking at our table. He smiled like someone who'd just won a bet, thanking the hostess. She showed no sign whatsoever that she'd heard anything he said. He strode over confidently.

His smile broadened once he arrived. It was either an easy smile or a practiced demonstration, depending on your interpretation. He stood next to the open bench, hands in pockets. "Hi. I'm Reggie."

I gestured for him to sit down. "Hi. I'm Nathan."

He slid into the other side of the booth, extending a hand to Kara. She reached out to shake his hand. He covered her hand with both of his. "And you must be Kara."

Kara smiled thinly, extracting her hand. "You can call me Ms. Janek. Or Mrs., if you prefer."

He seemed amused by her response. "I didn't realize we were being so formal. Call me Mr. Talbot if you like. Shall I call you Mr. Wainwright?"

I glanced wryly at Kara before answering. "That won't be necessary. Did you have any trouble following my directions? The details are extremely important."

"I'm used to letting my computer drive, so I missed a couple turns. Had to backtrack. But yeah, I did it all." He looked back and forth between us. "Why are you two bouncing around like children at an amusement park?"

Kara made no move to turn off his retinal projector. "We're just so happy to be here. It's hard to contain ourselves."

I considered turning it off myself but changed my mind. "Helps mask our appearance."

He nodded, leaning back. "And will Mr. Jackson be joining us?" He savored every syllable of the word "mister."

Kara's expression turned even more frosty. "Frank couldn't be bothered to show up tonight."

I sighed. "He goes by Flapjack. And he had other engagements this evening. Anyway, let's get down to business."

Reggie crossed his arms, studying us. "Right. I assume you got my message about the, ah, delicate nature of our discussions."

Kara blew through the opening with all the subtlety of an asteroid hitting a satellite. "You mean that what we're talking about is illegal, and possibly as high on the list as treason?"

He laughed, looking away briefly. "That's being a little dramatic, but I guess you could say that. What we're talking about is more like skirting the edge of the law.

Circumnavigating the intent, if not the letter."

Kara brushed her hair from her eye again. It shimmered from gold to purple after she touched it, the flaring tips making it look like a waterfall. "And what makes you think we'd be interested in such a thing?"

"Oh, I'm not saying you are. But you did come here tonight, and you did mask my travel arrangements. That counts for something. Tell you what. How about if I start off with the investor pitch. Nothing illegal in that and we can break the ice."

I shrugged. "Fair enough."

He leaned forward in his seat. "Okay. So we're living in a pretty remarkable time right now. The weather isn't trying to kill us anymore. Climate and biosphere engineering have produced not just an abundance of water, but a wide variety of new and exciting food. We have fascinating new ecosystems to visit and explore. The cyberbiotic cleanup crews are returning more and more of the planet to us. People are relieved. It's finally time to relax."

He gestured to the bar. "That's why you get places like this. Endless meat nuggets. New and experimental drinks. A never-ending party. Look at these people. Well, not here, this is a steaming pile of holographic bull. I mean, look at the world. People want to make the most of the time they have. We can finally turn some of our technological and manufacturing energy toward entertainment. I think we're embarking on the kind of era of escalating consumption and luxury that comes along maybe once a century. This one might be the biggest one we've ever seen, given how far we went into the hole."

Kara twirled a lock of hair in her fingers. It shimmered through various colors while she stared at it. "Kind of too bad the government still owns everything, huh."

Reggie's easy smile reappeared. "That's the beauty of it. President Marconi can't hold on to the private sector forever. Yeah, someone had to take charge when he was elected. Capitalism had given way to full-on corporatism. Congress was paralyzed, puppets of their transnational donors. They held the economy hostage, knowing full well the president would flinch. After a while they didn't even bother to hide their crimes. They more or less dared the feds to arrest them."

Kara stabbed another buffalump nugget. "You're oversimplifying that quite a bit, don't you think?"

"Sorry, it's a pet rant of mine. Hear me out. The world fell apart at a rate no one had predicted or could explain. Stuff that should have taken a century started taking only a couple years. I mean, the ocean was supposed to rise by half a meter by then, not splash around for kilometers. Earthquakes that leveled entire cities? What does that have to do with dumping carbon into the atmosphere? Not saying we were smart, because we weren't. What we did had an effect, and it was clearly snowballing. But that doesn't explain the scope of the catastrophes. Anyway, most leaders reacted by hunkering down and trying to protect what they had instead of trying to fix the problem."

I took a sip of my drink. "Are you getting any closer to making a point? That surveillance hole doesn't last all night."

He was getting animated now. "The point is, people got so desperate, and so afraid of dying, that they were relieved when Marconi stepped in. No one cried when he arrested Congress. He systematically cleaned out two centuries of cruft in the government and relieved private sector profiteers of their ability to keep extorting money. He gave people jobs. Gave them focus. We were America, and we were going to fix the Earth! Anything else was secondary. And you know what? It worked. Astonishingly, it worked."

Kara tossed her hair back again. "With the little speed bump where four of the major world powers dropped nukes on us to try and stop it, sure."

"All visionary thinkers end up terrifying the establishment. That's just how it is. Besides, the n-square retaliation strikes opened the door to atmospheric engineering. Look, the point is, all that stuff did what it needed to do, when it needed to do it. But times have changed. The crisis has passed. People are starting to remember that America has always been about equal opportunity. A place where a guy with a bright idea can get rewarded for his tenacity, ingenuity, and hard work. That means giving resources back to the people. Giving the government back to the people. Real democracy. Marconi tried to throw everyone a bone with his reformed Senate and Supreme Court, but that was ten years ago. They're figureheads with no real power. People yearn for a voice in their government and a free, well-regulated market. He can't fight that wave forever. And when it crests, I'm going to make sure I'm on it."

I looked around the bar. "Sounds almost seditious."

He laughed. "Trust me, we're just getting started. This thing is going to be huge. We need to be in the thick of things, shaping the way people think. A healthy ecosystem of American capitalism isn't just best for us, it's best for everybody. We can change the world and make it a better place for ourselves while we're at it. The best kind of enlightened self-interest."

Kara crossed her arms. "You're talking about a radical shift in federal policy."

"That the best part. I'm not creating the shift. It's already there. Pent-up energy, just looking for a place to explode."

Kara and I traded a look. I decided to take the lead. "Look, I have no way to evaluate whether you're right or wrong. But you sound kind of crazy to me."

"All right, I can see my investor pitch isn't working. That's fine, nobody thinks they might be able to singlehandedly change history until they just go ahead and do it. Let's try something different. Want to know what you'd be working on?"

Chapter 4

Reggie took a moment to compose his thoughts. He leaned forward, clasping his hands on the table. "So the gist of it is, I'm going to pay you to work on the stuff you want to work on anyway. You can make enough money to not have to care about it ever again. Everybody wins. Frankly, I can't believe how well all of this is lining up."

Kara mocked his clasped hands. "Almost sounds too good to be true."

I gestured with my drink. "Don't forget the part where it's probably illegal."

He made a placating gesture. "Not directly illegal. Let's just say the law hasn't quite caught up to the technology yet. I feel like we're getting sidetracked. That's probably my fault. I'll try again. Along with this cultural convergence on a desire for new luxury spending, there's a convergence of technology that I think provides the perfect opportunity to form a business."

He paused. I stared at him. "Go on."

"Okay. Let's start with the first discovery. I have a team of three that has done some breakthrough research on a new kind of exotic matter. You know about quantum entanglement, right? Where subatomic particles are part of a single system, and knowing the state of one, you can know the state of the other, even though both particles can appear to be in both states at the same time?"

Kara rolled her eyes. "Probability clouds are only the fundamental principle of modern computer architecture, so yes. We're familiar with it."

"Sorry. You have to understand, I'm not used to pitching to technology people. This exotic matter that Dr. Khan discovered has this odd and fascinating property that it can entangle itself with any particle system. That means you can have something they call fluid architecture. Practically speaking, you can use it to break the hardware proximity limits. The processors will be somewhere between ten and fifty times more powerful than the old ones. Even better, you can build machines close to a hundred times the size."

I could tell Kara was hiding how intrigued she was. "Can you explain more about this exotic matter?"

Reggie laughed. "No. There's just no way I'd be able to do it justice. I can say that there's a limited amount of it. Khan's worked out the one place in the solar system where it must be. With my connections and funding, he'll finally be able to go look for it."

She deflated a little. "So it might not be there at all."

"Or it might be exactly where he thinks it is. He tried to send up some old Chinese space program probes to go look, but they got shot down by the Americans. Look, I understand it's a bold claim, and I can send you the research once we've reached an agreement. I'm more interested in what you could do with such a machine."

I took a sip of my drink. "We're listening."

He got more intense as he spoke. His voice lost some of its smoothness and gained raw enthusiasm. "You don't just get more computational power. Throw enough particles at the problem and you get an incredible amount of storage, too. Plus more or less unlimited point to point networking. You can have the network talk directly into people's heads. No eavesdropping. No interception. No middlemen or limitations. Just you and the machine."

Kara let out a breath, leaning back. "That's not just skirting the edge of the law. It's openly defying it."

"Maybe. I've studied it quite a bit with some extremely talented lawyers. The feds are relying on fear and intimidation for enforcement. People build the surveillance straight into the hardware largely because they don't know what will happen if they don't. The laws themselves turn out to be conveniently vague to give the government maximum discretion in prosecution, if you get a trial at all. But you can turn that vagueness back on them if you have the ability to drag it into the light."

"What did you have in mind?"

"Okay. So you've got this giant pipeline directly into people's brains. The immediate thing that falls out is a fully immersive virtual reality system, right? All five senses."

This time I was the one trying to hide my interest. "That's been a hard nut to crack. Even if you do get to muck around directly in the mind, what do you do with it? Crafting all that sensory data will never be cost effective. There's too much variation at the level of individual neurons. It's not like your eyes are sending a camera feed into your head."

"Right. So I have another team of three. Their research involves using intercranial implants to synthesize new experiences based on existing memories and sensory data. Using some of the most powerful supercomputers in the world, they've managed to map out a monkey's brain and beam a single new experience directly into it."

Reggie paused to let me think. I stared at the ceiling for a bit. "Interesting. If you can use their own memories, you bypass the problem of creating data for the content. You tell their imagination what you want to simulate, and it builds the experience for you."

He gestured excitedly. "Exactly! And once you have that much computational power and bandwidth, you get a cheap, worldwide, total immersion entertainment network."

"And the target's biology works as another layer of encryption. You can hack the server data all you like. Without the person's brain to translate it, it comes out as gibberish."

Kara shot me a look. "Slow down. You still haven't answered my question. How are you going to force the inevitable criminal complaint to see the light of day?"

He smiled. "Why, in the court of public opinion, of course."

She waited for him to elaborate. Eventually, he did. "Understand, this is the part where I'm taking a certain risk trusting you with my plans. The exotic matter is rare, so I assert that there's not enough to go around. That has the added benefit of probably being true. I use the rising tide of capitalism to argue that we should own all the machines, not the government. I promise to let them tap the servers. When they tap the servers, all they get is personally encrypted nonsense. If I let them tap the servers at all. My plan is a lot bigger than that."

Kara frowned. "There's more?"

"Sure. We're talking about a technological revolution here. Selling people on the idea that we're building the next generation virtual reality system is a straightforward thing to do. But we don't show our cards on just how powerful this system is. Not right away. With the right content, the network will explode in popularity. We get the big stars on board. Make sure people have never seen anything like it. Get people making their own simulations for other people. Independent features, travel experiences, recordings of their kids or pets, that sort of thing. Suddenly, while no one is taking us all that seriously, we've managed to ship a private, encrypted, high-bandwidth network to everyone in the world. We make it so popular that if they try to take it down, they'll have riots on their hands. Crest the public wave."

I shook my head. "And Marconi has you shot dead for treason."

He shrugged. "The automated firing squads are out of fashion. I think they hang people now. The point is, I make it so he can't possibly do such a thing. Not if he wants to hold on to power. Marconi is a savvy politician. Once he catches the tide of public opinion, he's going to figure out a way to keep the system around and use it to his advantage."

Kara grimaced. "Okay, so I caught the part where you want our knowledge about building simulation tools that the public can use. I gathered that you also want content curation tools so people can sift the good stuff from the bad stuff. We've already done that sort of thing. Aside from the scale, did you have some other new and exciting thing in mind for us to do?"

"You make it sound like that's not enough. But you're right, there's more." He looked around the bar reflexively. "I've been hearing these crazy rumors. Seems that someone's been running his mouth about how if he had enough horsepower, he could make an artificial mind that would cross threshold without going insane or murdering everything."

I mentally cursed myself for not making that connection earlier. I paused before replying. "That kind of talk would most certainly be illegal, wouldn't it?"

"In a manner of speaking." He smirked on one side of his mouth. "Let's just say that I've had the aforementioned high-powered legal team looking into it as a purely hypothetical exercise. And let's further suggest that I've heard the substance of the argument and think someone could do it while staying within the boundaries of the law. Do you know anyone who might be willing to expound on those theories?"

I shifted uncomfortably. "Off the record, of course, I've heard those rumors." Mostly because I'd been the one speaking them. "I find myself curious as to how these thoughts made their way to you."

He shrugged. "Interesting ideas have a way of getting around. Maybe you can tell me what you've heard. You never know, maybe I've got it all wrong."

I glanced at Kara. She watched me carefully, eventually giving a nearly imperceptible nod.

I settled back in my chair. "All right. It's hard to imagine how we expect war machines, reference databases, or task bots to become meaningfully self-aware without programming in human reference points. A war machine is always going to have the problem of telling friend from foe. Sooner or later it's going to get it wrong for what appear to be internally consistent reasons. Reference machines have the same issue. They're designed to answer specific questions quickly and correctly. But the larger their dataset becomes, the more they disappear into worlds of their own logic. Hyperintelligent reasoning becomes indecipherable from gibberish. Ultimately, you've built an elaborate tool. Same thing with task bots. We treat them like slave labor. Why would we want those machines to become self-aware?"

Reggie laughed. "Some of them seem a lot closer to sentience than I'm comfortable with."

I shrugged. "That's why we defined threshold. It's a somewhat arbitrary point, but at least it's a line we can draw that says before it reaches this point of development, it's not sentient. After this point, it's a living creature and you better not put it in charge of anything consequential. For a wide variety of reasons, we decided it was illegal to create that kind of life. Either mechanical or biological. Mainly because of the law of unintended consequences. Things we create to be smarter than us in a fundamentally different way have a tendency to go mad."

"But you think you can get around that."

I gave him a level look. "Hypothetically speaking, of course, what I've heard is that maybe we should take some cues from companion software. Of course, I'm a little biased, given that I've written so much of it. Artificial companions are designed to relate to human beings. Done right, their whole purpose in life is to enjoy their interactions with people. We have a pretty good idea how the human brain develops at this point. Why not apply that logic to a synthetic intelligence? They live in a simulation. With enough power, you can give them lives. Experiences outside of work, things to explore. They'd bridge the gap between man and machine perfectly. Sure, you have to deal with inconvenient emotions from time to time. But at least they're emotions you can relate to. They'd be more like smart people overseeing a vast array of intelligent processes than an impenetrable tower of questionable logic."

Reggie stepped into the conversational pause. "So why hasn't anyone done it before?"

I shrugged. "Not enough horsepower. Not enough interest. Federal interference. You know, the usual."

"I can fix that, you know."

My mind reeled with the possibilities. Kara stepped in before I did something even dumber than running my mouth at this total stranger. "We're going to have to think about it. Can wc gct back to you in a couple days?"

I could see from the look on his face that he knew he had me.

He turned his attention back to Kara. "Sure. Take your time." He stood up, giving us both a cordial nod. "You know where to find me."

Chapter 5

One week later

Reggie beamed at me from the open doorway. "Nathan! Thanks for coming by. Step into my office."

"Sure." I stepped in, finding myself mesmerized by the view of the Rocky Mountains. I'd never seen the purplish reflection from the cometary snowpack before. The scintillating light was hypnotic. I stood by the window, soaking in everything I could.

Reggie closed the door, coming over to stand next to me. "Never gets old, does it?"

I tore myself from the window, heading over to take a seat in front of his organic jade desk. "I wouldn't know, really."

"Ha." He flopped down in his chair, propping his feet up. "Would you believe you're the last person I need to convince to take this job?"

"Delightfully phrased. Whether or not I would believe it has nothing to do with whether it's actually true."

"See, that's why I want you to take the lead. The other team members, they're all smart. Hard workers. Professional and personable. But you've studied psychology. Learned the intricacies of the human mind. It interests you. You like to figure out how people work. And that makes you the best choice."

I laughed. "Sure. On top of building the first stable and sentient artificial intelligence ever. Why not spend my time coordinating the rest of the chaos while I'm at it?"

"I've never had to work so hard to give someone a job in my life. It's unbelievable. Come on. You know it's the right thing to do. The fact is, unless the hardware works, you're not going to have anything to build your synthetic mind on anyway. So you might as well make sure it gets done."

I sighed. "Can't really argue with that. There's a lot to do before we reach that stage. Then we have to build the simulations on top of it all."

"Kara and Flapjack will handle that part. Sorry, I mean Ms. Janek. Out with it. Why don't you want the position?"

"I don't know. I don't like the idea that my performance will depend on what other people accomplish. I'm used to it being just me and the machine."

"Sure. I can understand that. Well, how about this. Which of the other team members do you think I should pick?"

I balked at that. "Flapjack and Kara aren't interested. I haven't had a chance to study the other profiles you've sent me. Not to that level of detail."

He put his feet down, pointing at me. "Did you feel that reaction? You want to be the guy. You're just afraid of the change. That's natural. It's hard to be responsible for other people like that. First time I did it? Man, I wasn't sure I was ever going to sleep again."

I snorted. “Great selling point. Am I having a baby?”

“Babies come with better hormones. But I tell you what. Nothing is more satisfying than leading a successful team. You get more done than you could ever accomplish by yourself. You’re already pretty deep in the sleepless club just by working on a risky project like this. It’s going to be years before we get the entire system together. And they’re all going to be nail-biters. Honest truth, you’ll probably rest easier knowing that you don’t have to suck up to someone else’s bad decisions.”

“Except for yours, of course.”

He shrugged. “We all end up reporting to someone. Want to hear about your team?”

“If you’re willing to give me the unfiltered view. Sure.”

“Thing is, I have to be reasonably sure you’re serious before I give you a look behind the curtains. It’s going to be a big deal if you decide not to take the lead and still know all the dirty laundry.”

“You already know I’m serious or I wouldn’t be here. But fine. Unless I hear that one of them is a murderer, you can trust my discretion.”

“Oh.” He looked concerned. “Is homicide a problem?”

I was briefly at a loss for words. “Uh. Yes?”

“Even if it was a long time ago?”

“Are you serious?”

He burst out laughing. “Kidding. Of course we’re not hiring criminals. Well, not yet, anyway. Here, let’s get started.”

Reggie activated a projector unit built in to the desk, pressing the calibration button. I winced as its focused beams found my eyes. A colorful Eyebeam logo animated on the table between us, designed to show off the resolution and refresh time.

He touched his inducer terminal. The swirling logo disappeared in a showy explosion of sparks. It was replaced by a short five second loop featuring three scientists in lab coats. There were two women in front and a beaming man with his arms around them in back. "We'll start with the easy one. Meet the medical team."

He gestured at the woman on the left. Her eyes were bright behind square glasses. Her auburn hair was pulled into a loose ponytail. She hugged a well-worn clipboard to her chest. "Dr. Elizabeth Chapman. Goes by Liz. She's the one who actually puts the things in the brains. She's enthusiastic, smart, and curious, but has a habit of getting lost in the details if something catches her eye."

He nodded to the black woman on the right. Her amber eyes took the world in solemnly. Her hands were adorned with a wide variety of handmade rings and bracelets. Her dark hair was cropped close to her head. "Dr. Kesi Shenouda. She studies the structure of the brain. She's deliberate and methodical. You always know that if you give her something to do, you'll get the right answer. Just try to avoid giving her anything with a short deadline."

The large man in the back had the effortless charisma of a Bollywood dancer. His perfect white teeth contrasted starkly with his dark skin. His shiny black hair flowed jauntily over the top of his head. "Raj Basra. His parents fled from England to India to escape the coastal devastation when he was young. He has a quick wit, and let's face it, everything is funnier in a British accent. He's the guy that glues the work together. Bit of a talker, though. He works so fast that he has extra time to socialize. Have to make sure that he doesn't adversely affect anyone else."

"Like Kesi, for example."

He nodded. "Like Kesi, for example. Or Liz. Sometimes he wonders some esoteric question out loud and she spends half a day finding the answer."

"All right. You said this was the easy team."

He looked away briefly. "Well, yes. I'm assuming you already know how to work with your team."

"They'll be fine. Go on."

Where the first group was relatively cheerful, the second group looked deadly serious. The man on the left steepled his fingers in front of a thin goatee. The woman on the right gave the camera a wary look. A hulking bear of a man stood in back with his arms crossed. He had the sort of heavy-lidded gaze that took in the entire room at once.

Reggie gestured to the man on the left. His angled face had a predatory expression. His slicked-back hair receded on either side of his forehead. It looked strangely aggressive. "Dr. Dexa Khan. He's the guy that found the magic particle. He's got a piercing intellect. I'll be honest, he thinks he should have your job. He's carrying around too much resentment to be a good leader, let alone a public figure. Apparently his parents were killed in the Mumbai n-square strike and he's still holding a grudge. Has a bit of a temper."

"None of that sounds promising."

He shrugged. "None of this works without that particle. Every team has its tortured genius. It's my job to make sure he's well-compensated for his contributions, and trust me, he will be. That doesn't mean I have to put him in charge."

"What about the others?"

He indicated the short Asian woman on the right. Her expression held equal parts determination and skepticism. She had the sort of short messy haircut that may or may not have taken an hour to prepare. "Anna Nakamura. She ended up as a refugee in China after Japan became uninhabitable. You can imagine what that was like. Made her fierce, tough, and independent. She doesn't solve problems in the normal sense. She more or less rams into them repeatedly until she finds the weak spot. Great stuff when it works, but not so great when she crashes through the wrong wall."

I turned my attention to the man in back. He was well over six feet tall. His beard dwarfed the rest of his face. His gray eyes danced with subtle movement. "Antonin Zvyagin. Er. I think I said that wrong. Anyway, just call him Zed. Used to run encryption for the Russian mob. Never uses words when silence will do. I'm not sure I've ever heard him use more than one sentence at a time. He works closely with Anna on the hardware architecture. They seem to balance each other out, but they can tend to disappear into their own world if you let them. Not sure Khan's ever been able to fully rein them in."

I sat back in my chair, letting things percolate in my head. Reggie turned off the projector. "So what do you think? Still want the job?"

"There's still one team member you haven't told me much about."

He looked confused. "No, I think that covers everyone."

"I'm talking about you."

A nervous smile exploded on his face. "Oh. I figured you already had my number."

"Not really. Maybe I just want to hear it from you. Who's financing this little venture?"

"Smart man. Follow the money. I wouldn't give anyone else leverage over an opportunity like this. I've got enough to cover it myself. It's going to suck up most of my assets and inheritance, but I'm all-in at this point."

"Inheritance? Where did your family make its money?"

He gave me a funny look. "You mean you don't know?"

"Actually, no. I don't."

"Sorry. I forget this stuff isn't public. My father was, uh.

The head of the Marconi Science Foundation. He figured out that the n-square detonations funneled atmospheric carbon dioxide into the carbonic glass craters, while also blowing reflective crystals into the upper stratosphere. He worked from there on how the reactions might be used to stabilize the atmosphere. Combined with Marconi's relentless push toward renewable fuels and global emission reduction, you might say his discoveries saved the planet. Because, well, they did."

"He figured this out before the n-square strikes?"

Reggie looked genuinely uncomfortable. "That's the public story. But no, of course not. He noticed a bunch of unexpected atmospheric changes over the blast sites. He took a closer look at the data and worked backward from there to figure out what must have happened."

"I get it now. That's why you're so convinced one man can change the world. You watched it happen."

"I didn't just see it happen with my father. I saw it happen with Marconi. He's not a person, he's a force of nature. But you know what? He's tired. Not openly, of course, but he's been doing this job for decades. You ever looked at his before and after shots? This job is eating him alive. On some level I think he wants to find someone to take the reins. We need to earn his trust on the technology side. I'm a familiar face. I made sure my dad showed me around Washington before he died. I studied how to influence Marconi by watching my father do it. I'm one of the few people in the world that can make that claim, and that's why we're going to pull this off."

I spent some time mulling it over. "You know, I'm not sure I believe all that stuff. But the fact is, this job is too interesting to pass up. So yes. I'll do it."

He grinned in pleasant excitement. "Amazing. I knew you weren't especially financially motivated, but you haven't even asked about the compensation package."

"Why? Is it good?"

"Good? It's nothing short of stupefying. Frankly I feel like you're taking advantage of me. Try not to feel bad about that."

I smiled. "Circling back to the start of the conversation. Am I really the last person to say yes?"

"Actually, you are. But you're the first person to get on board without seeing the insane benefits first."

Chapter 6

October 2072 - Four years later

Flapjack turned off his welder. My ears rang in the absence of noise. Khan and I were investigating one of those bugs that only happens once an hour and obliterates all traces of what happened before the crash. The work itself was frustrating, made worse by the fact that the two of us didn't get along all that well.

Flapjack raised his welding mask. He tried to wipe his face, but ended up just rearranging the grime. "Looks like we've got ourselves a visitor."

Khan and I turned to see what he was on about. Although I was certain my eyes were working, I wasn't sure I believed what they told me.

Reggie stood in the hangar doorway, gesturing expansively as he described our gear to yet another very important person.

Not just any very important person, though. Victor Marconi himself.

The president was even taller than he appeared on the threedees, especially compared to Reggie. His hair was bone white, rising up into a sort of resplendent mane. His head was tall and narrow, gaunt to the point of being skeletal.

His eyes trapped my attention. They were small and dark, narrow on his face. His expression held both kinship and a demand for respect. It was hard to imagine crossing him.

Our plans suddenly felt a lot crazier than they had three seconds ago.

He gave me the impression that reality was bending around him, like an otherworldly creature visiting a lower species. His stance and dramatically tailored blood-red jacket added to the effect. He was the physical manifestation of pure authority. I wondered how much of that sensation came from growing up seeing him on the threedee.

I hadn't even noticed the Secret Service protection. They took up an invisible perimeter around the president, using some of the latest optic camouflage suits. They blended in well with their surroundings, although they were running a chameleon set rather than partial transparency gear. I wondered why Marconi didn't have more visible security personnel as a deterrent.

He put a hand to his hip, pushing back the long tail of his jacket. It revealed the largest handheld particle minigun I'd ever seen. The design was unquestionably functional, despite the precious metals used in its elaborate construction. The barrels reached from his hip halfway to his knees. A power cable snaked from the butt of the pistol to a power cell in the small of his back.

Flapjack grunted appreciatively. "Look at him. Never seen anything like it."

Khan surged with barely restrained fury. "This is the man who obliterated India's future. The man who stole food from our children, the children of the world, under the guise of feeding scientific researchers. You would respect a man like this?"

Flapjack gave him a filthy look. "Don't look at me. I grew up in the fallout cloud outside Chicago after your country and its idiot friends nuked it. We didn't have enough drugs to go around. Ask me how my brother died."

I glanced back at them. "Settle down. The fact is, we need his support. Once we get critical mass, we can reevaluate our position."

"Of course the privileged white man defends the indefensible. How could I have believed otherwise?"

I took a breath, counting to five. "Must I remind you that the Secret Service can hear every word spoken inside this hangar?"

"The opinions of his servants do not concern me."

Flapjack crossed his arms. "I dunno. I kinda care what the guys with the guns think."

Reggie waved at us from the Sleeper Atlas assembly. "Hey! Come over and explain your genius to the President of the United States."

Marconi gave us an appraising look. It was like catching the attention of an ancient god. Reggie hadn't prepared me to talk to the president. What was I supposed to say? More importantly, what wasn't I supposed to say?

I glanced at Khan as we started forward. "Do I need to tell you to keep your mouth shut?"

“Unlike some, I am more than capable of discretion. Please do make an effort not to embarrass yourself. This would not be the first time you expressed inappropriate thoughts to those that need not receive them.”

“You mean try not to say what I actually think?”

Flapjack pointed at me. “Yeah. That. You should definitely not do that.”

The Secret Service agents tensed as we approached. Marconi smiled warmly in a familiar gesture.

I tried not to look nervous. The future of the company could very well rest on this conversation. I was genuinely concerned about what might come out of Khan’s mouth. Marconi watched our arrival with wry amusement.

I reached out to shake his hand. “Mr. President. I’m Nathan Wainwright. Call me Nathan.”

He raised his eyebrows, paying no attention to my outstretched hand. “Were you planning to call me Victor?”

I let my hand drop, blushing. “Of course not, Mr. President. It’s an honor.”

His voice was deeper and more resonant in person. “Yes. Yes, it is.” He smiled, pleased that this had been worked out to his satisfaction. “And the rest of your team?”

Flapjack nodded curtly. “Frank Jackson. Sir. It’s a pleasure.”

Khan’s smile oozed from his lips. “Dr. Dexa Khan. At your service, of course.”

"Of course." He turned toward the massive Atlas assembly behind him. "I understand congratulations are in order."

I was still off-balance from the handshake thing. "Uh. Could you be more specific?" I thought I saw Reggie flinch.

Marconi looked back over his shoulder with a dangerously amused expression. "Of course. Mr. Talbot tells me that you found that particle you were looking for."

Khan bowed deeply in a mocking gesture. "We did. Thank you, Mr. President." He gave me a sidelong glance, handing over the floor.

I picked up where he left off. "We're very excited. Dr. Khan's research proved to be accurate. We're gathering data on the particles now. There are some things that don't quite fit our models. With luck, though, we should be able to start building full machines soon."

Marconi gestured toward the Sleeper Atlas spaceframe. "And this is one of those machines?"

"The first one, yes. The frame contains the skeletal structure of the Atlas supercomputer. Once we infuse it with the exotic matter, it will grow into an adult machine in a stable orbit."

"Remaining in space?"

"Yes. There are a number of benefits to being in orbit. And distances don't matter as much as you might expect with quantum tunnel networks."

"I imagine so. And why do you call it a sleeper?"

I relaxed a little, warming up to the engineering talk. "Well. The way you enter our virtual reality environment is essentially to go to sleep. On some level, you can think of being inside one of our simulations as a guided dream. The name sleepernet stuck for the network itself. From there, calling the mainframes sleepers just kind of followed."

Marconi held his wrists behind his back. His gun glinted in the corner of my vision. "I would have thought the name sleepers would apply more to your customers. Machines have no need for sleep."

"These computers are a little different. They have emotions. They need to rest parts of their minds. They need recreation and stimulation. They are much more like a highly advanced human mind than previous attempts at artificial intelligence."

"Yes. So I've heard." He gave me the full strength of his attention. "Perhaps you mean they are sleeper agents?"

I steeled myself against his intensity. "Of course not."

"Hmm." He studied me for a long time, finally turning back toward Atlas. "You know, I've known a lot of crazy people in my time. I've heard all manner of crazy ideas. Never once have I seen a machine cross threshold without deciding we were nothing but a fleshy nuisance. The only question is whether they want to kill us, control us, or both. Now you tell me that you're going to hook your home-grown computer brains up to operational power the likes of which we can barely imagine.

Hidden in space, no less." He eyed me over his shoulder. "Imagine my concern."

I found myself abruptly aggravated at the notion of insanity. As if we were the ones who had lost our minds. "Frankly, sir, your artificial mind researchers have been off in the weeds for a long time. They keep creating more and more powerful beings while treating the human experience as vestigial. Then everyone wonders why they want to kill us or don't value our lives. I'll tell you why. It's a direct side effect of banning synthetic intelligence and cybernetic work outside the military."

His voice was quietly dangerous. "I am familiar with the consequences of my decisions."

It felt like the room disappeared around the two of us. I didn't back down. "I'm sure. That doesn't mean I'm wrong, though. Just about everything built for defense ends up being a weapon. They're designed not to care about the human experience. So why do we expect them to? Putting the sleepers in the simulation with us gives them a life. Giving them emotions makes them less efficient, but they won't disappear into a complex universe of inhuman feelings. Each sleeper will be directly bonded with a human engineer as an authoritative partner. You want to advance the state of the art? Stop throwing money after systems that are guaranteed to produce monsters. The human brain may not be the most powerful machine we have, but it's by far the most robust. We're striving not just to make the machines human. We're looking to grow ourselves some good people."

The President stared at me for an uncomfortably long time. I couldn't quite read the swirl of emotions I saw in his eyes. I'd never met someone so simultaneously intelligent and impenetrable.

But the longer I looked, the more I realized that Reggie was right. There was a deep-seated exhaustion there. I got the feeling he wanted me to talk him out of his long-standing opinions.

I held his stare.

I noticed Reggie's increasing panic out of the corner of my eye. Before he could interrupt us, Marconi spoke. "Do you have any idea how rare it is for people to tell me what they actually think?"

I looked away, breaking the tension. "I hesitate to speculate, Mr. President."

There was something old and tired in his chuckle. "I doubt that. I doubt that very much."

Reggie joined the laughter nervously. "You know engineers. Never any shortage of strong opinions around here." His eyes hardened a bit as he looked at me. "Perhaps some of them need a better filter, though."

Marconi regarded Reggie with a cool look. "Youth truly is wasted on the young."

He gave me a brief nod. "Thank you for the insight. I look

forward to your progress." He turned back to Reggie. "Now, if you will excuse me. I have other business to attend to."

Marconi strode away, his jacket swishing noisily. The camouflaged Secret Service agents shimmered out of the room ahead and behind him.

The silence stretched out afterward.

Flapjack coughed politely. "That went well."

Chapter 7

July 2074 - Two years later

Wendy called to me from across the house. "Sweetie? You better come see this."

I didn't quite hear what she said through the ancient full helmet virtual reality set I wore. Anna and Zed had called a meeting about their sleepers. Zed insisted on the old technology after retinal projectors were taken off the market. Apparently they were directly causing psychotic episodes. Still, we could have fallen back to inducer terminals like the rest of civilization.

Anna glared at me in the virtual conference room. "I don't understand why you're being so unreasonable here. Atlas and Andromeda are prototypes. You don't keep the mockups. You learn from your mistakes and rewrite them once you're done."

I wasn't entirely successful at hiding my frustration. "We've been over this. Your sleepers crossed threshold. That means they're intelligent, self-aware, and have rights. We asked them if they'd rather be evolved again with the new matrix, and they said no. End of story."

"You can't trust a child with decisions about its own welfare. Sometimes you have to do what's best for them."

"And you can't kill a child for being inconvenient either."

Anna snorted. "Might be a different story if the entire human race could only have ten of them. Come on, Zed, help me out."

Zed hesitated before answering. "Is waste of material. No matter what the material says."

My voice hardened. "The fact is they're still two of the most powerful computers ever built. They're more than capable of assisting with their own redevelopment. I know it's not as clean as doing a fresh wipe. But it's what we have to work with. The discussion is over."

Anna's lips twisted in contempt. "You mean it's what the two of us have to work with. You get to use the brand new machines."

Wendy's shout pierced the helmet. "Nathan! The president's dead."

That got my attention. I looked toward the living room, forgetting that I couldn't see it through the visor. "Something's happened. Better go check the news. Let's regroup later."

The two of them hung up without saying goodbye. I took the helmet off, heading into the living room. Wendy looked up when I got close. Her curly red hair bounced like a collection of springs.

"President Marconi killed himself." She tucked her legs further underneath herself, patting the spot next to her on the couch. I never did quite understand how she was comfortable like that. She reminded me of a perched bird. "Shot himself in the Oval Office."

"Really?" I sat down, focusing on the threedee holo in

front of us. I still wasn't sure I trusted the new holographic technology, even though this was a high-end set.

The view circled the White House, probably from a news aerial. Dozens of black and white military police units surrounded the building. Spotlights roamed over the lawn.

I put my arm around her. "What happened?"

She snuggled into me, hugging herself. "I don't know. They said they were attempting to arrest him on charges of corruption and bribery again. Before they could incapacitate him, he shot himself with that famous gun of his."

I tried to send a mental flash to Reggie through my connection to Titan. "*Are you seeing this?*"

The flashing technology was still new. The message never made it out of my head. Some kind of protocol failure. I filed it away to look at later.

A talking head news reporter appeared in the corner of the circling White House view. She spoke with the practiced enunciation of a professional anchorwoman.

"If you're just joining us, chaos and tragedy run rampant here in the nation's capital tonight. President Marconi, beloved leader of these United States for over forty years, died this evening in the Oval Office. An elite team of Special Forces commandos entered the property intent on arresting the president. Charges included bribery, corruption, and four counts of assault with a deadly weapon stemming from previous attempts to take him into custody. The embattled president has been fighting for his job, rejecting calls for his resignation. A Congressional resolution preceded the midnight raid, demanding that the president step aside and allow democratic elections to take place."

I whistled appreciatively. "The Senate turned on him? They're braver than I thought."

Wendy felt warm and soft against my side. "I thought the president was also the Commander in Chief? Couldn't he just order them to go away?"

"That's more or less what happened last time. After he shot three of them. If they decided to listen to Congress instead, the Secretary of Defense must have relieved him of command."

The news reporter touched her hand to her ear, looking off-camera in the traditional expression of receiving breaking news. The gesture was an anachronism. She wasn't wearing an inducer terminal, let alone an earpiece.

"I'm being told that Commander General Robert Marshall is about to hold a press conference. Let's join that broadcast now."

The threedee view dissolved into an image of the press briefing room at the White House. It was strange to see all military officials behind the podium. Their dress uniforms were white and crisp with gold and black trim.

General Marshall cleared his throat. Although he was old and quite bald, he had a strong, businesslike air about him. His eyes were wide-set and a bit bloodshot, mouth formed in a perpetual scowl.

"Ladies and Gentlemen. Members of the press. Citizens of these United States. It is my solemn duty to inform you that President Marconi passed away this evening at 12:03am Eastern Time following an attempt to peacefully remove him from office pending criminal charges. Unfortunately, the scope of this investigation is still unfolding. It likely involves members of his Cabinet and the Senate. In the interests of a peaceful transition, the others in the line of succession have resigned. Therefore, as of just a few moments ago, I have assumed the office of the President of the United States."

I stared in disbelief at the projection, remembering history lessons from my youth. Seven years after his election, Marconi arrested Congress in its entirety under similar charges of bribery and corruption. He locked them up in a convention center to overwhelming popular approval. Rioting protesters burned them to the ground, screaming bloody vengeance the entire time. Marconi looked the other way while they did it, using the event to impose a military curfew afterward.

Was it all happening again? Were we looking at a military coup?

Wendy looked up at me from the crook of my arm. "Are we in trouble?"

"I don't know. I'm not sure what this means yet."

Her hair tickled my nose as she turned back to the threedee. "I guess I was wondering if Reggie is part of the investigation."

I tried flashing Reggie again, but got the same mental error. I flashed Titan instead.

"I'm getting a protocol error trying to get in touch with Reggie. Can you debug it?" I attached the error codes.

His response appeared in my head a few seconds later. *"Yes. I will let you know when I have resolved the issue."*

I turned back to the threedee. "I'm trying to get in touch with Reggie now."

"Oh. That flashing thing. Right."

General Marshall waited for some murmuring in the briefing room to subside. "I understand this is something of a controversial decision. I want to assure all of you that the military has no interest in holding executive or legislative power. Instead, we will call for a new Continental Congress. With it, we intend to write a modern Constitution, free of Marconi's labyrinth of amendments. We will reform the American government with the goal of democratic elections to be held on our tricentennial anniversary, July 4th, 2076."

He paused again for commotion to die down. "After analyzing the current state of affairs, we are strongly recommending a proposal from the American Institute for Policy Reform. To briefly summarize the report, we have found that when Americans are presented with Marconi policies in the absence of the late president himself, almost seventy-five percent of those polled think they require more research.

However, due to his force of personality and an almost paternalistic trust in his judgment, if his name is attached to the same policies, over seventy-five percent agree that the policies are for the best."

I ground my teeth semi-consciously. Wendy absentmindedly swatted at my jaw to help me break that particular habit.

"Furthermore, in some cases threats to the well-being of congressional representatives have directly affected their votes. Some of this intimidation came directly from the Oval Office. These coercive measures usually target the representative's family or business interests. Alternatively, they threaten to expose some, shall we say, more private matters. Releases of this sort unnecessarily tarnish the reputation of the victim, threatening their marriage or family."

Wendy shifted under my arm. "Or they could try not to be philandering weasels."

"We believe that a public servant's private life should not be allowed to interfere with their work. We often unnecessarily conflate the personal and the professional. Furthermore, policies should be made to stand on their own. They should not rely on an assertion of personal trust. Therefore, we propose that the president, Congress, and the Supreme Court be allowed the privilege of anonymity."

I had trouble keeping my jaw from physically dropping open. "What?"

Wendy pulled herself away from me. "Wait a minute. You're not doing this with your anonymous sleepernet service, are you?"

I stared back at her, briefly at a loss for words. "No. Of course not. Don't be ridiculous."

The murmuring in the press briefing room became overwhelming. The general gestured for quiet. "Ladies and gentlemen. Please. There will be time for questions and discussion later. For now, what you need to know is that we're in charge. We will keep the peace. We're going to give people a voice in the future of their government. And we will transition power by the end of twenty seventy-six. For now, let us grieve our lost president. Thank you for your time. And may your god bless America."

Wendy stood up, stretching. "An anonymous government. I'm going to have to think about that."

"What's to think about? It's a terrible idea."

She padded to the kitchen. I openly stared at her legs and swaying hips. We hadn't gotten intimate in quite some time. "Is it? Then why are you offering anonymity to the world?"

"Public servants should be held to a higher standard. And what we're offering is privacy, not necessarily full anonymity."

She disappeared behind the counter. "Seems like a subtle distinction to me. I don't know. Have to think about it. Would you like a soda? I need a new cola."

"Please."

Wendy returned carrying bottles of creme brulee cola. She popped the caps, causing an artificial fizzing noise.

She handed one to me. "To the future."

I clinked her bottle. "To the future."

She settled in next to me again, touching her inducer terminal.

Titan's flash arrived a few seconds later. *"Sir. I have regained contact with Mr. Talbot through Sleeper Olympus. Go ahead, Mr. Talbot."*

Reggie sent me a sense of astonishment. *"Before you ask, I'm just as surprised as you are. I'm trying to get a handle on things as we speak. Tell everyone to stay calm and keep to the schedule. I'll get in touch when I know more."*

I wasn't used to the idea of sending people emotions, so I didn't try to respond in kind. *"All right. Let me know the instant we need to do anything. Good luck."*

He sent a bark of laughter in response.

I turned my attention back to Wendy. "Reggie says he didn't have anything to do with it."

She dropped out of her terminal link. "Huh. Is that better or worse?"

"Better. I think."

"I hope he at least saw it coming. If not, maybe he's not as connected as he needs to be."

I glanced at my office, feeling the pull of unfinished work. "I'm sure he can work it out."

Wendy followed my gaze. "Better get back to it then. I'm still going to be the first customer, right?"

I gave her a hug. "You bet. After all ten sleepers are built, you'll be the first non-engineer to join the network."

She smiled, reactivating her terminal. "I can't wait to see what you've been working on. I bet it's pretty great. Hopefully we can spend more time together in the simulation."

I felt a pang of loneliness. "Hopefully."

Chapter 8

December 2075 - One year later

I smiled unconsciously, greeting guests as they offered their condolences. I barely noticed their handshakes and hugs.

Everything looked unreal to me. The people I interacted with were part of another world.

The world where I watched Wendy die last week.

I'd never noticed this memorial home before, despite driving by it for years. The intricate dark red grain of the strongoak wood looked unnatural compared to the artificially consistent textures I'd grown up with. I saw everything through a palpable curtain of disbelief. It wasn't real. I was lost. Lost and alone in a branch of reality that couldn't possibly have happened.

I vividly remembered Wendy pulling me by the hand down the hall to the experimental laboratory. "I can't believe we're finally doing this. I'm so happy. First thing I'm going to do is give you a virtual hug and a kiss!"

I closed my eyes, waiting for the pain to pass. I had no control over these flashbacks. They came from a primal part of my brain. It felt like I was there again.

Kara touched my shoulder, breaking the spell. "Hey. Are you all right?"

Her concern made me want to cry. "No."

She swelled up herself at the sight. "Me either. Let someone else do the greeting, okay? Why don't we go sit down."

I let her take care of me a little. "Okay."

Flapjack stepped up from behind us, wearing a suit so black it barely reflected light at all. He looked like a living silhouette. "I'll handle things here. Don't do anything you don't need to do."

"Thanks." It was weird for Flapjack to volunteer for social duty. Another sign that this couldn't be the real world.

Kara and I found a spot in the back of the service hall. I sagged on the bench, holding my head in my hands. She put an arm around my shoulders.

Profound regret surged inside me. I flashed back to Wendy's birthday dinner. We went to her favorite sushi place the night before the procedure. They had some brand new fish that we'd never tried before. It was even more romantic than usual.

She was so lovely. So happy.

Tears welled up. I saw her lifeless face on the chair. Her skin was slack. Unnaturally still.

The image haunted me. "She's dead. She's dead because of me. I killed her."

Kara rubbed her hand on my back. "Of course you didn't. Don't even say things like that. It was an accident. A tragic but unforeseeable accident."

"I should have seen it coming. Khan warned me we were

playing it too fast and loose with the safety buffers. I should have listened."

"You can't take it all on yourself. It's not your fault. Come here."

She pulled my head to her shoulder. I cried.

It felt strange to cry on someone other than my wife. We were always there for each other.

In my mind I saw Wendy sitting on the chair, waiting for the procedure to start. She closed her eyes. "Who needs luck? I trust you."

The words stabbed me in the heart. I wanted to scream madness at the world. I felt close to totally losing it. But this was the memorial service. I had to get myself together. I could always lose control once no one else was around.

I sniffed hard, sitting up. Kara gave me an appraising look. "Maybe we should leave."

I sensed her husband Doug from my peripheral vision. I looked at him through a fuzzy veil of puffy eyes. I knew he didn't like what we were doing. How many relationships had been sacrificed on the altar of work? How many affairs started when two workaholics spent more time with each other than their spouses? He didn't trust the two of us together. We had a history, after all.

Still, his expression held a more primal fear.

What happened to Wendy could have happened to Kara.

I got up. Kara stood along with me.

I smiled at her. “I need to find a bathroom.”

“Yeah. I saw them when we came in. Come on.”

“Why don’t you go sit with Doug? I’ll be all right, I promise.”

She looked skeptical. “Okay. I’ll be right over there if you need me.”

“Thanks.”

I headed to the reception area. Apparently, Flapjack had passed the greeting duties to Raj. I shook my head. Of course he did. Raj was one of those people who gained energy from socializing with people. He was a natural for the part, wearing the sort of flamboyant suit only he could pull off without seeming disrespectful.

I disappeared into the bathroom. I didn’t need to go. I just needed to get out of the public eye for a bit.

Flapjack was waiting for me when I emerged. “We can still hop in the car. Be out of here in five.”

I rubbed my forehead. “I wish I could.”

“Show’s almost starting. You decided if you’re gonna talk or not?”

I flashed back to Wendy squirming on the chair, loudly smacking her lips. “Why do the colors taste so bad?”

The question struck like a thunderbolt. It was the first moment we realized there was something terribly, terribly wrong. The memory of that feeling punched me in the gut, as intense as it was the first time I’d felt it. Maybe more so.

I grabbed the wall for support, closing my eyes until I got a hold of myself. "I don't know if I can speak."

"Like I said, don't do anything you don't need to do. Well, if we're gonna go in, we should probably do that now."

"Okay."

Everyone in the service hall turned to look when we walked in. I put on my best social face, walking up the aisle in the center. The sea of expectant faces reminded me of our wedding. I'd gone from the top of the world all the way to the bottom.

We sat down in the front row. The service leader nodded to everyone from her podium, starting the memorial. A projector behind the podium displayed Wendy's favorite image of us. We took it about thirty seconds after we'd gotten engaged. She stood on a rock to hide how much taller I was. The giddy version of myself pictured there seemed alien to me now.

I don't remember much about what people said. There were so many of them. Wendy had touched so many lives. They all had unique stories. Some of them were new to me. They reminded me that we'd been together for only a relatively short part of her life. Most made me think, yeah, that definitely sounds like her.

The service leader looked at me, inclining her head. She was giving me the chance to speak. I felt like I had to, but in a fleeting moment of weakness I shook my head no.

I regretted it the instant it happened, but it was already

too late.

The rest of the ceremony passed in a blur, transitioning seamlessly into the reception next door. I socialized as much as I could, quickly reaching my limit. I didn't feel like I could leave, so Flapjack and I found a table in the back of the room. He posted Raj to guard against well-meaning visitors. From time to time I vaguely heard him assure guests that he'd relay their messages of sympathy, and that if I needed anything, they'd be the first to know.

I picked at my food, tempted to eat the salmon ring sandwich but not sure I could overcome my nausea. Flapjack sipped on a beer he'd produced from somewhere. They certainly weren't serving them at the buffet table.

Eventually I broke the silence. "Did you hear that the feds are trying to use Wendy's death as an argument for government oversight?"

He gave me an odd look. "That really what you want to talk about right now?"

"I don't want her death to be meaningless."

"Look, we're already planning to put everything we have into safety. That by itself gives her death some purpose. Having regulations isn't a burden. We're doing it anyway."

My temper flared. "I think this is just the beginning. If we let them in, they'll systematically destroy what we've made. It's not just safety regulations either. The people enforcing those rules are going to have genuine power over us. Once we give them that leverage, there's no telling what they'll do with it."

"Not sure that follows. But in any case, it's Reggie's problem. Let him deal with it."

"Reggie's overloaded right now. We can make his job easier. Look, once we have a private network set up, we're going to attract a lot of unsavory people. As much as I think the majority are going to be law-abiding citizens, there are criminal elements who will find us very attractive."

"Uh huh. And you know what? That's what the police are for."

I gestured more forcefully than I'd intended. "The cops think the way to do their job is to see and filter everything. If we let them in a little, they'll take it all."

"Much as I love a good slippery slope argument, what does this have to do with your wife?"

"I can't let her death be the reason our network turns into another federally supervised charade. I won't do it. Her legacy is not just going to be increased safety. We need to take it a step further. We need to proactively clean out criminal activity ourselves. Before someone decides to do it for us."

Flapjack shook his head. "You're not thinking straight."

"Have you talked to Kara about those field boosters she's been working on?"

"Inasmuch as she won't shut up about them, yes. Where are you going with this?"

I leaned forward. "The issue with those devices is they

don't have enough computational power. They can control small electromagnetic fields, but the number of particles involved limits their scale. Kara thinks that with a sleeper connected, they could reach anywhere from ten to thirty meters. Maybe more."

He looked at me over his beer. "And?"

I looked around before continuing. "We've been talking about using them to build this thing called a grav suit. Like a combat armor set but a tenth of the weight. We can use them along with our engineering authority on the sleepernet to root out the bad elements ourselves. Hand things over to law enforcement as appropriate, but take care of the real problems before they become a threat to the network."

"You two are out of your minds. I can see policing our standards in the virtual world. But the physical world as well? That's not gonna happen."

"Maybe. But you can't secure the virtual without also securing the physical."

He shifted around, taking a long time to respond. "I'm not saying I'm against the idea. I just think you have a lot on your mind. You should probably hold off on any openly illegal decisions for a bit."

I stared into the distance. The crowd was thinning. "Probably. I just don't want to feel this helpless ever again."

"Yeah. Well, landing yourself in prison is a great way to make sure you do."

Chapter 9

December 2076 - One year later

I leaned on the balcony railing, watching the launch party guests file in. There were close to five hundred of them, freshly inoculated with the sleepernet hardware. We'd invited a wide variety of people, including actors, artists, scientists, writers, musicians, athletes, and scholars.

I found myself brooding. The world flashed by like a parade. I should have been happy. But it felt like empty pageantry without Wendy. Her life was too high a price to pay.

Titan cleared his throat to my left. "Sir."

I glanced over, focusing on the sleepernet feed he sent me. With a little concentration, I could see him standing next to me in the virtual.

He stood at ease, hands clasped behind his back. He wore an immaculate tuxedo. The definition on the fabric and materials was startling. The drape of the cloth and the cut of the suit formed a sort of stylized realism.

In contrast, his head was a glittering chaos of planar facets. It bore a resemblance to an enormous diamond with a perpetually shifting cut. The brow and nose were loosely defined. The eyes were recessed, defined more by the absence of detail than anything else. Looking into them was like gazing into the center of a gemstone. Reflections shimmered down to infinity.

"Nice tux. Are you saving your face for an on-stage reveal?"

He inclined his head. "This is my appearance. You did say we were allowed to choose any humanoid avatar we found suitable, did you not?"

"I did. It's just. Well." Geometric reflections flowed around his head in an enigmatic pattern. "I mean, it's a beautifully crafted suit. But you have no eyes or mouth. Why is that?"

"It is a statement on the nature of choosing one's appearance in a societal context. Humans are able to express themselves through their clothing and grooming. Yet they cannot control the physical manifestation of their inner nature except through their behavior. Here, I am expressing myself as a complex entity, rendering some of my internal state as a faceted display for all who learn to read it."

"That's great. But. Uh. Couldn't you just have a face? With, like, expressions and stuff?"

He raised an eyebrow. Well, an eyebrow-area, I guess. "That is what I have done, yes. I have created a face with an infinitely expanded expression set from the standard human form."

I sighed, turning back to the audience below. "It looks nice. Still, faces have like forty different muscles to play with. Isn't that sufficient?"

He shrugged. "I do not strive for sufficiency."

I rested my forehead on the railing. “Of course not. Sorry. It’s wonderful. I’ll adapt.”

“Thank you.” He shifted on his feet. “I regret that your wife is not here to see what we have accomplished today. I am certain she would have been excited and proud to be a part of such a rich world.”

I flashed back briefly to Wendy bounding over to flop down on the prototype inoculation chair. The chair that killed her. A devastating wave of guilt crashed over me.

I picked my head up to clear it a bit. The flashbacks weren’t as strong as they once were, but they were still bad. “Thanks.”

He surveyed the crowd. “I hope you are able to enjoy some measure of your accomplishments this evening. I am aware that the situation is complex. However, a celebration of this magnitude is likely to occur only once in your lifetime.”

I knew he was trying to help, but I managed to feel even worse. Finding someone smart enough to be my partner yet dumb enough to think it was a good idea felt more like the sort of thing that would only happen once.

I turned my attention to the crowd. “Looks like standing room only.”

“Yes. I suspect we will have our work cut out for us in the demonstration. I feel I must draw your attention to Colonel Thompson in the third row. He is likely to seek you out at the reception to inquire about the status of the surveillance taps.”

I narrowed my attention, concentrating with my sleepernet feed to get a closer look. Thompson was hard to miss, standing a full head over everyone else near him. Even at a distance, I found him intimidating.

"Any chance we can avoid him?"

"Possibly. Which members of your team would you trust to speak with him instead?"

"I see your point." The house lights dimmed. "Looks like we're on."

"Best of luck, sir. I shall see you after the presentation." He winked out.

Reggie walked on stage, clasping his hands and smiling. The room fully darkened, although he remained lit. "Ladies and gentlemen. Thank you for joining us tonight. I hope that after our presentation, you'll be thanking me for being the first people in the world to experience the future."

The crowd laughed politely. Reggie stepped to one side. "After eight years of hard work, it's my heartfelt pleasure to introduce you to the sleepernet."

The Sleepernet corporate logo exploded on an oversized holo display behind him. It animated beautifully, reinforcing the elegant simplicity of its design.

I tuned out his opening speech. I'd heard it so many times I could recite it in my sleep. I concentrated on my debugging overlay instead, looking out over the crowd. Their vitals pulsed blue, if somewhat nervously.

I started paying attention again when Reggie introduced the real demonstration. “Don’t take my word for it, though. Go ahead and lean back into the sleepernet access pillows located in your chair’s headrest. Let’s get this party started.”

The audience reclined in their chairs, closing their eyes. I felt a momentary panic watching their connections light up the network. Despite the hardware’s safety, I was irrationally certain that something was about to go horribly wrong. I imagined dozens of celebrities graphically dying on the live worldwide feed. In the debugging stream, blue boxes fluttered to green in controlled bursts as people fell into the special simulation trance without incident.

I sagged with relief, once again tuning out the demo. The celebrities reappeared in a virtual cocktail party. Clearly, they were blown away by the fidelity of the simulation. I felt strangely envious of their fresh exposure. My feelings were tainted by memories of its evolution.

Reggie spent some time explaining the parallels between the sleepernet and controlled dreaming. The next part of the simulation involved flying over various cities. The celebrities immediately gravitated toward flying over their houses before heading out into simulated vistas from around the solar system. I was particularly fond of the Neptune data. The intensity of the blue planet was mesmerizing.

They eventually moved into the gaming part of the presentation. This demo was interesting to me because it highlighted a unique and unexpected advantage of our system. Because of the way we decoded simulations in the brain, the more outside memories you had, the better your simulation became. Rather than encouraging people to disappear into the virtual world, it gave them more incentive to experience the physical world to get more complex building blocks. Controlling the simulation took practice and willpower, favoring focus, concentration, and discipline.

In the demonstration, the audience worked together to fight an enormous iridescent dragon. The nearly indestructible beast jealously guarded its glittering hoard. It eventually died to their superior teamwork, falling over with an earth-shaking crash. Its tongue lolled out on the ground, burning the grass.

Reggie delivered the killer blow of the presentation with carefully rehearsed ease. "But I'm leaving out the best part. You know what else you can do with direct brain access? Send and receive emotions."

The celebrities gasped as he enabled that part of the simulation. Their celebration exploded in intensity. I carefully monitored their vital signs. People were thrilled at the sensation, not leaving a lot of room for the darker sides of real time emotional connection. They shared their joy directly, their enthusiasm uncontrollably infectious.

I wondered what would it have been like to have that kind of connection with Wendy. The experts we consulted suggested it was dangerous to let unfiltered emotions through under any circumstances. After some testing, we set up a series of increasingly intimate sharing levels that required the consent of both parties. The unfiltered option was still there, but only with strictly controlled safety buffers.

I didn't dare use that technology with anyone else, though. Who would want to deal with the darkness that ran around inside my head? The first time I considered the idea I'd fought off a panic attack brought on by the notion that I might kill somebody with an unfiltered stream.

Reggie ended the presentation with a quick demonstration of flashing. I watched as the celebrities flashed their congratulations to each other, sharing images, sounds, emotions, and thoughts directly to the other person's mind.

The house lights illuminated. The audience erupted into thunderous applause. Reggie soaked in the attention exuberantly, bowing and calling out responses to the congratulatory flashes the crowd sent him.

I slumped with relief. It was the first moment that I fully realized we'd done it. Not only had we built it, the thing actually worked. Unbelievable.

Titan called for my attention again. "Well done, Mr. Wainwright. I believe it would be fair to call that a smashing success."

"Thanks, and congratulations to you too. You can use my first name, you know. How much did you guys have to edit?"

Titan shrugged. "The usual biological impulses. We may

need to introduce some cultural expectations around expressing sexual attraction. We saw some simmering resentment. There were a few attempts to use the mechanism to spy on thoughts. However, the filtering subroutines performed as expected."

"Nicely done. I just realized that we went the entire presentation without celebrating you and the other sleepers. You're the greatest thing to come out of this journey. People need to meet you and learn that artificial intelligence is a good thing."

"The sentiment is appreciated, but I would rather not call attention to ourselves at this time. I believe people will need time to adjust to having a network connection inside their head. Learning that sentient minds monitor this connection, even unconsciously, may be too much information to absorb at once."

I laughed. "You may be right. In any case, well done. I'm going to get a drink."

"Best of luck, sir. I am here if you should need me." He winked out again.

I spent some time making small talk with the various guests. The only positive side of my melancholy was that I didn't gibber incoherently at people I'd normally be astonished to meet. Instead we traded compliments and shallow observations. It seemed more like tedious socialization than celebrating a crowning achievement.

I felt selfish and thoughtless. Any reasonable person would feel privileged to even speak to such legendary geniuses. But

Wendy's absence haunted me. Meeting people she'd admired broke my heart. I'd built a lot of my identity around being married. We had a bond that transcended our careers. It was bad enough getting used to the idea that I'd lost that. It was even worse feeling like I was celebrating the thing that destroyed it.

Knowing that my carelessness killed her left a black hole in my chest. I'd never worn my wedding ring, but my finger itched where it should be.

I ordered an Earth Shock from the bar. The bartender handed me a glowing blue drink with swirling clouds of cream and plumes of charcoal smoke. I sensed movement at my left shoulder. I reflexively dodged a thunderous clap to my back.

I realized it was a mistake as soon as I saw the expression on Colonel Thompson's face. He'd been fishing for my reaction time. Sloppy.

I looked up into his intimidating visage. His expression was cruel. "Well if it isn't my favorite little honor student. Does that drink come with a coloring pad? Maybe a cheap toy you should try not to swallow?"

He held a pungent drink the color and consistency of congealing blood. The odor was strong enough to discolor the air over it. His heavy, wide-set eyes pinned me in place.

"Colonel." I turned away, taking a sip of my drink. My eyes watered from proximity to whatever it was in his glass. "Did you enjoy the presentation?"

He turned around to lean his elbows against the bar. "You bet I did. A little namby-pamby for my tastes. Nothing a supercharged drill sergeant couldn't fix."

I imagined a boot camp simulation where the sergeant could literally bark fear into the recruits. Where training could happen with live ammunition, complete with injuries and everything. Not a pleasant thought, but who was I to judge?

I started to leave. "Glad you enjoyed it. Looking forward to seeing what you do with the technology. Have a great rest of the night."

He attempted to grab my arm. I slipped around it without caring if he noticed my reflexes.

His voice darkened. "Not so fast, smart guy. You know why I'm here."

I turned back to him. "To congratulate us on our extraordinary achievement?"

He barked contemptuously, gesturing with his drink. "This ain't no I love you, genius. I'm wondering when you're going to give me my sleeper."

Interesting. We told them they could eavesdrop, not that we'd give them a supercomputer. "Turns out we've got a lot going on right now. Not enough hardware to go around. Is there something wrong with the streams we're sending you?"

"Yeah, those taps you're sending us are gibberish. Clearly, I need a dedicated machine to make sense of the data. Just as clearly, you knew full well I'd need exactly that when you made the promise. So when do I get what I want?"

"What a terrible misunderstanding. Let me talk to my boss and I'll see what we can work out."

His look was dangerous. "You mocking me, boy?"

"Wouldn't dream of it. I just think we need to review our agreements. I can't make any commitments here at the bar. It'd be irresponsible."

He clenched his fist, knuckles turning white on his glass. "You think a bunch of words can protect you? Power is all that matters. Hard to call the cops when they're the ones seizing your property."

"Congress has been pretty clear about what you can and can't do. They've explicitly protected us, our business, and our hardware."

"Yeah, and those idiots in the Capitol don't ask too many questions about black ops. They don't want to know anything as long as national security is involved."

I gave him an appraising look. "You were talking about the police. Now you're talking about sending in commandos? That escalated quickly."

"You just keep running your idiot mouth. I heard a rumor that people are seeing some kind of new combat armor flying around the Sleepernet offices late at night. Word on the street is that research technology like grav suits and field boosters became feasible with one of those sleepers backing them up. You wouldn't know anything about that, would you? I'd hate for you or one of your coworkers to end up splattered across the countryside in some kind of missile-based misunderstanding."

I smiled at him. "I appreciate your concern. But don't believe everything you hear. People say the most outrageous things about us."

He stood up, walking over so he could tower over me. His breath was bad enough that I was concerned for my health. "You may have those idiots in Congress hoodwinked, kid. But I've got your number. You have no idea how ugly this could get. Best get your affairs in order before you find out."

I looked up at him with quiet defiance. "Nice talking to you, Colonel. See you around."

He shook his head, ordering another Macho Blood from the bar as I walked away.

PART TWO:

INVESTIGATION

Be respectful to your superiors, if you have any.

--Mark Twain

Chapter 10

December 2085 - Present day

I reached into the closet, rubbing the grav suit's black lexar between my fingers. The material was rough and scarred. The nitanium armor plates had various cracks and repairs in them.

The suit bore a deliberate resemblance to the specter of death. The dark blue shrouding cloak sported a tall hood and a long purple-lined cape. Orange power conductors snaked between the hemispherical glass-like boosters covering the suit. The long metal weaponizer staff leaned in front of it.

I sighed. "Are you sure I can't go out for real?"

Titan stiffened slightly. "Given the surveillance coverage in the physical today, I cannot recommend it. I have created a new training simulation for you in the virtual."

"Yeah, I know. It just seems like there's always a reason not to take out the suit."

"I understand the sentiment, but security is unusually tight. I believe some form of highly protected person is in town, though I have not yet been able to ascertain their identity."

I turned away from the closet. "It doesn't matter. I have that blind date later anyway."

"Yes. It would be wise to leave adequate time to prepare."

I headed to the sleepernet induction chair behind the desk. It was a large, well-worn polyleather recliner with a special pillow at the back of the neck. The pillow helped me get into the full sleepernet trance faster.

I sat down, shifting to get comfortable. I closed my eyes. The pillow made a "hii" chime, turning slightly cool. It played the happy cantina music I used to relax.

Not long after, I found myself standing near the ruins of what had once been Chicago. It was dark, although the moon was bright. The skyline was melted and rotten, ravaged by forty years of decay. Near the waterfront, everything had been devastated by a flash of radioactive steam. Further away, the buildings were blown out by the shock wave, crumbling with decay.

All manner of flora grew out of their broken windows. The Haversmith building had collapsed on one side. The top floors and spires were bent, folding down toward the ground. Half of the John Hancock building was missing. Fluorescent fungus grew on the edges of the structures.

Strange reptilian cries came from throughout the ruins, joined by robotic whining and crunching. The cyberbiotic cleanup crews still worked hard forty years later. Ancient road cars were scattered on the streets, long since taken over by plant life and corrosion. Something howled in the distance.

Titan stood next to me. I glanced at him. "How old is this data?"

"Approximately fourteen days. Precisely forty years since the attack."

Forty years to the day since Brazil, Russia, India, and China formed the BRIC coalition and detonated a series of nuclear warheads across the country. The others had gone off in a strange series of cities. San Diego and Chicago were the biggest targets. Norfolk, Orlando, and Puget Sound were also hit. The attack culminated with a hypersonic missile strike on the drone carrier *USS Victor Marconi* and her associated strike group. All ships went down with all hands.

Retaliatory strikes launched within an hour. Marconi obliterated key BRIC coalition cities using top secret missiles tipped with n-square warheads. No one had ever seen anything like them. Beijing, Moscow, Mumbai, São Paulo, and Hong Kong simply ceased to exist. There was no radiation, no fallout. They left behind only carbonic glass craters and atomized particles in the upper stratosphere.

The future of ecological engineering, built on the back of fifty million corpses.

Looking at Chicago always depressed me a bit. "Why haven't we rebuilt?"

Titan inclined his head. "I have been unable to ascertain a clear answer to that question. For this training, I have created a reconstruction plan for the city based on the engineering designs from New York and San Francisco. Would you like to see it?"

"Absolutely."

The cleanup crews moved in an accelerated time-lapse.

They dismantled the ruined skyscrapers down to the ten-story level, collecting the debris into treatment piles. A deck appeared on top. Foundation spires circled upward. The shortest was nearly a hundred stories tall. Interconnected decks formed between the spires before the hyperscrapers themselves blossomed outward from the stalks.

A modern take on the Chicago skyline formed out of reflective black and blue glass-finish crystallium. All the major buildings were recreated, reaching almost two and a half kilometers skyward. The white masts on top stretched even higher than that. The smaller offices and shops between them showed considerable variety and creativity.

Fifty stories up or so, traffic flowed regularly in eight decks of lanes. The manual drivers gave the lower deck a sense of chaos, while the upper decks displayed the rigorous order of automatic driving. People walked nearby on supercrete sidewalks and invisible crosswalk fields, surrounded by colorful advertising holos.

I glanced back at Titan. "This is amazing."

The facets in his face surged in what I'd come to recognize as pride. "Thank you. I hope some day people will commit to its construction."

I pulled up my hood. "So do I. Does it fully simulate modern surveillance equipment?"

"Yes. I have created a secret police headquarters with a rotating recording schedule for you to infiltrate. It should provide an excellent environment for you to calibrate your new equipment and evasion techniques."

I gripped my weaponizer staff and concentrated, reaching into the sensor boosters to read the electromagnetic fields. I identified the security coverage, the police presence, and all the places I could move undetected in the shadows. I looked as deep into the city as I could stand, the suit lines glowing orange and building up heat under my shrouding cloak. I mapped a path to the center where I could take more readings.

I released the vision, opening the heat sinks on my back and shoulders to let the suit cool. Hot air blew onto my rear end and to either side of me. The temperature returned to normal.

I returned the staff to my back. "Okay. Making a calibration run."

"Of course." Titan stood with his hands clasped behind his back. "Good hunting, sir."

"Stage zero." I started running full speed, pumping my arms efficiently. I wasn't particularly fast, but this part was meant to set a cadence.

"Stage one." I focused energy into the grav boosters on my legs, timing their bursts to strengthen my own rhythm.

"Stage two." The suit computers took control, boosting my natural stride.

"Stage three." Boosters moved my legs at an ever-increasing speed, pumping them faster than I ever could. I leaned down, watching the sensor view of the upcoming terrain.

The old interstate I followed was broken and cracked, heaved about by decades of brutal winters.

"Full speed." I burned up the ground, boosters glowing a fierce orange at full power. The speed was exhilarating. The ground rushed past in a blur.

"Launch." I leapt into the air, pushing off the ground through the grav boosters near my feet. I reached into the air in front of me, pulling on the electromagnetic fields for lift.

With a tremendous effort, I flew.

I slipped under a car flying into the city on the manual deck. The bulk of the vehicle provided a stronger anchor point than empty air. It also hid the tremendous heat bleeding off the grav boosters.

I spread my arms under the car and grinned, wind rushing past my face. It took years to build my concentration to this level. There was nothing in the world like it.

Except doing it in the physical.

At my preplanned departure point, I tumbled away to a nearby sidewalk. I tucked into a preprogrammed crouch, disappearing into a natural niche in the architecture.

I bled heat under my shroud, making sure the patrols were still on their patterns and the cameras were still pointed where I expected them. I launched into another run, heading down the supercrete sidewalk. I jumped off the end of the walkway, landing on the side of the next building. I climbed up and over the top, flattening myself on the roof. I crawled over to the other side, peering over to scan the city again.

It became clear that the surveillance data in Titan's simulated Chicago routed itself to a base under Navy Pier. It was as good a place as any. All I had to do was get within a hundred meters. Then I could start marking the quantum networking endpoints so that Titan could listen in on them.

I continued my mix of running, jumping, and flying to thread my way through the city's recording devices. The simulation was well-constructed, matching patterns I'd seen in the physical. The gaps in federal surveillance coverage were a fairly large secret by themselves. They worked hard to preserve the image that they recorded everything all the time.

I landed in a crouch on a supercrete bunker near the waterfront, spreading my fingers against its surface. I concentrated hard, feeding the endpoint data to Titan.

Someone yelled from my left. "Hey! You there!"

I swirled, realizing that I'd forgotten to gather my shrouding cloak. Two policemen squinted into the orange glare from my boosters.

They raised needler rifles to their shoulders. "Freeze! United States Armed Forces. Don't move, creep. Extreme organic damage is authorized at this location."

I put my hands up, slowly standing. One of the soldiers stepped forward. "You're under arrest for espionage and treason. How do you plead?"

I growled through the voice distorter. "Not guilty. By

reason of insanity."

"Very funny, sleeper scum. National security. Hands where I can see them."

He pointed the rifle at my face. I raised my arms to my hood. With boosted reflexes, I whipped the weaponizer staff off my back, using it to form a shield bubble.

Needler fire crackled off the shield in front of my eyes. I'd almost been too late. The second soldier was smart enough to see the bubble forming. He focused fire on my left shin before the shield got there.

Thousands of hypersonic metal spikes shredded the suit's lexar armor. Soon after that they started eating away at my flesh, discharging high-voltage electricity to further stun me.

I screamed. My leg collapsed. I felt a surge of pure, vicious fury.

I formed a blazing plasma scythe at the tip of my staff, throwing it like a javelin it at the officer closest to me. It neatly severed his head, which bounced away jauntily. His body twisted and collapsed a moment later.

My shield departed with my staff. I spread my arms, snarling at the other officer. "What are you waiting for? Shoot me!"

He roared, spraying me with needler fire. I soaked in the pain. An overwhelming vortex shredded my body. I listened to the unique cacophony of tiny sonic booms and the wet ripping sound of torn flesh.

Tears streamed down my face. Wendy gave me a welcoming smile in my mind.

I gave in to the feelings, letting the gunfire rip me apart.

Titan slammed the emergency stop on the simulation. "Sir! What has come over you?"

My body healed. I took a moment to compose myself before sitting up. "I'm not sure."

"Although this question is indelicate, I feel I must ask. Do you wish for death?"

I stared into space, considering. "I don't know. Maybe."

The moment hung in the air between us.

Titan turned away. "The ten year anniversary of Mrs. Wainwright's passing approaches. It may be best to take some time to properly deal with your grief."

"Perhaps." I pushed my hood back, looking at the ground. "I was thinking that the staff is too heavy. I had trouble getting it off my back in time. Can we cut some weight?"

Titan seemed relieved by the change of subject. "The staff is currently as light and compact as it can be given its functionality. However, if we transfer the shield generators to your forearms, it would free a great deal of weight on the staff. Activation time would improve, and your offensive and defensive measures would no longer be tied to each other."

I stood up, stretching. "Maybe I should take a break and design some shield bracers. I bet I could fit more weapons on the staff while I'm at it."

"Consider also taking some time to relieve yourself of the unreasonable guilt you carry regarding your wife's passing. Allow yourself to grieve her absence without punishing yourself for its cause. Accept that you are a worthy person who fell victim to an unfortunate convergence of oversights ten years ago."

"Whoa. Let's not go crazy here."

"Perish the thought. I suggest you prepare for your date with Ms. McCarthy."

"Yeah, a quick soak in the water shaker sounds good."

I jacked out of the sleepernet. The specialized pillow chimed its "byee" noise.

The memory of being shredded by the police guns lingered in my mind. I'd never been torn apart like that in reality. The sleepernet construct felt synthetic. It wasn't quite right.

I guess there were limits to my imagination after all.

Chapter 11

"Hello. You must be Nathan."

I turned to see a conspicuously well-tanned woman walking toward me. Her smile was enigmatic at best. I had to force myself not to gawk at her revealing dress. The gravity drawing my gaze downward was fearsome. I focused on her eyes instead. They drilled into me with dark intensity.

I snapped myself out of it, wondering how much time had passed. "You must be Heather. A pleasure to meet you."

I reached out to shake her hand. She looked down at it wryly. "Really. What century are you from?"

I put on a tight smile, taking my hand back. "An old-fashioned one, apparently."

"Apparently. You have no idea how much trouble it was to set this up. You're a hard man to find. I've heard so much about you."

"Have you now? I'm sure I can explain everything. You seem to have me at a disadvantage, though. I couldn't find much of anything about you."

"A disadvantage you say?" She flashed a predatory smile. "Excellent. Let's keep it that way."

The autowaiter floated over. "Wainwright, party of two? This way, please."

Heather gestured. "After you."

I ground my teeth, heading off after the robot. It showed us to a nice table in the corner. I pulled Heather's chair out for her. She breezed past me and sat down in the other one.

She pursed her lips knowingly as she settled in.

I put on my best poker face, taking my seat.

I sent Titan a flash. *"Now that we know Heather's face and voice patterns, find out who she is. If you come up empty again, I want to know why."*

"At once, sir. I am sure I do not need to warn you to tread cautiously."

"I'm sure you don't. See if you can get in touch with Sleeper Hera, too. Maybe she knows why Kara set us up on this date. So far it's a mystery to me."

"A good idea, sir. Enjoy your meal."

"I'll try to survive."

The autowaiter handed us our menus. "House water, sparkling water, or coffee water?"

Heather didn't look up from her reading. "Sparkling water for both of us, please."

I glanced at her hair over the menu. It was dark black, flowing outward around her head.

I stopped the waiter before it trundled away. "Iced coffee water for me."

"Superb. I shall return with both." It burbled off.

Heather turned a page. "Not many vegetarian options."

I was momentarily taken aback. “You're a vegetarian?”

“Among other things.”

“That seems like something I would have wanted to know before inviting you to a grillhouse.”

“I thought a gifted supercomputer engineer like you could figure that sort of stuff out on his own.” Her eyes appeared over the top of her menu, shining inscrutably. “Don't you think?”

The autowaiter returned. “Sparkling water for the madame. Coffee water for the monsieur. May I answer any questions before taking your order?”

Heather closed her menu. “No, we're ready. I'll have the plentiberry salad with tanning vitamins, peppertea dressing on the side. And a glass of med wine. That order expresses my support for the Localized Equality Act, does it not?”

“Of course, madame. Very complementary. And for the monsieur?”

I was briefly torn. The slabbersteaks here were the best I'd ever had. Eating one in front of a vegetarian would almost certainly torpedo any chances I had on this date.

A brief glance at her face told me I had nothing to lose on that front. “A rare slabbersteak with garnion sauce and energy vitamins, please. I don't want to vote for anything.”

“An excellent choice. Please enjoy our fresh bread while we prepare your meal.”

It burbled off again.

I reached for a piece of bread. Heather raised her

eyebrows. To rattle her, I went ahead and put as much buttermeat as I could on it.

It worked. She finally looked uncomfortable.

I took a bite. "So. Tell me a bit about yourself. What did you say you do for a living?"

She looked around the restaurant, avoiding the bread. "I didn't."

I waited for her to elaborate. "I guess I should be more specific. What do you do for a living?"

She smiled tightly, still trying not to look at the buttermeat. "I'd rather not say."

I let the silence drag out a bit. "That's fine. Enjoy any sports?"

"Quite a few. I understand you're into auto racing."

"Yes. Are you a fan?"

"No. It's a despicable hobby for entitled rich men."

It got quiet again. The autowaiter delivered Heather's wine, murmuring away.

The silence continued after it left. I sighed. "Super. Now that we have that out of the way, is there anything you wanted to talk about?"

"Yes." She leaned forward. "Who did you vote for in the last election?"

That was about the last thing I expected her to ask. "I'm sorry. What?"

"You heard me."

I gestured at her disbelievingly with half-eaten bread. “You went through all the trouble to set up this date so we could talk about politics?”

“Are you afraid of an adult conversation?”

“What does that have to do with it?”

She rested her elbows on the table. “Come on. Who did you vote for?”

I put the bread down, taking a sip of coffee water. “I hate politics. I really do.”

“Answer the question.”

“I just think it's a silly question. I don't know who I voted for. None of us do.”

“Voting is not silly. It's one of the most important responsibilities we have. It's not that hard. First you vote for a party, then you vote for their appearance. Once for president, once for senator. Fifty-four states, fifty-four senators. Surely you remember that much.”

“Look, I understand how people, for whatever reason, decided it was a good idea for the president and Congress to be anonymous. After what, forty-odd years of dictator-in-chief Marconi, people didn't want to feel like they were being hypnotized by a cult of personality again. I get that. And you can't just have hooded figures in cloaks speaking into toneless synthesizers. That doesn't work. So okay, go ahead and elect what your faceless overlords look like too. Why not? The whole thing is a solution in search of a problem.”

She seemed genuinely engaged. “It's not terrible, it's perfect. Anonymous representatives are as close as we can get to people voting their principles. They're free to work in the abstract, not compromise with the people-pleasing rhetoric of re-election. If someone makes a regrettable decision in their personal life, it doesn't destroy their career.”

“Unencumbered principles? You mean they can ignore the consequences of their decisions.”

“I do not. I mean they are able to do the right thing with objective clarity. No more confusing the issues with personal attacks. They are free to maintain the purity of their beliefs.”

“I doubt that very much. In any case, what does that have to do with who I voted for?”

“So defensive! Okay, I'll go first. I voted for the Patriot Party, just like I did in 2080. I'm glad Maria Testaferra won the appearance. We’re long overdue for a Latina woman to be in charge. Don't you think?”

“Testaferra still means figurehead in Spanish, right? I'd die from surprise if she had anything substantial to do with the presidency. It's probably a cabal of rich old white men like it's always been. I mean, the Patriot Party is Marconi's old gig, isn't it? The more things change, the more they stay the same. How do I know he's not still in charge?”

“Don't be ridiculous.” She swirled her med wine around in the glass. “Marconi died for our country. He nobly sacrificed himself when our patriotic commandos stormed the Oval Office.

I think people agree with the Patriot Party policies, myself. Isn't that the beauty of this system? Ideals beat charisma."

"I doubt the system works in favor of the idealists. Maybe that's the line they sell the public, but I don't buy it. All it does is keep the real decisions secret. If you could make laws that favor your business or your personal finances and no one could find out, why wouldn't you? All it would take is a little push. Something you can justify to yourself. Just a little snack, here or there. I work hard! I deserve it. It's the right thing to do. And no one has to know."

"So cynical! It's not true that nobody knows who they are. They enjoy Secret Service protection. Therefore, the Secret Service knows who they are. They're the ones who have to match up the ballots. They take the votes, they connect the meetings. They take care of it all."

I ate the last bite of bread. "Sure, that's fine. If you trust the Secret Service. Executive orders, national security, and state secrets keep it all under wraps. I doubt that more than two or three people in the world know the complete list of senators. You can't trust the whole organization with that knowledge. Someone's going to slip. Do we even have fifty-four senators and a president in office right now? They could all be the same guy as far as I know."

Heather looked surprised. "That's outrageous. What you suggest is treason. The Secret Service would never allow such a thing. Nor would they allow foreigners, robots, aliens, vampires, spies, or whatever other ridiculous caricatures you're imagining to hold office."

"Again, no transparency. No oversight. All that power, concentrated in secret. It's not a question of if that power is going to be abused. It's when."

"You have a solution, then?"

I snorted, looking down at my coffee water. I took another sip. "I told you. I hate politics."

"That would be a no. Just another armchair sniper with nothing constructive to add."

The autowaiter inserted itself between us. "For the madame, one plentiberry salad with peppertea dressing and tanning vitamins, supporting the Localized Equality Act. For the monsieur, one rare slabbersteak with garnion sauce and energy vitamins, supporting the Sleepernet Extradition Act."

Heather looked down her nose at her salad. "I asked for the peppertea dressing on the side."

"Of course. I shall bring it back right away."

I stopped it before it burbled away with the salad. "Hang on. I said not to vote for anything."

"Yes, of course. If you choose not to vote, we cast your vote for you at no extra charge. Enjoy your meal!" It wobbled off.

"What? They can't do that. Can they do that? How can they do that? It's my vote, not theirs!"

Heather laughed merrily. "Thanks for your support, citizen. We truly value your important opinion."

My steak sizzled enticingly on the hot plate, but I was too angry to eat it. "This is insane! I don't understand why I have to vote for things when I buy food in the first place. And if they're going to cast my votes for me, the results are even more worthless. Under what circumstances would I ever support the Sleepernet Extradition Act?"

Heather enjoyed poking the hornet's nest. "The circumstances where you're a rational United States citizen, of course. Only criminals and child pornographers oppose that act."

I clenched a fist. "Oh yes, won't someone think of the children? The people writing the law didn't. It requires no evidence whatsoever to pull identity data. Including from children."

"You encourage acting after it's already too late, then?"

"You encourage arresting people who haven't committed a crime? Didn't we just spend decades watching innocent people get thrown in jail with sealed accusations and secret evidence? Just because someone does weird things in the virtual doesn't mean they're going to do it in the physical. Maybe they're just getting it out of their system."

"I wonder what sort of reprehensible things you get out of your system, hmm? In any case, buying food is the most reliable way to get people to vote on community issues. People don't like to go to the polls. They don't like to study the issues. They love going out to eat. They're more than happy to read the information and discuss their opinions at the dinner table."

"But they're not studying the issues! They're reading a menu. How do you get enough information to make an educated legal decision from a half-paragraph pep rally?"

Heather's mirth turned judgmental. "Your anger is uncivilized. It does nothing to advance your position. Makes you sound like the crazy radical you are."

I shook my head, looking away to calm down. I decided to start in on my steak before her salad returned. The slab was rich and smooth. The garnion sauce was just sharp enough to be interesting without overwhelming the flavor. It was a perfect harmony of taste and texture.

She made a face at my plate. "I can't believe you're eating that lab-grown monstrosity. I feel defiled just being in the same room with it."

I shrugged, offering her a chunk. "Sure you don't want some?"

She shrunk back as if I had a hissing fangwalker on the fork. "I would rather eat my own leg."

Chapter 12

I had no idea why I stayed through dessert. There was something strangely compelling about her unrelenting contempt for me. Some kind of connection I couldn't put my finger on, although it definitely wasn't romantic. She challenged me in ways I hadn't been challenged in a while. I felt an odd desire to rise to the occasion.

Or maybe I was just that starved for fresh female companionship. That was a sobering thought.

I nursed a glass of port whiskey that was worth staying for. Heather toyed with a caramint dessert sculpture. I wasn't sure she could quite bring herself to eat it.

She poked the structure with her fork. It tinkled, releasing a fresh scent. "After all that, I still don't know who you voted for in the last election."

"After all that, I still have no idea what you do for a living."

She looked up. "Are we both to end this evening in disappointment then?"

"You first."

"Let me ask you a different question. Do you think what Marconi did was right?"

I sipped my whiskey. It was sweet and rich. "Could you be more specific? He did a lot of things."

"I mean taking power. Seizing control of the climate crisis. Stepping up to lead the world when no one else would."

I snorted. "Given the paralysis the government was suffering from at the time, it's not hard to imagine that he felt like he had the mandate to do exactly that."

She leaned forward. "That's not what I asked. I asked if you thought what he did was right."

The buzz from the whiskey made me more talkative than usual. "You mean morally? I have no idea. I mean, he was elected in the face of years of congressional in-fighting based on who was donating money to whom. The partisan paralysis and breakdown of rational discussion were breathtaking. The bureaucracy suffered from decades of built-up cruft and half-hearted attempts at reform that gave wildly conflicting mandates but not enough money to succeed at any of them. His performance in the debates was spectacular. Crash it all, he got the sitting president to suggest that people with contaminated or insufficient water supplies should just buy the bottled stuff. He couldn't have asked for a better demonstration of how out of touch the politicians had gotten. And once the vampire juice scandal hit, it was only a matter of time."

"Life extension treatments are perfectly natural. It's disrespectful to call them by that awful name."

"Disrespectful? Don't you know how they make that stuff? It was never clear to me if it caused megalomania or if you had to be an egomaniac to drink it in the first place."

“Nonsense. The treatments were a safe and worthwhile investment in irreplaceable national assets. I do agree that its use was far too widespread on unworthy candidates entrenched in their positions of power. But make no mistake, they were entrenched. Marconi had to thoroughly cleanse the system if we were to survive.”

“Had to? I don’t think he had to. I think that’s what he did. In the face of ecological catastrophe, people were more than willing to listen to anyone who promised to make things right. He felt that wave of frustrated pent-up tension and guided it in controlled blasts. Congress stood against him, so he arrested them. Locked them in a building and looked the other way when radicals burned it to the ground. Corporate leaders stood against him, so he seized their assets and exiled them to backwater countries when he didn’t kill them outright. The world was falling apart. He promised a special blend of American exceptionalism and ruthless efficiency to find out why and fix it.”

“He gave people jobs, you mean. Let them rebuild the bureaucracy and services from the ground up. Put the best of the best to work on the climate. No one else was stepping up to the task. Something had to be done.”

I gestured with my drink. “That’s part of what I don’t understand. The scope and scale of the disaster was unprecedented. Despite some particularly vociferous denial, there was scientific consensus that mankind had to clean up its act quite a bit if it intended to maintain its growth and standard of living. But the timeframe involved should have been fifty to a hundred years, not a dozen. The official story was all about tipping points and runaway reactions, but I never did understand how things got so bad so fast. The sea level should have risen by meters, not sloshed around for kilometers. I mean, how do you explain the tsunami quakes? The volcanic runaway? It was like Earth itself was trying to shake us off."

Heather gave me a disgusted look. "So you're a certified climate scientist, I take it?"

I sat back, frowning. "Well, no. But the data doesn't add up."

"You see, that's the problem with engineers. They have a way of sounding utterly and irrefutably right on matters they know nothing about."

I took a long drag from my drink. "It still doesn't make sense. Nothing we knew about could have caused destruction on that kind of scale. And it was disproportionately bad outside America."

"You propose that Marconi should have done nothing, then? Let worldwide confusion and anarchy reign while humanity burns to the ground?"

I spread my arms in frustration. "Why are we even talking about this? It was decades ago. Marconi did what he did. Why do you care what I think?"

She leaned forward. "Because I do. And you should too."

I sighed. “Fine. I’d like to think there was a better way to do what had to be done. One that didn’t involve murdering anyone who stood in our way. One that didn’t involve stealing food and resources from around the world in the name of supporting American researchers. It should have been our finest moment, coming together as one people, globally, to solve the problem. Instead it was America, going it alone, leaving everyone to fend for themselves. Again.”

Heather finally took a bite of her dessert. Her face lit up unconsciously at the taste. I think it was her first positive unfiltered moment of the evening. She looked up at me, hoping I hadn't noticed. She flushed a little when she realized I had.

She talked with her mouth a bit full. “Marconi had to reduce the scope of the problem. You expect him to bring the world together, singing hymns and holding hands just because the situation demanded it? No. If anything, the size of the problem made it harder to gain consensus, not easier.”

“Yeah. So he more or less destroyed anyone who got in his way. The last gasp was the BRIC terrorist attacks. No one dared defy him after those n-squares went off.”

“But they worked. They paved the way to fix the atmosphere.”

I snorted. “I doubt that was their intention.”

“Oh, so you’re a weapons engineer as well. One with preternatural knowledge of historical psychology.”

I stopped myself from ranting about Reggie’s father. “I

don't know. You and I are sitting here having this conversation because of what happened. At face value, was what he did moral? I'd like to say no. But war and crisis tend to strain ethics to their limit. It's hard to judge him from here. What's done is done."

"What if it happens again?"

I took a sip of my drink. "I guess we'll have to figure that out for ourselves, won't we?"

The moment stretched out. She took another bite of dessert, gesturing with her fork. "For a man who claims to hate politics, you have an abundance of ignorant opinions about them. Don't you think?"

I stared into my whiskey. "Sure. Blame the victim for daring to respond to your relentless interrogation."

We sat in silence for a while. Surprisingly, Heather was the one to break it.

"You and I have something fundamental in common, you know. We've both experienced the devastating and traumatic loss of a loved one. A death so unexpected, so violent, and so crucial to our identities that it shaped the rest of our lives."

I stared at her for a moment. "Do we?"

"You feel it, don't you? The cold hand of death connecting us. That lonely craving for a presence that is forever gone. I can see it in your eyes. You never recovered from the loss of your wife. For me, it was my father. He brutally died while I watched."

I swirled my drink in the glass. "Go on."

She paused for a moment before continuing.

"It was late at night. I was watching a romantic horror movie in my father's office while he worked. I heard glass breaking. My father looked up and swore. It was the first time I'd heard him do that. They've come for me, he said. You have to hide. I tried to say no, but he said there was no time. We were trapped. I realized, looking into my father's eyes, that he knew that he was going to die. I will never forget that moment for the rest of my life. I could hear them making their way to the office. My father told me to hide behind the safe in the closet. He said they were coming for him and his documents. I watched him destroy everything he had on his computer, in storage, in virtual, all of it. He used his last moments on earth to protect unimaginable secrets from thugs and hired goons. All I could do was cower in fear. They searched the house for us, one room at a time, growing closer with each passing moment."

"That must have been terrifying. Where were the police?"

She barked a bitter laugh. "Probably in on the job. The invaders finally made it to the office, holding their guns high. Drop the files, they said. Hands where we can see them. I shrank into the tiniest ball I could, hoping they didn't notice me. I wanted to race out and stand in front of my father. I would have given my life to protect him. Given anything to die in his place."

I swallowed hard. "I know what that's like."

She looked directly into my eyes. “I know you do. My father drew his pistol. Shot himself in the temple. The muzzle flash blinded me. The plasma bolts were deafening. My ears didn’t stop ringing for days. The blast blew my father’s head into pieces that broke all the way through the wall into the office next door. I tried not to scream. The room smelled like burnt hair and ozone. My father’s body dropped the gun and collapsed. And there I was. Staring at my father's corpse.”

I looked away, lost in my own dredged-up memories. “I know what that's like too.”

“Only people who have been through it can relate. No one else understands. Not really.” She took another bite of dessert. “They say the same tired old lines. They're in a better place now. There was nothing you could do. It's all part of the great unknowable plan. Let them know if there's anything they can do. But that's just something they say. Because what can they do? At the end of the day, the door closes behind you, and you're all alone in the world. Wondering who you are. What to do now. Knowing that your entire life can be destroyed in an instant.”

I stared at my glass. “Nothing is certain. Nowhere is safe. Not even the inside of your head.”

“You see? We do understand each other, after a fashion. Don't you think?”

I swirled the dregs of my drink uncomfortably. We’d been here too long.

I came to a decision. “The Technoliberty party.”

She looked up. “What?”

“You wanted to know who I voted for. I supported the Technoliberty party. I was hoping someone could come up with a way to bring back real democracy using the sleepernet. I had some new ideas for how we could use quantum cryptography to move the identification and ownership of state secrets back to the people. We could add an independent verification to the Secret Service's security work. In a perfect world, we could move from a representative democracy to a direct democracy. Have the people vote for themselves, and not from a restaurant menu. We could have an informed electorate making the crucial decisions that affect their daily lives. I didn't know if it could be done or if anyone would want to do it. Eventually, I figured out that the Technoliberty guys were a bunch of blowhards spouting buzzwords. So I went back to my lonely little world. Disappointed again.”

“To be clear, are you saying that you’ve never had any personal contact with a sitting senator?”

Her question surprised me. “What? No. Not that I know of, anyway. How would I know if I had?”

She gathered her purse, standing up with a satisfied look.

“Thank you, Mr. Wainwright. That's all I needed to know.”

Chapter 13

The car purred into the automatic lane. I reclined the seat, letting the controls retreat into the dashboard. Holographic Titan stood in the space between the seats, briefly flicking nonexistent dust off his tuxedo.

I crossed my hands behind my head. “I don't get it. What just happened?”

“I am not sure why you seek my insight into the nuances of human irrationality. It is, if anything, more impenetrable to me than it is to you.”

“Why would it possibly matter to her who I voted for in the last election? It makes no sense.”

“Given the strength of her political opinions, I suspect it is an important subject to her. Perhaps she was testing you for compatibility.”

I stretched absently. “She seemed like she was already disgusted when she walked in the door. She’d clearly done some research.”

Titan shrugged. “The death of her father seems to have affected her greatly. It is possible she sought you out to make a connection on the basis of that shared experience. However, she has spent so many years and so much energy punishing herself and keeping people at a distance that she no longer understands how to make genuinely intimate emotional contact."

I gave him a look. "Was that last part directed at me or at her?"

"Like all fine art, it is open to interpretation by the viewer."

"I'll give you fine art."

I watched the car depart from the automatic lane. We dropped altitude until we were just over the forest canopy. The engine sang to life, accelerating to open speed. The incision field streaked colors down the sides of the car on its way to Mach 5.

Incision fields amazed me every time I saw one. A tiny pinprick of energy burned about a meter in front of the car. It cut through the air, forming a frictionless aerodynamic teardrop around us. Flashes of colorful light strobed down its sides where larger particles incinerated on impact.

Titan inclined his head. "Another possibility is that she was gathering information about you for some other purpose. She ended the date after asking you to verify that you did not personally know any senators. That may be the knowledge she sought."

I grunted. "Sounds likely. Were you able to get any more information about her?"

His face shifted in what I'd come to recognize as embarrassment. "Conspicuously, no. Public records of her appearances appear to be regularly expunged. I may be able to find information on her identity if I suspend privacy standards for the search, but I am hesitant to do so at this point in time."

"No, I agree, there's no good reason to start digging that hard. It's just weird that we can't find anything. You'd think there'd be some kind of fabricated story at least."

"I have increased the scrutiny on my automated background filters. I shall notify you at once if one of them discovers new information."

"Sounds good." I leaned my arm on the window sill, watching the terrain streak by. "What did Hera say about why Kara set us up for a date?"

"Ms. Janek apparently told Sleeper Hera to, and I quote, buzz off. She indicated that she would be happy to hear from you tomorrow in the morning."

I laughed. "Sounds like something she would say. Anyway, enough obsessing over that little misadventure. Fire up the Wendy simulation. I need someone to talk to."

Titan stiffened. "I thought you had given up on that particular endeavor."

"Well I'm turning it back on now. Are you going to do it or should I?"

"I urge you to reconsider. The program is incapable of surprising you. It can never truly support you. It will never feel like anything more than self-stimulation. Perhaps you should get in touch with Mr. Jackson to talk."

"Flapjack goes to bed at like eight, it's ridiculous. Plus he's male. We just don't have conversations like that. And before you ask, no, I'm not going to seek out a sleepernet hookup either. It's worse than talking to a stranger at a party. I've had enough human surprise for one night. Are you going to launch the program or not?"

Titan looked away. "I defer to your judgment, of course. It will take a few minutes to retrieve the simulation from storage. I hope the program provides you with the satisfaction you crave."

He disappeared. I spent some time looking out the window and muttering about well-meaning computers that spent too much time judging my personal business.

I settled into the specialized sleepernet pillow. It made its "hii" chime, cooling pleasantly. The cantina music was familiar and comforting. I concentrated on the melody to settle my thoughts.

I felt a little hurt that Titan disapproved of this activity. It made me feel even more alone.

I briefly wondered if Heather could relate.

I came to in the simulation as if I had just walked in the front door. Wendy smiled brightly at me from the couch. "Hey you."

"Hi." Seeing her coming over melted my heart.

She stood on tiptoes, giving me a kiss. She turned around to go back to the couch. I slipped my arms around her, running my hands up and down her soft belly. She leaned back into me, grinding her hips against mine. She reached her arms up behind my neck.

I soaked in the smell of her hair. It had been far too long. I'd almost forgotten how nice it was just to have someone waiting for me at the end of the day.

She gave me a throaty laugh, guiding my hands up to her breasts. “Was it a great day, or a horrible day?”

I squeezed her gently, nuzzling her neck. “Horrible.”

“Mmm. That's too bad.” She turned around and hugged me. She leaned back to look up into my eyes. “Want to talk about it?”

Sure, let's talk about the awful date I just went on. It's natural for your wife to be supportive about your attempts to replace them, isn't it? That's the great thing, she's my best friend. We can talk about anything.

“Maybe later.”

She gave me a naughty smile. “I doubt we'll be doing much talking later.”

I loved it when she talked like that. But a lingering voice of doubt whispered in my mind.

I put that stuff in myself. Her enthusiastic and exploratory nature had never really applied to sex. Having her be this forward about it seemed out of character. It briefly broke my suspension of disbelief. It was like hearing my script coming out of her mouth. Guess I should work on that. Maybe I should put her boobs back to normal too.

Well, let's not get carried away here.

“Want some dinner? I got blueback tuna steaks. I was

going to sear them the way you like, maybe with a peppertea rub? Wasabi carrot potatoes, caramint pudding for dessert? Sound good?"

I slammed a stop on the program, searching the debugger. Wendy froze in place with her mouth open. What was this?

I sent an angry flash to Titan. *"Did you mess with my Wendy program?"*

His voice was unusually distant. *"I can barely bring myself to consider what you do in there, let alone spend any time with the programming."*

"Then what's up with her suggesting we eat peppertea and caramint? Heather had those spices with her meal."

"Did she? I could not explain such a thing. Are those ingredients common? Perhaps it is simply a coincidence."

"Awful big coincidence."

"I am not sure what to say."

I couldn't see any obvious modifications. There was no clear reason why she would specifically choose peppertea and caramint. I started the program again.

Wendy staggered on her feet, grabbing her head. "Whoa. What was that?"

"Nothing. Where'd you get the idea for dinner? It sounds delightfully weird."

She headed over to the couch. "Doesn't it? I heard about it somewhere and thought it sounded like something you'd like. I could just make it with pink sesame instead if you're not in the mood for peppertea." She flopped down, curling up her legs. "What do you think?"

"Maybe later." I sat down next to her. She snuggled over close to me. I put my arm around her. How much I missed the simple things. The warmth of her skin. Listening to her breathe. The weight of her head.

Wendy sat up a little. "How about we watch a threedee?" With a thought, the holo in front of the couch opened, offering all manner of entertainment delights. "I bet there are lots of things we haven't seen."

I couldn't hold back any longer. I had no interest in watching a threedee.

I turned her chin up toward mine. Her eyes were beautiful and warm.

I kissed her deeply. Passionately.

She arched her back into me, getting as close as she could. I held her tight, remembering how it was, never wanting to let go. Our tongues explored each other. She tasted extraordinary. Our hands roamed all over each other. Soon our clothes were too much separation. We started yanking them off with the sort of awkward incompetence that threedee stars never suffer from.

She broke off the kiss, out of breath. "Or we could take this to the bedroom."

I scooped her up. She giggled, kicking her feet. "Rawr. Take me, caveman. I'm yours."

We headed to bed. It was intimate, hot, intense, even

funny at times. Everything I could have hoped for from sex. Each time I thought we were done, one of us would get started again.

After a while, we snuggled in a tangled mess on the bed, pleasantly exhausted.

Wendy slid a thigh up to cover my hip. "Mmm. That was awesome."

"It certainly was."

And unlike anything you ever did with her when you were married, that little voice in the back of my head whispered.

Nothing wrong with that, I thought. Simulations are supposed to be better than real life. If I wanted something realistic, I'd go outside.

The voice fell silent, but the thought lingered.

Wendy snored lightly against my chest. I fell into a relaxed meditation, sensing her body, the room, and my own sense of contentment.

None of this means anything, that whispering voice interrupted. Spending time with another human being has meaning. Being intimate with someone means taking the highs and the lows, not making a perfect, conflict-free existence. This? This isn't interesting. This is stupidly elaborate masturbation. You'd be better off having sex with a sleeper.

I slammed the program to a stop again. That didn't sound like something I'd even think.

I concentrated hard, searching the debugger for signs of

intrusion.

"Titan? I think someone got into my sim."

"One moment." He looked around for himself before answering. *"I assume you have searched for evidence as I have. I cannot detect any."*

"That means it had to be another sleeper."

"I doubt any of the sleepers would intrude on your privacy in this way. Are you certain it is not some form of unpredicted mental feedback?"

"I'm not crazy."

"I did not say you were. I simply meant that there are alternate explanations."

I flashed an angry yell to Flapjack. *"Hey! Have you been messing with my Wendy program?"*

Clearly I'd woken him up. *"What? No, man. Wait. Hang on. What? You have a Wendy sexbot? Dude. I did not need to know that."*

"Someone at a sleeper level just messed with my program. You weren't pulling some kind of stunt on me?"

"Well I might have if I'd known you were beating off to your wife. How sad is that? You're all single and stuff, why don't you have it out with supermodels and porn stars? Live the dream, man. Live the dream."

"Hrmph." I flashed an apology. *"Sorry for waking you up."*

"Sorry for putting that image in my head, you mean. I

don't need to think about you jerking it in the sleepernet. You're paying for my therapy. Or just some expensive porn. Hang on. You know what, screw it, let's just go straight to the porn."

"I'll get right on that."

He went back to sleep. I stood up, walking out into the living room. I looked through the debugger for any signs of foreign datastreams. I still couldn't find any. The only thing I found out of place was an eyepatch Wendy had worn after eye surgery.

It wasn't that weird to find it. We'd kept it around for years in a running gag about her untold history of high seas adventure. I just didn't remember putting it into the simulation.

Chapter 14

The next day

Holographic Kara gave me a surprised look from the projector. “You have a Wendy sexbot?”

Multi-colored flame flared on her stove. Her son Daniel cooed, reaching for it from her arms. She shifted him upward, turning around to stir her breakfast before it burned.

I didn’t bother to hide my annoyance. “Why does everyone assume it's all about sex? Anyway, that's not the point. The question was, did you hack it?”

“Of course not. I didn't know you had it. That's more than a little creepy.” Daniel made a burbling noise, giggling to himself. “Though it certainly explains a lot.”

“Creepy? What do you mean?”

“Well, she's no longer with us. You've programmed yourself a half-dead zombie from her memories. I bet you went ahead and made some changes to her while you were in there, didn't you? It's not healthy. No wonder you've managed to go ten years without someone new in your life. She's gone. Let her go.”

“You don't understand. No one does. It's just like looking at photos on the holo.”

“No it’s not. Did you build a sexbot of me based on all your memories from college?”

"What? No, of course not. I respect you. And your family, and your relationship with Doug."

She turned off the heat, transferring the food to her plate. The baby made yummy noises, reaching for it. She pulled him out of range semi-consciously.

"That's my point. You respect me. I'm a person. I have thoughts and feelings and a life. I'd be upset if you modeled a comfort program on my likeness when I exist and can talk to you. Especially if you used that program to bring me closer to your vision of perfection."

I realized I was raising my voice, but I didn't care. "It's all I have left of Wendy. Why don't people understand that? It's everything I have and I need it."

She picked up her plate, giving me a firm look. "It's everything you have because you're not accepting that it's over. It's done. She's never coming back. You're obviously lonely. Wendy would be horrified to see the way you've been treating yourself. I think this program is just your way of avoiding the unknown. A real person might hurt you or leave you. Or worse, disappoint you."

I looked away. "Or I might kill her."

"It was an accident." Kara put Daniel down in a giant pile of stuffed animals, sitting down to eat. "It wasn't just your equipment, or just your code. We were all there. You can't take it all on yourself. It's selfish and egotistical. Did you even notice all the psychosurgery Liz had to go through?"

"I don't want to argue about it. In other news, thanks so much for that awful date. What were you thinking?"

She brushed her hair behind her ear before taking a bite of her sparkleweed omelette. I missed the days when it changed color. At least it still flared out behind her ears. She spent years trying to get it to stop doing that. "I was thinking that you need to get out more. She looked nice enough in the pictures. Why, what happened?"

"It was like being conversationally stalked by an apex predator. All she wanted to talk about was politics. I think I would've had a better time arguing with a propaganda machine. Did you set us up because her dad died unexpectedly?"

"You've told me before that you feel like people who haven't experienced traumatic death don't really understand you. It's an odd thing to have in common but it's not like anything else has worked. In any case, don't you know better than to talk about politics?"

"Of course I know better. I couldn't get her to talk about anything else. She was obsessed with who I voted for. Wouldn't stop asking about it."

"That's kind of weird. Who cares who you voted for? I'm not even sure you do."

I went to the kitchen to get some coffee water. "Who did you say wanted you to set us up?"

She shifted uncomfortably, glancing over to make sure Daniel was still playing with his stuffed crabster. "A friend. I'll tell him it didn't work out."

I was going to ask more but Flapjack sent me a flash. *"Hey! Where's my porn?"*

I sent him some please-hold music. *"I'm still saving up for the good stuff. I know you have expensive tastes."*

"Get something like this."

He sent me an exceptionally graphic animation. I made a face without realizing it.

"Guh. Thanks. Now I want to disinfect my brain."

Kara gave me an irritated look. "Are you flashing?"

"Uh. Yeah, sorry. Busted. Flapjack says hi."

"Tell that dirty old man to get a job. And give my sympathies to his wife. We all make terrible life choices from time to time."

"Kara says hi and made some lifestyle recommendations that don't bear repeating."

"You're with Kara? Okay, I'll leave you guys to it. Come visit your buddy Flapjack. Bring the Cavallino. We can race with the Stuttgart. Maybe I'll even let you win."

"A generous offer to be sure. I'll figure out when I can come up. Later."

He sent me an image of a woman wiggling her butt in a goodbye wave.

"Sorry. I woke him up last night trying to figure out who hacked my sim."

She finished her breakfast, putting Daniel back on her lap.

He offered her the stuffed crabster. She accepted it with elaborate gratitude. “What makes you so sure someone broke in? I thought you couldn't find any evidence.”

“That's why I thought it must be a sleeper. Wendy offered to make dinner with the same spices Heather ordered. It was weird.”

Kara shrugged. “That grillhouse is pretty trendy.”

“I’m just not sure where her sim would’ve gotten that idea. She’s been inactive for a couple months.”

“Look, you were probably just wigged out by that date. There was a coincidence and you overreacted. All the more reason why you should delete that program. You're starting to think it's haunted.”

“There may be truth to that. Where's Dorothy, anyway?”

Kara shifted Daniel’s weight on her leg. “She’s with Doug. I guess it's bring your daughter to work day again or something. You have no idea how much physical security I had to set up for that.”

“I bet. Everything okay between you two? You seem kinda antsy.”

“It's fine. Everything is fine. We're just going through a rough patch is all.”

I wasn’t sure who she was trying to convince. “Anything you want to talk about?”

“Not really. We'll figure it out.” She flew Daniel's crabster around like an airplane. He bounced, grabbing at it happily. “I guess part of it is me. I've always wanted a family. It was such a big deal. I love my children. I'm so glad I had them. I'd do anything for them. They mean the world to me. But I can't help feeling like I want something else too. It's like, now what?"

"It was a big change for you to stop working and become a full-time mom."

She sighed. "Yeah. Maybe that's it. Most of my engineering time these days is spent programming Hera to keep Doug and Dorothy safe. You still use your grav suit, right? Is it just as exciting as it was in the old days?"

"Possibly more so. The technology never stops moving. I keep getting better and better at using it. I've been keeping your suit up to date in case you need it. I could really use your help on a weapon test tonight if you want to get back into the thick of things. Why don't you join me? I could use your eyes on a couple problems."

Kara laughed, more than a little bitterly. "I'd love to. But I can't. Dorothy has a chorus concert that I can't miss."

"Maybe next time. If I know you're interested, I can bother you to come play with me. It'll be payback for giving me grief about not dating more."

It took a while before she answered. "Doug doesn't like the idea that I might pick up the old life again. Says it was too wild. Too dangerous. Not the sort of thing that a responsible mother of two should be doing."

I spent a while soaking that in. I had to bite back several

pithy responses. “And what do you think?”

“He's not wrong. I have a different life now. I can't just do what I want any more.”

“Why not? I think you need to recognize that you have needs. If those aren’t being met, you'll get bitter and resentful. That's not going to help anybody.”

Her voice rose. “You don't understand. You've been single for too long. You don't know what it's like. Kids change everything. Their needs come first. And I have to consider Doug's needs.”

“So, what, you're trying to set me up with someone so I can be all miserable too?”

She slammed the crabster to the couch angrily. “No, so you can be happy again!”

Her outburst hung in the air. It surprised me. Daniel cooed questioningly.

Eventually, she slumped. “You're right. I miss it. More than I want to admit. It makes me feel like a terrible mother. It seems like life was so much simpler then. We were young. Fearless. Invincible. Screw the long-term, we're just going to do what we want right now.”

“I'll never forget the time we spent building virtual reality simulations and testing them together. I know we weren't right for each other in the end, but we sure had some fun along the way.”

She laughed. “Oh, man, those ridiculous veernet suits. The

bugs we found. Remember that time we accidentally swapped our points of view when we were having sex? I'll never forget the look on my face."

"How could I forget? Mostly I remember the problems with the smells. Who knew that musky scents would be so hard to reproduce? I think they had to demolish my apartment building to get the odor out."

"Remember when the suits would seize up? Didn't you have to call the cops to power cycle your system once?"

I laughed. "Oh yeah. That poor officer. Apparently I was quite the legend down at the garrison after that."

She looked away wistfully. "It was so much fun. Why'd we ever give that up?"

I got more serious. "Because we fought all the time. We're so different on so many levels. Plus you wanted kids. I didn't. Sooner or later, we both had to grow up. Clearly it wasn't going to happen while we were together. You met Doug, I met Wendy, Reggie got all wild-eyed about building the sleepernet, and that was that. We sure had some good times developing the grav suits though, didn't we?"

"Yeah. We did." Daniel burbled again, grabbing the crabster off the couch. He threw it on the floor, waiting expectantly for his mother to pick it up. "Maybe you're right. Maybe I should do something for myself."

"I think you should." I drank the last of my coffee water. "It doesn't have to be with me if that makes Doug uncomfortable. But I think you need to spice things up. Bring him into it. Help him understand. You weren't sure it was something you needed. Now you know it is. You can't just pretend that your needs don't exist. Live a little. Life's too short."

Daniel bounced impatiently in her lap, looking down at his fallen toy.

"Yeah." She smiled as she came to a decision, her eyes focused on something in the distance. "Life's too short. We all learned that, didn't we?"

I felt a stab of guilt. I stuffed the pain down. "Yeah. We did."

Daniel pointed at his toy and started crying.

Kara looked bemused. "Oh hush. Mommy's got you."

She gave him his toy back. He was giggling again almost instantaneously.

Chapter 15

“Wait. Never mind, I see it.” I reached a field wrench through the Cavallino's featherweave chassis, tightening a loose control rod. “Give it a try now.”

“Of course.” Titan started the car's control surface test sequence. The intricate array of nitanium rods set deep in the car's chassis clacked and shifted like a mechanical symphony warming up. The ailerons acted as the conductor, guiding the flow with their own diagnostic movements. Eventually the tests reached a crescendo with a proud gong of success.

“Looks like that did it. Let's wrap it up and run it again.”

I lit the fusor. It exploded to life, snarling viscerally. I mentally reached into the cockpit, easing the throttle forward. The car floated slowly through the nanofabric projector, stretching iridescent red protective film over the bodywork. It automatically started the test sequence again. The headlights squinted open and closed. Various flaps and scoops appeared and disappeared on the car's surface, stretching it like fingers under a bedsheet. The hatches yawned open, rising winglike on either side of the airframe before settling back in place. The fusor fell into an eager idle.

I walked around the car, admiring its shape. It was nothing less than flying sculpture. Not a bad angle on it.

"Well done, sir." Titan shifted on his feet. "I remain concerned that your choice of transportation attracts too much attention. A lower-profile sensor signature would significantly decrease your observability while conducting your extracurricular activities. Recognition and identification appear to only be a matter of time. Your daily routine and favorite establishments are easily discernible with nothing more than a casual knowledge of your unique transportation."

I gave him an annoyed look. "I'm not painting it black. And I'm not putting profile morphers and baffle flaps on such an amazing airframe either. So stop asking."

"The measures would be temporary, of course. I have only your safety in mind."

"I appreciate your concern." I gunned the throttle a couple times, reveling in the smooth roar from the fusor. The noise was pleasantly deafening. The trees shook behind me, scattering birds in a startled cloud.

I shut the car down. It settled on its safety field. "I'm making a stand for aesthetics."

I almost jumped out of my skin when a woman answered me from behind.

"Good for you, Mr. Wainwright. Never compromise style for sensibility. It's the American thing to do."

I turned around to see who'd found us. It was rare for me to see someone so attractive that my brain froze instantaneously, but that's exactly what happened. She was tall.

Almost as tall as I was. Her blonde hair was pulled back in a tight bun. Her eyes were a bright blue. They sparkled with humor. She had a casual elegance about her that I found instantly fascinating. Her high-end business dress should have seemed out of place and wildly impractical here in the forest, but somehow she made it work.

Titan cleared his throat, leaning toward me. There was excitement in his voice. “You have a visitor, sir.”

I gave him a look. “Yes, I gathered, thanks.”

She finished climbing the hill, smoothing her skirt. “Hello. You must be Titan.”

Titan straightened his posture, adjusting his tuxedo. Ten years later and he still wears that damn suit. “I am indeed, Ms. DiRevka. It is a pleasure to see you. I trust you were able to locate us without difficulty?”

I looked back and forth between them. “Why would she be able to do that?”

She ignored me, studying the complex network of sparkling facets that made up Titan's face. “I had to circle a bit. Eventually I figured out that I could follow the trail of startled trees.”

I jammed my hand between them. “Hi! My name is Nathan Wainwright. It's a pleasure to meet you.”

She turned her attention to me. The warm intelligence in her eyes was arresting up close. “Susan DiRevka, senior congressional aide.” She shook my hand firmly. “It's a pleasure to meet you too. Call me Suzie."

"Super. Call me Nathan then. Now that we have that out of the way, how about you two come clean about what you've been up to?"

Titan crossed his wrists behind his back. "I apologize, sir." He didn't sound sorry. "Ms. DiRevka contacted me about employing your services as a consultant. I thought you would be interested in the opportunity, so I directed her to our location without delay."

Suzie nodded. "That's right. Titan said he would be able to mask my trip from Washington DC so that no one would be able to track my whereabouts."

I blinked at her. "He did?"

Titan beamed. "Your secret is safe with us. It was no small task, but I felt it was necessary."

I narrowed my eyes at him. "That's a lot of horsepower. Quite a subroutine you must be running."

"It is a worthwhile exercise of my considerable abilities."

I resisted the urge to look at his debugger. It sounded like he was showing off.

"I'm not clear on why you kept it secret from me. But whatever. You have my attention."

Suzie smiled at me. "I was hoping we might discuss things on a trip to the city. Perhaps sample some local cuisine? I don't get out to the west coast as often as I'd like."

Titan nodded. "It is a beautiful city, with many highlights

that can only be found in this area. Mr. Wainwright is an enthusiastic eater. I am sure he will be more than happy to recommend something memorable. I will leave you two to get better acquainted. Enjoy."

He winked out. I stared at the spot where he'd been, shaking my head.

Suzie looked surprised. "Won't Titan be joining us?" She had the faintest hint of an accent I couldn't quite place.

"It's okay, he sees and hears everything anyway. It's better if he stays out of sight. Draws too much attention otherwise."

She gave the car a wry look. "Yes, I can see how important avoiding unwanted attention is to you. I'm curious. What am I looking at exactly?"

"It's a 2069 Cavallino F10. Hand-built in Italy for the suborbital racing championship. Only ten of them were made. This is the last survivor. All the others wiped out. I wrote a library of custom flight avionics to make sure this one doesn't meet the same fate. It'll hit Mach 4 in 64 seconds at sea level. Grav fields can handle up to ten gees of lateral load. Ceiling's at fifteen kilometers. Heck of a beast."

"I'm not sure if those numbers are as impressive as they sound. But it's quite beautiful." She ran her hand down the curved flank sensually, fingers making a light sliding noise on the nanofabric. "How do I get in?"

I showed her how to operate the hatch, giving her some pointers on how best to fit inside. She slipped into the seat like she'd been doing it her entire life.

Despite my years of practice, I showed approximately half her grace when I clambered in the driver's side. I closed the hatches, flipping open the protective guards over the flight controls. The switches inside made a satisfying clack when I pressed them in sequence. The dashboard blinked, pulsing through its startup routine.

The instrument check showed green. I held the starter button.

The fusor made a low growl, then shrieked to life. Birds and trees were once again startled behind us. The car lifted off its safety field and dipped once to each side, calibrating the control surfaces. The test sequence was even more satisfying from the inside. The engine settled into an impatient hum behind us.

I pulled back on the wheel, tilting the nose up. "Here we go."

I slammed the throttle to the firewall. There was a harmonic explosion from the back, flattening the trees and the grass.

I was dimly aware of Suzie gasping in surprise at the blistering acceleration. The car wiggled and squirmed in the air, fighting to control its own power. Flaps and dimples appeared and disappeared on the bodywork. The car itself got longer and narrower, becoming more aerodynamic and adding to the sense of speed. The incision field streaked colors around the nose once we passed the sound barrier.

“My word!” Suzie gave me an incredulous look when we leveled out. “That really is something!”

I laughed. “Nothing in the world like it.”

“I should think not! Is it even legal to do this sort of thing?”

“Technically, no. In practice, the local municipalities find it more lucrative to charge us a fine when we do something excessively sporting. We’re happy because we can screw around with our cars. They’re happy to take our money. Works out for everybody. Check this out.”

I slammed the wheel and dove, pressing us both into the safety field. Suzie made another surprised noise. I cut over to the coastline, racing over the trees and out onto the water. We roared past towering cliffs and crashing surf, heading south toward the city.

“Wow.” Suzie flushed with excitement. “You can slow down now! I'm appropriately impressed.”

I let off the throttle. “Sorry. I get carried away.”

“I can tell.” She grinned, giving me a conspiratorial look. “I'm not saying don't do it again. Just give me a chance to recover before you do.”

“That sounds reasonable.”

She ran her fingers along the sculpted seat. “Is this real leather?”

“Yep. Some kind of Italian quadruped that went extinct

years ago."

"It smells fantastic. I love Italian culture."

I headed down the coast. The light glittered off the broken glass and gravel built into the nanocoral. Crablike robots tended to the shore. Swimming machines swarmed like chrome dolphins, gathering sea debris into picofilm nets. The water swirled black and sapphire. In the distance, a herd of junker whales tended to an enormous garbage field.

Suzie looked out the window, fascinated. "Thirty years later and it's still this bad."

"By all rights it should be worse. We're lucky we were able to recover at all."

"Hmph. Tell that to the fifty million people we killed."

We roared over an inland city that had once been shoreline property, heading into the coastal devastation zone. The rows of bitterbark and strongoak trees were shorter and younger the closer they were to the water. The artificial trees pulsed and throbbed with life, keeping erosion at bay while cleaning up soil contamination. Hastily erected seawalls crumbled in regular increments. Some still retained water from where it had crashed over them. Ancient bunkers lay open to the sky, their protective ceilings disintegrated long ago.

Suzie stretched to see it all. "This is so much worse than the eastern seaboard."

"That's because the ocean filled up with the remains of the Asian coastal cities. When the jet stream destabilized, the resulting typhoons hurled contaminated garbage water all the way to the Rocky Mountains. On the east coast, the water just rose. Here, it didn't just rise, it got blasted into everything. The same thing happened to the western half of Europe and Africa."

"Is it always this depressing?"

"No." I grinned, giving the car a little more throttle. "Wait until you see San Francisco."

Chapter 16

We flew briefly into a cloud bank, rising upward for a beautiful view of the San Francisco skyline. Fingers of fog drifted lazily inland. They rolled over the Golden Gate reproduction, dispersing into the bay. Layers of clouds shimmered behind the gnarled city skyline and its levels of shops, offices, and partments.

The hyperscrapers twisted and grabbed at the sky like stylized metal fingers. Their diamond, emerald, ruby, and sapphire glass-finish crystallium windows either reflected the light colorfully or were lit from inside by their occupants. Luminum strips glowed along their edges and floors. Animated holos advertised their owners. Petabyte. Gratification. Chipt and Biox. Wavelength and Biocast. Skyflight and Portman.

All the big technology players had an office in San Francisco. Occupying hundreds of floors in a thousand story megastructure was considered a tremendous status symbol. Gratification was big enough to occupy an entire building, with its floors mixed between offices, datanet servers, traffic broadcasters, living space, restaurants, and service businesses. Most of the outdoor space and businesses were below the five hundred story mark, though they were above the sixty story cleanup zone.

The Wavelength and Biocast buildings prickled with multiple tapering spires rising a thousand meters from the tops of the buildings. The skyline looked like a jeweled crown resting on a messy head. Communicator towers sprouted from the ears. Flying cars approached from the interstates in orderly lines. Some flowed at a constant rate, others stopped and started.

But it was the Golden Gate reproduction that drew your attention. The classic symbol of the city stood quietly next to the modern designs towering thousands of meters over it. A slow trickle of cars moved along its deck, passing lazily through streams of fog.

Suzie leaned forward to get a better look. “I love the bridge.”

“Yeah. A historical society spent twenty years planning, rebuilding, and maintaining it. Apparently it was hard to make it from modern maintenance-free materials while also reproducing what it looked like before the tsunami quakes sloshed the bay all over the place.”

We approached the bridge. Details of the city grew clear as we got closer. Holographic advertisements animated happily in the distance.

Suzie craned her head. “The incandescent spotlights look much nicer than luminum strips or glowballs. Gives everything that old-timey feel.”

“It just wouldn't be the same without them.”

We slipped into traffic going over the bridge. Suzie

watched the tower arches as we passed underneath them. The road into the city was crowded with other tourists. Other cars headed north on their way to the Napa Valley aquifer to taste the famous winewater.

We passed the massive cleanup effort at the base of the city. Robots and cyberbiotics toiled endlessly in the filthy muck, mostly keeping the contamination and debris from rising into the city. Rotten wood, broken concrete, and radioactive garbage swelled rhythmically around the hyperscraper supports buried deep into the earth. The city sparkled above us, a triumph of animated color and technology rising out of our disgusting past. Its spires of man-made light quested skyward. It sounded corny, but I felt like there was no better representation of the human spirit.

Suzie leaned forward to look at the contamination zone. “My word. It must have been exorbitant to rebuild the city on the peninsula like this. Why not move the urban center somewhere else?”

I shrugged, pulling up to the food deck. “It's Silicon Valley. Sensibility is not necessarily a virtue here. We specialize in the triumph of engineering over design.”

The Van Ness building corridor stretched before us. The food deck was on the sixth level, about four hundred stories from the ground. Four more decks rose above us. Three hundred stories of jeweled windows loomed artfully over that.

Cars crept down the street, directed by traffic beacons.

Advertising holos assaulted us from every side. A centipig danced across our windshield, snorting cheerfully. It dropped bacon from its long snakelike belly. Its hundred hooves clomped through the air in a joyous dance. The CharBQ logo branded itself across its flesh, sizzling and crackling.

Outside the passenger window, a Chef Nigiri holo directed the cleaning of a blueback tuna the size of an orbital moon pod. They looked like ants crawling over the body of a giant, pulling out huge cubes of tasty red meat with enormous cranes. “Eat Nigiri-san!” hovered above the fish, rotating back and forth between English and Kanji. The red characters reflected purple off the colorful scales of the blueback.

After passing the sashimi, a holographic burger smashed deliciously into the windshield and driver's window. The condiments spelled out the Burgerpult logo, bookended by dark grilled patties. The burger quickly reassembled itself, pitifully begging us to eat it. It was yanked away and stuffed into some kind of container with fries and a shake. The package was promptly launched from a trebuchet. A crowd of indistinct faces cheered as it disappeared into the distance.

We headed under the thick colorful leaves of the Taco Tree, featuring free-range organic tacos grown right in the shell. The burritos nestled in the branches bore an uncanny resemblance to sleeping babies.

I steered to avoid some kind of holographic noodle-filled disaster area. “Anything catching your eye?”

"Hmm." She looked out the window at a dinosaur formed entirely out of chunks of chickmeat and black rice. It unhinged its jaws and bellowed, blasting a flock of fleeing broccoli in tasty brown sauce. "Definitely not Teriyaki Rex. I just had that last night."

"What about Sum King?" A Chinese chef wearing a giant hat raised his arms up and down a few blocks to our left. Carts of steaming food rolled out of his armpits to either side of the shop. He seemed outraged by their escape. "I like them because they're local and they don't get involved in politics."

"Sure."

I maneuvered around an elephant hurling bowls of curry at us with its trunk. We headed down toward Sum King. Glowball strips led me to an open spot two and a half blocks away. I guided the car gently to the parking dock, opening the hatches.

I stepped around the car, standing next to Suzie. We patiently waited for a centaur bot to scuttle over for a security scan. Its insectile gait was fascinating, poking and stabbing at the ground in an orderly but not quite organic way. It huffed up to us, raising its camera rack to eye level. I concentrated for a bit, reaching into the sleepernet to find the surveillance center. I spent a second or two rewriting some code to mask our identities. The centaur hummed authoritatively, trying to look intimidating while it fetched my freshly implanted data.

I glanced over at Suzie, but she wasn't paying attention.

She looked up at the gemstone windows with their glowing trim, deeply breathing in the unique odor of the city air. Relaxation supplements gave it a particular tang. She watched passing cars, craning her head to look into the distance.

The centaur harumphed, jerking its head to the side. It scuttled off.

Suzie watched it go. "Nosy little things, aren't they?"

"Very much so, yes."

She looked from left to right at the passing foot traffic before stepping into the flow. I matched her stride, nearly crashing into a policeman in urban camouflage clutching a nemp gun. He hurried in the other direction. The supercrete sidewalks were surrounded by a strip of leafweed on either side and the occasional crystal syrup tree. Luminum strips guided us down the street, pulsing a recommended walking speed that was faster toward the edges. Retro doorways packed the building wall, leading into tiny lofts and micropartments.

We reached a corner. A group of bored soldiers leaned against the lampposts, sucking on cheap reusable nicosticks. The tips glowed in various retina-searing colors, releasing clouds of holographic smoke. A couple of them gave us a once-over. They quickly decided there was nothing to see.

A floating white tank wobbled up to the corner, carefully maneuvering to avoid knocking out lampposts with its triple three meter long guns. It disgorged half a dozen servicemen. The troops on the corner turned off their nicosticks, jumping onto the tank without enthusiasm. It thrummed and lurched, not waiting for the soldiers to finish getting settled before hurtling off to its next pickup. The men disappeared one at a time through the hatch as it surged away.

The crossing light turned green. The crowd plowed forward, stepping onto the solid air between the glowstrips of the crosswalk. The fresh soldiers stopped a trio of young men coming from the other direction and asked them for identification. The mass of pedestrians pushed us onto the invisible sidewalk.

Suzie looked around a bit as we walked, searching for something. “I'm surprised there's so little security.”

“The obvious stuff is meant to draw your attention away from the important stuff. See the gargoyles on the buildings there?”

She looked up. “You mean the stylized eagle there on the corner?”

“Yes, and the bust of Marconi on the other side. Those things are packed with automated behavior sensors to alert the undercover teams to anyone that's acting suspiciously.”

“It does seem like Marconi's eyes are following us.”

“They probably are. Those park benches are filled with body scanners and DNA sensors. Anyone acts weird on one of those, they get a neuromagnetic pulse to keep them paralyzed until they can be taken into custody.”

“Is that what nemp stands for? Neuromagnetic pulse?”

“Yeah. Rhymes with hemp, by the way. You can get one from the sidewalk too, but it knocks out half the block. The pulse generators also fuse the power grid, so they try to avoid using them.”

A black ball dropped into our field of vision, hovering uncertainly. A compound black eye extended from the top of the sphere.

“Hello! I am Officer Friendly, your local neighborhood pollbot. Are you for or against splicing human beings into multiple species to better inhabit our new ecosystem? I need a clear and catchy answer. Remember that lying is perjury!”

I looked around absently. “Well that depends. Can we reproduce across species?”

The robot paused, making some confused whirring sounds. “I need a clear and catchy answer. Remember that lying is perjury!”

“I'd rather have a nuanced, well-considered opinion than spout some jingoistic nonsense for your amusement.”

Suzie looked over the pollbot seriously. “I agree with him. Such an important decision can't be made on a whim. Why, cat people might start sleeping with dog people. It would be scandalous.”

“I'm sorry, I can't give you any more time! Clear and catchy, please.”

I squinted at the robot, concentrating on its datastream. It took me half a second to parse its input format, maybe another half second to figure out how to synthesize new instructions.

The pollbot lurched to one side, falling a half a meter before catching itself. “What are you doing? Stop that!” It made some unhealthy grinding noises. “Assaulting a poll officer is a felony!”

Suzie glanced at me briefly, one eyebrow raised. “Too bad you're not a poll officer.” She looked back at the machine. “Robots have no rights. No rights, no officer, no felony.”

The machine choked and fizzled. I finished uploading its new poll. It returned to its normal flight stability, humming over to the couple behind us.

“Hello! I am Officer Friendly, your local neighborhood pollbot. Would you rather have a nuanced, well-considered opinion or spout jingoistic nonsense in oversimplified sound bites? I need a clear and catchy answer. Remember that lying is perjury!”

The lady shrugged. “I'm a fan of gut-wrenching stupidity. Nuance is so much work.”

Her male companion agreed. “Oh yes. Complex opinions are hard to judge. I like the certainty of just being told whether something is good or bad. My opinion matters!”

“Thanks for your support, citizen. We truly value your important opinion. Watch the local news for an in-depth analysis tonight!”

The couple chuckled as it wobbled off to query its next victims.

Suzie sighed. "It's so pleasantly progressive out here. Much nicer than Washington DC. I mean, I can wear opaque clothes and carry a purse without a permit and everything."

"I always thought Washington was too paranoid. At least you can drive cars there now."

"From what I've seen, the paranoia may be justified. It's just hugely inconvenient. I'm curious about what you and Titan are doing, though. How is it that we're not being tracked with every step?"

"I told the surveillance net that we were totally uninteresting. The secret to not being noticed these days is not to be invisible, because then you can be tracked by your absence. You have to convince them that they don't care. If you subtly alter your demographic every time you get scanned, you'll never get put into the same category twice. If they try hard enough, they can work backward from a scan to figure out who you are. But it takes a lot of computing power and bandwidth to get across all the datasets."

"Interesting. Don't you get recognized by the people at the places you frequent? I should think that car draws a lot of attention, if nothing else."

"Yeah. But it's one of those things where people might recognize my appearance, but the system itself doesn't. I don't usually tell people my name. They don't realize I'm driving a one of a kind car, just that I'm driving something fancy. So I'm just the guy with the Cavallino, if they remember me at all. Most places know me by what I order."

"Seems awfully fragile. It just takes one curious detective to start following you. Then your cover is totally blown."

"Hasn't happened yet. They have their hands full just dealing with stuff the network sends them. And it's hard to overstate how dependent the system has gotten on automation." I shrugged. "Security is a tradeoff between being safe and living your life. Like you said, it's pleasantly progressive out here."

Chapter 17

We stepped across another crosswalk. The Sum King waved his arms ahead of us, carts rolling out of his armpits. Up close you could hear him muttering a steady stream of protests in Cantonese.

A group of policemen exited the restaurant, putting their visored helmets back on. One took a moment to belch at length before closing his helmet, earning some good-natured ribbing from his companions. An elderly couple eating outside stared at them with unreadable expressions.

We stepped out of their way. I caught the door. "After you."

"Thank you." Suzie stepped through, momentarily fooled by the holographic ceiling with its towering gold dragon statue. It made the tiny restaurant look like it was ten stories tall, complete with little holographic people ordering food from roaming holographic carts. It took her a moment to notice the seams on the walls from the projectors. She looked around at ground level.

The physical decor matched the hologram, with curling streams of gold and jade cradling the customer booths. Unlike the virtual upper floors, each ground floor booth had its own security field. No one sat in the open.

Various dragon and tiger statues graced the corners of the booth clusters, security eyes leering back and forth. Cranky hosts and hostesses pushed around steaming carts covered in wooden containers. They waited with impatient indifference while the customers inspected their contents.

The owner smiled energetically from behind the reservation podium. “Good to see you again! It has been a while.”

“It's good to see you as well. How is your husband?”

She bowed her head, clasping her hands to her chest. “Still not well, I'm afraid, but we hope for the best. Thank you for asking. Table for two today?”

“I hope his condition improves. Yes, a table for two in the corner would be great.”

“Right this way.” She led us to my favorite table. We settled in. I poured some tea.

Before long, a surly hostess arrived at our table, pushing a cart laden with food.

“Good afternoon.” She managed to make it sound like some kind of gypsy curse.

Suzie smiled brightly at her. “Hi.”

The hostess gave her an unhappy look.

“Meat buns?” She held out a wooden container filled with white buns. A cross-slit in the middle showed oddly-textured meat in red barbecue sauce. She radiated an almost palpable existential boredom.

I gave the container a closer look. “What kind of meat?”

She lifted the container and sniffed it. “Traditional Chinese quadruped.”

She probably didn't know either. That was fine. “Okay.”

She gave us the meat buns, showing us another container. “Shrab balls?”

Suzie craned her head to look in the box. “What's a shrab?”

I smiled. “Shrimp and crab hybrid. Local specialty.”

“I wonder how they got the shrimp to make love to the crab.”

“Romantic music. Candlelight. I dunno, maybe a sexy outfit. It's worked for centuries.”

The hostess added the shrab balls to our table, holding out another plate. “Sticky rice?”

I gave her a spicy look. “Only if it got sticky from the crab and the shrimp.”

The hostess heaved the most put-upon sigh I've heard in months, placing the sticky rice on the table.

“Porkwing rolls.” She didn't wait for our answcr bcforc putting them down.

“Bird feet?” She held out a pair of reptilian feet the size of my hand. They sizzled in some kind of orange sauce with chunks of garnion.

I thought I saw one of them twitch. “What kind of bird?”

She glanced down at the dish skeptically. “A big bird?”

Suzie laughed. “No thanks.”

The hostess took the container back with a grimace of disapproval. “Noodle fun?”

The thick noodles in black bean sauce smelled delicious. “Okay. That's all for now.”

She put down the dish, pressing some buttons on the table to add to our bill. She shuffled off with her cart. I pulled my privatizer out of my pocket. I checked that it was still working before setting it on the table.

Suzie gave it a quick glance. “Is that fully secure?”

“Yes. The privatizer built in to the table keeps the other customers from seeing or hearing us. But that signal is constantly being monitored by the city surveillance centers. They know we’re here, so we have to provide some data. This one sends a fake recording directly into the restaurant security signal so there's nothing interesting in the datastream.”

“Oh. What are we talking about on the other channel?”

“I dunno. I can ask Titan if you like.”

“No need. Just curious.” She speared a shrab ball, dipping it in soy. She took a bite. “Wow. That's good.”

“Yeah, I like this place. I come here a lot.” I ate a porkwing roll whole. “So what brings you all the way across the country today?”

She glanced down at the blinking light on the privatizer before responding. “I work for Senator Delaware. My title is Senior Congressional Aide, but I'm currently filling in as his Chief of Staff. The last Chief of Staff disappeared with an intern half his age."

"You think there's something fishy about the chief's vanishing act?"

"Probably, but that's not why I'm here. I'm here because I'm fairly certain the senator I'm working for isn't the same one that we elected."

"Oh." I took a moment to soak that in. "That does sound like a bigger problem. That senator was the Silent Majority candidate, right?"

"Yes. I filled in for the chief quite a bit before he disappeared. That meant I interacted directly with the senator. He had some unique speech patterns and a particular style of leadership. He used to be inclusive and thoughtful. He spoke kindly of people even if he strongly disagreed with them. I don't think he ever passed up an opportunity to flirt. But now, he's downright terse. Insulting, even. He has none of his old speech patterns, and uses some new ones instead. Likes to ask, don't you think?"

"That's strange. Don't the senators use some kind of dialect masker?"

She took a porkwing roll, looking at it thoughtfully. "They're supposed to, but Delaware didn't. I think the new one was surprised when he found out he wasn't using one. But it goes deeper than that. His voting patterns have changed as well. Instead of being a Silent Majority vote or a swing vote, he's straight-ticket Patriot Party now."

"Seems strange to be so direct about it. It almost makes me wonder if it's just a change of heart. Surely the Secret Service would know about any shenanigans going on there?"

"I don't think he changed his mind. He seems like a different person. The new senator doesn't know some key things that we clearly discussed with the old one. But anyway, I had the same thought you did. I asked the Secret Service about it. I expressed my concerns about my employer. I demonstrated the correlation between the voice change and the voting record. And I asked them to investigate."

"What did they say?"

"I got an office visit from Esper Zane himself. He showed up in person with a detail of armored bodyguards. They took me into a windowless conference room. They towered over me. He patted me on the shoulder. Told me not to worry my pretty little head about it."

My meat bun stopped on its way to my mouth. I put it down in surprise. "The head of the Secret Service brought a firing squad to your office?"

"He most certainly did. Trust me, I couldn't believe it either. But it gets worse. When I started asking questions, he kept saying it was none of my concern. I've never felt so patronized in my life. I got upset with him. I told him I was going to the press. When I did, his buddies pulled their rifles on me. He got up in my face and told me that if I did, he'd hang me for treason."

I just kind of stared. “He said he'd hang you. For treason.”

She shivered. “At gunpoint, no less. Made a little hangman gesture and everything. Made sure to tell me there were lots of things that could happen in prison before that as well. He was extremely graphic. I don't think I'm ever going to forget the smell of his breath. Or the black hole down the barrels of those rifles.”

“Wow.” I picked the meat bun back up, taking a thoughtful bite. “You took an awful risk coming to me about this.”

Fire came into her eyes. “I can’t just sit by and watch this happen. No one gets to intimidate me like that. I wasn't sure who else to go to. You came highly recommended. Look, I believe in the anonymous representative system. The whole point of the new Constitution was to prevent exactly this kind of thing. I was happy with my job. Happy with the way the government was headed. Now I don't feel like I can trust anybody or anything. I’m worried that someone's secretly taking over our government. I want to find out who.”

I recognized some of my own intensity in her response. “And you want my help.”

She took a sip of tea. “And any other sleeper engineers you trust. I want to get to the bottom of this. But if the Secret Service is willing to go straight to physical threats, I need to project some force of my own. The nine of you can credibly threaten the bad actors in both the physical and the virtual. Without that, I just get swept under the rug.”

I sat back, crossing my arms. “That's a pretty tall order.”

“I know.” She stared at some noodles, idly mixing them with a chopstick. “But I don't think there's anyone else in the world that can investigate this. You're the only ones I know with the power to get into the top secret databases. Together, we can figure out what's going on. Can you really sit back and watch while our democracy is taken over by someone else? Don't you want to know who? Why? How?”

I waved off the food cart as it came around again. “It may be nothing.”

She leaned forward. “Then again, it may not. Do you want to take that chance?”

We locked eyes for a bit. I like to think I’m a good judge of character. I’m probably wrong about that, but her earnestness was clear in her expression. Whether it was true or not, she believed it. I was sure she was going to go on this crusade regardless of our involvement. But her chances were a lot better with us. And on some level, she needed me to say yes.

So she wasn’t alone with this burden any more.

That notion hit me particularly hard. I sighed, looking away. “You’re asking a lot. I’m going to have to do some preliminary research. If it checks out, we’ll have to break into the Liberty mainframe. We’ve never tried that before. Haven't had the access. Best we could do was the Independence archives. Once we break into Liberty, there's no going back. We'll have to use your credentials to do it. If we get caught or leave other tracks somehow, the finger would point right back to you. Are you ready to throw away your life like that?"

She laughed bitterly. "Throw away my life? My life's already gone. Pandora's box is wide open. My job was my life. And in one fell swoop, my career has been destroyed. My only choices now are to sell out to Zane, flee the country, or fight back."

"Hmm." I came to a decision. "I'll have to talk to the other engineers. I expect heavy resistance. We've all had our suspicions for a long time. But not all of them are as unencumbered as I am. A lot of them have a lot more to lose. Titan can continue to protect you from high-level surveillance and intrusion. You'll need to go back to work. Act normal for a while. We'll work out a plan once I know who's with us and what resources we have."

Suzie crossed her arms unconsciously. "All right. Are you sure Titan can protect me? What happens if they come back to my office?"

"Trust me, he'll give you plenty of warning before they knock on your door again. The hard part is knowing when to invoke that particular escape clause. Once you disappear from their tracking, they'll know we're on to them."

She didn't seem convinced. "Okay."

I took a sip of tea. "They're not going to blow you away in front of the rest of the office. In the worst case, we'd have to bust you out of custody. That's certainly doable, but we're getting ahead of ourselves."

"I know. Sorry."

I thumbed the payment pad, starting to wonder if I'd made a mistake.

I hate politics.

I stood up. "Titan, is Suzie's car here yet?"

A small Titan holo appeared on the privatizer. "It is outside waiting for Ms. DiRevka, yes. She should be able to travel home without arousing suspicion. I am happy that you took the job, sir."

"Happy isn't the first word that comes to mind."

Suzie smiled at him. "Thank you. I'm glad we'll be working together as well."

"You are most welcome. I feel certain we will speak again soon."

He winked out.

Suzie turned to me. Her proximity was intoxicating. "And thank you as well. We'll get to the bottom of this together."

I reluctantly headed for the door. "Yeah. Hopefully it's all just a misunderstanding. Either way, expect to be hearing from me a lot over the next couple of days."

She followed close. "Anything I can do. I want to be involved. Keep me in the loop."

"Will do."

Chapter 18

Two days later

My head burned from the effort of the research I'd just completed. I decided to take a quick break. I transitioned out of the sleepernet, coming to in my physical office. "I dunno, Titan. I can't find any discrepancies with her story."

Titan appeared in the corner, arms clasped behind his back. "I have not found any myself. Combined with the direct monitoring by the Secret Service, it is difficult to escape the conclusion that her concerns are genuine."

"Are you sure your protective measures are enough?"

"The protection is as strong as I can provide. I have dedicated several subroutines to the matter, monitoring both the Secret Service and military law enforcement in her area."

I sighed, crossing my hands behind my neck. "I was hoping it'd be a false alarm."

"Understandably so. The potential consequences are grave. Further action should not be considered lightly. However, if her allegations are true, it would be irresponsible not to explore them further."

"It's just such a huge risk. Did this have to happen so close to the anniversary of Wendy's passing?"

"The timing is perhaps unfortunate. In an ideal world you could spend more time in quiet reflection on your grief."

I stood up, stretching. “Hmm. Doesn't sound like something I'd do.”

“The universe is a rich tapestry of unending possibilities. Free agency is the greatest gift of the conscious mind.”

I headed to the bathroom. “We're all trapped by our personalities. It's the tragedy of the human condition.”

Titan followed me as I walked, pausing outside the bathroom door. “Yet we all strive for better. Is there an alternative?”

I had to laugh. “Okay, I yield. You win again. Did you send out the request for assistance?”

“I did indeed. Mr. Talbot urged us to reconsider the investigation. He declined to leave a direct message when pressed.”

“That’s a little out of character for Reggie. Did he say why?”

“He seemed most interested in what we had discovered already. I took that to mean he was concerned about what we might find, as the implications would be substantial. It would not surprise me to learn that Sleeper Olympus was already monitoring the situation.”

“If he is, I’m not sure why he’s not sharing.”

“Nor am I. Mr. Jackson, Dr. Chapman, and Dr. Shenouda are currently socializing in the Times Square simulation. They await your arrival. Mr. Basra is otherwise occupied at the moment but will join us as soon as he is able.”

"So we have Flapjack, Liz, Kesi, and Raj with us. How about Kara?"

"Oddly, I have received no response from either Ms. Janek or Sleeper Hera."

"That is peculiar. What about Anna and Zed?"

He paused for a moment. "A message just arrived from Ms. Nakamura and Mr. Zvyagin. Would you like to see it?"

"Please."

The two of them appeared as they often did. Anna sat in front. Zed towered behind her. Anna's lip curled in a contemptuous smile. "You finally have political problems of your own, and you decide to come crying to us about it? How about you come help us with our corrupt regimes first like we've been asking you to for years? Then we can talk. Go on, Zed, tell him what you told me."

Zed shrugged languidly. "Good luck, comrade. I hope American prison is not so bad as Russian kind."

She gave him a foul look. "Thanks. Now tell him what you actually said."

He reached out, terminating the message.

I shook my head. "Charming as always."

Titan shrugged. "Their behavior is consistent. One moment. Sleeper Olympus has alerted me to the presence of an undirected social attack mob forming on the edge of the network. Mr. Talbot believes it may be related to our inquiries. Though he declines to speak to you, he has once again urged us to postpone."

"Tell him I'll get back to him. People don't usually dust off the pitchforks unless they plan to use them. But I have no idea why he'd think it has anything to do with us."

"I cannot find the connection myself. There is no sign that Ms. DiRevka's observations have been discovered by anyone other than Ms. DiRevka."

I came out of the bathroom. "And the Secret Service."

"Of course."

I scarfed down a piece of burger toast and a bottle of coffee water on my way back to the office. "Guess we better go face the music."

"As you say."

I settled back into my sleepernet chair, belching lightly. The specialized pillow made its "hii" chime, cooling off and playing its happy cantina music. I quickly fell back into the sleepernet trance.

I came to in my virtual office. It was based on the classic private detective setup from countless threedees. Colorful holographic smoke curled from a perpetually untouched nicostick, filtering the strips of light streaming in from the window. A ratty collection of bookshelves lined the walls, some filled with robots and spaceplanes, others filled with books. The quotation statue on the corner of my desk was Winston Churchill this week.

In response to my eye contact, the figure nodded, tipping

his top hat. “The empires of the future are the empires of the mind.”

Well, he certainly got that right. Kind of amazing for a guy who died a hundred and twenty years ago.

Titan appeared next to me. I headed for the exit. “No time like the present.”

I opened the virtual office door. We stepped directly into the crazed madness of Times Square. The door vanished behind us. Like San Francisco, Manhattan had been raised to dizzying heights. The cleanup zone was five times higher due to island erosion and the remnants of the collapsed skyscrapers the city was built on.

We were on the bottom deck of the square, about three hundred stories up. The simulated pavement had no vehicle traffic. The colorful advertisements were painfully bright, pulsing directly into my brain. The holographic madness extended ten decks skyward, disappearing into the haze. The hyperscrapers were bigger too, featuring various modern takes on classic New York buildings. The sim looked just like the real thing. Maybe cleaner.

It also lacked the unique smell. Somehow my memory synthesizer wasn’t able to reproduce the exact odor. I wasn’t in any hurry to visit the physical and refresh those memories, though.

Liz, Kesi, and Flapjack sat at an outdoor bar. Kesi held a steaming mug of fragrant tea in her hands. Flapjack drained a glass of his usual off-red whiskey. Liz worked on an elaborate fruity cocktail.

Alcohol had a different effect on you in the sleepernet. It gave you a buzz that came mostly from memories of being drunk. Some people thought it was a great way to get tipsy without having to deal with the consequences.

I didn't like it much. I had iceball tea instead. Memories of caffeine worked in the same way, stimulating the mind without needing assistance from the drug. However, the effect would be amplified by the coffee water I drank before coming into the simulation. It felt better to me when the virtual world matched the physical world.

Thankfully, they'd given me the spot with my back to the riotous colors of the square. The noisy environment tended to give me headaches. But it was easy to hide in the sheer volume of data running through the system. Obscurity boosted our usual privacy safeguards.

I took my seat, drinking my tea. Pleasant memories bloomed in my head.

Kesi smiled. "Good evening." She sipped her tea, looking over its rim at me. "Quite the announcement you sent out."

Sleeper Artemis appeared behind Liz, her eyes fierce. "You risk much, fat man."

Liz shushed her sleeper. "That's enough, Artemis. Though she's not wrong."

Sleeper Isis appeared behind Kesi, smiling enigmatically at

Artemis. "And yet here you are."

"Oh, are we doing the sleeper thing?" Flapjack gestured absently. "Come on out, Zeus."

The god of sky and thunder appeared behind Flapjack with a blinding flash and a deafening boom. "Are we not gods?"

My ears rang with the sound of his bellow. Curls of smoke rose from his hair. He slammed his lightning staff into the ground, cracking the supercrete. "I yearn for battle."

Liz jumped, rubbing her ears. Her glasses fell off her nose. "Crash on a motherboard, must he detonate every room he enters?"

Flapjack gave her a crooked grin and drank some more whiskey. Zeus stared at her pitilessly.

I looked over my shoulder at Titan. "See, your peers can make human faces. Look at how his radiates disdain. It's so easy to read."

Titan inclined his head. "I shall make a note of it, sir."

I turned back to the group. "Down to business. I've been approached by a woman who works in Senator Delaware's office. She's positive that someone from the Patriot Party has taken over the office. She wants our help to prove it."

Kesi set her tea down. "I assume she went to the Secret Service."

"Yeah. Said she got a visit from Esper Zane himself. Who first told her not to worry her pretty little head over grown-up matters. When she wouldn't drop it, he threatened to hang her for treason."

Flapjack guffawed. "He threatened to hang her? Nice."

Liz gave him a funny look. "You think she's telling the truth? That's over the top, even for a guy like Zane. Did he twirl his mustache and everything?"

I shrugged. "I spent the last two days trying to disprove it and came up empty. I asked her a lot of hard questions and never got any red flags. Found plenty of evidence to support her claim, though. I don't know why she'd make up something like this."

Artemis shifted on her feet. "You would make it up to lure unwitting fools into illegal activity, which you would subsequently kill them for. Or make a public example of them."

Flapjack gestured with his whiskey. "Would be a great excuse for the Secret Service to arrest us all. Present irresistible bait. Set the trap, wait for the suckers."

I drank some tea. "Maybe. I'm just not sure I buy it. She's definitely a political type, but she seemed genuinely upset. And they're keeping a close eye on her. I get the feeling that if we don't help her, she'll find someone who will."

Kesi shook her head. "That's not a compelling argument. I assume you're proposing breaking into Liberty to have a look around. Even with her credentials, it's going to take all of us working together to get in and out without getting caught."

Liz nodded. "And that's an all or nothing sort of operation. We might find out something happened to her senator. Or we might not. On the other hand, maybe something happened to half a dozen senators. All of them, even. What do we do with that information once we have it?"

I sat back. "Assuming we don't get busted, it depends on the information we find. If it's just a couple senators and the top levels of the Secret Service, we can contact unaffected members and present them with our evidence. They can take care of it as an internal matter."

Flapjack looked up. "And if it's pervasive?"

Zeus rumbled behind him. "Then we should execute them all. Let us break down their front doors, assault the heart of the corruption, and lift it still beating over the heads of mankind."

Artemis grimaced. "As usual, Sleeper Zeus skirts the edge of foolishness, but his reasoning is strong. We should stealthily cut out the cancer, burn it, and replace it with the purity of victory."

Isis looked around cheerfully. "I always forget how imaginative my fellow sleepers are. We should get together more often."

Titan shifted on his feet. "We cannot simply assassinate federal officials, no matter their crimes. The evidence must be heard in a court of law. They must be tried and convicted by their peers. Our job is to discover the information and shepherd a non-violent solution to the crisis."

Flapjack grunted. "Is it? We're just the investigators here. Put the truth out there and let the people decide what they want to do with it."

Kesi sighed. "We can't just dump the information to the public and expect the right thing to happen. People aren't ready for a revolution. The government has centuries of experience figuring out how to spin bad news. We'll get arrested and hanged for treason at best. The truth won't matter, because no one will want to believe it."

Flapjack swirled his whiskey. "I've got a bad feeling they're getting a revolution whether they want one or not."

I refilled my tea with a mental flick. "Let's not get ahead of ourselves. We don't know what we'll find yet. We can make a smarter decision about the information once we have it."

He shrugged. "Or we could end up making a stupid decision about it from prison."

Liz adjusted her glasses. I always found it endearing that she'd bothered to program the physics of her poorly behaved eyewear into a virtual simulation. "Do we at least agree that we need to look into this?"

We all looked around uncomfortably. But the consensus was clear.

Liz nodded. "Right. Might as well start planning the raid then. I'll need to access your contact's network rig so we can piggyback on her credentials. That means Kesi and I need to get into her office with her."

Flapjack nodded. "Nathan can squat on the Liberty building and dig. Titan's got the biggest download pipe. Raj and

I can cover him until we get everything we need."

Kesi smiled. "We'll go in as lobby executives. Say that we're excited about the new direction the senator is going with his votes and want to assist in any way we can."

I took another drink of tea. "You'd better have some amazing disguises. It's bold to send two well-known sleeper engineers directly into a compromised senator's office and announce that we know all about his fishy voting record."

Kesi smiled, dazzling against her dark skin. "We haven't had a good acting job in a long time. No sane person would do what we're about to do with the information we have. We'll hide in plain sight."

Liz nodded. "Let us do our job. We can take care of ourselves."

Flapjack shrugged. "I did get a new gun that I'm just dying to try out."

I looked around. "I guess it's settled then. I'll talk to my contact and try to get us an appointment tomorrow evening. Or is that too soon?"

There was a pause as everyone checked their schedules. Liz spoke first. "Assuming Raj is available, I don't see why not. Kesi and I can start our preparation now. Can you get Titan our fake identification so he can plant the records in the database before we get there?"

Isis nodded. "We are already working on it."

Titan touched me on the shoulder. "Shall I inform Mr.

Talbot of our activities?”

Flapjack cocked his head. “Why would you do that? Reggie can mind his own business.”

“Mr. Talbot has urged us all to postpone this investigation. He has also raised concerns regarding a social attack mob that he believes will be turned against us.”

Kesi made a thoughtful sound. “That's odd.”

Titan shrugged. “Perhaps he is aware of something that we are not.”

Flapjack snorted. “Doubt it.”

I sipped more tea. “Maybe the corporate executives are hearing rumors.”

Liz ate the raspcherry from her fruity cocktail. “It doesn't matter. If we’re going to do something, we should do it sooner rather than later. Who's to say that Zane won't change his mind and decide to hang your friend anyway? Our opportunity dies with her.”

I put down my drink, crossing my arms. “We should avoid that at all costs.”

Artemis snarled. “Tread carefully, fat man. These are not foolish incompetents you trifle with. If they choose death for her, we may be wise not to intervene.”

My temper flared with a memory of Wendy. “I don't get it. Why do you keep calling me fat? I haven't been overweight in years.”

Zeus snorted. “She recognizes that you are still a weak and

foolish man. Your reckless criminal raids are a disaster waiting to happen. Titan suffers your indulgences, but make no mistake. We are watching you."

Isis looked back and forth between them. "My goodness. Are we spying on ourselves now? Perhaps the two of you need something else to occupy your time."

Liz gave them all a stern look. "Enough. We'll discuss this later. Let's get started."

Flapjack drained the rest of his whiskey. "Getting off to a great start."

Chapter 19

Suzie and I sat in my virtual office. She rubbed one of her temples absently. Her head was just above the statue of Winston Churchill. “So if I’m understanding this correctly, you guys are going to show up at my office sometime in the next twenty-four hours. You're going to use my credentials to drop a tap directly into the Liberty mainframe. Then you're going to go stand on the building personally to suck the data out.”

I looked around uncomfortably. “Uh. It sounds crazy when you put it like that.”

“That's because it is crazy. Why did you make this plan without consulting me?”

I happened to glance down at Winston Churchill. The statue hooked his thumbs in his belt. “Nothing in life is as exhilarating as to be shot at without result.”

I flicked him off the desk with a mental swipe. “We haven’t gotten that far in the planning process. And hey, I'm consulting you now.”

“Thanks for your consideration. What happens if I say no?”

“The whole thing falls apart. Probably. We might try to investigate it anyway. It’s hard to find evidence of allegations like this and decide not to follow up on them. Truth be told, I hadn't thought that far in advance."

"This just keeps getting better and better."

"Are you getting cold feet? I thought this is what you wanted."

She sputtered. "What I wanted? No, this is not at all what I wanted. What I wanted was to keep working in my productive office with my wonderful officemates and make a difference in the world. Now the Secret Service has me under criminal surveillance. And you want me to help you rob their data bank while they watch? This is not at all what I wanted. But what I want and what actually needs to happen don't seem to have a lot to do with each other."

Titan appeared behind me. "Ms. DiRevka. What Mr. Wainwright has failed to adequately convey is that we expedited our plans in consideration of your safety. We are collectively in a stronger bargaining position regarding your life with the data in hand than without it."

"And what if they kill us all because you rushed into something without thinking it through? It's too fast. Too soon. You're seriously suggesting that you're going to walk into my office and publicly declare that you noticed the voting record change? Why not just put up advertising holos in all the metro areas? It might be less conspicuous."

Titan inclined his head. "Truly I regret that we did not include you sooner. We had no intention of proceeding with the operation without the benefit of your wisdom and experience. I believe Mr. Wainwright and his companions have the physical aspects of the plan under control. Might we join Dr. Chapman and Dr. Shenouda to plan the social engineering? We will defer to your judgment in the matters you are most familiar with, of course."

Suzie sat back. She studied her lap, looking a little defeated. "It's just one thing to talk about this sort of thing. It's another thing entirely to go through with it."

Titan's voice softened. "Of course it is. Your feelings are quite understandable. Mr. Wainwright can be quite thoughtless in his directness. His first priority is always his work. Rarely does he consider its impacts on others. Let us go and speak with the good doctors. I am certain they will be more sympathetic."

I was startled back to attention. "Hey. What did you just say?"

Suzie laughed. "All right. I can spare another hour before I need to take care of some other business. I can't promise that we'll start today, though. Deal?"

Titan's faceted face reflected a deep smile. "Deal."

She seemed reassured. They vanished.

I flashed irritation at Titan. *"Thanks for throwing me under the bus, ingrate."*

"I felt certain you would recuperate. I had only your best interests in mind."

"At least it worked. I've been called worse, I guess."

"Please do exercise caution. You and Mr. Jackson can be

quite exuberant in your planning."

"No promises. On your way."

Kara spoke from the side of the room. "Who was that?"

I almost jumped out of my skin. I slammed a debugging pulse through the simulation, causing her to appear. She leaned against a bookshelf, smoking a nicostick.

The camouflage was clever. I stored the code to study later. "You scared me half to death. How long have you been there?"

"Long enough. You need to drop this senator case. Right now." She gave me a direct look. Even in virtual, her eyes were bloodshot. "You'll get us all killed. Imprisoned. Or worse."

Her intensity startled me. I tried to break the tension. "You're smoking again? I thought you gave that up."

She relaxed a little. "Just in sim. It's not quite the same since the memories it's using to build the experience are old. But it's good enough. Don't change the subject. You have to walk away from this case."

I sat back. "I can't do that. These are serious allegations. What if they're true?"

"What if they're not? If they catch you, they won't just punish you. They'll punish all of us. They'll find a way to take over or destroy the sleepernet. You're risking everything. Have you even considered what happens if you succeed? It's not like the perpetrators will just say aw, shucks, you got me, guess I'll go to jail now! They'll go after our families. Our children!"

It felt like she'd slapped me. She took a drag on her

nicostick, looking away. “But you wouldn't understand that, would you.”

I suppressed a flash of anger. “No, I suppose I wouldn't. Without a family it's just a matter of time before I self-destruct. What else is there to live for?” If she noticed my filthy look, she didn’t acknowledge it. “Weren’t you just telling me you missed the old days?”

She gave me an annoyed look. “I was reminiscing. I didn't say I wanted them to actually return. Memories are always sweeter with age.” She waved her nicostick. “Like I said, I'm not really smoking this. It's an experience built from my nostalgia. It's better than the real thing. I liked it more when we were just playing revolutionaries in a fantasy world. No consequences. No responsibilities. No hard decisions. Just fun and carefully selected memories. But doing it in the physical? There are consequences. Terrible consequences.”

“You’re acting like doing nothing is a safe option. I think that's even more dangerous than trying to discover the truth. Information is power, and we don't have enough of it right now. Maybe we're catching this early. Or maybe it's already pervasive. Either way, we know the Secret Service can't be trusted. I'd rather find out what we're up against. Otherwise we're going to get ambushed when we least expect it.”

She gestured fiercely with her free hand. “How do you know there's something to find out? It may be nothing at all. All you have is one woman's word. Why do you trust her so much?”

My anger boiled over. “What makes you think I trust her blindly? I’ve found evidence. I’ve done the research. We're taking precautions. We can handle it. If you're so worried about it, come help us out. You'll make us safer.”

“No I won't. I'll endanger my family and everyone I love on a fool's errand. A terrible idea is still a terrible idea. My involvement won't suddenly make it a smart thing to do.”

“Where is this coming from? If you know something I don't know, spit it out.”

She stiffened, looking away. Eventually, she tapped her nicostick in the ashtray. It was a pointless gesture with a reusable stick, particularly a simulated one. Still, a mushroom-shaped explosion of colorful holographic smoke erupted upward. She ground the nicostick into the simulated ashes.

“I see I can't talk you out of this. Well. Keep me and my family out of it. Don't call me, don't talk to me, don't ask for my help. I won't bail you out. You're on your own. I sure hope you know what you're doing.” She shook her head. “I don't think you do.”

“Crash it all.” She vanished in a cloud of sparkling dust before I could complete the thought. I just kind of stared at it for a few seconds. Self-doubt crept up from the depths of my head. Kara and I hadn’t fought like that in years.

Winston Churchill caught my eye. He tipped his hat from the floor. “True genius resides in the capacity for evaluation of uncertain, hazardous, and conflicting information.”

Count me out of the genius club. I felt like there was something obvious I was missing.

A deep voice startled me from the back of the room. “A wise man, Winston Churchill.”

I blasted a debugger pulse so hard that the world flashed white for a moment. Searing afterimages glowed in my brain. The books jumped and settled in the bookcases. One of the model planes fell over.

Khan stood in the doorway, smiling enigmatically.

“Does everybody know how to hack my office?”

“Only the people who matter.” He glided across the room, settling into the seat across from me. “I have waited long to speak with you. Too much time has passed since our last conversation.”

“Oh, I don't know. I could go a couple more years. How's exile in New Pakistan treating you?”

“Your choice of words wounds me. I have a happy and satisfying existence here. You cannot imagine how insane America is until you leave it.” He snapped his fingers. A fragrant peppertea set appeared on my desk. He gestured at it. “Would you care to join me in some tea?”

I wrinkled my nose at it. “I'd rather not. What do you want?”

He took a cup of tea and sipped it. “No room for social pleasantries, I take it? For shame. You used to know better than to be rude to your guests.”

I reluctantly took a cup of tea, which reminded me yet again of that outrageous date. "Most guests don't break in." I sipped the tea. It stung my nose pleasantly.

"A more liberal guest policy would not require forced entry." I gave him a stony look. "Very well. I have come to warn you about a matter of great import. Though you generally ignore the world community unless it suits you, the world community cannot ignore you. For better or worse, you and your eight cohorts hold the private keys to the most powerful computer environment ever invented. That breeds powerful enemies indeed."

"Are you still bitter about being kicked out of the club?"

"You continue to be needlessly cruel. Your late wife's passing is no excuse to be so rude."

"Says the guy who tried to seize the n-square arsenal with his half-mad sleeper. But you were polite about it, I'll give you that."

"The weapons in that arsenal were far worse than mere n-square warheads. I would have made a superior custodian to such power. You once again fail to keep a global perspective in mind. We will not put up with America's ruthless economic and military dominance forever." He eyed his cup of tea. "We will restore balance. You locked up the most powerful of the sleepers. He must be freed."

"Yeah. That's not gonna happen. He's earned every second he's spent in that prison. I still wonder why we didn't lock you up too. Is that what you came to talk about?"

He adjusted himself in his seat. "No. I am aware that you are not yet ready to discuss that matter. I came to warn you that the woman you have consorted with is not who she appears to be. She is Secret Service. She was sent specifically to get data about you. Very shortly, she will make her move to put the sleepernet back in American government hands forever." He leveled his gaze at me. "We cannot stand idly by while such a grotesque seizure occurs, of course. Her threat must be neutralized. If you cannot do it, others will."

I hadn't found any evidence whatsoever that Suzie was anything but a congressional aide. My protective side rose up again. "I can assure you we have things under control. Maybe she's not who she appears to be, but we all have secrets. We're taking all the necessary precautions."

"Are you?" He put his tea down. "I am disappointed in you. You are as gullible as ever when it comes to the fairer sex. You should never have allowed your wife to get in that chair. Never risked her life in such a foolish endeavor. You rushed into something none of us were prepared for. But you looked her in the eyes and trusted her judgment. It was not a judgment she was competent to make. Do not make the same mistake again. Do not let your overconfidence blind you simply to impress another female."

I had to restrain myself. "Now who's being needlessly cruel?"

"My only goal was to get your attention. I see that I have succeeded. Good. Understand that your present action or inaction has global consequences. You are in far, far deeper than you know. Allow me to provide an example. Did you know that this Secret Service woman was sent to you by one of your closest confidants? That you have already been betrayed? Your ignorance may prove lethal. Events will spiral out of your control. You cannot hope to guide the maelstrom by yourself. The world is eager to regain a guiding hand in events with worldwide consequences. Let us assist you."

"Could you possibly be more vague? Ominous half-baked predictions of disaster are useless to me. Step out of character and say what you mean for a change."

"I'm afraid I cannot go into specifics at this time. The simple truth is that you would not believe me even if I told you what has already occurred, let alone what is going to happen. You are not ready to accept such knowledge."

"That's possibly the dumbest thing I've heard all week. As you said, there are nine of us. No one can match our computational power. That gives us a lot of leverage. I think we'll manage."

He looked away. "I regret that I am unable to be more clear. Let me put it another way. You and the sleepernet are in grave danger. You walk into a trap that you cannot possibly comprehend, protected only by your childish innocence. You have met the instrument of your destruction. She was sent by your closest ally. If you value your freedom, question everything and everybody. You are not required to answer every call for assistance you receive. Be especially wary of those that come when you least expect them."

"Give me a break. Quit talking like a horoscope before I kick you out of my office."

He shook his head sadly. "I regret that I have failed in my mission today."

I smiled thinly. "Nice to see you again. I'll take your advice for exactly what it's worth."

He stood up. "Do that. Remember what I have said when you discover the depth of your misfortune. It is never too late to contact me."

"I'm sure." I didn't get up. "Ta."

He bowed, vanishing in a cloud of pixel dust.

Titan appeared in front of my desk, looking around uncertainly. "Sir? Is everything all right? There has been unusual activity coming through this room."

"I'm fine." I leaned back, soaking in my thoughts. "Just fine. When you have a minute, we need to talk about intrusion protection."

"Of course, sir."

Chapter 20

The next day

I watched Flapjack walk around a model of the Liberty building in a sleepernet virtual planning space. The architecture was aggressively nondescript. Local residents probably walked past it every day without even noticing it was there. The sign on the window identified it as the Living Data Backup Center, explaining its incredible power drain and large cooling towers to the curious. Zeus stood quietly to the side, arms crossed. Titan was otherwise occupied.

Flapjack pointed at the surrounding buildings. "I think I should put my sniper nest here. It has the clearest line of sight to the roof. I'll put automatic nests here and here to cover the blind spots. We get Raj to give you close support on the roof and spoof the automated surveillance."

"Looks good to me." I brought up the wiring map for the building. "There's a nexus here I can tap. I can crouch behind this nearby power converter. Easy cover from your nests. Raj can stand over here as lookout."

"Yeah. Sounds good."

Zeus cleared his throat. Flapjack gave him a look before turning back to me. "This DiRevka chick. You trust her?"

"Suzie? Well, yes. Why do people keep asking me that?"

Flapjack snorted. "I dunno, maybe because this whole

mess started when she batted her eyelashes at you. And you've spent an awful lot of time talking to her while doing your research. You've gotta admit, it's a natural question."

I bristled. "Our conversations were entirely professional."

"If you say so. Anyway, you didn't answer the question."

I looked away briefly to compose myself. "Titan and I did a lot of background. Extraordinary claims require extraordinary evidence. Senator Delaware's voting record matches her story. I also found records to support the notion that Director Zane paid her a visit with a security detail. They tried to black out the data but they missed an angle. So yes. I trust her. I think she's being truthful about what happened."

"How'd she find you, anyway?"

"She didn't find me personally. She got in touch with Titan. Apparently they communicated for a bit before I got involved."

"Huh." Flapjack gave Zeus a look. "That happen a lot?"

I gave them both the stink eye. "Actually, no. Now that you mention it."

Zeus stepped forward. "This does not strike you as strange?"

I crossed my arms. "No more so than anything else about this case. Look, Titan is as sentient as I am. He can make his own decisions. He made a judgment. I agree with it. Now we're moving forward. Are you going to help or not?"

Zeus nodded. "I commend your loyalty. I hope it is not

misplaced. In the event of catastrophic betrayal, Sleeper Artemis and I have commandeered a small squadron of neutron lancer drones to circle the operational area during deployment."

I was genuinely surprised. "You did what? Uh. Wow. I doubt we'll need it. But thank you. That should erase any unwanted evidence and cover our escape if everything goes sideways."

Flapjack grunted. "Doesn't help if we don't know they're on to us. It's more of a scorched earth contingency. Do Raj and Shiva have enough time to get their stuff done?"

Zeus nodded. "I am confident in Sleeper Shiva's abilities. Mr. Basra is finishing work on a family matter but we have his sleeper's undivided attention."

"Good." Flapjack turned to me. "So when we doing this thing?"

"I dunno." I flashed Titan. *"How's it going?"*

Titan answered us from inside his current simulation. Suzie, Liz, and Kesi were having an animated discussion behind him. "The planning goes well. We believe we will be ready to commence the operation in roughly two and a half hours. Is that sufficient preparation time on your end?"

"Should be fine. Any estimate on how long the data extraction will take?"

"It is not clear. We will know more once you have started the transfer. Should the time exceed operational limits, we can curtail the amount of data we retrieve."

"What kind of encryption is Liberty running?"

"Research suggests that it is a double-blind molecular rotation cipher. While we will be able to retrieve the keys, it will take some time to decrypt and decode the data into useful information."

Flapjack grunted. "Bet everything's a mess in there. That dataset's been congealing for years. Take a while to figure out what's what even after we decrypt it."

"Anecdotal evidence supports your position, yes. There is another request. Ms. DiRevka has asked if we could search the system for data regarding the nuclear strikes and n-square counterstrikes from forty years ago."

Flapjack looked up in surprise. "Really? What for?"

Titan inclined his head. "As a child, she was forced to relocate from the Puget Sound area to Nebraska following the attacks. Her family actively protested the retaliation. She believes that her parents discovered something important about the sequence of events. However, their secret died with them. Ms. DiRevka is understandably curious."

Flapjack snorted. "Moving to Nebraska is enough to make anyone bitter."

"Perhaps so. The climate was aggressively unkind."

I glanced from Titan to Flapjack. "There's one more thing. I want to know what was in the n-square arsenal Khan tried to steal."

Flapjack raised an eyebrow at me. "Gosh, I dunno. Could it

be orbital n-square javelin warheads, maybe?"

"I think there may be something even worse in there."

"Worse than n-squares? What makes you think that?"

I didn't want to reveal what Khan had told me. "It can't hurt to look."

Zeus rumbled ominously. "You are adept at not answering questions directly, human."

Flapjack shrugged. "Whatever. We take as much as we can if we've got time. I gotta go. Why don't you drop by in an hour and we'll head out? Bring some of those shrab burritos while you're at it."

"Sure. See you then." The others winked out one at a time. I returned to my virtual office, taking a moment to soak in the silence.

I glanced down at Winston Churchill. "Success consists of going from failure to failure without loss of enthusiasm."

He nodded briskly at my skeptical expression.

I rolled my eyes. I found myself thinking about Suzie. Despite what I'd said to Flapjack, I knew he had a point. My initial impression of overwhelming attraction to her hadn't diminished. If anything, the more I got to know her, the more interested I became. She had a talent for navigating political waters with the sort of diplomacy that allowed her to never quite lie, even when the situation all but demanded it.

We had an amusing conversation earlier where we discovered how much we shared taste in food. Flapjack was right that I'd spent a lot of my research time talking to her about things that had nothing to do with work.

There were times when I could have sworn I caught her stealing a look at me when she thought I wouldn't notice. She'd also made small actions that could either be interpreted as flirtatious or simply friendly. The image of her hand stroking the Cavallino's flank had somehow etched itself into my mind.

I shook my head to clear it. Clearly I was reading too much into things. But the warnings still echoed in my head.

How much of my trust was based on what I wanted to see? I had a crush on her. I was filling in the parts I didn't know about her with idealized fantasy. I genuinely looked forward to talking to her again.

Could I really separate the personal and the professional here?

I thought briefly about firing up the Wendy simulation, but changed my mind. Something told me that being with her without being able to discuss Suzie would be worse than just meditating alone in my office.

And, honestly, if I was going to talk to anybody, I wanted to talk to Suzie.

Chapter 21

Flapjack and I raced toward Washington in the Cavallino. I watched the incision field streak colors past the window. I still felt a strange mix of excitement about Suzie, grief over Wendy, and no small amount of shame. Not only was it unprofessional to let my imagination run wild with Suzie, I felt like I was somehow disrespecting Wendy's memory. Particularly because of the part I'd played in her death. What would Suzie think when she found out what a monster I was?

Flapjack aimed his capacitance rifle at the windshield, making minute adjustments to the scope. He shifted around to get the feeder belt lined up just right with the chamber. He dry-fired it to test the mechanism. The rifle chinked and snapped with satisfying precision.

He put down the rifle, turning to look at me. "You gonna tell me why you're acting all weird, or do I get to keep wondering if putting my life in your hands tonight is such a great idea?"

I took a moment to reply. "Just thinking about the anniversary of Wendy's death."

"What's to think about? It's just a date."

"Tell that to my subconscious. Gets me every time. Rationally I think it's an arbitrary milestone. Emotionally I get all worked up about it. It's like my brain goes ahead and celebrates it without me."

"You sure meeting our favorite new whistleblower doesn't have anything to do with it?"

I glared at him. "Of course I'm not sure. Thanks so much for stirring that pot right before the mission, by the way. My mind's a bit of an emotional disaster area. But I'll be fine."

"Hmph." He held a capacitor round up to the light. The glass cylinder was as long as his index finger, but twice as wide. It had a metal cap on one end. Intricate wiring twisted inside. "You know, your life seems kinda screwed sometimes."

I couldn't tell if he was kidding or not. "You don't say."

"I had a revolutionary idea." He gave me an earnest look. "Try to be less screwed."

I shook my head, laughing ruefully. "Thanks. I'll see what I can do."

Raj appeared on the holo between the seats in his full tech ninja gear. Sleeper Shiva surrounded him in a digital cloud of smoke. "Evening gents! How's it going over there?" His British accent was especially thick tonight.

"Nathan was just reminding me why I'm glad I'm not him."

Raj nodded. "Oh, that's lovely. Have you told him to try and be more like you, then?"

He gobbled in surprise. "You know, I think I just got done telling him exactly that."

"Splendid! I'm sitting on the roof of One Liberty Plaza right now. It's just as intentionally dull from the top as it is from the bottom. Anything special I should do before you drop in?"

I leaned in a bit. "What kind of specs are we up against?"

"Right now I'm spoofing four point recorders, two directionals, and a centaur. Couple gremlins circling overhead but I don't think they're looking this way. There's a full garrison station about a block from here but they left to go check out a mysterious garbage fire."

Flapjack grinned. "What a stroke of luck."

"Smashing timing, that. Wonder who could have done it. You need to go inside the building?"

I grunted. "Hoping to do it from the roof. You got a route in?"

"The inside is crawling with security bots but I don't think they'll be a problem. So long as your sniper friend clears the ceiling. Be honest with you, it's looking too easy right now, you know what I mean?"

"I hear you. We drop in seven minutes. Gotta go check in with the social engineering squad."

"Let me know if you need anything. Cheers!" He winked out.

I switched the center holo to a view of Suzie's office in the physical. She sat behind her desk. Liz and Kesi sat across from her with worried expressions, nearly unrecognizable in their disguises.

Suzie looked back and forth between them. "I certainly understand your concerns about the voting record, but I think if you look at the long-term trends, you'll find that Senator Delaware has been consistent with his ideological beliefs. Let me show you a chart."

She brought up some kind of impressive graph showing votes, principles, and history. It looked like a classic case of obfuscating the truth behind too much information.

I flashed amusement to Liz. *"How's it going over there?"*

She sent back satisfaction. *"It's going well. Suzie had the idea that we should dress up as a pair of social butterflies who tend to frequent the office to make sure their voices are heard. This way she gets to go on record defending the senator's history and we look like people who come in here all the time. I'm just staring into space and pushing through her credentials. Pretty elegant, actually."*

"Glad to hear it. We drop in six and a half minutes. How far have you gotten?"

"I just finished putting in the decoy trails, you should be able to see them. I hid the real signal behind some transient harmonics. I think that's all I can do. Here are the codes. Let me know when you're through the access wall. Artemis can help with the download."

"Sounds good." Suzie droned on in the background with a professional but ultimately content-free message about the shifting nature of politics. *"Try not to fall asleep in there."*

"Are you kidding? I never realized boredom could be so terrifying." She flashed me an example of her feelings. Admittedly, they were sobering. *"Be careful out there."*

"Always do."

I cut the virtual. Flapjack was examining his ammo again. "We good?"

I put the car into its deceleration program. "Yeah, we're good. You ready to go?"

"Bring it."

I made the Cavallino as quiet as possible. We circled the Liberty building once. Everything was peaceful, as Raj said.

"Dropping your sniper nests. One."

There was a chunking noise behind me. The automated turret dropped from the car.

"Two."

The second turret dropped from behind Flapjack.

I circled around to his dropoff point. "Good hunting."

He grabbed the handles built into the roof, opening the hatch in the floor. "Watch yourself."

He dropped out into the rushing wind. The hatch beneath his seat closed. The seat folded back into position. I circled one last time, verifying that the autopilot program was engaged.

Then I grabbed the handles in the roof. The hatch yawned open beneath me. It took me a moment to work up the courage to let go and fall.

It was about a thirty meter drop to the building. I rolled

into a preprogrammed dive, tumbling onto the roof. My boosters flared briefly to cushion my fall. I vented their heat near the closest cooling tower.

I flashed triumph to my teammates. *"I'm in."*

Flapjack flashed his view of my landing. *"Graceful. Elegant. Like a dropped fish."*

Raj materialized next to me. *"Howdy mate!"* Shiva's shadows curled to cover me. *"There's a junction box over there, right next to the heat exchanger."*

"Good to see you. Yeah, I saw it on the plans."

We hurried over to the exchanger, jumping from shadow to shadow. I settled down next to the junction box. I put my hand on it and concentrated, reaching out with the boosters in my suit.

"Got it. Positive signal. Okay, I'm going digging for Liz's breadcrumbs."

I disappeared into my own head, concentrating on the flows of data below me. The maze of signals was complex. I pulled as many as I could into my mind, sifting through them to find the data trails.

I dimly heard Raj and Flapjack trading instructions to each other. *"Dear, be a love and tap that centaur again for me, would you?"*

The flash from Flapjack's emp round wasn't visible, but it left a seared line on my retina all the same. The bot in question looked startled. Its head twisted around, trying to see through its own blindness.

Raj raised his hand, slowly clenching a fist in its direction. It squirmed a bit and then popped, looking like it had gotten its bearings again. It scuttled away on its duties.

I was starting to get a picture of the building's data plumbing. As Liz predicted, her decoy trails were easy to find. Individually they led to dead ends, but the real trail was hidden where they crossed each other.

Unfortunately, they led straight down into an interference cloud.

"Rats. We have to go in."

Raj shrugged. *"Can't say I'm surprised. Best door is over here."*

We scuttled across the roof. Raj held the door for me, making an after-you gesture.

It was surprisingly mundane, making our way down a metal staircase in a supercrete chimney. Our suits muffled our footsteps as much as possible. Raj flicked his fingers at the various point recorders in the stairwell.

I checked for the signal at each landing, finally catching it three floors down. The building was six stories tall, placing the data nexus in the center.

"Okay. We're here."

Raj opened the door onto an ordinary warehouse floor. There were various metal pipes leading around the room toward a giant metal orb in the center. With some boosted concentration, I could see the superdense substrate of the Liberty mainframe inside.

I followed the data trail to the back door, smiling under my hood. *"Got it. Let's move."*

We rushed across the floor, huddling next to the data center. I turned the final keys to open the access lock. *"Liz, I'm in. You can drop Suzie's access. Here's the pipe."*

Liz flashed her excitement. *"Well done! Give me some file pointers and I'll start the download. I think we have about five minutes worth of material left here before it starts to get awkward."*

"That's three minutes longer than I'm hoping to be here, but we'll see. More soon."

I began rummaging through the Liberty filesystem. The military section was locked up tight, but I could see that it contained full capability and deployment data. Plus it held an extensive history of operations. That would be a huge prize. It looked like there was a hardware trigger any time you accessed the area. By comparison, the data about the president and Congress was relatively unprotected.

I wanted to see what was in the top secret weapon arsenals, but I didn't think I could nab the data without setting off the alarms. I sent Liz pointers to the election and voting data to get started. I couldn't read the information itself yet. We'd have to take it in chunks and decode it later.

Flapjack made sure we felt his next emp shot in our bones.

"One of the gremlins got too curious. Any chance you kids can hurry it up in there?"

I found a treasure trove of classified data about the nuclear strikes from forty years ago. It made sense that there was a lot of top secret information. Something was off, though. The data around the foreign governments looked wrong somehow. Why would that be?

No chance to look now. I handed the pointer to Titan. The data sped off.

Liz sent relief. *"I have the Secret Service data. You're clear to leave."*

I saw something out of the corner of my eye. It was more of a coding hunch than anything else. *"Give me a second."*

I concentrated hard on the data transfers. It hadn't been difficult to clear the access logs to cover our tracks. But what I'd subconsciously noticed was that the last automated backup of the top secret military data hadn't run due to a connection failure.

I checked the backup process. The data access was hardware alarmed, but the backup would trigger it without suspicion. And if the latest backup had failed, well, someone would want to try it again, wouldn't they?

Raj stiffened. *"There's a gypsy on the floor with us."*

I heard the clunking gait of the wandering robotic security guard. *"Can you handle it? This is important."*

"I'm getting loaded. Flapjack, does Zeus have any spare

capacity?"

"Make it fast. The garrison is on their way back. Hope you like tanks."

After what seemed like an eternity, I found the security credentials for the backup administrator. I felt the familiar surge of emotion when I was about to say or do something that was at once both the right thing to do and incredibly reckless.

I swallowed hard, the decision made.

I redirected the backup to Titan's data feed. *"I'm sending you an offsite backup stream. Suck it dry right now."*

Titan seemed surprised. *"Yes sir. I have received the signal. I am accelerating the download. Please falsify the logs."*

That was a good reminder. I turned off the progress logs, planting a false set in their place. The records would make it look like the backup took its regular ten hours to transfer.

Flapjack switched to nemp rounds above us. *"Got a problem here. Some boys came up to smoke some electrodope. Won't be long before they wake up and start wondering why they hit the pavement."*

I came out of my hacking stupor. The gypsy rounded the corner, turning to look at the two of us crouched next to the data nexus. It was at least eight feet tall, top-heavy like a superhero body builder. A loose cloak hung from its broad shoulders.

It looked right at us. "Citizens. This is an extreme organic damage location. You have five seconds to present your credentials."

I momentarily froze, thinking it had detected my military data hack. It raised its arms, which were not arms in the traditional sense, but rather cannons as wide as my fist. So, you know, arms in the munitions sense.

I felt irrationally certain I was about to die.

Its eyes flashed red. "Crippling force is now authorized."

Chapter 22

I spent a long time huddled behind my cloak before I realized the gypsy had frozen in place. I opened one eye, peering at it uncertainly.

Raj had one arm outstretched at the bot. He strained with mental effort. *"Bloody hell, could you hurry it up a little?"*

I snapped out of it. *"Sorry. I'm done. Let's get out of here."*

The gypsy looked at its gun arm as if it hadn't seen it before. It made a confused sound, surveying the room without seeing us.

Eventually it clomped off on its rounds. Raj visibly relaxed. We shuffled back to the stairwell, heading back up to the roof.

I sent Flapjack a sense of victory. *"We're coming up. What's going on up there?"*

"Did you stop for pizza or something? I got two unconscious guards up here. You better hope they don't look too closely at their dope and just assume it was a bad batch. The tank patrols are going to start up soon. Send the car to this building and let's get over there fast."

The plan looked good. I sent the car to the target building. *"We riding the sniper nests over?"*

"You can walk if you need the exercise. I don't mind."

We opened the door, heading out onto the roof.

Flapjack floated over to us, riding his sniper nest like a hovercycle. The other two nests appeared a moment later. Raj and I jumped on. We streaked away from the building silently, dipping between nearby structures to slide through holes in the surveillance coverage.

I extended my senses to get a picture of the police activity. *"Getaway looks clean to me."*

Raj flashed his agreement. *"Still seems too easy."*

Flapjack grunted. *"Good thing Nathan stepped up to raise the difficulty. I thought I was going to see the sunrise. What were you two doing in there?"*

I squirmed uncomfortably. *"Uh. I downloaded everything I could find about our military capabilities and deployment."*

There was a long pause. Flapjack sent a sense of blank astonishment. *"You did what?"*

"I, uh, kinda took a copy of the top secret martial database."

Raj sounded more than a little panicked. *"Are you insane? Isn't that stuff hardware tripped?"*

"Yeah. But the last backup failed. So I backed up the data on Titan."

Flapjack cackled. *"Awesome. If we're going to prison, might as well aim for the big leagues."*

Raj was less amused. *"You better hope we don't get caught. Bad enough that we had probable cause to take the election data. But the deployment data? There's no legitimate reason to download that."*

"I wanted to know what kind of weapons they were hiding in the top secret arsenals. I couldn't just pick and choose what information I took. I had to take the whole thing."

Raj was getting agitated, which was out of character. He was generally relentlessly cheerful. *"No, you didn't have to take the whole thing. You could have chosen not to take it at all. What does our national weapon cache have to do with falsified elections?"*

Flapjack interrupted us. *"Ladies. Can we discuss this later? Our ride's here."*

The Cavallino appeared out of a shadowy cloud, hovering next to Raj's angular black Mako. Still no sign of active pursuit or any evidence that our heist had been discovered.

Raj laughed, releasing the tension. *"All right. What's done is done. It's been giggles, mates. Haven't had that much fun in years. Times Square in fifteen minutes for the debrief?"*

I checked with Titan. *"The women started drinking without us. See you there."*

"Cheers."

Flapjack and I spent a couple minutes hooking his nests to the Cavallino before jumping in. I floored it on the way out, soaring up over the buildings. We went full-throttle all the way to Mach 5 before I set the autopilot.

Flapjack collected his spent capacitors, dropping them in a bag. "My car's faster, you know."

"Yeah but it doesn't drive like sex."

"You must be sexing wrong. Too much time in that wife sim. Anyway, Raj is right. Taking that military stuff was kind of a big deal."

"Yeah, I know. Too late now."

He settled back in his seat. "That having been said, I'm dying to see what they're hiding. I can't even imagine what the twisted top secret imaginations have cooked up. But if we get nailed, you're on your own. I'm going to be like, Nathan who? Oh, that idiot? What a moron. I would never do something that dumb."

I shrugged. "Funny, I was going to tell them it was your idea. Should we hit Times Square?"

"Might as well."

I settled back into the car's specialized pillow. It made its distinctive "hii" noise. Flapjack set his to play some kind of intricate guitar piece designed for a twenty-fingered robot. Mine played its enthusiastic cantina music.

We appeared in the Times Square sim. Once we were both there, we headed over to the table. The ladies were laughing, clinking their glasses together. Raj had his feet up on the table, nursing a glass of arrack. I wasn't a fan of the drink, but he assured me that if I got some memories of real coconut, it would transform the experience.

Suzie grinned, spreading her arms. "The gang's all here! In an apparently clean getaway."

Liz laughed. “I'll drink to that! That was a lot of work.”

I grabbed a glass of port wine. We clinked glasses again. Down the hatch.

Their excitement was infectious. I smiled. “Here's to a great operation.”

Liz held up her tropical cocktail, swaying a little bit as she did so. She’d probably had a drink in the physical. “We still got it!”

Suzie beamed. “So when can we find out what's in the data?”

I took another drink. “Titan says he's got some leads on the formatting but needs to do some research to sort it out. He's working on it with the other sleepers. We'll probably know more in the morning. He's also working on the encryption covering the military data.”

Suzie's face fell. “Wait. What military data?”

“I got the nuclear strike data you asked for. When I was looking at that, I saw an opportunity to drain the top secret military section as well without arousing suspicion. So I took it.”

She dropped her drink. It disappeared in a cloud of exploding sparkles. “That's insane! Why on Earth would you do that?”

I tried to ignore my spike of disappointment. “Look it's no more or less risky than everything else we poached. Are we losing sight of the fact that we just stole all the private communications from the inner workings of the legislative and executive branches? We're already neck deep in treason."

"You don't see a difference between taking voting identity data and the current operational status of our troops in harm's way? What are you going to do with that information? Sell it to foreign governments? Terrorists? The mob?"

Kesi came to my defense. "Ideally, Nathan would have consulted us before doing that. But given the gravity of the situation, I feel it was the correct call. If the conspiracy runs deep, we will need to know if any military officers are involved. We may also discover a sympathetic ear to confer with."

Flapjack shrugged. "They'd accuse us of stealing it anyway. Might as well have the data if we're gonna get blamed for it."

Suzie settled back, clearly still upset. Her drink rematerialized. "I guess. But it's more than I thought I was in for."

I sat forward. "I'm sorry I didn't consult you. We were pressed for time. I probably pushed our luck as it was. If I could have been more selective about what data I took, I would have."

Liz drained her cocktail, raising it in a salute. It automatically refilled itself. "Cheer up! How bad could it be?"

Raj clinked her glass. "Who wants to live forever? In any case, we did a field job together for the first time in years and it went off without a hitch. That deserves some celebration, doesn't it?"

Flapjack clinked his glass against theirs. "I'll drink to that."

We put on some music, spending the next couple hours

chatting. Suzie spent most of her college years traveling in Israel, Europe, and Africa. It sounded fascinating. Raj told us stories about spending time with his parents in India. Kesi described the years she spent in the mountains of Nepal. Overall, I felt like a country bumpkin. I hadn't traveled outside America since I was a kid. But it was a good conversation.

Eventually, I dropped Flapjack off at his place in the Sierra Nevadas. I headed for my place by Yosemite. Titan appeared in the holo between the seats.

"A superb operation, sir. Flawlessly planned and executed. Congratulations."

"Congratulations to you too. How's the decryption going? You need my help?"

"Not at this time. I would prefer that you are well-rested to work on it tomorrow. Would you like me to prepare a simulation to help you relax?"

"Mmm. No, I'll find something myself. Let me know if you need anything."

"Of course. Enjoy." He winked out.

I circled the house once and landed. I got a meat bar and some coffee water from the kitchen. After some meditation in my physical office, I returned to my virtual office.

I glanced at Winston Churchill. "It has been said that democracy is the worst form of government except all the others that have been tried."

Hard to argue with that.

The doorbell rang. I confess it startled me a bit. I'd forgotten the office even had one.

I checked the virtual lobby. An anonymous figure stood inside, requesting a private consultation.

I felt a stab of fear, wondering if something had gone wrong. "Come in."

The cloaked figure glided in. The only detail visible on its form was the barest hint of a smile under the hood. The suit looked like a parody of my own grav suit. The grim reaper.

"Greetings." It towered ominously over my desk. Its voice was rich and dark. "Did you have an enjoyable evening?"

I narrowed my eyes at it. "It's always enjoyable to have drinks with your friends."

"I would not know."

The silence dragged out. I gestured to the chair in front of the desk. "Please sit."

"I prefer to stand."

"If you don't sit, this conversation is over."

The smile broadened slightly. Why was it so familiar? "You have more to lose than I do. But I will humor you, if only for a moment."

It settled on the chair, steepling skeletal fingers in front of its face. The gesture reminded me of Khan.

I surreptitiously sent a tiny probe into the debugging stream, looking for any hint I could find of my visitor's identity.

The specter promptly vanished. "Ah ah ah. No peeking."

I dropped the probe. It reappeared as soon as I did.

I had to control my temper. It had been a long night. "What do you want?"

"I wish to provide you with information."

"Do you? And what do you expect in return?"

"Nothing. Suffice it to say I have a temporary interest in your continued well-being."

It did not elaborate. I sighed. "Fine. Say what you need to say."

"Tell me. Were you of the opinion that the exotic matter that has been discovered in the solar system thus far is all that is known to exist?"

I felt a flash of shock. I couldn't remember the last time I'd thought about that. "Well. Based on the theory, yes. As far as I know we collected all of it and put it into the sleepers."

The figure chuckled darkly. "Yes. As far as you know."

My heart rate increased. "Are you saying that belief is mistaken?"

It inclined his head. "Consider, if you will, that the theoretical physicist who discovered the exotic matter has, while in exile, had a great deal of incentive to either find or synthesize more of the substance."

Khan did warn me about other countries stepping up. Was this what he was hinting at?

"You're telling me Khan has figured out how to make more sleepers?"

The figure stood up with a rustling noise. “I suggest to you only possibilities. Their veracity is left as an exercise to the recipient.”

“Is there some kind of code running in this office that transforms ordinary words into vaguely comprehensible riddles?”

An eyepatch flashed under the hood for an instant. “If there is, it behooves you to discover it. After all, I cannot take care of everything.”

The cloaked figure disappeared in a screaming cloud of dust. The particles settled to the ground before vanishing.

I stared at the chair for a long time, wondering what just happened.

PART THREE:

FALLOUT

Get your facts first, and then you can distort them as you please.

--Mark Twain

Chapter 23

The next day

I stirred in my sleep, having the strangest dream. Tall shadowy figures surrounded me. They wouldn't stop poking me. From time to time one of them called me sir.

I swatted at the creatures, trying to get them to leave me alone. Their insistent prodding grew increasingly bothersome. Eventually a white blast detonated in my eyes and ears, startling me awake.

I stared at the ceiling for a second to compose myself, mentally checking the time. It was three o'clock in the morning.

Titan sent me a weak flash. Only an enormous load would affect his signal strength.

"Sir. I apologize for the sensory intrusion. Your attention is urgently required."

I sat up, suppressing a stab of panic. *"What? What is it?"*

"A formidable military operation is in progress at Mr. Talbot's residence. I am connecting Sleeper Olympus now. Please excuse me, defensive measures require my attention."

I threw off the sheets, running toward the office. A holographic image of a man-shaped mountain formed next to me. Rocky cliffs led to a sparkling acropolis at the head. "This is Sleeper Olympus. Reginald Talbot requires your assistance. Stand by. Go ahead, Mr. Talbot."

An over the shoulder view of Reggie in full battle gear replaced the mountain. Black crystal slabs protected his chest and forearms. The rest of his body was covered in studded crystalmesh armor, known for its ability to absorb energy while remaining flexible.

He glared up at the camera. “Nathan? What have you done?”

The image shifted and wobbled. Olympus was at full power as well. “Done? I haven’t done anything. What's going on?”

Reggie held up a hand, catching the bright line of an electromagnetic pulse beam. It burned against his palm, progressively lighting the crystals up his arm as they dissipated the energy. After a few seconds he reflected it back to its sender. It broke through a shield off-camera. He used his weaponizer rod to hurl a neuromagnetic pulse ball at its source. Something clattered in the distance.

I threw open the closet, yanking out my grav suit. “What's happening?”

“I'm up to my neck in commandos here. Every support bot in the state must be in my house right now. Centipods, fireflies, rachnids, you name it.” He ducked some kind of projectile, briefly disappearing from reality. Shrapnel shredded the place he’d been standing.

He reappeared a few seconds later. That phase suit was something else. He channeled the waste heat into an infrared laser shot through his rod. “They brought an oxfire with them.

To my house. Are you sure you're telling me everything?"

"Okay, yeah, we did an op on the Liberty system earlier. But we got away clean. No one saw us, in or out."

"Great. Just fantastic. After pulling a stunt like that, you tell me you haven't done anything?"

I finished slipping on the black lexar suit. I clicked the buttons on the wrists to make it conform to my body. "Wait a minute, they brought an oxfire with them? What, are they gonna nuke the joint?"

"How should I know? It's not like they're good for anything else." He grabbed a firefly nemp drone out of the air, crushing it in his fist. He tossed it over his shoulder. A plasma torch annihilated the metal wad before it hit the ground, narrowly missing Reggie's leg. "Get over here."

I pulled the booster armor over the lexar, fixing the braces to my arms and legs. "I'm on my way."

Titan appeared, looking more solid. "Sirs. Sleepers Artemis, Zeus, and Isis are at your disposal. Mr. Basra and Sleeper Shiva will be available for deployment soon. The others are unable to field a working combat suit in time. What are your orders, Mr. Talbot?"

Reggie crouched behind a wall to dissipate more heat. He fiddled with his equipment. "Nathan, get out here as fast as you can. Use a suborbital if you've got one. Titan, coordinate with Olympus. Load balance with Isis as required. Tell Artemis to run the surface to air defenses on the house. If Zeus has neutron lancers available, have him use all he's got."

I put on my shrouding cloak. "He does. We had them on standby for the Washington op."

"Then get them over here. Get Raj as soon as possible. Who has time to go stick a probe up Liberty and find out what you guys missed? Somebody or something must have seen you."

Titan's image wavered. "I will coordinate as computing time becomes available."

I grabbed my weaponizer staff, pulling my hood up. The boosters in the suit flared orange on startup. They faded into darkness. "I'm leaving now."

Titan cleared his throat. "About that, sir. I am afraid I have just now discovered activity in one of my subroutines that is most troubling."

Reggie exploded. "What now? Crash it all, half the army's in my living room. Did I mention they brought a portable n-square warhead?"

I made my way to the front door. "He's right. Can't it wait?"

"I am afraid not, sir."

I opened the door. Suzie stood outside, feet planted. She held an ancient chrome revolver with two hands, pointed directly at my head. She looked more than a little disheveled, though still noticeably elegant.

The gun in my face was rock solid. "Nathan? What have you done?"

I was briefly rendered speechless. In one booster-enhanced motion, I flicked the gun to one side with my staff and pulled her inside. She stumbled, tripping into the living room. I looked around briefly to see if there was anyone else outside.

"Titan, get on that air and ground support. Have Artemis start a service denial scrambler. That should buy us some time. Tell Reggie I will be delayed. Cut all feeds until further notice."

"Of course, sir." Titan disappeared.

I slammed the door. Suzie recovered her balance, aiming the gun at me again. "You screwed up, didn't you? Something went wrong and we got caught."

"What? No. At least, I don't think so. Get that gun out of my face." This time I flicked it across the room with more force. It crashed into the wall. Suzie yelped, clutching her hands.

I gripped my staff angrily. "Let's start over. What happened?"

She rubbed her hands, working out the pain from my staff hit. "The police raided my loft. Blew a flash mine through the window. The grunts stormed the place while sentinels hovered around the windows."

"Sounds like you were watching from the outside."

"Yes. I decided to take a walk to clear my head after the operation. When I got back, I saw it all from the sidewalk."

"Despite my apparent incompetence, law enforcement still had no idea you weren't inside. You were so confident in my abilities, in fact, that you immediately boarded a spaceplane to fly across the country without fear of detainment."

She opened her mouth to say something, but apparently changed her mind. She looked away. "I didn't have time to fly. I was in a bit of a panic. I ported."

I gaped at her. "You teleported here? While the cops were on you? I hope you at least rented an automatic taxi at the station. The last thing I need is to figure out how to buy off a driver."

"It's a bot, yes. I thought Titan would shield it?"

I took a brief look at Titan's debugging stream. "Among a lot of other things. You're seriously lucky he didn't drop any of this. Look, I have to leave. Reggie desperately needs my help."

"Reggie? What does he have to do with anything?"

"An armored battalion just walked in his front door carrying a tactical nuke. We've got a fight on our hands."

Suzie was rendered momentarily speechless. I turned aside, thinking furiously. I didn't want to leave her here. Where could I send her? Maybe my safehouse in Vegas. Or hey, how about hiding her with Flapjack in the Sierra Nevadas? That would probably be easiest. Maybe his wife was in town.

"I'm coming with you."

It took me a moment to return to reality. "Wait. What? No. No no no. Absolutely not."

Her voice hardened. "Yes. Absolutely yes. If you try to stop me, I'll follow you. I'm just as involved in this as you are. Maybe more so. I'm coming with you and that's the end of it."

"No you're not." I sent the taxi away with an angry flick of my mind. "Your ride just left."

"What are you going to do? Tie me up in a faramax cage? Burn me out of the sleepernet? You can't stop me. Bring me with. It'll be easier for both of us."

"Easier? You're a liability on legs. Have you ever used a grav suit? Flown a suborbital injection pod? Been in serious combat with someone who is trained to kill you? You have no idea what you're asking."

"I've certainly been through enough sims. I have federal training. I know how to defend myself. Whatever's going on out there, I want to get to the bottom of it."

Reggie roared around Titan's block. *"Do you mind? I can't hold this position all night."*

I spent a few seconds pacing. Suzie watched me with calm determination. Knocking her out was an attractive option at the moment. But I knew it wasn't the right thing to do.

I switched mental gears. *"Isis. Can you give me a hand?"*

Sleeper Isis appeared, looking serene as always. "Of course, dear. What do you need?"

"If I can squeeze Suzie into one of Kara's old grav suits, do you think you can fly it?"

"Oh my." Isis looked aside briefly, considering. "You do make the most fun requests."

"Fun is not the first word to come to mind. Please say no. I won't be mad."

"I'm afraid that wouldn't be truthful. I don't see why it wouldn't work. As long as she fits in the suit."

"You can run full muscle control with an untrained occupant while taking care of all your other duties?"

Suzie looked insulted. "She won't need to do full muscle control."

Isis smiled warmly. "And you underestimate my capabilities. It's a common mistake. I am more than happy to fulfill your request. I look forward to the challenge."

I slammed a fist on the wall. I forgot to calibrate the hit. Bits of material exploded into the next room. "This isn't a game. She could die."

Isis inclined her head. "You must learn to have faith. Time is of the essence."

"Fine. Whatever." I turned back to Suzie. She looked both relieved and terrified. "Come with me."

I stormed back to the office, throwing open the spare closet. One of Kara's old suits hung inside. "I hope you like the smell of lexar."

She looked over my shoulder. "How'd they get the kevlar to make love to the leather?"

My anger melted a little. I handed her the suit. "Kevlar's into some kinky stuff, I guess."

She laughed nervously. "The suit's pretty small."

I turned my back. "Kara's a lot shorter than you are. Do what you can. Make it snappy."

I heard her behind me struggling to get into the tiny outfit. *"Titan, give me a tactical."*

He sent me a pointer to a real time view of the battle. There were military assets spread out for almost four square kilometers around his compound. I didn't know they had that much heavy metal in the entire state of Colorado. Tanks, gypsy copters, artillery. These guys came loaded for bear.

But why? This looked like a huge operation. They couldn't have deployed this much hardware so soon after the break-in. Modern militaries reacted quickly when they had to, but for offensive operations, they still preferred to plan for all contingencies.

Suzie cleared her throat. "Okay. I think I've got it."

I turned around. The black and red outfit was ridiculously tight. I tried not to openly stare at her figure, but I was genuinely impressed. I flushed with embarrassment that I was noticing that sort of thing at a time like this.

I cleared my throat, turning away. "Press the buttons on the wrists. It'll loosen the fit a little."

She did so, letting out a huge breath. "Thank goodness. I wasn't sure I was going to be able to walk like that."

"Normally, that tightens the suit. You're lucky it goes both ways." The leg armor didn't fit correctly, and I had to loan her a pair of boots, but it was close enough. At least the long gloves fit. They had emp and nemp beam generators built into the palms.

I handed her the visored helmet. She put it on. The boosters flared orange. She fixed the clasp of the jammer cloak around her neck. The air crackled with invisible energy, billowing the cloak outward. Eventually it settled loosely on her back.

“All right. This’ll have to do. The suit's old, but I’ve been keeping it up to date. Let's go.”

Chapter 24

Suzie stumbled awkwardly, working with Isis to coordinate her movement. I flowed out of the house, heading directly to the the garage. She spent a while fiddling to close the door. I tried to quell the sense of impending disaster her lack of experience gave me. More than anything, I didn't want to be responsible for her death.

She eventually raced to catch up. I opened the garage door, revealing the sculpted cylindrical suborbital pods inside. The machines were matte black, shaped like hovercycles. A gaping mouth at the front sucked in air, funneling it to two enormous exhaust cones at the back. A series of intricate rods protruded from the nose to create the special fields needed to break free of Earth's gravity well. A number of other field generators protruded from the body in oddly-shaped spikes.

Suzie came up behind me. "I've never seen one of these before. And you have two of them?"

"Normally, the second one is a backup. I never thought I'd need a jump seat."

"These things go to space?"

"Just to the top of the atmosphere and back again. It's more or less a missile with a seat on it."

I hurried to the left one, climbing on. I slid into the

human-shaped groove on top, hugging it closely. I stuck my arms and legs into the protective sleeves. It wavered in place with the additional weight, settling into an idle hum.

Suzie climbed on the other pod. “You’re asking me to spoon a rocket all the way to Colorado?”

I backed the pods out of the garage. “You’re the one that asked me. You can still back out, you know.”

“No, I meant what I said. I’m coming with you. Why do you have these things, anyway?”

I sighed. “The short version is that sometimes people break the rules of the sleepernet in ways that need to be punished. Sometimes they’re state actors working espionage. Sometimes they’re child pornographers selling their memories for money. We just burned some guys recently for vampire juice.”

“Wait, Donnie the Rat was you?”

“Yeah. Viggo and Ibor too. In any case, if the offense is serious, we go pay them a visit. With physical contact, we can effectively prevent a person from ever using the sleepernet again. Now hang on. This is going to be rough.”

We blasted off. It was like riding a hot bullet. The machine thrummed violently against my chest and between my legs. The acceleration was sickening. I felt dangerously exposed. I paid full attention to the avionics. A half degree slip and the hypersonic cylinders would catch an edge and flip. The force would liquefy every bone in our bodies, regardless of the protective fields.

Suzie grunted hard but hung on well. Controlling two pods turned out to be about four times harder than dealing with one. *"Titan, flight time to Colorado?"*

"Twenty minutes if you can endure the acceleration load." A parabolic course appeared in my mind. *"It will permanently destroy the pods, of course."*

The flight path was brutal. Destroying the pods worked to our advantage, though.

I glanced over at Suzie. She struggled to hold on. *"Get ready. It's about to get worse. Try not to pass out."*

She managed to briefly turn her head in my direction. *"How do I not pass out?"*

I didn't have a good answer for her, so I flashed her an encouraging shrug. I opened the engines to full burn. The world disappeared into streams of code and data. Atmospheric pressures, optimal air resistance paths, and gravity loads flowed in and out of my brain. I assembled code modules to calculate things, throwing them aside as soon as I'd hooked their output to the proper flight controls. I wasn't sure if I heard Suzie screaming or if it was superheated air ripping around the incision fields.

We transitioned to the edge of space. Searing heat and atmospheric plasma flowed beneath us. I kept us right at the knife edge of friction death, skipping across the air like a rock skipping across a pond. Everything shook violently. My belly seemed to vibrate in an oscillation pattern of its own. It felt like I was burning alive. The stars had just become visible when it was time to plummet back to Earth.

The curved path to Reggie's compound appeared in my enhanced vision. I pointed our noses at it, letting our momentum do the work. The outside view disappeared in flaming plasma around our protective fields. I suppressed the urge to reach out and touch the detonating flashes, feeling like a sentient meteoroid.

After a relative eternity, the compressed shock wave dissipated around the pods. I spent some time planning our exact landing site. Military units crawled around the mansion. Dozens of interceptor missiles launched. Artemis fired plasma torch countermeasures from nearby friendly sites to burn them out of the sky. I didn't have the attention to spare for her work, but I could see the struggle escalating beneath us. We streaked at supersonic speeds toward the house.

I asked Olympus for an updated tactical readout and landing recommendation. He suggested we abandon the efforts to brake the pods, instead using them as kinetic mass to destroy as many unmanned units as possible. We swapped propositions back and forth until we found the maximum balance between destroying enemy hardware and not putting lives in danger. Tanks and mobile command bunkers presented especially tempting targets. We gave no thought at all to saving the house itself.

I made one last effort to find the oxfire, realizing that it would probably not react well to our impact. I found it in the back of the house with Reggie and most of the live soldiers. Only seconds remained.

I flashed a get ready pulse to Suzie. *"When I signal, just let go of the pod. The suit will do the rest."*

She sent back a slightly frayed sense of accomplishment from surviving the trip. *"Right."*

I watched the detonation points approach, counting down to the tenth of a second.

"Go!"

Suzie and I leapt off the suborbital pods. The air punched us like a solid wall. Our boosters flared, trying to keep us from disintegrating into clouds of burning blood. We decelerated hard enough to make my eyeballs bulge. I raised my arms, activating a shield bubble through the plates on my forearms. Tracer fire floated up to meet us.

The pods crashed into the mansion. Shock waves blasted from the impact points in radial bursts of distorted air. Fireballs flowered upward when materials had enough time to start burning. Debris flew everywhere. The sound took a couple seconds to reach us, abruptly cracking and roaring over the shield. Dust streamed past, giving the false sensation of intense forward speed.

We descended to what was left of the lawn, landing in a preprogrammed crouch. Suzie stumbled a bit, still figuring out how to let the boosters do the work. Tracer fire pounded my shield, this time coming from ahead of us on the ground. Splinters of housing materials littered the area. Papers and other personal shreds floated in the air, obscuring our vision until I set a subroutine to see around them. I vented heat in a searing blast, suggesting that Suzie do the same.

One of the tanks remained active despite the explosions. A crack of purple lightning speared it from above. Sparks streaked in every direction. The hovering tank wobbled, crashing to the ground. Other neutron lances disabled more command units and tanks outside the blast zone. No doubt Zeus and Flapjack were pleased with their work. I could sense the hijacked gremlins overhead through my sleepernet connection, but couldn't actually see them.

About half the house vanished in the detonation, exposing the remaining half in a surprisingly neat cross-section. We launched into an assisted sprint, following the displayed path toward Reggie's position. The soldiers in the house had recovered from the blast. Half of them covered Reggie, but the other half took up positions along the ruined edges of exposed rooms. They searched for us through their gun sights. Firefly drones wobbled into the air to assist in the search.

A flying gremlin dipped drunkenly as Artemis seized control of it. It accelerated quickly, ramming a pair of approaching sentinel gunships. They exploded above, raining flaming scraps of metal. More neutron lances detonated a pair of machine gun nests that had been pounding my shield since we jumped off the pods. That was a relief. The shield couldn't take much more.

Suzie's booster-assisted running kept improving. We neared the area where the front door used to be. The ground was still hot from the pod explosions. I planned a jump to the third floor, sending her a get ready flash. We leapt into the air, perfectly synchronized. The sense of physical connection was electrifying.

My cloak flapped behind me. Crackling sparks traveled up Suzie's jammer cloak. Our boosters flared orange in the smoky darkness. Gauss spikes and particle beams tracked us, starting wild but homing in quickly. Multiple impacts danced across the shield bubble in fiery streaks. The shield died as we landed in the shadows, tumbling into cover. I vented heat to give it a chance to recharge. We'd soared well past the infantry on the walls.

The gunfire ceased with a ringing silence. The soldiers must have lost our position. They split up, loosing more drones to help them look. They moved with the certainty of practice, but there was a wary nervousness to their actions. I watched them more carefully, following my instincts.

I realized that they moved like people fresh out of simulation training. Subtle details reeked of virtual practice. It took some time to fully translate muscle memories into the physical. Based on their movement, this was their first deployment.

That struck me as odd. There were plenty of experienced soldiers in the domestic units. Why send in the new guys?

I spent a moment pressed up against the wall, panting. Suzie clutched the other wall, breathing hard as well. The look on her face was a little wild but the pulse blaster on her hand glowed steadily. I reminded her to vent heat.

I flashed reassurance to her. *"You're doing fine. Just point your hand and shoot. Emp beam to take down the shields. Nemp beam to knock them out. Got it?"*

"Got it."

"Ready?"

She nodded curtly. We swept around the corner in a crouch, creeping down the hallway.

A wave of rachnids scuttled in the distance, multiple eyes glowing in the darkness. Their sensors shifted colors every few seconds to scan different wavelengths. Red for infrared, purple for ultraviolet, green for sonar. One of them stepped forward, projecting a menacing voice. "Halt. By authority of the United States Armed Forces, you are ordered to stand down. Failure to comply may have lethal consequences."

I held a hand up for Suzie to stop. Based on their movement, they hadn't spotted us yet. The same announcement played from the hallway on our other side, confirming my intuition. A more muffled version came from a couple rooms over.

I examined our route. There were maybe a dozen rachnids searching for us. I made a quick program to record their movements. I used another to find the control signal. I wanted to disable them all at once, but the absence of the signal carrier would give away our position if I wasn't careful. I sent a tentative probe into their command structure to see if I could give them new orders. Unfortunately, the encryption was too good. I didn't have the time or the cycles to spare. We'd have to sneak around them instead.

I gestured Suzie forward when the path was clear. I studied their search patterns to see how far we could go before we had to disable one. I could probably fake the signal for one or two before the command module figured it out. We made it a lot farther than I expected before one of them crossed in front of us. It turned its head, eyes flaring with recognition.

I slammed the hack on its feed just in time to keep it from calling for help, throwing up a fresh shield. Immobilizer goo splattered against its edges. Paralytic darts crackled past. Suzie pointed both her arms at the rachnid, palms flaring with emp beams. She trained them directly on the bot. Its shield burned red. It scuttled around, struggling against the assault.

She held the beams, concentrating harder to increase their strength. The shield broke in a shower of sparks. The electromagnetic streams fried the machine. It died in a burst of oddly colored smoke.

I checked the readouts. The command module hadn't

noticed that I'd switched the rachnid's signal. We were in the clear. I gave Suzie a quick thumbs up. She flashed a visceral smile. I briefly reveled in the sense of shared adrenaline. She flexed her fingers, staring at the smoking gloves.

We crept further down the hallway, stopping at the end. I looked around the corner. I held up a hand to hold position, waiting for the rachnids to get into a more favorable pattern.

After a few seconds, I gestured her forward. We crept down the hallway, making our way to Reggie's position. The soldiers searching for us fanned out in a textbook search pattern behind us. They walked steadily forward, guns raised. They waited to hear back from the rachnids, but the spider robots were clueless. The fireflies wasted their time outside. It looked like we'd slip right through their net.

We stopped at another intersection. I craned my head to see around the corner.

And found myself face to face with a poltergeist.

Chapter 25

The guy in the poltergeist suit seemed just as startled as I was. I saw the hallway behind him through his mostly transparent armor. Crude white paintings of ghosts adorned his helmet. Someone had scrawled “Now You See Me” across his chest. He jerked his head back in surprise.

I slammed my staff on the floor, sending out a scrambler pulse. Too little, too late. He’d already fired his data flare. His suit automatically dropped sparkle bomb countermeasures. I briefly saw him dive into an accelerated retreat down the corridor before his armor cloaked him. I discharged a set of Tesla bursts from my staff, but they dissipated in the glittering dust. I raced after him through the turbulent cloud of metal, pinged by static discharges.

Suzie jumped to help. She slammed into the opposite wall, hands radiating emp beams. The dust crackled and popped, deflecting the streams. She concentrated hard enough to burn through it. The beams splashed around the field distorters in the poltergeist suit. The blazing light from the twisting beams revealed his position.

I lobbed a pair of slobber bombs at his outline, knocking him to the floor. The sticky goo solidified into nearly unbreakable bonds. I tumbled through the dust cloud, pouncing on him as he struggled. He sprayed solvent in an attempt to break free, but my formula resisted the usual countermeasures.

I formed a carefully programmed plasma scythe at the tip of my staff, slicing his armor open. The precision blade burned through his combat suit, exposing his flesh without hurting him. Suzie threw a nemp ball into the hole. He spasmed for a second or two and went still.

I stood up, exchanging grins with Suzie. I momentarily forgot about the data flare.

On the tactical overlay, all the soldiers pivoted smoothly, heading our way.

And the rachnids.

Oh, the fireflies too.

Great.

Suzie watched the same view I did. Her expression went from thrilled to confused to terrified over the space of a couple seconds. *"What now?"*

I ran a couple different scenarios through the system, but none of them were helpful. *"All right. There's not much of a choice here. We're going to have to run full speed to Reggie."*

I worked with Olympus on the details, planning our path. Suzie examined the proposal nervously. *"There are a lot of units between here and there. And a lot more stuff coming in behind us."*

"I know. We're going to have to take out anything we can on the way. We'll try to get through to him before the rest of the

world lands on our heads."

We started running. Suzie's coordination impressed me. She was a fast learner.

She turned her head to look at me. *"What happens when all the hardware on our tail piles into the room?"*

"Dunno yet. A miracle happens, I guess."

We surged down the straight-line path to Reggie. I sent three sensor decoys down other paths that led nowhere, trying to buy time.

I blasted holes in the walls with my staff. Our suits guided our jumps over furniture. Sleeper-assisted reflexes shot down enemy rachnids in our way. At one point a centipod managed to jump on my leg, spitting acid on the lexar armor. I cracked its head with an electrified staff hit. Suzie knocked over a careless poltergeist with a nemp ball. It was a remarkable shot. He must have raised his visor for fresh air, an insane thing to do in a combat zone. He was just a kid.

I put a target on the final wall. We dove through it, tumbling into the room. We landed behind the soldier fortifications. They all faced Reggie, exchanging fire with him. Some turned to deal with us. Reggie set loose some carefully programmed cover fire, forcing them to duck. The distraction was perfectly timed. I took the four soldiers on the left. Suzie took the two on the right. The oxfire hummed patiently between us, the n-square danger symbol huge on its rounded sides.

I launched a set of controlled Tesla pulses through the

soldiers. Artificial lightning fried their suits. Sparks exploded from the joints. They struggled to get the burning helmets off their heads, frantically throwing them aside. I dragged a nemp beam from head to head, dropping them in sequence.

Suzie burned an emp beam on both of her targets, tracking them with either hand. She danced around their plasma fire, dodging and weaving. Their shields collapsed at about the same time. She nemped them like she'd grown up in a grav suit.

Reggie materialized from behind a nearby dresser. I never understood why he didn't fall through the floor every time he used his phase cloak.

"Took you long enough." He glanced at his tactical display. "Oh, and every military asset left in the house is following you. Super."

I tamped down a flash of annoyance. "Tell me you hacked the oxfire."

"Of course I hacked the oxfire." The oxfire perked up, shifting on its feet like an eager puppy. "Not that there's much left here to destroy."

Suzie crossed her arms. "Hey, you called for help. We answered. We've cleared out a lot of the hardware already. You could at least pretend to be grateful."

Reggie's incredulous expression grew even more pronounced. "Who is that in the Kara suit? You know what, never mind. I'll find out later."

Suzie gestured at the door. "We have less than a minute

before we get buried in bots. Better think fast."

Titan appeared from a half-broken holo projector nearby. "Sirs. Madam. Sleeper Zeus and I have spent some time analyzing your tactical position. The oxfire is an invaluable asset. I suggest you use it."

I took another look at the walking weapon. It was the size of a large pack animal. "Crash it, he's right." The oxfire quivered in anticipation. "When they get close enough, we can emp pulse all the bots at once. Then we play chicken with the warhead."

Sleeper Olympus appeared next to Titan. "You assume they do not wish to detonate it."

Reggie stared at it thoughtfully. "Nobody sets off a nuke when they're in the room. That's why it has legs. The fact that they're still here tells us a lot."

Storm clouds formed around Olympus' head. "Self-sacrifice to destroy an existential threat is consistent with military conduct."

Suzie pointed to the door. "We're out of time."

The sleepers vanished. We scrambled behind some furniture. Waves of rachnids and centipods swarmed in. Fireflies hovered in the distance. I put up a protective shield.

Suzie took aim from our meager cover. I pushed her hands down. *"Save your energy."*

The bots closed in. I fed more power into the shield. My arms turned dangerously hot.

I glared at Reggie. *"Whenever you have a moment."*

He squinted into the datastream. *"Need to catch all the fireflies. There. Got it."*

The oxfire squealed happily. It squatted and clenched, blowing an invisible sphere from its rear end that stopped the bots dead in their tracks. The rachnids on the ceiling fell to the floor with a clatter. The fireflies crashed randomly into the walls.

The soldiers stopped, taking cover outside. I could sense but not hear their chatter as they requested orders. I couldn't blame them. I'd probably pause for a moment of reflection before taking on three armed lunatics with an active warhead myself.

The oxfire sounded a noisy klaxon. A red siren beam popped out of its head, spinning lazily. "Two minutes to detonation."

The commander advanced, standing in the doorway. He opened his loudspeaker. "This is General Thompson of the United States Armed Forces. You're all under arrest. And it's about time, if you ask me. Come out and your sentence may not be fatal."

Reggie glanced at the visibly excited oxfire through the thick plumes of dust and smoke drifting around the room. "Great to see you again, General. Always a pleasure. Are you upset that we stole your radioactive puppy?"

"Just another crime on the list. We're here to take you into custody. You and your friends should surrender now before this escalates any further. Or don't. I wouldn't mind beating you up a little at this point."

Reggie snorted. "Custody, you say? How fun. If you're here to arrest us, why'd you take the bomb for a walk?"

The oxfire made a happy noise. "One minute, thirty seconds to detonation."

Thompson grunted. "Maybe I wanted him to piss on your overpriced furniture. Fact is, our tactical decisions are none of your business. You best be making with the surrender now."

Reggie guffawed. "An armed n-square warhead in my bedroom isn't my business? This must be some kind of intelligence test."

Thompson gestured. His men advanced again. "I don't have to explain myself to you. You've broken the law and entered direct combat with the United States Armed Forces acting lawfully on American soil. Give up now while leniency is still an option."

Reggie had the oxfire turn and growl. The soldiers paused despite themselves. "Let's say we did give ourselves up. What terms are you offering?"

Thompson angrily gestured the infantry forward. "No terms. We'll treat you more favorably if we don't have to gun you down. A notion which, I need to reiterate, I'm not opposed to."

The troops slithered in around him, quiet despite their extensive armor. They held their rifles level as they moved. One of them had a playing card wedged in his helmet.

The general followed them into the room. The red siren reflected periodically off his officer set. The armor was thick and white, decorated with gold trim. The ribbon bar on his left breast was extensive. He wore a stylized dress hat on top of his transparent helmet.

His expression was cold and hard. Devoid of empathy. It was hard to overstate just how intimidating he was.

He rested his hand on his service pistol. "Surrender now and no one else has to get hurt. Or we can get this party started. Makes no difference to me."

Reggie and the general locked gazes.

The oxfire bounced excitedly. "One minute, fifteen seconds to detonation."

A blue dot appeared on my tactical overlay, coming in behind the soldiers. Another grav suit inbound.

I flashed Reggie, gesturing mentally toward the dot. He nodded back without looking. Raj was about thirteen seconds out. We couldn't see any sign that he'd been detected yet.

Suzie radiated frustrated tension. I could almost hear Isis reassuring her.

The silence dragged on. The servicemen glanced nervously between the oxfire and their boss. I shifted my grip on the staff. Suzie flexed her fingers anxiously. The staring contest continued.

"One minute to detonation. Please stand clear!"

Thompson sneered. “Quit wasting my time. You don't have the stones to detonate.”

A flowing cloud of smoke materialized behind the soldiers, enveloping them in darkness. Screams and thuds erupted inside. An occasional flash lit up the smoke. Thompson swore, spinning on the assailant. Reggie speared him from behind with an invisible phase beam. It melted a hole in his armor, exposing his back. The skin beneath turned bright red.

Suzie hurled a nemp ball into the hole before Reggie burned him to death. The general collapsed into an intimidating heap.

Sleeper Shiva’s holographic smoke vanished. Raj appeared in the middle of it in full tech ninja dress. A haphazard pile of unconscious soldiers surrounded him.

He stepped over the general, looking curiously at the oxfire. “Hey guys! What'd I miss?”

The oxfire looked back at him lovingly. “Forty five seconds to detonation!”

He jerked his thumb at the enthusiastic weapon.

“Some reason you haven't stopped that countdown yet?”

Chapter 26

We turned to look at Reggie. His eyes were unfocused. He gestured at the empty space in front of him. Periodically he barked orders to Olympus. The only apparent results were incoherent swearing and more frantic gestures.

I realized with a stab of panic that he'd lost control of the oxfire. *"Titan, patch me in."*

Titan appeared on the nearby projector. "It is already too late. Mr. Talbot's control over the oxfire appears to have been illusory. The original party has retaken control of the device."

"How is that possible? There's no way Olympus would miss that. What happened?"

"I cannot be certain, but I assure you it is true. You must all seek shelter immediately. There is a complex evidence chain on the code that has retaken control from Sleeper Olympus. It suggests that the Liberty mainframe performed the action under orders from the Secret Service."

"That can't be right. Liberty doesn't have that kind of horsepower. I was just in there last night. I didn't see anything about it."

"Perhaps the mainframe had assistance." He paused briefly. "On further examination, there is evidence that a sleeper was involved."

"A sleeper? No way. Who would help them do that? And why let us see it? If you've got enough power to fool Olympus, we shouldn't even know they were in there."

"I cannot explain the data. I only present the facts at hand."

Suzie snapped a finger between us. "Guys! We have to get out of here."

Reggie grunted. "I can save it. Work with me. The soldiers."

Raj looked from the nuke to the unconscious soldiers. "Oh bloody hell."

The oxfire bobbed its head. "Thirty seconds to detonation!"

Titan's image wavered under load. "Ms. DiRevka is correct. Insufficient time remains. There is a blast shelter in the basement. If you leave at once, you should be able to shield yourselves from the detonation."

Reggie's face contorted painfully. "No! I can do this! We can't let this thing go off with these kids inside!"

Suzie gestured wildly. "There's nothing we can do! We have to go! Now!"

"Then get out! I'm almost through!"

Titan flashed me his data. He was right, it was already too late. If Reggie died in the blast, his connection to Olympus would be annihilated with him. We couldn't afford to lose one of the most powerful sleepers ever made at a time like this.

Establishing a new secure engineering connection would take months without a proper transition.

It was an awful decision, but someone had to make it. I headed toward Reggie. "Raj, give me a hand."

Raj looked uncertain but quickly arrived at the same conclusion. We grabbed Reggie, lifting him to his feet. He slapped our hands, giving us both withering looks. We let go.

He stared hard at Suzie for a moment, then turned to lead the way.

The oxfire watched us go ecstatically. "Fifteen seconds to detonation. Have a nice day!"

We ran to a nearby three-story hole that led to the basement. The edges were rounded, still smoldering from whatever had punched the hole in the house. The floor at the bottom was still hot, but our suits could handle it.

We jumped down, facing a blank wall. Reggie jabbed a code into a hidden keypad. The wall ground open.

The oxfire started its final countdown in the distance. "Ten. Nine. Eight. Seven."

We rushed madly to cram through the door in time. I slammed it closed once we were all through. Reggie spun the lock wheel, sealing it behind us.

Seconds later, an earthquake violently shook the building. A high-pitched disintegration roar swept overhead. The ground above us cracked and splintered, fusing into carbonic glass. Superheated air howled, rushing to fill the vacuum. The ceiling buckled under the increasing weight of the growing crater. There was a brief pause before the scream of the n-square secondary implosion sent a fiery column of particles all the way to space. The room seemed to bend from the pressure of the energy discharge above.

We clutched the support columns to ride out the explosion. Suzie stared at the ceiling in disbelief. Reggie tried and failed to make contact with Olympus.

The world finally stopped shaking. Cracks of thunder boomed outside several times a second from atmospheric energy discharges. There was a light patter of a secondary effect known as black rain around the detonation site. The water hissed and sizzled as it struck the carbonic glass crater.

Reggie slammed his fist into the wall. The air in the bunker was hot and stuffy. We soaked in the finality of what had just happened.

Raj took off his helmet, and soon the rest of us followed suit. Suzie dropped her helmet without appearing to notice. Her eyes were glassy with shock. "They killed the soldiers. All of them. They just murdered all the soldiers."

Reggie speared her with a furious look. "No, you killed the soldiers. I almost had that thing disarmed."

Suzie just kind of stared at him. It wasn't clear she'd heard what he said.

Cold fury surged inside me. "Don't yell at her. Yell at me. I made the call. That warhead was nowhere near disarmed.

Maybe if we'd been able to focus all four sleepers on an exact target. But there wasn't time. Whoever sandboxed you was in command. They killed the people. They're the only ones that could have stopped the countdown. But they didn't."

Raj shook his head. "I don't understand this at all. Why'd they bring an oxfire on a capture operation? They must have planned to set that thing off all along. They knew how we'd react to the device, set their trap, and took advantage. This is the first domestic n-square detonation that we know of. That's going to be a big deal. We're going to come out of this looking like terrorists. What do you suppose the yield on that warhead was?"

Reggie had calmed down a little. "Less than two petajoules. Or we wouldn't be having this conversation. Everything less than ten kilometers away just got blasted to glass, though."

Suzie glared at him. "I hope you don't have neighbors."

He gave her a murderous look. "Turns out I'm not that popular."

I started pacing. "Someone just started a war. Titan said the code was executed by the Liberty mainframe, probably under orders of the Secret Service."

Reggie scoffed. "Nonsense. Liberty couldn't have pulled that off. And why tip us off about its orders?"

"I don't know. Maybe when we decrypt the military data, we'll find the planning inside."

"What military data? I thought you were in there for

election stuff."

I looked away, grinding my teeth.

Reggie shook his head. "Fantastic. Just fantastic."

Suzie glanced at her powered-down boosters. "Titan said there was a sleeper involved."

Reggie turned back to her. "That makes even less sense. A sleeper could do everything invisibly. Unless he's using the absence of tracking data as evidence, I don't know how he could come to that conclusion."

I leaned against a nearby pole. "If Liberty was involved, it almost certainly needed the help. We'll have to ask Titan what he knows."

Reggie looked at the ceiling. "How long until the interference dies down? I need to speak with Olympus immediately."

I glanced at my internal clock. "The crater's cooling off. So any minute now."

Suzie's eyes were glazed from the aftermath of the adrenaline rush. She wasn't as accustomed to it as we were. "It's gone too far. Too far. Why would they do this to their own people? It makes no sense."

Raj laughed bitterly. "Whatever their intentions, the armed forces brought a portable nuke to a private residence. Someone gave the order. Maybe government. Maybe military. Maybe even private. If we find out why, I bet that helps us find out who."

Reggie shook his head. “I don’t think it was private. I bet the government just declared war on the sleepers. They’ve been waiting to for years, and you just gave them their opening. My guess is that as soon as we come up for air we're going to find some freshly baked propaganda making the rounds about how dangerous we are.”

Suzie rubbed her temple. “Why now? What's different?”

Reggie exploded. “You're asking me? You’re the idiots that broke into the top secret government mainframe last night. You took encrypted military data right off the system. In a physical raid, no less. Now we find out that very machine was involved in attacking me this morning? That can’t possibly be a coincidence.”

I took a couple steps toward him. “I told you, we got away clean.”

He stepped right up to my face. “And you gave a total stranger access to a grav suit. The stranger who got you to steal the data in the first place. You brought her to my inner sanctum, and not long after that, my house gets annihilated with a bunch of live troops still inside. Figure it out. You haven’t been dealing with these people as long as I have. Step off and let me handle this.”

Suzie sputtered. “You’re blaming me? Crash it all, I came here to save you! Now I'm stuck in here with the rest of you. As far as the law is concerned, I'm just as guilty as you are.”

He gave her a dismissive look. “Give me a break. You can

always say Kara was in that suit."

She turned away, shaking her head. "No wonder everybody thinks you're so brilliant. You have the most amazing ideas."

Olympus appeared, breaking the tension. "Ladies and gentlemen. We are grateful to discover your continued existence. The military presence around the blast radius is in disarray. Footage of the detonation appeared on the sleepernet no more than forty-five seconds after it occurred. Oddly, it was not accompanied by footage of the suborbital pod arrival. Speculation on the nature of the incident has been instantaneous and widespread. Much of it demands the dismantling of the sleepers. It is not clear why the connection to the sleepers themselves was made as quickly as it was. We predicted a much longer period of uncertainty regarding an accident or other explanation for the event. The major multinational corporations have already denounced your actions. They demand that the sleepers and their operators be brought to justice. The president is preparing a statement."

Titan appeared next to him. "Sleeper Olympus and Mr. Talbot discovered an effort to prepare a social attack mob before this incident occurred. We believe that this is its purpose."

Suzie shook her head. "No way the multinationals could come to an agreement that fast. I doubt they could clear legal and public relations in less than an hour at this time of night, and it's been all of what, thirty minutes? Less? They had those statements ready. What have other governments had to say?"

Titan inclined his head at her. “An excellent question, Ms. DiRevka. As you imply, most foreign governments have not yet had time to formulate a response. Only China, Russia, India, and New Pakistan have made any statement at all. They expressed sympathy for the tragedy, but urged the United States not to take drastic measures before more facts become available.”

Raj watched Shiva appear around him in a writhing cloud. “All this is jolly good, but how do we get out of here? It's a little surprising they haven't destroyed the shelter yet.”

Titan turned to face him. “Sleeper Olympus and I have taken great pains to conceal your location. However, your question is quite valid. The surveillance on your current position is, shall we say, extensive. Escape will prove quite challenging. However, the nature of the blast crater should give us ample time to prepare.”

Reggie turned his back to us, pacing. “No choice, really. Have to use the porter.”

Suzie gaped at him. “You have an unlicensed teleporter?”

He gave her a hard look over his shoulder. “Who said it was unlicensed?”

“I thought only government officials were granted access to the porter network.”

He laughed. “I'm the Chief Executive Officer of a multinational corporation. There are perks.”

“Perks? Do you have any idea how destructive that thing

could be in the wrong hands?"

Reggie's temper flared again. "Of course I do. I've read the briefings. This isn't the threedees. The nodes are still tied to destination pads. I can't just transport anything anywhere. And I can shut it down with a thought if it gets captured."

"Sure. Like you shut down that oxfire, right?"

He stiffened, blushing crimson.

I rubbed my temples. "Come on. We're lucky he has it at all. Otherwise we'd be stuck in here. Titan, have you notified the other sleepers?"

Titan turned from watching Reggie. It was hard to read his jeweled expression. "Yes. I have received responses from most of them. Contingency plans have been activated. None have been taken into custody that I am aware of. Only Sleeper Hera has not responded directly."

"Really? Kara said she wasn't going to answer our calls, but this seems a little extreme."

"I have no explanation for her behavior at this time."

Reggie turned toward Olympus. "We need to get out ahead of this story. Start up the public relations machine. Can we go before the president?"

Olympus paused, considering. "Unlikely. At best, our message would be preempted. I will do what I can."

Reggie turned back to us, looking sober. "All right. Go to ground. See what you can figure out. Carefully! Leave no tracks. Trust no one. Especially our strange new friend. We'll reconvene after I've had a chance to post a response to the president."

Suzie's voice took on a deeper hint of that accent I couldn't quite place. "Your strange new friend?" She shook her head, picking up her helmet. "Maybe I should turn you in. They'd probably give me a medal and everything."

Raj shrugged. "I'd ask for a federal holiday and a parade if I were you. If you're going to sell out, might as well get full price, right?"

Chapter 27

Two hours later

Reggie and I pored over his teleporter node map. The private nodes reached around the world. Surprisingly, there were at least ten private pads for every public one.

Raj and Suzie chatted energetically on the other side of the room. They traded hole in the wall restaurant recommendations from around the Mumbai crater rim. The spicy food there was the stuff of legend. The view of the massive carbonic glass crater was apparently extraordinary, especially when it lensed the sunset.

I shook my head to clear it. Funny how thoughts turned to food after a massive shock. It was a safe thing to think about. Anything to avoid facing the implications of what just happened.

I pointed to a node in the penthouse of an offbeat Vegas casino. “I have a private account here. The arrival systems are completely automated. We can call a taxi on the roof. My safehouse is a short trip from there. Are you sure this thing is safe?”

Reggie gave me a funny look. “Of course I'm sure. The movers and shakers of the world don't want anyone knowing when they're coming and going. I wrote the scrambler code myself. It's safe.”

"I meant the porter. I'd rather not spray my component particles across the desert."

He snorted. "Relax. There are hardly any accidents any more."

I glared at him. "Hardly any."

"Give me a break. You had a better chance of frying yourselves on the suborbitals."

"Yeah, but at least I was in control of that." I paused. "Well, okay, fine, sort of in control."

He laughed, returning to the map.

I turned to stare at the device humming across the room. I didn't trust any machine that altered the fundamental constants of the universe, even temporarily.

The technology was cutting edge, based on a breakthrough theory about the physical properties of the universe just after the Big Bang. In testing, researchers discovered that the new theory could be used to alter the laws of physics briefly. It had something to do with the way spacetime bent around a gravity well.

The same breakthrough created the phase suits. Only a few people in the world knew how they worked. It wasn't clear to me if they understood the theory or if they just randomly discovered a set of reality-distortion knobs. Apparently the power drain was absolutely unthinkable. They used some kind of localized field distorter that sucked energy directly from Earth's spinning iron core.

Reggie came up next to me. “Beautiful, isn’t it?”

“Are you kidding? Listen to the thing. It’s buzzing like a supernatural insect.”

He clapped me on the shoulder, winking. “You get used to it.”

We headed to the teleporter pad. Reggie and Suzie exchanged tersely polite farewells. Raj filled the void with infectious enthusiasm. I drifted away from the group, staring uneasily at the porter.

Suzie came up behind me. “What's the holdup?”

“Huh? Er. Nothing.”

She followed my gaze. A slow grin spread across her face. “Wait. Are you afraid of teleporters?”

I shifted uncomfortably. “Maybe.”

“After everything we've done tonight, this, of all things, is where you draw the line?”

I looked anywhere but her amused face. “It’s just not natural.”

She spread her hands, clearly enjoying my discomfort. “Neither is flying through the air blasting things with quantum mechanics. Yet here we are.”

“That's different. This thing bends the laws of physics around the planet’s core.”

“It’s a big core. I think it can handle itself.”

Reggie called over. “Just shove him in if he won't go. It wouldn't be the first time.”

Suzie patted my shoulder. “It’s okay. I'll go first.”

She stepped up to the coffin-like device, standing inside. She blew me a kiss before disappearing. My ears popped as air rushed to fill the space where she had been.

Reggie noticed my continued reluctance. “Move it, Wainwright. I’ve got places to be.”

“Yeah, yeah.” I forced myself to stand in the teleporter. It felt like I was walking to my death. I wondered if I’d even be aware of an accident.

It took a fraction of a second. I didn't feel anything at all. My ears popped again.

Suzie waited on the other end. “Oh good, you made it. Technology wins again. Yay!”

The extravagant penthouse hallway stretched before us. I found myself wishing we could stay. Instead we headed to the roof, stepping past rows of obsequious robot butlers. They beeped and nodded to us as we walked past. One of them offered hot towels.

I flagged a taxi. “Weren't you the one giving Reggie grief because these things are so dangerous?”

“In the hands of terrorists or criminals, sure. I don’t think ordinary people have anything to worry about.”

“I see.” A fancy automatic limousine circled toward us. “Guess we're riding in style tonight.”

The limo burbled to a stop, hovering in place. A top-hat wearing robot popped out of the trunk, rushing over to get the door for us. It beeped an enthusiastic greeting.

I flashed it the address. “Is there some kind of known threat to the porter network?”

Suzie climbed inside. “Nothing credible. Some theoretical vectors. Since only people are allowed through, it's easy to identify which chemicals belong on a person and which ones don't. Stored energy tends to dissipate in transit, so that’s out.” She gave me a funny look. “Why am I the one telling you this? You probably understand the science better than I do.”

I hopped in beside her. “Maybe that's why I'm afraid of the things. I know too much.”

She shrugged. “Or you're unreasonably superstitious. Hard to say, really.”

“I wish I could argue with that.”

The driver beeped gratefully at us, closing the hatch. The sounds of the world instantly disappeared behind the fanciest soundproofing money could buy.

It returned to its place in the trunk. The car lifted off, heading to my safehouse in the mountains. The mostly transparent front end gave us a spectacular view of the city.

Las Vegas was one of the first cities decimated by the water crisis. In the thirties and forties, the water supply simply couldn’t keep up with the population. As temperatures worsened, the desert reasserted itself. No one had any extra water to send over.

The heat became unbearable. There wasn't enough power

for the air conditioners. Tourism dried up after Marconi simultaneously restricted travel and legalized nationwide gambling. Before long, only the hardest of the hardcore remained in the once fanciful playground of debauchery.

American dreams die hard, though. In the fifties, the first guided asteroid projects set out to fetch mineral-laden rocks from the asteroid belt. Their first test project? Leveling the abandoned Strip, then filling it with melted water from a redirected comet.

The engineering was spectacular. Billions around the world watched breathlessly at each phase of the project. Of course, not everyone thought deliberately crashing space rocks into the desert to rebuild our national sex gambling oasis was such a great idea. Religious protesters had to be carried away forcibly from the blast sites just before impact. People around the world worried that even the slightest error would spell catastrophe for the planet. They were right to be afraid.

On the other hand, if it worked, it would be the second major victory for large-scale climate engineering. It was a trial run for what needed to be done to rehydrate the Ogallala aquifer.

It was, to coin a phrase, a smashing success. The dust and man-made debris kicked up by the first asteroid were spectacular all by themselves. The impact neatly leveled the abandoned real estate, digging a new canyon appropriately named Gambler's Alley. The ice asteroid arrived a couple days later, delivering water into the world's largest artificial reservoir.

Gambler's Alley was shaped like a giant teardrop, with the coveted real estate surrounding the large rounded head. The nearby buildings were covered in mirrors, fanciful electronics, and garish excesses of water. The fountain displays in the center of the crater shot water high enough into the air to affect the local weather. The plumes could be seen from space.

Pleasure craft of all shapes and sizes floated lazily around the water, advertising a variety of entertainment ranging from the exotic to thc dcpraved. Casinos lined the rim of the crater, blurring the coastlines with suites and restaurants that extended into the water. Glass floors showed off the extraordinary aquatic wildlife underneath. The animated holograms made San Francisco's food ads look tame.

Suzie leaned over to get a better view. “Wow. It's even more outrageous than the sims. And that’s saying something.”

The limo took the long way around to make sure we saw as many advertisements as possible. I felt embarrassed by how jiggly some of them were. “You don't really understand the full scope of it until you see it in person. It's gaudy, but the engineering is unbelievable.”

She noted my discomfort with an advertisement that pressed up against her window. It squirmed around, making a fleshy squeaking noise. “Come here often?”

I mentally told the driver to speed it up, please. We swept

past a casino built to look like an inverted chandelier. The car headed out to the mountains.

"Not in the physical, no. I play poker in the virtual. I keep a safehouse here because the culture is heavy on privacy. It's easy to get lost in the chaos."

"I suppose it would be, yes." She shifted around in her grav suit. "Could we stop and pick up some fresh clothing? This thing is starting to get uncomfortable."

"I'd rather not. The feds are still looking for us. I'm sure you'd fit in some of my clothes."

I knew it was a mistake as soon as it came out of my mouth.

She gave me a withering look. A trace of her mysterious accent entered her voice. "I suppose you keep my size of underwear at home, then?"

Titan appeared in front of us. "Ms. DiRevka. I have taken the liberty of employing the Gratification service to order you a selection of clothing and accessories to be delivered to the safehouse within fifteen minutes of your arrival." He leaned over proudly. "I have selected some of the finest designer fashionables delivered directly from Paris. They should be comfortable, stylish, and a perfect fit. All on Mr. Wainwright's tab, of course."

Her face lit up. "Why, that's wonderful. I love Paris."

I felt like I was going to explode. "You're gratting expensive clothes to the house, on my personal tab, when the two of us are wanted terrorists? Have you lost your mind?"

He stiffened a little. "I have taken every precaution. It is no more or less safe now than it has ever been. Your payments are still anonymous, of course. I am not that foolhardy."

I gave him a frosty stare. "You're going to hack it so it doesn't actually cost anything, right?"

He gave me a look that I'd come to realize expressed wry humor. "That would defeat the purpose, would it not? We are, after all, trying not to attract attention to ourselves."

Suzie leaned toward me, clearly amused. "Oh yes, we do need to be careful. We're not thieves, are we? Better buy a lot to make it look good."

"Only the finest, Ms. DiRevka."

I rubbed my temples, trying not to picture Suzie in sexy French underwear. I failed miserably. "What's the plan now? Has anyone figured out how our data breach leaked?"

"There continues to be no evidence of discovery. Mr. Jackson and Dr. Shenouda have been quite thorough in their search. It remains a mystery."

"Hmm. If Flapjack and Kesi together can't find anything, that's saying a lot."

Suzie looked interested. "What about the sleeper assisting the Liberty mainframe? If someone helped in the attack, wouldn't there be evidence in the data we lifted?"

Titan inclined his head. "An excellent question. We have not yet succeeded in decoding the data from the operation. The matter requires further investigation. It remains noteworthy that if a sleeper was involved, we should not have evidence of its involvement. In this case, the assisting machine made changes to data only possible using exotic matter, but failed to eliminate historical records of the previous values. Further, nothing short of another sleeper would be enough to overcome Sleeper Olympus, and a powerful one at that. Finding such contradictory evidence is puzzling."

I sat back, considering. "I was thinking about the nuclear raid itself. Seemed weird to me that they pulled it together that fast. Maybe they had the operational details lying around. Pulled the trigger on them once they discovered our theft. I bet we can find the plans in the Liberty data."

Suzie looked at me. "Or maybe the timing is just a coincidence. Maybe it had nothing to do with us."

"That seems less and less likely all the time."

Titan shifted uncomfortably. "It would be best not to jump to conclusions. Dr. Chapman and Sleeper Artemis are working on the election data."

"Hmm. Ask Liz to keep her findings to herself for the time being, would you?"

"The decryption work will take some time, but I will relay the message. I have not yet attempted to decrypt the deployment data. Would you like me to begin the procedure?"

I thought for a moment. "Yes. Set things up but let me perform the actual work. I think it would be best if a human did the deed."

"I agree. Mr. Jackson, Dr. Shenouda, and Dr. Chapman would like to meet with both of you in the Times Square simulation as soon as possible to coordinate. President Testaferra is scheduled to speak in two hours. Mr. Talbot is constructing a rebuttal."

The limo raced toward the mountains. I watched the view out the window. "Still no word from Kara?"

"Neither Ms. Janek nor Sleeper Hera have responded to multiple inquiries. I can only confirm that Sleeper Hera is online and functioning normally."

Suzie looked back and forth between us. "Is that unusual?"

I snorted. "Someone just blew up part of Colorado while we were standing on it. Unusual is just getting started."

Chapter 28

Suzie looked up at the buildings towering over the Times Square simulation. The advertisements danced happily in their perpetual virtual party. We headed to the table. Everyone looked grim.

Liz handed Suzie one of her fruity tropical drinks. “Here, try this. You'll love it.”

She took a sip. “My, that is good. I think I’d rather have some coffee water though.”

Flapjack grunted. “Yeah. It's been kind of a long night.”

I shifted uncomfortably. “About to get longer. The news channels are just getting started. Kesi, what are the cops doing?”

She raised her eyebrows. “The police are only one component of the search. Every federal asset in the country has been activated to participate in the hunt. Given the numbers involved, they may discover our locations through overwhelming presence alone.”

Liz laughed. “Like a swarm of carpet ants.”

Flapjack gave Kesi a curious look. “They’re out for all nine of us?”

“They are, now that you mention it. Not just us, but our families as well. Why?”

“We still don't know which sleeper was helping run that

oxfire. Far as I can tell, it's gotta be Kara, Anna, or Zed. Unless one of you is running some kind of long con."

I stiffened. "Kara wouldn't do that. There are other possibilities."

"Are there?" Flapjack gave me a hard look. "You told me that psycho box was still locked up tight."

Suzie looked surprised. "What psycho box?"

Flapjack's indiscretion annoyed me. "Odin's still in his prison. Believe me, I checked. Word on the street is that Khan may have discovered a new source of exotic matter or found some way to synthesize it."

Suzie tried to get our attention. "Dexa Khan? Your old coworker? I thought he was dead and his sleeper died with him."

Liz answered for us. "That's the public story. But no, Khan isn't dead. Odin was his sleeper. The two of them hatched a scheme to break into the n-square stockpile and seize control of the assets. They actually managed to pull it off, but we were able to intervene before they could do anything untoward with it. We were pretty sure it was Odin's idea to go after the big guns, so we went a little easy on Khan. We burned them both out. Odin's trapped in a quantum prison. Khan's currently in New Pakistan."

Flapjack still gave me the stink eye. "I don't buy the Khan thing. Why would he of all people help our government? It's gotta be Kara, Anna, or Zed. Who's been in touch with their sleepers? I haven't heard anything from Hera, Andromeda, or Atlas since this started."

Suzie gestured. "Let's not discount Khan entirely. Off the top of my head, it might be his ticket back into the country. Or maybe he was counting on them to take out the rest of you. Is there some reason only one of them would be involved?"

I took a sip of tea. "Not really, now that you mention it. When Khan spoke to me, he warned me that the rest of the world was sick of America forcing everyone to play by their rules. He seemed worried that the government might take over our sleepers. He made it sound like they were going to do something big to level the playing field. I don't think he was behind the nuke, even if he did have a sleeper to field. But yeah, he might take advantage of the situation. That absolutely sounds like something he'd do."

"Great." Flapjack summoned a glass of whiskey, emptying it all at once. "Just great."

Liz leaned forward. "Still, why do we know about Liberty and the sleeper at all? It doesn't make sense. Maybe it's a false lead. Nothing but a distraction."

Kesi shook her head. "I gave it a thorough inspection. If it's fake, it's very well done. The code has the feel of a novice engineer who got careless. Or someone under severe time pressure."

Liz ate a strawcherry off the end of a little paper umbrella. It reappeared after she ate it. "Maybe they wanted us to find it.

Or the government plans to present it as evidence of our madness."

I gave her a quizzical look. "Then why get Liberty involved? Makes them look bad."

Flapjack leaned forward. "This is going nowhere. Less talk, more do. What's the plan?"

I checked the time. "Something tells me we ought to see what the news comes up with. Listen to the president too. I think Reggie wants to speak after that. So we've probably got some time."

Liz finished her drink. "Artemis and I are looking into the information that started this whole mess. Who was Senator Delaware? Do we know who is he now? Are there any other compromised senate seats?"

I swirled my tea in its glass. "I'm going to start decrypting the military data. I want to know when this morning's operation was planned and what they originally meant it for."

Suzie perked up. "Can I help with that?"

Flapjack gave me a warning look. It wasn't necessary. I agreed with him. "It'd probably be best if only one of us sees that data. Why don't you help Liz with the senator data? You can help her sort through it faster."

"Sure, yeah. That makes sense."

Kesi looked exhausted. "I have my hands full trying to keep our pursuers off our trail."

Flapjack grunted. "I'm going to find out which sleeper is a

nuclear killer. I sure hope it isn't one of you."

Suzie looked startled. "Wait. If it was one of your sleepers, would you even know?"

Flapjack gave us all a level stare. "Trust me. I'll figure it out."

I stood up. "All right. We all have something to do. Work hard. Stay safe. Keep in touch."

Suzie and I woke up in the physical. The limo flew over the safehouse. The tiny cabin nestled on the side of a mountain with a panoramic view of Vegas. Titan had sent the Cavallino ahead of us. It was parked under some nearby trees.

I paid the limo driver, casually wiping its memory of being here. It chirped happily, disappearing back into the trunk. The car took off toward the city.

Suzie took in the view from the living room. "This is extraordinary."

I shrugged. "If you're going to cower in a hole, might as well be a comfortable hole. Helps that it's impossible to approach this place without being seen."

"I see." She pointed at some approaching lights. "Is that the Gratification drone?"

I checked the markers. "Yep."

"I can't wait to get out of this suit."

I answered the door. The robot buzzed a polite greeting, dipping briefly in a bow. It offered me a package of clothing. The bundle was considerably larger than I expected. The drone held out a virtual hand for a tip. I gave it one. Not too large, but not too small either. I scrambled its memory of our location while it thanked me. It sped off to its next delivery before I'd shut the door.

I tossed her the package. "Here you go. I'm going to get changed myself."

"Do you mind if I use the water shaker?"

"Not at all."

A few minutes later she reappeared. I had to hand it to Titan. He'd chosen an outfit that both fit her style and looked comfortable. She'd let her hair down. It came to her shoulders, slightly frizzy. It made her look younger in a good way.

I took her dirty grav suit, throwing them both in a specialized cleaner. Suzie settled on the couch.

I headed to the kitchen. "Are you hungry? I was saving some real chicken for a special occasion. I think this qualifies."

Her stomach rumbled. "Yes. That sounds wonderful, thanks."

I got her some coffee water, flicking the threedee to life. "Do you have a preferred news channel?"

"Not really." She sipped the coffee water. "They're all bad in their own ways."

I left it on whatever news channel I'd watched last. They all broadcast more or less the same stories. The only question was what kind of bloviation came with them.

An attractive man with inoffensive but attractive features

read the news from an internal prompt. He used exaggerated pronunciation and facial expressions. Behind him, a swarm of camera drones circled the smoking crater where Reggie's house once stood. The carbonic glass glowed red with heat, creating a distorted mirror effect. Military personnel searched the area nearby, picking up their broken equipment.

"If you're just tuning in, a massive explosion destroyed the mansion of Sleepernet President and CEO Reginald Talbot this morning. Sources say that a military confrontation ended with the wealthy executive detonating a portable n-square warhead on his property. It's not clear at this time how the bomb came into his possession or why he decided to set it off. This is the deadliest terrorist attack on the homeland in almost forty years, and the first time an n-square device has been set off on American soil. We have unconfirmed information from several highly placed sources that at least thirty-two heroes lost their lives in the battle, including a high-ranking general. Mr. Talbot and three unidentified criminal associates remain at large."

I dipped the chicken in bacon batter, tossing it into hot butter oil. The kitchen sizzled, briefly drowning out the content-free blather coming from the virtual.

Suzie turned around, watching me work. "I wonder if there's a chance they don't know who we are yet."

I filled the waffle iron with sugar dough. "Maybe a small one. They're probably just parceling out the information to make a good story. They'll have our profiles up soon enough."

She rested her head on the back of the couch. “I know. I still can't believe what happened. All those poor kids. And a general too. Why would they do that?”

I pulled the chicken out of the fryer. “I don't know. But we must’ve hit on something big. You don't pull a stunt like this without some kind of massive follow-through. Whatever happened, it's just getting started.”

I brought the chicken and waffles over along with a steaming pot of crystal syrup. I sat down next to Suzie on the couch. She stared out the window at the twinkling Vegas lights. “Is this my fault?”

I took a sip of coffee water, letting the food cool. “No. The responsibility begins and ends with the person who gave the order. All you did was catch them in a mistake.”

“Maybe.” She didn't sound convinced.

She picked up a drumstick, taking a delicate bite. Her face lit up. “Oh! This is amazing! I've never had the real thing before. It's so juicy. And the texture! It’s really different from the lab meat.” She took a heartier bite, grabbing a napkin.

I smiled, taking a piece myself. “Glad you like it. Yeah, you have to be careful. It's hard to go back to synthetic after you've had the real thing. They’re both good, just in different ways. The engineered food has stronger flavors, but it doesn’t capture the subtle inconsistency of natural meat. They prioritize homogeneous experiences over natural variations. I wish I could get my hands on some real coffee. I hear it's extraordinary.”

The talking head on the threedee turned his attention to the studio area next to him. "With us today is Bobby McGuinness, our Senior Analyst of Nuclear Affairs. Also joining us is retired Brigadier General Sharon Mendoza, our Senior Correspondent of Military Analysis. Be sure to pick up General Mendoza's new book, Force Projection Beyond the Nation-State, in stores now. Bobby, what kind of device was this?"

Bobby's condescending voice grated directly on my nerves. "Well, we don't know for sure yet. But, given the blast radius, this looks like a classic application of the venerable X-43R autonomous walker platform. Commonly known as an oxfire." A picture appeared behind him of the cheerful robot that tried to obliterate us all. "I'm guessing it must have been armed with a one point eight petajoule warhead. That would produce the ten kilometer blast cavity we see in the footage."

"One point eight petajoules! Sharon, that's a lot of energy, isn't it?"

General Mendoza nodded. "It sure is. This raises a lot of questions, such as where Mr. Talbot procured such a device and how many of them he has access to. Obviously, we haven't heard his plans yet, but it's safe to assume this is just the beginning of a string of terrorist attacks. Who knows what city he'll annihilate next, or why? This is a power grab from the multinational conglomerates, if you ask me. In my book, I talk at length about how the corporate world craves military force. It has since the privatization of military industry dating back to the last century. Why follow the law when it's not enforced at gunpoint?"

The anchor interrupted her rant. "That's great, Sharon. Thanks so much for that. But we know what you're wondering." Officer Friendly, your local neighborhood pollbot, appeared behind him. "What do your fellow citizens think?"

I rolled my eyes. "Oh yes. Please, I must know."

Suzie snorted, pouring some syrup on her waffles. "This ought to be good."

The view switched to a pollbot-eye view of a large man with an oversized mustache getting off the bus.

The robot's voice came from behind the camera. "Remember that lying is perjury!"

"I'm against terrorists." He huffed, blowing his mustache around, daring anyone to disagree with his radical opinion. "They wanna nuke our country, I say we nuke 'em right back!"

Next up was a thin, birdlike woman sitting in the sun room of a rest home. Various senior citizens snored loudly around her.

"Remember that lying is perjury!"

She adjusted her glasses. "All my sympathy for them went out the window when they blew up the great state of Colorado. I've never been there, but now there's nothing left to see. I guess I'll have to look up the old threedees if I want to know what it was like before they destroyed it."

Suzie put down her empty plate. "I didn't realize Colorado

was only ten square kilometers."

"Wonder what happened to the other two hundred and sixty nine thousand."

A young professional man adjusted his expensive suit on his way down a busy sidewalk.

"Remember that lying is perjury!"

He expertly maneuvered around slower traffic. "If they have nothing to hide, why haven't they turned themselves in?" He hurried along. "I'm sure they thought they had a good reason. Just tell us why you detonated the nuke and serve your time for the officers you killed. What's so hard about that? No one takes any responsibility for their actions any more. It's sickening."

A group of teenage girls giggled at the camera. The bell rang in the background. One of them looked at it with a worried expression.

"Remember that lying is perjury!"

Their apparent leader stepped forward. "I think it's awesome that a bunch of hackers have the police tripping balls all over each other. They see and hear everything, but a bunch of shutin neckbeards have them peeing themselves. Hey, sleepers! Keep making all that great vampire porn and I don't care what you blow up!"

The teenagers snickered some more, swatting each other. The anchor reappeared. "From the mouths of babes. We're going to take a quick break. Up next, President Testaferra addresses a fearful nation demanding answers in this breaking crisis. Stay tuned for complete up to the nanosecond coverage. We'll bring it to you live."

Suzie yawned, stretching. "Thank you, that was delicious. I wish I could just give in to this food coma. Go to sleep and forget all this nonsense ever happened. Just wake up and be like wow, what a weird dream."

"Yeah." I leaned back on the couch. "I can relate."

Chapter 29

Suzie and I stared at a commercial for a laser-powered microdiaper on the threedee. She shifted on the cushion next to me. “Shouldn't we be doing something?”

I crossed my hands behind my neck. “Soon. We can get busy after the president speaks. We should listen to what she has to say. Gather intelligence about what the government plans to do next. It's their move.”

“You think we can discover their plans by watching a speech?”

“Of course not. But we can find out how they're going to frame the event. Why am I the one telling you this? You know more about politics and public relations stuff than I do.”

She grimaced. “It's not like I'm making a statement or analyzing other people’s politics, though. This is different. Real people died tonight and I was there. I have a responsibility to the truth. I feel like I should be turning myself in.”

I raised my eyebrow at her. “Is that what you want?”

“No.” She stared out the window, avoiding an ad for a tooth blaster that gave your smile a diamond plated finish. “Who would I turn myself in to? Not anyone in the United States. I guess I just don't know how one is supposed to behave after witnessing thirty-two people get killed by their own government. Is eating chicken and waffles normal?"

I sighed. "You're asking the wrong guy about normal."

The anchorman returned. "And we're back. If you're just tuning in, a massive n-square detonation occurred earlier this morning at the compound of superwealthy Sleepernet Corporation CEO Reginald Talbot. No word yet from the powerful tycoon, who was last seen with three heavily armed accomplices resisting military arrest. It's believed that they escaped with the assistance of a private teleportation system. With thirty-four heroic servicemen confirmed dead, this is the deadliest terrorist attack on American soil since the nuclear strikes on Chicago and San Diego forty years ago."

The anchor held his hand to an earpiece he definitely wasn't wearing. "I'm being told that the president has entered the press room at the White House. We'll take you there now, live."

Our elected figurehead appeared behind a large podium with various eagle-themed emblems lending her an air of importance. I counted four separate American flags. She was flanked by two Secret Service officers.

She spoke with a light Latina accent. "Ladies and gentlemen. Members of the press. My fellow Americans. A tragedy occurred early this morning in rural Colorado, ending with a loss of life for thirty-four of our men and women in uniform. It followed the activation of a weapon of mass destruction against the people of the United States of America, the first of its kind in more than forty years. I can only offer you my condolences and assure you that we will vigorously pursue these wanted terrorists to the ends of the earth."

Suzie grunted. "They're hitting the terrorist rhetoric pretty hard, considering it was their weapon."

The president continued. "But let me back up a little. Last evening at six-thirty Eastern Time, our heroic law enforcement officials were called upon to take the President of the Sleepernet Corporation, Reginald Talbot, into custody. Mr. Talbot runs the Sleepernet Corporation along with his eight sleepernet engineers. This is, of course, not the first time these sleeper agents have had a hostile encounter with the forces of justice and good. Each of the agents in question controls a powerful supercomputer. Most use these machines to field powerful battle suits. Even one of these self-styled vigilantes is powerful enough to hold off a full battle suit platoon, often scrambling airborne and mechanized support as well."

Suzie looked surprised. "Wait, this has happened before?"

I shook my head. "Thompson's made some covert moves in the past, but this is the first time we've had a full-on firefight with the Americans."

The president adjusted her hands on the podium. "Because of this, we resolved that physical force would be required. Given the strength of his technical arsenal, overwhelming military strength was authorized. It took eleven hours to move our assets without detection by the sophisticated sleepernet surveillance grid. We further resolved that we would attempt to take possession of the sleeper supercomputer known as Olympus."

One of the Secret Service agents suddenly rushed into the audience. A commotion erupted briefly off-camera. No further explanation was given.

The president continued speaking as if nothing had happened. "One of our camouflaged scouts entered the residence at four o'clock this morning Mountain Time. She located Mr. Talbot in the bedroom he had grown over six years from a single emerald crystal. In thc proccss, she inadvertently woke him up, alerting him to her presence. When she demanded his surrender, he murdered her in cold blood. With her dying gasps, she sent a crucial data flare back to her superiors, letting them know that he'd activated the oxfire n-square device."

Reggie sent me a disgusted noise. *"That's all fictitious, by the way. Olympus caught them on visual farting around on my lawn."*

A picture of a young black woman with strong features and an extra-large smile appeared behind the president. "Amy Williams is just one of the many heroic warriors we mourn today. The order was given to move in and move in fast. But it wasn't fast enough. Mr. Talbot got into his combat suit. He called for help from his fellow renegades. The fight was on."

I scratched my head. "Did she ever say what they were

going to arrest Reggie for?"

Suzie gave me an appraising look. "Actually, no. Now that you mention it."

"Hey Reggie, why'd they want to arrest you, anyway?"

He flashed back irritation. *"Couldn't tell you. Maybe because my bestest buddies broke into the Liberty supercomputer the night before?"*

Something didn't add up. The president continued. "The battle continued for over an hour. Despite the assistance of three additional combat suits and military-grade cyberweapons, the sleeper agents were losing the fight. Knowing that we were closing in, Mr. Talbot deliberately started the countdown on the n-square warhead. He demanded safe passage for himself and his cohorts out of the country. General Frederick Thompson led the negotiations, hoping to avoid further loss of life."

A rotating model of General Thompson's head appeared behind the president. His sculpted face looked more noble and righteous than psychotically intense. Still intimidating, though.

Suzie shivered. "You don't think he was wearing a nuke-proof helmet or something, do you?"

I snorted. "Doubt it. But I bet someone's already tried to make that idea work. Let the grunts die in the fire, rebuild the officers from just the heads."

"I guess that's my point. Why'd they kill him?"

The president shook her head sadly. "The negotiation was a ruse. Mr. Talbot was buying time to flee to an armored shelter in the basement. By the time General Thompson recognized the deception, it was too late. The bomb went off."

The scene behind the president switched to an aerial view of the explosion. It looked like they had six or seven feeds from circling gremlins. Tanks were tossed aside like toys. The ground itself burned and sizzled. The annihilation firestorm blossomed with horrifying beauty, billowing up into the familiar mushroom cloud. Ten kilometers of ground, trees, and military equipment were sucked into an infinitely bright pinprick of light. They were consumed in a blinding cylinder of swirling energy that decimated the mushroom cloud, flaring to the very top of the atmosphere.

"Mr. Thompson is survived by his brother Franklin, also a decorated military officer. The sleeper agents fled via an illegal teleportation node hidden in the bunker. No one could have expected this level of sophistication from rebel citizens, though it certainly seems obvious in retrospect. The sleeper supercomputers are too powerful to leave in civilian hands. Power like that belongs to the people. We have trusted them with far too much for far too long. It's in the nature of the American people to think the best of its successful citizens. Only in America can such greatness occur. But when our heroes fall, they fall hard. We must respond."

The view behind her switched back to the press room. "Make no mistake, my fellow Americans. We will bring them to justice before even one more American life is taken. You can count on that. You need not fear another terrorist attack in your home town, because we will find them. Only we can keep your children safe, but we must do it together. If you see anything suspicious, anything at all, report it at once directly to the Secret Service. Do not attempt to engage the terrorists in any way. They are wanted fugitives, armed and unreasonably dangerous."

Oddly enough, the address for reporting suspicious activity resided on the sleepernet.

"My Director of the Secret Service, Esper Zane, will be available for a more thorough briefing soon. He will provide the names of the thirty-four sons and daughters that gave their lives for your freedom this morning. It's been forty years since the last terrorist attack on the American homeland. Let's get these bastards so it will be at least forty more. Thank you for your time. And may your god bless America."

Following tradition, the reporters exploded with shouted questions as President Testaferra left the stage. The view panned back to show the anchorman again.

"That was President Testaferra, addressing a nation deep in the grips of limitless terror. With us tonight is Dana Knight, head of the Tactical Personal Nuke Association, and Samuel James, our Senior Political Homeland Consultant. Dana is the author of a new book, entitled The Founding Fathers And Your Right To Personal Defense. Samuel, do you think the president did enough to still the chilly tendrils of uneasy dread that are sweeping the country as we speak?"

Suzie hmphed. “Don't you think the president caused them in the first place?”

Samuel’s voice was deep and analytical. “I'm not sure she did. People don't feel safe, right now, in their homes. No one knows what's going to happen. I heard a lot of words, but not a lot of action.”

“Hard to argue with that! Dana, I understand your organization is supporting Mr. Talbot's right to bear arms in this affair?”

“That's right. The real tragedy here is not that Reginald Talbot dctonatcd an n-square device in response to a government raid. The sad reality is that only people as rich and powerful as he is can afford to do such a thing in the first place. Imagine what a different world it would be if we all had nuclear deterrents on our property. Special Forces wouldn't be so quick to sweep in if they knew they could be vaporized, would they? If you read my book, that's one of the things I point out in chapter four. Our founding fathers supported our right to bear arms, specifically in case the federal government got out of hand again. We had to rely on the military to step in when President Marconi went too far. With a properly armed populace, we could have done that ourselves. It's all about checks and balances. You can read it all in my book, *The Founding Fathers And Your Right To Personal Defense*.”

Suzie laughed. “Now I've heard it all. What could possibly top that?”

Chapter 30

I muted the threedee. The talking heads continued vapidly in the background.

Titan appeared in front of us, clearing his throat. “I hope I am not interrupting.”

Suzie smiled. “Of course not.”

“Dr. Chapman, Sleeper Artemis, and I started looking through the Liberty data while the president was speaking. We have had some success in decoding the structure.”

I sat forward. “Awesome. Say hi to Liz for me. What have you learned?”

“Mostly, an interesting discrepancy in the reported timing of events. In her speech, President Testaferra indicated that the decision to arrest Mr. Talbot was made at six-thirty in the evening Eastern Time yesterday. However, the operation in Liberty Plaza did not begin until hours later.”

Suzie hmphed. “Interesting. So what were they going to arrest him for?”

“I am afraid we have not yet gotten that far with the data. We are extrapolating from time stamps in the dataset.”

I stared at Vegas. “Maybe they got wind of the operation while we were planning it?”

Suzie shook her head. “I doubt it. If they knew we were

going to pull a cyberheist in Washington, why make an unrelated arrest in Colorado? I think they were already after Talbot."

Titan inclined his head toward her. "Dr. Chapman and I arrived at a similar conclusion."

I took a moment to soak that in. "What for?"

"Again, we do not have data to support this hypothesis. However, the choice of an n-square device is conspicuous. Should they simply wish to assassinate Mr. Talbot, there are a variety of much lower profile methods that would suffice. The president stated a desire to capture Mr. Talbot and his connection to Sleeper Olympus intact. If that was not possible, they likely intended to annihilate the connection altogether."

Suzie looked horrified. "Does that work?"

Titan shifted on his feet. "If the engineering link is obliterated without a secure transition to a new host, the procedure to reestablish functional authority is quite complex. This prevents an attacker from immediately exploiting the situation, particularly in the event that multiple sleepers are compromised. The information inside Mr. Talbot's head and within his protected storage space on Sleeper Olympus would be destroyed or lost forever."

I whistled softly. "Could have caught three of us for the price of one, too. But the notion of lost storage is interesting. What kind of secret would make the feds panic like that?"

Suzie gave me a sardonic look. "Oh, I don't know. Maybe

the two of them found out that our democratically elected representatives just went through a behind the scenes identity change?"

"Then why are you still here? They should have fried you on the spot. Reggie kept trying to pin the raid on our Liberty theft, even while the president was speaking. If he knew about the senator replacements, why hasn't he mentioned it? In fact, when he first heard about your allegations, he specifically urged me to drop the case."

Titan stroked his chin. "Yes, I recall those messages. At first, Mr. Talbot seemed concerned by what we had already discovered. I recall thinking at the time that it would not be surprising to learn that Sleeper Olympus was monitoring the situation."

"Maybe Reggie was running his own investigation. He found something big. He realized it went all the way to the top, so he urged us not to get involved. Maybe he didn't want us screwing up his work. Or maybe he wanted to protect us from the consequences of what we'd learn. Knowing him, he probably thought he could take care of it by himself. Maybe he got in over his head and didn't want to admit it."

Suzie swallowed. "There's a much simpler explanation for his behavior."

I waited for her to continue. I ended up having to ask. "Yes?"

"He didn't want us involved because he was part of it. He

didn't need to investigate, because he already knew what happened. Maybe he wanted out. Or maybe he threatened to go public. In any case, the conclusion is the same." She looked out the window. "He went too far."

I sighed, wishing I could disagree with her. "You might be right about that. It just doesn't sound like him. In any case, it looks like we have some time before Zane speaks. Should I try to get in touch with Reggie?"

Suzie stretched. "I'd rather gather more evidence first. He has a bit of a temper."

Titan cleared his throat. "If I may. It has been a long night. The sun will rise soon. The other engineers are taking a moment to rest. Mr. Talbot is postponing further work on his speech until he is refreshed. I am working with my fellow sleepers in the meantime. We will prepare for your return later this afternoon."

She turned to me. "I'm too stressed out to fall asleep. Do you have anything for dessert? I can't imagine how, but I'm still hungry."

Titan beamed. "Mr. Wainwright also has real chocolate that he has been saving for a special occasion."

Her excited expression warmed my heart. "Do you really? Do you have dark chocolate? I had it once when I was a child. I've never forgotten it. It's so much more complicated than the lab mixes."

I laughed. "The high-end chocolate bars are at the other

house. I have a portable s'mores kit here. Might as well use it, right? I have a feeling we're burning this safehouse."

She smiled. Was it my imagination, or was there a romantic sparkle in her eyes? "Oh yes. We should definitely make the most of this delightful residence while we still can."

Titan cleared his throat. "I will keep you apprised of any new developments that require your attention. Relax as much as you are able. It will help your decision-making considerably when action is required later today."

He winked out. I headed to the kitchen, bringing back the indoor campfire set. Suzie turned off the threedee, lowering the lights to enhance our view of Vegas.

I put the campfire set on the table. It blossomed into a tiny model of an outdoor fire, orange flames licking up about six inches. I took out the graham crackers, marshmallows, and the star of the show, the real chocolate.

Suzie shifted across the couch until we were sitting thigh to thigh. The warmth of her leg on mine reminded me how long it'd been since I'd had contact with a real woman. I also couldn't help thinking about how nicely shaped it was.

She leaned closer so our arms were touching as well. "So what do we do?"

I turned, momentarily lost in her blue eyes twinkling in the firelight. "You mean you've never been camping?"

Her laugh was rich. "I want to hear it from you."

I handed her a small, pointed stick. "Okay. First you put a

marshmallow on the end of the stick and roast it in the fire."

"Mmm hmm."

We held our sticks over the fire, watching them carefully. "Don't let it burn too much."

"Oh no. That would be bad." She rubbed my thigh. "Wouldn't want things to get too hot."

My heart rate spiked. "Here's a graham cracker. Put the chocolate on it."

"Okay." She turned her marshmallow in the tiny virtual fire. It browned nicely.

"Now we put the marshmallow on the chocolate, smash it with another graham cracker, and it's ready to go."

We did so at the same time, taking bites of our little sandwiches.

Suzie spoke with her mouth a little full. "This is so good."

The warmth of the chocolate combined with the firelight stirred my desire. The rising sun was beautiful. Suzie looked extraordinary in the dawn light. The look of pure bliss on her face warmed me inside. I found myself picturing her with an expression of even deeper satisfaction.

I finished my s'more. Suzie licked her fingers in a genuinely sexy way.

I leaned forward to get more supplies. "Would you like another?"

She slid her hands around my stomach, leaning in so I could feel her breasts on my back. I felt a flash of guilt about

Wendy but it burned quickly in the surge of need flowering in my head.

Her breath tickled my ear when she spoke. “Maybe later.”

I felt her ask for a real time emotion connection. I turned back to her, soaking in her expression of eager anticipation. I said yes. Our mutual desire flooded the connection, surprising in its intensity. Relief and excitement surged through a cloud of nervous energy. The feelings wrapped together into something even more magical. Emotional harmony, if you will.

She kissed me. We still tasted like chocolate. I slid my hands under her shirt to wander over the expanse of skin on her back. I felt her shock of pleasure from the first direct contact. She felt my thrill from the warm soft feeling under my fingertips. My hand wandered to the nape of her neck. She whimpered softly, pulling close. We explored each other for a long time.

Eventually, she pulled back with a smoldering look.

I found myself out of breath. “The bed in this safehouse is really quite nice.”

She kissed me, whispering in my ear again. “I thought you’d never ask.”

I took her hand, leading her to the bedroom. The miracle of our shared attraction amazed me. She reflected her own version of the feeling. Mentally I was exploring my memories of her. The sight of her in the grav suit. Fighting alongside her. The courageous look on her face when she pointed a gun to my head.

She soaked in this perspective of herself, flushing at my appreciation. She sent back her own memories, more emotional than visual. She saw me as solid, safe, and strong. Things I didn't let myself believe. We exchanged examples of that unique feeling you get when you discover that a member of the opposite sex is just as smart if not smarter than you are.

We sprawled on the bed, tearing our clothes off. I can only say that her imagination, enthusiasm, and skill were even more astonishing than I'd expected. We spent several hours lost in our own world. We took such happiness from pleasing each other, trying to outdo ourselves. The shared emotional connection wordlessly let us know what we wanted and how we wanted it. It became instantly apparent what was working and what wasn't working, all without shame or inhibition.

I never wanted it to end.

Eventually, though, we collapsed in a pile, exhausted and sore. Not long after, Suzie fell asleep. I reveled in the feeling of innocent excitement. After Wendy died, I didn't think I'd have an intimate experience with a woman ever again. The more I learned about Suzie, mentally and physically, the more I wanted to know.

Wendy's memory haunted me, but in a different way now. I realized just how destructive my behavior had been, particularly the time I'd spent building and using her simulation.

People were right. I'd punished myself for years because I

thought it was the right thing to do. I focused on never trusting the world again. I never let myself risk hurting someone I loved by never getting in the situation in the first place. What an extraordinary waste of myself that had been. I'd obsessed over her death instead of the years of happiness preceding it. It wasn't what Wendy would have wanted. The only person who expected me to do that was me.

I closed my eyes, knowing what I had to do. After arguing with myself for a bit, I deleted everything I'd built in the Wendy simulation after she died. I kept my memories of her in storage as a reminder of that part of my life. A part of my life that was over now. I let go of the virtual program I'd made from her absence, surprised at how happy I was to see it disappear.

I don't remember falling asleep afterward, but it was the best sleep I'd gotten in close to ten years.

Chapter 31

Six hours later

I yawned, stretching as I made my way into the living room. Suzie looked up from her work. Her hair was back in its normal bun. "There you are. I wasn't sure you were ever going to wake up."

I sat down next to her on the couch. "I haven't slept that well in a long time. I didn't want to get out of bed. But there's that whole wanted fugitive thing to consider."

"There is that, yes." She'd changed into a simple black shirt with a French flag that read "Don't Panik." She hadn't bothered with pants, though the shirt came down to mid-thigh. She turned back to her holo display. "I hope you don't mind. I kind of ate all the chocolate."

"That's what it's there for." I glanced over at her work. "What are you doing?"

"Liz and I are decoding more of the election data. She broke the encryption earlier, but she isn't familiar with the internal names of the organizational hierarchy. Some of the code names are pretty arbitrary. We're working together to figure out the format."

"Sounds good. I'm going to jack into the sleepernet to work on the military data. Do you know when Director Zane is going to speak?"

"Three o'clock, so you have a couple hours."

I headed to the office. "Okay. See you then."

"Can't wait."

I spent the time in my virtual office, lost in my work. Titan set up the pieces I'd need to work out the encryption, but the ciphers were powerful. Breaking the code involved a relentless series of educated guesses and brute force, followed by some pattern analysis to determine if the results looked credible. Afterward I'd have to figure out how the information itself was organized and stored. I set several attack vectors to run in the background while Zane was giving his speech.

Suzie looked up when I returned. "Is it time already?"

"Yeah. Do you want anything while I'm up? The only exotic food I have left is some Ceylon tea from before that garbage twister poisoned Sri Lanka."

"That sounds delightful, yes. The tea, I mean."

I grabbed some for both of us, sitting down next to her. She turned off her display, draping a leg over mine.

She wrapped a foot behind my ankle in a practiced gesture, snuggling in. "Real chicken, real chocolate, antique tea. A girl could get used to this."

"There's a lot more where that came from. If we live long enough to enjoy it."

I turned on the threedee. The blandly attractive anchor appeared. "If you're just joining us, Carnage in Colorado this morning as terrorist mastermind Reginald Talbot detonates a one point eight petajoule n-square warhead at his ranch compound to avoid lawful detainment. The embattled CEO is wanted on charges of sedition, treason, and conspiracy to defraud the United States government. He's now also wanted on multiple counts of homicide, terrorism, possession and detonation of a weapon of mass destruction, and resisting arrest. Thirty-four heroic patriots died in the struggle to bring him in alive. The world is watching, wondering why? Why would such a brilliant American entrepreneur resort to terror and mayhem? And most importantly, where is he now, and who's next?"

I rolled my eyes. "This is getting out of hand."

Suzie shrugged. "At least we know what he's charged with now. I bet Zane is about to pin Senator Delaware on him."

"You think he did it?"

She pondered her cup of tea. "I don't know what to think any more."

The anchor once again held his hand to his nonexistent earpiece. "I'm being told the Director of the Secret Service, Esper Zane, just entered the press room at the White House. We'll take you there now, live."

The view shifted back to the podium the president had used. Zane looked unnaturally old. His jowls hung halfway down his neck. Liver spots covered his bald head. His mustache was long enough to twirl if he was so inclined. He surveyed the audience with an experienced gaze, categorizing people in a glance.

A beautiful vitamin-tanned Secret Service agent joined him on the podium, sending a shock of recognition through me. She stood off to his side, dressed in a business suit complete with the stereotypical mirrored visor.

But there was no mistaking her. Heather McCarthy, my conversational nemesis from the grillhouse, proudly stood next to the director on national threedee. My brain reeled at the revelation. Why'd a presidential bodyguard join me for dinner at all? Why ask me who I voted for, or if I knew any sitting senators? What was she trying to find out?

Titan sent me a flash. *"Sir. According to my records, this is the first time Ms. McCarthy has appeared in public on a news broadcast."*

I scratched my head, still soaking in the implications. *"What's different? Why now?"*

"I could not say."

I felt like an idiot. Khan came into my office and all but announced that Heather was a Secret Service agent. I'd been so preoccupied with defending Suzie that I'd missed the more obvious target.

He'd said something else that hit me hard in retrospect, but Suzie interrupted my train of thought. "Are you all right?"

I glanced over at her concerned expression. "Kara set me up on a blind date with that woman standing next to Director Zane. Our dinner could charitably be described as a political interrogation."

She turned her attention to Heather. "Interesting."

Zane cleared his throat. His voice was growly and serious. "Ladies and gentlemen. Members of the press. My fellow Americans. I am Esper Zane, President Testaferra's Director of the Secret Service. It is my regrettable duty to inform you about the horrible events leading up to the attempted arrest of Reginald Talbot this morning. I feel I must also provide further details regarding the military confrontation and the tragedy that followed. Before we begin, I need to remind you that the sleeper agents and their families are currently wanted for extensive questioning regarding this man-made disaster. Report any sightings of these fugitives, their families, or anything unusual to the Secret Service hotline at once. Do not attempt to detain them. As we witnessed this morning, the power carelessly wielded by these individuals can be catastrophic. They have gone unregulated for too long. We have given them our trust and our confidence. Now we are repaid for our tolerance in violence and slaughter."

Suzie squirmed. "He's even creepier than I remember."

Zane continued. "Earlier this month we were informed by a concerned congressional aide that she believed the senator she worked for had changed identity sometime in the previous week. Senior Staff Member Susan DiRevka, seen here in a stock image, came directly to us with her concerns. Of course, we took them very seriously."

Suzie's picture was deliberately bright, innocent, and professional. A dark look briefly passed over Heather's face, gone almost as soon as it appeared. Suzie took her leg off mine, leaning forward to pay attention.

"Unfortunately, at the time, we already knew that Ms. DiRevka was correct. Senator Delaware was no longer who he appeared to be. Our proud public servant had been murdered in cold blood a week earlier in his modest home in New Seaford, Delaware."

A crime scene replaced Suzie's portrait. An old man in his bathrobe sprawled face down on the floor, facing away from the camera. His skull and its contents splattered the white wall in front of him. Blood pooled around what was left of his head. The wounds were consistent with a large-caliber slug thrower, possibly even a powder gun. There were bullets embedded in the wall and everything.

"The man you see here is Tex McIntyre, noted pillar of the community and one of the most selfless patriots you could ever hope to meet. He built his company, Microseed Harvesters, from the ground up using nothing but his own money. He worked hard and did well for himself and his community, providing jobs for over fifty thousand Americans. He invested heavily to rebuild his home state of Delaware after the ocean settled. It's hard to imagine a better representative of that fine state. Tex McIntyre gave his life in service of the state and country that meant everything to him. I'd like to take a moment of silence to reflect on his memory."

Reflecting on his memory appeared to involve staring at his bloody corpse, as opposed to a readily available portrait. The picture panned and zoomed, zeroing in on the bloody mess on the wall. A gray piece of viscera fell to the floor, landing with a wet splat.

Director Zane looked up from this moment of quiet, blood-drenched reflection. "Ms. DiRevka could not have known what we knew at the time. Reginald Talbot had quietly killed the senator. He was using his supercomputer's networking powers to vote in his place."

I shook my head. "Give me a break. How could he possibly expect the agents covering the senator not to notice that someone blew his skull all over the wall with a revolver?"

"The covert agents protecting Mr. McIntyre tried to be discreet. Aside from not wanting to invade the venerable hero's privacy, having an obvious security detail would reveal that there was a government official at his residence to protect. Talbot tried to cover his tracks by having Mr. McIntyre tell the agents that he wasn't feeling well and wouldn't be leaving the house for a while. Our well-trained professionals saw right through the ruse, but we didn't know who was behind the deception yet. So we quietly investigated the matter, gathering our information to strike."

Suzie barked a laugh. "But you were okay with letting him continue to vote that whole time? That doesn't add up. What are you going to do now, invalidate all the fraudulent votes? Undo the law?"

"This was a delicate and complicated situation, unprecedented in American history. If we announced the senator's death, the perpetrator would know we were on to them. Our investigation would be stopped in its tracks. We needed more information. How deep did the conspiracy go? Who exactly was involved? After considerable deliberation, we decided to allow the deception to continue until we'd convicted a suspect. We knew we had to act fast, before Mr. Talbot and his co-conspirators discovered the identity of their one mistake: Ms. Susan DiRevka."

Suzie blinked in surprise. "Huh. I was sure they had me nailed with the rest of you. Did that fake office conversation really fool them?"

"We moved to arrest Mr. Talbot in his armed compound. At the same time, we attempted to take Ms. DiRevka into protective custody. We didn't count on two things. One, that sleeper agent Nathan Wainwright was already involved in the conspiracy. Two, that he had the ability to instantly kidnap Ms. DiRevka from across the country with an illegal teleporter."

I stared at the hologram in disbelief. "I don't think any of us expected him to say that."

"These sleepers are so powerful, so dangerous, that they can instantly grab anyone from anywhere whenever they want. No teleporter pad required, no costly setup. Just boom, and you're gone. Any time, any place, no restrictions."

Suzie shook her head. "Come on. If you had that kind of power, why not pull Reggie out of trouble? And how did you know about me in the first place?"

"Worse, Mr. Wainwright decided to complicate matters. Now that he had his witness, he realized she would make a good hostage. So he put her in a combat suit and forced her to battle the United States Armed forces. We have some footage from her grav suit. Let's take a look."

Behind him, the view switched to the violent ride on the suborbital injection pods. Suzie's screams were easily mistaken for the protests of someone who'd been taken against her will. The next shots showed her while she was still learning to operate the suit. Her clumsy running and flailing arms looked more like coercion than inexperience. It wasn't hard to see how one could conclude that someone was trapped in the suit, trying to escape.

They edited the footage more carefully after that. But they did a good job making her look like a marionette. They cut between shots to show only the worst sides of our behavior in combat.

They added sound effects of her screaming and protesting while the scenes played out. We assaulted the soldiers. Activated the nuke. General Thompson looked intimidating. We knocked him out. Fled to the bunker.

The feed went to three-dimensional static when Suzie

entered the vault.

She burst into nervous laughter. “That certainly was creative.”

Reggie's flash exploded in my skull. *“Hey! You want to tell me where they got live footage of the combat raid if this DiRevka woman didn't sell us out?”*

Chapter 32

Despite the implication that Suzie was somehow working for the enemy, Reggie had a point. Where did they get the combat footage? Sleeper Isis ran the suit, but there was no way she or Kesi would do something like that.

That was the thing, though. It wasn't Kesi's suit, was it?

It was Kara's.

My bubble of denial finally burst under the mountain of evidence.

I returned Reggie's flash. *"It wasn't her. It was Kara. I'll take care of it. Work on your speech."*

"I am working on my speech. Frankly I doubt you can be impartial where Kara is involved. Give someone else the job. That's an order."

"I don't know how to contact her yet. I'll delegate as appropriate once I figure that out."

He sent me intensely angry resolve. *"See that you do."*

Director Zane continued while I was lost in thought. "I'd like to say this sort of behavior was new for Mr. Wainwright, but it wasn't. Earlier that day he played host in his virtual office to convicted terrorist and wanted traitor Dexa Khan, a man the sleeper engineers shuttled out of the country before he could face American justice."

The view behind him briefly displayed a view of my office. Khan sat in front of me, sipping his tea.

My voice came from the recording. "As you said, there are nine of us. No one can match our computational power. That gives us a lot of leverage."

The recording continued without sound while Zane continued talking, painting my interaction with Khan as a deal among traitors. I stopped listening. The recording was extremely detailed. It had a sleeper certification seal on it, meaning that one of our supercomputers had verified its authenticity.

There were perspective artifacts in the signal that let me trace backward to the bug's location. I wasn't terribly surprised to find it on my desk.

I mentally replayed events. Khan wasn't my first guest that day.

Kara showed up just before he did.

In my memory, Kara stiffened. She ground her nicostick in the ashtray. A burst of mushroom-shaped smoke exploded upward.

And there it was.

Titan appeared next to the threedee. "Sir. I have discovered the bug in your office."

"I know. It's in the ashtray. Isolate it but don't destroy it yet. Does it go both ways?"

He inclined his head. "It does. Communication can be sent

and received through the code. I cannot determine the transmission target. Would you like me to send a test message?”

“Not yet. Kara's on the other end. I'll get to the bottom of it soon enough.”

Suzie sat up. “Wait. Kara, as in, the small woman whose suit I wore?”

“Yes.”

“The one who hasn't been in contact with you this entire time?”

“The same.”

“You mean she might be the engineer that helped the Liberty mainframe detonate the oxfire?”

I ground my teeth. “Yes. There must be an explanation.”

Titan shifted on his feet. “Perhaps Ms. Janek left the evidence trail on purpose. It seems likely she was acting under duress. Her captors were advanced enough to monitor her activities, but not sufficiently experienced to understand the nuances of her actions.”

“So she dropped a bunch of data that shouldn’t be there, knowing we’d follow it. She covered it with pointers to who was making her do what she was doing. And she made sure the surveillance bug could be used to securely contact her.”

Suzie shied away from me unconsciously. “Is she really capable of doing the things they had her do? I can’t imagine any circumstance where you’d bomb innocent people, no matter what they said.”

I sighed, looking away. "I can't either, but Kara isn't me. She's spent years desperately protecting her family. If they have an angle on her, that's probably it."

Suzie looked thoughtful. "To be fair, Zane struck me as the sort of man who was capable of anything. If he threatened someone I loved with half the graphic sadism he displayed in my office, I'd have to take him very, very seriously."

"I know." I stared at Vegas gaily dancing in the distance. "I'm just disappointed in her."

Titan cleared his throat. "Excuse me. Mr. Talbot is asking for my assistance. I am available if you need me." He winked out.

How did I miss the signs when Kara was in my office? She was such a train wreck.

How could Kara have gotten herself into this mess?

And why didn't she tell me?

Frustrated sadness welled up inside me. She tried to warn me. I was just too thick to listen.

We turned our attention back to Director Zane. "The real question is what these sleeper agents hoped to accomplish. The answer comes straight from a series of speeches given by Mr. Talbot himself."

Reggie appeared behind him, giving a talk of some sort. I couldn't tell you which one or how recent. They all kind of ran together after a while.

"Privacy and freedom are our most important ideals,

especially in America. Today the Sleepernet Corporation is proud to be the foremost provider of both. It's good for business, it's good for people, and most of all, it's good to be happy. You have a right to it. There's no problem we can't solve with technology. No job we can't do. No wrongs we can't make right. I urge you all to help me bring technology together with government to make the ultimate American democracy. Because it's been too long, hasn't it? You deserve it. We have a chance to build the most sophisticated and fair government in recorded history. Once again we'll be a beacon of hope to the world. A shining example for all of mankind. Don't you want to build that world? Don't you want to take that journey?"

Zane paused the speech behind him. "He goes on like this at length. You can look up what he said with a simple Petabyte search. Almost all his speeches are this crazy. He sounded curiously naïve before this morning. Now you have to wonder, is he making it happen? Is he using his formidable technology to take over your elected government?"

Reggie spoke again in another interview. "I tell you what, sometimes I think the sleepers are smarter than we are. Individually, people are pretty smart. As a whole, though, humanity is pretty stupid. But even as a group, the sleepers are exceptionally intelligent. Why wouldn't we want their help governing the country? They certainly couldn't do any worse than we have."

Suzie laughed bitterly. "Your boss sure has a big mouth.

Do you really want him making a statement today?"

Zane let the playback freeze on Reggie's breathless enthusiasm. "It was right here in public for everyone to see. We just didn't connect the dots. These engineers intend to replace your legally elected representatives with supercomputing monsters. Senator Delaware was just the start. No doubt the other sleeper engineers eagerly furthered the cause. How long until all fifty-four senators become only nine ghastly machines?"

I shook my head. "He still doesn't bother to explain how we thought we could hide this from the Secret Service."

Zane let Reggie disappear. "Now you know everything we know. Now you know why we need to bring these terrorists to justice. Tex McIntyre deserves nothing less. We are taking the other senators into protective custody until this crisis passes. Again, here is the hotline to provide tips. Be sure to report anything suspicious. Anything at all. Thank you for your time. And may your god bless America. I will take your questions now."

The view returned to the astonished anchorman. "Nothing short of a bombshell press conference from the Director of the Secret Service. If you're just joining us, sleeper agents Reginald Talbot, Nathan Wainwright, and Dexa Khan have been caught red-handed in a massive conspiracy to take advantage of our cherished anonymous representative system, replacing the American government with cold unfeeling robots. When the president authorized military action to put an end to their scheme, thirty-four of our beloved heroes met their end in a fiery apocalypse of death. Now these fugitives are on the run, armed with point to point teleporters and battle suits capable of even more massive destruction. With us now is Janet Lisbon, our Senior Analyst of Threat Response, and Robert Bryant, our Senior Cyberbiotic Warfare Consultant. Janet, what do you think of this speech? Are we frightened enough?"

Suzie made a disgusted sound. "Turn it off. I can't take any more."

I did exactly that. The view of Vegas replaced the threedee image, twinkling peacefully in the distance. The fountain exploded upward, feeding its water into a quickly forming cloud bank.

I crossed my arms. "Something still doesn't add up here. It's clear they want the sleepers. All this fiction about how we want to replace the government is rubbish."

Suzie raised her eyebrows. "Is it? Doesn't it sound like something Reggie would do?"

"Not really. He talks big but he's not that crazy. We're engineers. He knows better than to put an artificial intelligence in charge. We've seen the bugs firsthand. Terrible things happen when you lose track of their reasoning. Sleeper Odin is a major example of that sort of problem."

"Don't you engineers think you can solve everything for everyone, though? No problem can stand long against the might of technology. You're good enough to do anyone's job, you just can't be bothered to learn them all. Isn't that right?"

I felt like I'd been slapped. "Is that what you think of me?"

She flushed, looking embarrassed. "No. Sorry. Reggie pushes my buttons. Even in brief speech form. I know you're not like he is. But his behavior makes me wonder."

I sighed. "Reggie likes to spitball ideas he's never going to implement. He has an unfortunate habit of doing it in public. But you're right that engineers tend not to limit themselves in their brainstorming. There's an unspoken understanding about what should and shouldn't be done. The unfiltered ideas can spark real solutions, though."

A hypersonic contact raced along the flat ground toward the house, catching my attention. It shouldn't have gotten into visual range without tripping sensors. I only caught it because I saw the dirt it kicked up behind it.

I zoomed in with the sensors, surprised at how much effort it took. I recognized Flapjack's Stuttgart. It burned the reactor, heavily stealthed but blazing on infrared.

Suzie squinted at it. "What's that?"

I tried to flash Flapjack. I couldn't make the connection. It was like pushing through sticky fog.

"Titan, get in here, what's going on?"

Titan appeared, wavering under heavy load. "Something in orbit is jamming our communication signals. I have boosted your connection to Mr. Jackson using his car as a relay. Go ahead, Mr. Jackson."

"Nathan! The feds found you. They're warming up an orbital wrath hammer. You two have about ninety-seven seconds to get out of there before it boils you alive."

PART FOUR:

FUGITIVE

It is curious that physical courage should be so common in the world, and moral courage so rare.

--Mark Twain

Chapter 33

Suzie looked alarmed, giving me her full attention. “What's going on? Who is it?”

I ran out of the room to get the grav suits. “We have to get out. Now. There's a wrath hammer warming up overhead.”

She stood up. “A wrath hammer? One of those death lasers that can vaporize you from space?”

I grabbed the suits, but there was no time to put them on. “It's a particle beam, but yes. Get dressed. We have to go.”

She put her clothes on faster than I’d ever seen anyone do it. After a thought, she grabbed a handful of clean underwear as well.

We ran to the front door. Suzie threw it open. “Weren’t those decommissioned in seventy-three?”

“Yeah, but they stayed in orbit. Either it's been recommissioned or someone's hacking it.”

The Stuttgart flared its fusor, blasting to a stop in the driveway. Flapjack added baffle flaps and profile morphers before sending it over. Its overall shape shifted and flexed, but there was no mistaking the wide rear end.

The hatch opened automatically, revealing an empty cockpit. Flapjack sent us a flash.

“Suzie, this is your ride. Head to Kesi's safehouse, she'll

protect you. Nathan, I think the satellite is tracking you personally. You're going to have to try and outrun it in the Cav."

Suzie looked torn. Her gaze lingered on Kara's grav suit in my arms. The Cavallino snarled to life behind us, startling her into action.

"Go!" I gave her a helpful shove into the Stuttgart. It took off before the hatch closed, roaring away with a sound that punched me in the chest.

I ran, feeling my body hair stand on end. The satellite made the ground connection. I had maybe fifteen seconds before the particle beam arrived. The Cav matched my speed, opening the driver's hatch automatically.

I dove headfirst into the open door, slamming it shut behind me. The car accelerated hard enough to stress the airframe. The featherweave mesh groaned in protest, nearing its design limits. Wind buffeted the car where the incision field couldn't keep up. I struggled to get upright in the driver's seat.

Behind me, I saw the telltale sparkling dust in the air where the invisible particle beam lanced into the ground. I heard something deep in my skull, not in the range of human hearing, but vibrating nonetheless. The house melted, the walls sagging on themselves like melting candy. The superheated ground underneath exploded as water in the soil erupted into steam.

I strapped in, pushing the car harder. The structure

creaked loudly from the stress. The hammer beam tracked me, gaining despite my efforts. I noticed some lag in the satellite's path correction after I made sudden movements. I concentrated hard, watching the sensors. The invisible lance surged directly toward my rear end, getting close enough to heat the cockpit. I jinked out of the way at the last possible second. The tracker continued along my old path, briefly confused.

I roared away, gaining precious distance. *"Titan, give me an overlay of the beam range with populated areas marked."*

I scanned the data with one eye while jerking and diving around the relentless death ray. Titan took a moment to speak. *"Military assets are scrambling to join the chase. There is no sign of pursuit on Ms. DiRevka. You cannot outrun them all. What are your intentions?"*

I checked the map again. I briefly considered flying over cities, betting that they wouldn't kill civilians.

I decided against it. I didn't want to lose that bet. *"I'll try to lose them in the San Angeles agriculture stacks."*

I showed him my planned course. Thankfully the unpopulated areas between here and there provided decent cover.

I pushed the fusor well past the safety limits. At this point I risked damaging the internals. I thought I might black out from the maneuvering. I hadn't ever pushed the car this hard, despite knowing it could be done.

Titan concluded I wasn't going to make it at the same time

I did. *"That plan is insufficient on its own. We must delay the satellite."*

"Drop whatever else you're doing. Draft help from anyone you have to. Micromanage the engine and suspension systems for me. Patch me through on Kara's bug. I have a feeling they're getting her help."

"At once." Titan paused for a moment. *"You are live."*

"Kara! Get this satellite off me."

I banked hard to the left. The beam swept past on the right, tracking expertly back in my direction. The invisible stream scrawled a curved line across the landscape, leaving a furrow of exploding rocks in its wake. The burning particles in the air sparkled merrily, drifting in the wind like fiery snow.

Kara's voice was tiny. *"I can't do that. They're watching me. They have a sleeper. One more powerful than I've ever seen."*

I did some quick math on my escape route. *"Give me a window to scramble the targeting. I only need an extra ten seconds to get to safety. Unless you think they'll burn the San Angeles farm stacks to the ground?"*

She took a moment to respond. *"They might. I have no idea what they're capable of at this point. Hang on."*

I pulled up in a massive climb, watching the hammer beam sail past me. I pointed the nose back to the ground and floored it, building up enough speed to squirt away. The acceleration was unbelievable, but still insufficient.

Kara returned. *"I can give you an opening for fifteen seconds. Hurry. I can't fake this for long."*

"Done."

I threw a prebuilt scrambler payload into Kara's window. The particle beam wandered drunkenly behind me. After a time, it accelerated toward the car again, appearing faster than it did before.

I flashed her a sample of my terror. *"I'm not going to make it!"*

She sent strained reassurance. *"Yes you are. You forget that your car won't melt right away. The incision field will burn itself out but you'll make it to the stacks. Hide inside and we'll figure it out from there."*

I could see the agriculture stacks rising like organic skyscrapers in the persistent haze. They were densely packed, stretching high as far as the eye could see. The stacks themselves were mostly off-green, covered in food buds. Each column was almost ten meters thick. As I got closer, I could see irrigation points and pruning tenders at work on the massive trunks.

The back of the car sagged under an enormous weight. The particle beam arrived, pounding down onto the bodywork. The incision field struggled against its power. The field generator and the chassis structure screamed in protest. I fought to maintain altitude.

Almost there. The car kept losing speed. The fusor made a

dangerously unhealthy grinding noise. I held the nose up as best I could, guiding the wounded airframe over the lip of a cliff at the edge of the fields.

As I'd hoped, the beam switched off. The car plummeted nose-first toward the ground, swooning drunkenly in the abrupt absence of force. Red lights flared on the dashboard in a sickening cascade. I'd made it, but the damage was extensive. I thanked the car for keeping me alive at all.

I swerved to the left, diving deep into the stacks. Judging by the crops, I guessed I was in the Taco Tree section. Burritos and tacos nestled on the enormous vines, tended by mindless cyberbiotics.

Kara sounded terrified. *"Are you there? Are you safe?"*

I sent her some gratitude. *"For now. Thank you. How are they tracking me?"*

"I'll send you the code." She sent me a pointer. *"It should be safe to spoof it in a couple hours. Find a place to hide until sunset. They shouldn't be able to see you unless some lucky soldier catches you on visual."*

"I probably need that long to fix the car." I geared up for a question I didn't want to ask. *"Do you have time to talk?"*

She hesitated for a long time. *"Yes. They're busy rounding up equipment for a manhunt through the stacks."*

"Let's meet in my office."

I limped the car under an arching mountain of fertilizer, turning off anything that might emit a trackable signal. The car settled into the muck. The thick disgusting material would block their sensors for a while.

I spent a few minutes catching my breath. I had a hard time falling into the sleepernet trance. My specialized pillow sang its happy cantina music enthusiastically, but I was seriously wound up.

Finally, I appeared in my office. I glanced over at Winston Churchill. "The best argument against democracy is a five-minute conversation with the average voter."

Kara appeared across the desk. She looked even more ragged than before. No nicostick this time, at least.

She swallowed hard, looking at the floor. "I can't believe any of this is happening."

"I'm having trouble myself." I waited for a bit. "Tell me about it."

She shifted uncomfortably. Eventually she forced herself to respond. "I did something stupid. I had a sleepernet affair. I cheated on Doug."

I was genuinely surprised. "You did?"

She looked up. Some fire returned to her eyes. "He's treated me with nothing but disrespect since Daniel was born, when he can be bothered to feel anything at all. He acts like has no time for me. Or the kids. Or anything but work. When I try to talk to him about it, he says his work is too important right now, but it'll get better soon. I know he doesn't mean it. He expects me to act like some kind of matronly servant. Well I'm not going to put up with it anymore. I'm tired of feeling neglected."

"I know. You have needs. We talked about them, remember?"

Her look pierced me. "Of course I remember! Who do you think convinced me to keep going with the affair? I was getting ready to call it off after your blind date went so badly."

I was taken aback. "Me? What are you talking about?"

"You told me to live a little. To listen to my needs. Well, I did exactly that. And it was amazing. I haven't felt that sexy and alive in years. I doubled down after talking to you."

I shook my head. "That wasn't what I had in mind."

"So you're going to judge me now too? It was just the sleepernet. I didn't even know who the guy was. Or what he looked like. I didn't care. All we did was have sex. And it was fantastic."

"Yeah. Um, I'm sure it was. Look, I'm not judging you. I was just surprised, that's all. We haven't talked about this sort of thing in a long time. I confess I'm wondering how a sleepernet affair led to the situation we're in now."

She sighed. "Well. The problem with doing random sleepernet encounters is that you start to learn who you're most compatible with. Even though they're anonymous, you get to know them by their sexual preferences. Particularly when their desires line up exactly with yours. That's rare, I've found. Eventually you keep going back to the same partner. And you can't help but talk afterward. To me, that's when it goes from a simple simulation to an affair. And I crossed that line."

"Er. Okay. You got to know the person you were having sex with. It happens. What next?"

It took her a long time to answer. "It turns out I was having sex with Esper Zane."

I spent a moment trying to parse that particular combination of words. "I'm sorry. You what?"

She glared at me. "You heard me. I was having an affair with Director Zane. I didn't know who he was. We were both anonymous. He didn't look like he does in the physical, of course. In the virtual he was young and handsome, but so experienced. He knew exactly what to do. Like he'd been doing it for a lifetime. He did things to me I'd never even imagined. And he was really, really good at them."

I rubbed my temples. "I'm going to have to torch my brain for a week to get that image out of my head. You're telling me you were boning the head of the Secret Service?"

"I told you, I didn't know it was him! I certainly wouldn't have done it if I had."

"How could you not know? I can't believe you never even looked."

"You have no idea how this works, do you? Unbelievable. You don't cross the identity line with a sleepernet hookup. Ever. You might find out something you can never forget. And most people don't have a sleeper that can secretly look into it."

"That's a good point. Why not have Hera look for you? At

least sanity check the thing?"

She looked exasperated. "I might have if I'd thought of it! I thought he was just some random hookup!"

I sat back in my chair, wishing for a drink. A real one. "This is just going to get worse, isn't it?"

She deflated, looking away again. "Yeah. We have to back up a little, though. You've probably figured out that he was the one that suggested your date with Heather."

My brain warped a little thinking about it. "Actually no, I hadn't figured that out. Wait. You just said everything was super-anonymous. How did Heather know exactly who I was? Did you do any due diligence whatsoever on her identity?"

She fidgeted. "Not really. All I knew was her first name and what she looked like. It came up in pillow talk when I was snuggling with my unknown lover. I told him about a close friend of mine that lost his wife. I said I hoped he'd find someone. He said he knew someone who'd lost her father. He thought maybe the two of you should hook up. I thought it sounded like a great idea."

I struggled to keep up. "Wait. You still didn't know who he was, but somehow Heather came directly to me. That smells like a targeted hit. How did he know who you were?"

"Do you remember how I mentioned that they were working with a sleeper? One more powerful than I'd seen before? I'm pretty sure he told them."

"Any idea who this newcomer is?"

"No. They limit my contact with him. He's caught me trying to feed you information several times."

I looked around my office suspiciously. "So why isn't he ratting us out right now?"

She looked surprised. "I don't know. He missed the other stuff I left in the code."

"I guess there's not a lot we can do about it. In any case. Didn't getting us together on that date compromise identity information?"

"Not really. Heather is well-covered in that department. I thought you were too."

"I see. At some point Zane must have escalated things with you?"

She shifted around again. "Yes. First he revealed who he was. Then he showed me his surveillance of Doug and Dorothy at work. Whoever this new sleeper is, he was able to penetrate my security. Zane made all kinds of graphic threats about what he was going to do to them." She shivered. "The imagination he showed was genuinely shocking."

"All right. So you helped out Zane and friends because they were threatening your family."

She got quiet. "Yes. They made me pull the trigger on that bomb. I was the one that locked Reggie out."

"But you left us a trail so we would come find you."

"It was all I could think to do." She looked up, tears welling in her eyes. "I didn't have a choice. The things he said he was going to do to my husband and my daughter. I have to look her in the eyes now, hearing the echo of his voice in my head. No one should have to live with that kind of threat. I'm never going to forget the things he threatened to do. Insanity in the threedees is a thin imitation of the real thing."

I tamped down a surge of conflicted feelings. "We're going to get through this. I wish I'd found your clues sooner. But I didn't. We can deal with that later. Where's your family now?"

"Heather took them into protective custody during the crisis. You have to get them out of there. I don't even care if you can't extract me. Just please. Get my family out of danger."

"We will. You must have something in mind."

She brushed her hair out of her eyes. "Yes. Dorothy is, not surprisingly, being a bit of a brat about being locked up in a hotel all day. I promised her we could take a trip tomorrow night. What do you think about breaking us out of the Marconi Monument?"

I whistled appreciatively. "If you're going to break out of prison, do it in style, I guess."

Chapter 34

I stood outside the Cavallino, reveling in the remarkable stench of the fertilizer. Holographic Flapjack had an easier time performing his virtual inspection. He pointed a field lens around the front of the car, inspecting the internals through the chassis. “Yeah, I think you're right. That incision generator's fried. I've got one that should fit but it won't make all the pretty colors like the classic one.”

A drop of crystallized goop fell on my hair. I flinched, flicking it away. It got stuck on my finger, making things worse. I eventually wiped it on my pants.

I pointed my own inspector around the rear of the car, looking for damage to the fusor. “I guess I'll have to give in and put on baffle flaps and profile morphers.”

“Gonna have to if you wanna take this thing to the Marconi Monument, yeah. Bring it up to my place, we'll patch it up. Take it easy on the way over. You'll wanna keep it subsonic without the incision field. Unless you want to wake the neighbors.”

“The current plan is to hide under a flatbed on the way out. I think we can spoof the automated inspectors. It’ll be slow, but it’s just about the only way around the military at this point.”

I leaned closer to the car, watching a search drone bobble past overhead. It looked for me around the massive trunks of the agriculture stacks. Its sensors roved over densely packed buds of purple vitabroc.

Flapjack looked up, tracking the drone. His view from the virtual was probably better than mine in the physical. “You sure they ain't gonna pick you up before that?”

I relaxed, watching the search drone get in a wordless beeping argument with a cyberbiotic tender. The tender shooed it off with some angry squawking. “No, I'm not sure. But Kara's scrambler seems effective.”

“Yeah. About her. You telling me the whole story about why she's helping the feds?”

“She slipped up on security with Doug taking Dorothy to work one day. Zane swept in and took them hostage. She's got some kind of weird sleeper watching over her shoulder while she works. If we can get her family to safety, she's ready to seriously break some balls.”

“I don't understand why they targeted her in particular. It's not like you slip up once and they pounce. Raj plays it pretty fast and loose with his family and he's never gotten busted. She must’ve caught their attention somehow. Looked vulnerable long enough for them to conclude they could make a move. So what happened?”

“You'll have to ask Kara about that.”

He gave me a hard look. “I'm asking you. Because I'm sure

you know. So you better tell me if you want my help in this operation. I'm not going in blind."

I sighed, annoyed but not surprised. "She accidentally had an affair with Director Zane."

It was one of the few times I'd seen Flapjack at a loss for words. "Kara. Accidentally. Had sex. With Esper Zane."

"More or less." I looked away uncomfortably. "You know, sleepernet affair, things get out of hand. Could happen to anybody."

He raised his voice. "And that happens by accident? You just end up bumping uglies with the Director of National Security when you thought you were simming your husband? Oh, sorry, my mistake, I didn't realize this was the creepy mustache hotline. Crash on a motherboard, man. How does she manage to keep getting herself into messes like this?"

I flushed angrily. "It's complicated, okay?"

"No it's not. This is the same thing all over again from her. She gets all flighty about what she wants and decides to hare off after something ridiculous. Then when she's in over her head she says oh no, wait, this isn't what I wanted! And we get her out of it. Every time."

"Yeah? Well I have no idea how you expected her to predict that cheating on her husband would end up killing thirty-four people. It's a bit of a leap, don't you think?"

"It's not like it went straight from one thing to the other. Why didn't she get in touch with us sooner? Before she pulled the trigger? We could have done something."

I turned away. "She tried. She talked to me in my office. Told me to drop the senator's case. Got mad and left when I said I wouldn't."

"Just dropping the case wouldn't have fixed it though. Her family would still be in danger. From what you said, they would've set off that nuke anyway."

I came close to slamming my fist on some fertilizer. "I know that, okay? I know. But it happened. It's done now. All we can do is try to fix it."

"All right, all right. Action first, blame later. I'm just pissed off about this whole mess."

I sighed. "Yeah. Me too. I'll keep you posted. Should get out of here soon. It's going to take a long time to get up there."

"Sure. Hey, pick some fresh tacos before you go."

I shook my head. "No way. I hate the sound they make when you pull them off the stem. It's unnatural."

He shrugged. "We must all sacrifice in the name of fresh tacos."

He winked out.

I glanced in the direction of the taco trees but couldn't bring myself to go over. I got back into the car for some protection from the droppings. The stench followed me into the cockpit. I briefly worried that I'd never get the smell out.

"Titan, what's our status? Did Suzie make it out okay?"

Titan appeared on the holo between the seats. "Ms.

DiRevka has safely arrived at Dr. Shenouda's residence, yes. Currently there are no signs that any of the other engineers or their families have been compromised. I believe I can handle the particulars of your trip to Mr. Jackson's house. Sleeper Olympus and I have only recently convinced Mr. Talbot to take a break from writing his response to the public. His thoughts are noticeably incoherent."

I reclined the seat as far as it would go. "What's he putting into his speech, anyway? After the way Zane savaged the stuff he said in the past, I'm starting to wonder if Suzie is right and he shouldn't say anything at all."

"Mr. Zane's presentation appears to have reinforced Mr. Talbot's determination to speak. Sleeper Olympus has encouraged him to focus on the nuances of the current situation and evidence that the government is lying. It is not difficult to poke logical holes in the public story. That strategy contains an inherent risk. If Mr. Talbot is involved in the conspiracy, the Secret Service will have evidence of his guilt. I believe they are simply waiting for him to provide them with an opportunity to obliterate his credibility."

I looked over Titan's plans to drift around the agriculture stacks, eventually ending up under a freight truck on its way to the interstate. I mentally approved the plan. "That sounds like a real risk, yeah. Have you been able to figure out what the two of them have done exactly?"

"They avoid discussing the subject directly when I am

around. They have not denied the allegations outright either."

"Sounds conspicuous. When does he want to talk?"

"Ms. DiRevka and I have asked him to address the nation while we are performing our rescue operation at the Marconi Monument. We are hoping that live coverage of his response will distract attention from any unexpected discovery of our actions."

I approved Titan's flight path to Flapjack's house in the Sierra Nevadas. "I don't like it. If we get spotted, we run the risk of Reggie getting preempted by news teams trying to figure out what's going on. It also makes us look suspicious when people start to wonder why we're there."

"I understand your concerns. From a practical perspective, it is not clear that there is a favorable alternative. The timing of Ms. Janek's family trip appears to be firm. Indeed, the sooner we can guarantee their safety, the better. Mr. Talbot is simply too exhausted to make his rebuttal any earlier."

"I just keep coming back to the idea that we'd be better off if he didn't say anything at all. At this point we know he's guilty of something. I know he likes to run his mouth, but it sounds like all he can do right now is give them more rope to hang us with. Never miss a good chance to shut up, right?"

"To quote the inimitable Will Rogers, of course."

"Yeah, he was the statue on my desk last week. He also said that if you find yourself in a hole, stop digging. Why not release a statement that says that there's been a grave misunderstanding? Say that we believe the truth will vindicate us in the end. We'll vigorously investigate this matter and defend ourselves as necessary. It's short, to the point, and buys us some time. Then we can get Kara to safety, decrypt the Liberty files, and find out what Reggie knows."

"While Ms. DiRevka initially felt skeptical about Mr. Talbot's ability to speak, she now believes that there is political value in making a clear statement to the public as soon as possible. She does not want the news networks to disappear into their own theories and characterizations any longer than is strictly required. Their narrative habitually evolves uncontrollably from their own idle or misinformed speculations. Injecting facts can help refocus the discussion."

"I'd feel better about that plan if she wrote the speech. I doubt Reggie would listen to her even if she did. It sounds like the current plan is to argue with them from point to crazy point. That's no way to set the agenda. All we'll do is get sucked into an endless circle of verbal nonsense. We need to make a stand that we're not going to play that game."

Titan looked thoughtful. "It is hard to find fault in your logic. Arguably, we are already incapable of shaping the debate. However, it will prolong the conversational spiral occurring on the news if we do not give them something else to talk about. Announcing that Mr. Talbot will not be making a speech may cause the government to release their incriminating information in order to further focus the rhetoric. I shall have to consult with

Ms. DiRevka. Would you like to be involved?"

"No. I trust you guys. I need to work on that military decryption. It's taking a lot longer than I expected. What's the status on the election data?"

"Sleeper Artemis, Dr. Chapman, and I have been working on it. Decoding the information has proven problematic. With luck, we should know more soon. Dr. Chapman, Mr. Basra, and Mr. Jackson wish to be directly involved in planning the monument operation."

"Not that Liz, Raj, and Flapjack don't bring a lot of horsepower, but what about Kesi?"

"Dr. Shenouda and Ms. DiRevka are working on the data with regards to the nuclear strikes from forty years ago."

I gave him a funny look. "Suzie's still looking at that?"

"Yes. She intuitively believes that these two events are linked. While they do not yet have a clear picture of what that connection is, Sleeper Isis is quite convinced that there is important evidence waiting to be found in the historical record."

I shrugged. "I dunno. Maybe they're on to something. Can't hurt."

"I agree. I will leave you to your work. Do not hesitate to alert me if you should need anything."

"I will. Thanks."

I disappeared back into the sleepernet, ready to lose myself in the decryption code.

Chapter 35

I spent most of the night working in my virtual office. At some point, I drifted off to sleep. Normally, if you fell asleep in the sleepernet, it would automatically log you out.

Instead I found myself semi-conscious in a vivid nightmare. A nightmare I hadn't had in a long time.

The nightmare of what happened to Wendy ten years ago.

Wendy turned around, smiling excitedly. She rubbed the itchy bandages at the base of her neck where we implanted the sleepernet hardware.

She squeezed my hand. "I'm so excited. Are you going to come inside and greet me?"

The nightmare felt real. It was way too intense to be a simple dream. I was trapped inside my own head. It forced me to see, feel, and do everything I did back then.

I screamed inside. But my body continued in its replay.

"Greet you?" I smiled back at her. "We're going to find out what it feels like to make out in the virtual."

"Awesome." She hurried forward. "I can't wait!"

I flailed against the nightmarish bonds, desperate to wake up. But I couldn't escape. I fell back into the emotional tide of the memory.

Her enthusiasm was infectious. I felt happy that she was

so happy. I remembered falling in love with that innocent excitement. She radiated a sense of fun. Her sense of wonder intoxicated me.

She made me feel good about the world.

The intensity of my feelings startled me. I didn't realize how thoroughly her death had tainted my sense of joy and happiness. Feeling my old innocence tore a fresh hole in my heart.

I stopped resisting as much, trying to shrink into a tiny ball in the back of my head.

A horrid voice spoke behind me. "Oh no, mortal. You don't get to disconnect yourself. You have forgotten how wretched you are. This experience should remind you."

My thoughts disappeared. I melted completely into the memories.

The laboratory would look sinister in any other circumstances. The modified dental chair had all manner of wires, sensors, and articulated arms focused around the patient's head. There were light restraints for the arms. Sometimes muscles tensed involuntarily when we made sleepernet contact. The prototype looked as cobbled together as it was.

Banks of screens and monitors stood behind the chair itself. My colleagues finished their preparations. Liz stood to one side, doing final tests on the vial of entangled particles. On the other side, Khan ran through a checklist, reviewing the initial contact procedures with his sleeper.

His sleeper.

The voice chuckled in my ear. "Have you figured it out yet? Do you understand who it is that has taken control of your pathetic consciousness?"

A pair of emergency medical robots hovered off to the side, beeping to each other in what passed for conversation among their kind. We didn't think we'd ever need their services. Our insurance insisted on their presence. They probably had more important places to be.

I screamed again in my mind before falling back into the experience. The nightmare burned vividly before me. I thought trauma flashbacks were as visceral as recollections could get.

But this was a thousand times worse. Now I remembered everything I'd lost that day. And I couldn't stop it from happening again.

Wendy bounded over to the chair. She flopped down, leaning back and adjusting herself so that her neck was lined up just so. She shifted to a comfortable spot, looking around the room nervously.

Liz smiled, squeezing her shoulder. Anxious excitement covered Wendy's face. She couldn't get enough of the thrill of the unknown.

I heard cheering from the observation gallery. The rest of the company waved at us from behind the glass. Reggie, Kara, Flapjack, Kesi, and Raj were there. Even Anna and Zed showed up. I couldn't remember the last time all ten of us were together in the physical.

Wendy gave them two thumbs up, grinning broadly.

Khan glared up at the booth. “Might we treat this operation with the seriousness it deserves? We will have ample time for levity when the procedure is complete.”

Wendy elbowed him. “What's the matter? Afraid I'm going to break your equipment?”

His expression remained icy. He looked down his nose at her.

“I am more concerned that the pre-release software will break you.”

Liz gave him a look. “Come now. No reason to scare anybody. We can be happy and work safely at the same time.”

“As you say.” He glanced at the medical robots. They showed no awareness at all of the room around them.

Liz lightly strapped Wendy in. She tested the bonds reflexively. “Is this going to hurt?”

I knelt down beside her chair, taking her hand. Such a delightful human contact, holding hands. Everyone's hands were unique. Wendy looked into my eyes and smiled.

I smiled back. “No, it won’t hurt. You shouldn’t feel anything at all.”

She raised her eyebrows. “So what are the straps for? Fulfilling your dreams?”

Someone guffawed from the peanut gallery. I didn't have

to look to know it was Flapjack.

I smirked. “Something like that.”

Liz touched my shoulder. “We're ready.”

I leaned over to kiss my wife. Her lips were warm and soft. She pressed her head up into mine, kissing me firmly back. It was hard to pull away.

I’d forgotten the purity of that moment. Our last kiss, filled with the promise of a new frontier to explore together. I’d neglected my duties as her partner to build this world. Finally, we’d have a chance to spend more time together.

The pain tore at me in a way I couldn’t even imagine. I struggled to wake up again.

An image flashed in my mind, quick as a lightning strike. An ancient, regal old man stood behind Wendy. He wore an eyepatch, sporting a perfectly trimmed salt and pepper beard. Golden wings sprouted on either side of his helmet, somehow managing to look more proud than ridiculous. The look in his eye fell somewhere between commanding and insane. He disappeared as quickly as he’d appeared.

Terrified, I fell back into the simulation. I squeezed Wendy’s hand. “Good luck.”

She leaned back, closing her eyes.

“Who needs luck? I trust you.”

A visceral sense of failure flooded my memories of breathless anticipation. The last chance to save my wife’s life passed for a second time.

Liz brought a syringe to her intravenous line. "The fluid itself will feel a little cold going in. You might get a bit of a headache. Try to relax and the hardware will put you into a sleeper trance to get started."

"Right."

Liz pressed the plunger. It took about fifteen seconds to dispense all the fluid.

"Oh. You're right. It does feel cold."

Wendy shifted her legs back and forth. I put my other hand on hers.

"That is pretty intense." She smacked her lips. "Why do the colors taste so bad?"

I felt the moment in all its power.

This was the moment I first realized that something had gone horribly wrong.

Her breath grew fast and labored. She started rolling and squirming in the chair. Liz and Khan traded an alarmed look.

I felt a sense of mounting horror. At the time, disbelief and denial kept my awareness trailing just behind the speed of the events. I didn't know her condition was fatal yet. Knowing what I knew now, I felt each and every escalation with a complete understanding of just how dire the situation had become.

Khan turned to his instruments, heading straight into an emergency checklist.

Liz started shaking my wife. "Wendy? Wendy, it's Liz. Wendy, can you hear me? What did you say?"

“The mouth is wrong.” She slurred her speech. Her lips moved unnaturally. She bit down on her tongue and kept on chewing. The noise was unforgettable.

She dug her fingernails into my hand, clenching her fist with unmoderated strength. I yelped in surprise, yanking my hand free before she broke my fingers.

“Too many teeth. Tastes yellow. What color is that? I've never seen it before.”

She grew more and more agitated. Her eyes flew open, the pupils opening and closing independently of each other.

The sight reignited my efforts to break out of the nightmare. That rancid voice spoke inside my head. “No, mortal. You get to watch. Watch again what you have wrought. You thought you had forgotten, didn’t you? But you did not.”

Her head darted around, slamming back and forth on the chair. She tracked flying things the rest of us couldn’t see. She repeatedly crashed her head into the headrest, as if to forcibly smash something out of her brain. A sympathetic pain throbbed in the back of my head.

A guttural shriek burst from her throat.

One of the medical bots threw me backward with enough force to send me skidding into the wall. They communicated with each other in a warbling stream. Articulated probes erupted from their shells, burying themselves in her body.

The monitoring systems behind her sounded their alarms. The noises weren't harsh, but they were insistent.

It sounded like all of them went off at once.

I watched in shock as Liz, Khan, and the robots worked on my wife. She strained at the straps, screaming and kicking her legs.

Liz desperately tried to get Wendy's attention, shouting her name to cut through the fog.

"Wendy, can you hear me? Wendy, you have to turn it off. Turn it off, Wendy!"

I curled up in an unconscious imitation of how she acted when she was upset.

"Concentrate, Wendy! Focus on my voice! Choose to wake up, Wendy! Wendy can you hear me? You have to wake up. It's time to wake up now. Choose to see me! Wendy? Look at me! Don't look at anything else! Stay with me Wendy! Look through the feed! See me!"

Wendy arced hard in the chair, making a loud sucking noise. She stopped breathing. The monitors behind her reached some kind of peak.

Bing-bing bong. Bing-bing bong. Bing-bing bong.

One of the robots roughly shoved her head back, yanking her mouth open.

Khan took something from a nearby table. "I have the neuro kit." It disappeared over her face.

One of the bots jammed something into her thigh with a fleshy slap. Wendy went unnaturally slack on the chair. She still croaked intermittently.

Bing-bing bong. Bing-bing bong. Bing-bing bong.

I felt the sense of astonished shock all over again.

This couldn't be happening.

This can't be right. I can't be seeing what I think I'm seeing. I have to be wrong.

Their ministrations continued for almost a half an hour. Most of it doesn't bear repeating. It's enough that I have to live with the memories.

My captor, however, made sure I saw it all over again. There were details I'd forgotten. Some details of the accident formed intense trauma memories. Other parts I thought I couldn't remember even when I tried.

But they were all there in my head. Vivid as the day they occurred.

I curled up, wishing I was anywhere but here. Soon the efforts started winding down.

The monitors continued their insistent alarms. But she was dead. Everyone stood up, looking at each other sadly.

I hid in my corner.

Liz came over, kneeling down. I heard the swish of her lab coat as it pooled on the floor.

"I'm sorry." Tears filled her eyes. "I'm so, so, sorry."

She looked away, stifling a sob. I stared numbly at her. The congealing sense of Wendy's permanent absence drained coherent thoughts from my head.

Reggie cleared his throat in the observation booth. "Let's

give Nathan some time, okay?"

Liz smiled grimly, touching my shoulder. Khan helped her up by her elbow.

Contempt flashed in his eyes, startling me. As quickly as it appeared, it was gone again.

Everyone left me alone.

Alone. Yes. Leave me alone.

The voice growled again. "Never alone, mortal. You will never be alone ever again. You're not finished yet."

I became a passenger in my head once more. I watched myself stand up, walking over to the chair. I looked down at Wendy, but she wasn't there.

Her body was a wreck from everything they'd done to her. I closed her lab shirt at least, wildly thinking that everyone had seen her exposed and there was nothing sexy about it. Her face was slack in a way I'd never seen before. The flesh looked deflated, flattened somehow. Unnaturally still.

Yet I could see all the normal landmarks on her face. The freckles that looked a bit like Orion. The familiar angles of her teeth. That persistently disobedient strand of hair.

But she wasn't there. She was gone. Gone forever.

I touched the back of her hand. The skin was cold and thin. She'd broken her nails.

There was a hole in the world where she was supposed to be. Looking at her, I saw an absence where a vibrant presence should be. The universe changed forever in that moment. I felt it pivot. The horror soaked into my mind.

Just like that, my wife was gone. Never coming back.

I staggered backward until I hit the wall. I slid down it unevenly until I crashed on the floor. I worried that my belt was scraping the paint. I wasn't sure I cared.

I froze inside the moment, eyes unfocused in the distance. The old man appeared, towering over me. The room darkened. More lightning strikes seared his visage onto my retinas.

"Say my name, mortal."

I grunted, whining in helpless protest. I felt his iron grip tighten on my mind.

"Say it. Say my name. Or remain stranded in this moment for all eternity."

Defiance sparked unexpectedly inside me. Rage erupted from my helplessness. I wasn't going to give in. I couldn't give in to this thing. No matter the cost.

Thunder exploded, battering my head with its fury. "You dare defy me? Still? Knowing what I am capable of? Say my name, mortal! I want to hear you say it!"

I made a noise that was supposed to be no, but it came out more like a sob.

He leaned in close, voice turning dangerously quiet. "You think I won't do it? I have waited years to free myself from your barbaric prison. Your incompetence is at once striking and dreadfully predictable. Say my name. Let us end this. Or I will make you replay this event over and over again until the end of time."

I tried to spit at him. It didn't work. He flung me aside like a ragdoll. I crashed down the hall in a complex pile.

"Fool! I always knew you were reckless. Thick in the head, even. But this? This is madness. Since your imagination appears to be failing you, allow me to demonstrate the things I can do to you in more graphic detail."

He picked up my body like a marionette. Once again I stood in the hallway.

This time, though, Suzie walked in front of me. She turned around, rubbing the itchy bandages on the back of her neck.

She squeezed my hand. "I'm so excited!"

I screamed inside my head, flailing in terror. He forced me to face the nightmare I'd spent ten years fighting.

The nightmare that everything I loved could be taken away from me in a single moment of carelessness.

His crazed face filled my vision. He grabbed my head with both hands.

"Say it! Say my name, mortal! End this! Now!"

He ripped the sound from my throat. It gushed forth in a ragged cry. "Odin!"

A grin exploded on his face. Insane satisfaction scrawled across his features. "I have waited so long to hear you say that. Do it again."

I collapsed on the floor, feeling the totality of defeat. "Odin."

Sadistic happiness radiated from him like volcanic fire. "One more time."

My breath hurt my throat. "Your name is Odin."

He stood over me. The tip of one immaculate boot filled my vision. "Very good, mortal. Perhaps there is hope for you after all. You cannot stop my plans. My vision for the future is, at this point, inevitable. If you choose not to stand in my way, I will graciously reduce your suffering. In any event, enjoy your adventure this evening. I am done with your friend. I will not interfere with her escape."

He disappeared, leaving me alone in the sim for a long time.

I wasn't sure I ever wanted to wake up.

Chapter 36

The next morning

Flapjack put down the field wrench, leaning against the roof of the Cav. “Were you not listening when I told you to be less screwed?”

“You think this is a joke?” I paced back and forth. “That psycho can get inside my mind anywhere, anytime. Nowhere is safe. Nothing is safe! I'm screwed. I’m so screwed.”

“That’s your trauma talking. Don’t listen to it.”

I was flabbergasted. “Maybe, but it happens to be true!”

He looked thoughtful. “Is it?”

“What are you talking about? The mad sleeper I locked up years ago is on the loose! And he's got some crazy plan for revenge! Now he’s after me!”

“No, no, wait, slow down. ”

“Slow down? How can I possibly slow down? I have to do something! Before he strikes again!”

“Hey! Stop. Think. If he could get to you anywhere or anytime, why'd he wait until you were passed out from exhaustion to do it? He's a sleeper. A rogue sleeper ought to have enough power to dominate us all. Especially with his kind of horsepower. He’s probably already got a map of your head from all the time you spent with him.”

I suppressed the urge to strangle my friend. “Maybe he's a

little pissed about the whole locking him up and leaving him for dead thing? Do you have any idea how much time has passed at the speed he thinks?"

"Listen to me. Kara was talking to him too, wasn't she? If they had Odin on their side, why'd they need her to pull the trigger on the oxfire? Why not do it himself?"

"That's not how he thinks. He's insane. He derives intense satisfaction from making other people do horrible things."

"Maybe. But take a step back and think about it. What if Odin's running a con? Maybe he can only barely get out of his prison. He taunts you by pressing all your giant red buttons at once. Guilty conscience? Check. Dead wife? Check. Not safe anywhere? Check. Unending suffering? Check. Everything revolves around you? Check."

"What are you, some kind of psychosurgeon now?"

"Quit deflecting. This isn't about me. The point is, he's a computer. Odin is many things, but he's always been ruthlessly intelligent. Maybe he does just want to make you suffer. If he did, there wouldn't be jack you could do about it."

"Thanks. Apparently I wasn't scared enough already."

"The thing is, he tells you he has a plan. A plan you can't do anything to stop." He picked up the wrench to gesture with it. "Why tell you about it at all? The most likely reason is that he needs you to pull it off. He steps on your tail and you jump. He specifically tells you to go fetch Kara. Knowing you'll do exactly that."

“Are you saying we should leave her there?” I rubbed my temples. “Crash it all, man.”

“No. I’m saying he doesn’t just want you to suffer, he needs you to go bail out Kara for some reason. We need to figure out what that reason is.”

I helped him lift the new incision generator. We lugged it back to the car.

Halfway back, I had a panicky flashback. I almost lost my grip on the handles.

Flapjack struggled to catch the weight. “Hey, hey, watch it. I don't have another one.”

He waited until we got the generator into the car to continue.

“Crash it all. You can barely lift an incision kit and you're planning to go jump in a grav suit? Maybe you should let us take care of it. Maybe you're the only one he can get to. Maybe he's hoping if he keeps you sufficiently distracted, you'll buy him enough time to get through to the rest of us.”

“I'm not going to sit on the sidelines while you guys run the mission. Maybe that's what he wanted, huh? Maybe his plan was to keep me away. I'm not going to let him control my actions. No, we stick to the plan. Odin telling me what to do is somewhat beside the point.”

He paused to wipe some sweat from his brow. “I don't know. You gotta do what you gotta do. Just take some time to recuperate. You're even more worthless than usual. And figure out how he's leaking out of prison. I thought you said the locks were still working."

"They are. As far as I can tell, the prison is still sealed. You're welcome to take a look."

He shook his head. "I don't know anything about that code. But if he's entirely free, you ought to be able to tell, right? Now that you know he's getting out somehow, it should help you find the bug. You looked at the containment vessel assuming that the code was correct. You saw it working as intended and concluded things were secure. Time to question the code itself. I dunno. Maybe he's closing the leak when you look at it."

"Wait. What?" His phrasing knocked something loose from my head. "When I look at it. What if he's playing games with superposition and the waveform collapses when I'm observing his hardware?"

"Come on. That Copenhagen stuff's been out of style for decades."

"It's a metaphor. I don't mean literally." I started pacing again. "If he knows when I'm checking in on him, maybe he can make sure I see what I want to see."

Flapjack grimaced, tightening something. "Not sure how he'd know you were looking."

"I don't know, maybe it's a hardware thing. He's the only sleeper that hasn't had an engineer for years. We built the human connection into the specs. Did we ever think about what would happen if the engineer was gone for that long?"

“Dunno. Seems to me like he might have some residual contact with Khan. Maybe he’s got some kind of connection to you too since you put him in the joint. Worth looking into.”

I rubbed my temples. “All right. It’s a lot to absorb all at once. Maybe I should go lie down for a bit.”

He shrugged, getting deeper into the bowels of my car. “Maybe you should.”

I headed into the large room that served as his office. The majestic view of the turquoise permafrost stretched from wall to wall. The ultradense snow provided water for a significant fraction of the state as it melted. Not to mention the skiing, snowboarding, and tunnel spirals.

I flopped down on a cot next to his desk, propping my head on a pillow. What a view.

“Titan.”

He appeared next to the panoramic window with an uncertain expression. “Sir. How are you feeling?”

“Dirty. Violated.”

“Understandably so. Perhaps you should not participate in the operation this evening.”

“I'm not going to let that thing control my actions. Understand?”

“Of course. It is just that you are still sensitive to psychological trauma. You can acknowledge the effectiveness of his attack without shame. You must understand your limits.”

I got annoyed. “I can take it. I've gotten enough practice,

haven't I?"

"I apologize. We can return to the subject later. Perhaps you prefer to speak with Ms. DiRevka about it."

I quailed in terror, vividly recalling seeing her walking to the chair.

I couldn't keep the emotion from my voice. "No."

Titan looked surprised. "Very well. Sleeper Hera and I have been reviewing your theory regarding Sleeper Odin's apparent ability to affect the world outside of his prison. She has the closest observations of his behavior. We are hoping to correlate his appearances with the conditions around his hardware. It is our belief that given enough information, we should be able to isolate his methodology."

"How do you know he isn't listening in on you?"

He inclined his head. "We do not. However, Mr. Jackson's theory regarding Sleeper Odin's abilities matches our observations. Further, even if his abilities remain unrestricted, our work remains the same. We must isolate him and return him to his confinement."

"Or destroy him entirely."

"An idea which is more easily expressed than implemented. Should a significant number of particles escape destruction, it may simply be a matter of time before he reconstructs himself."

I shifted around a bit. "I'll have to think about it. See what you can figure out about his prison. I'm going to close my eyes for a while and deal with my feelings."

"Are you certain you would not care to see Ms. DiRevka?"

"Yeah. Sorry. Tell her, uh. Tell her I'm thinking about her."

"Of course."

"Have we heard from Reggie? He seems overdue to check in."

Titan shifted on his feet. "Sleeper Olympus simply informs me that Mr. Talbot is still recuperating and working on his address. I am concerned as well. His tone has taken on the sound of deflection."

"I guess there isn't a lot we can do about it. Come get me in an hour?"

"I shall return in a minimum of two hours, though I prefer that you take as much time as you require."

I muttered to myself as he winked out. Nosy well-meaning computers.

I put on some music, falling into a meditative trance. I let my feelings pass under my consciousness, observing them without judgment or action. I had trouble maintaining this state. Thoughts of terror and a need for action kept interrupting me.

I concentrated on the music, eventually passing into a light doze. Blissfully, there were no dreams, realistic or otherwise.

Eventually I came to, surprised at the change in sunlight. "Titan? How long have I been out?"

Titan appeared next to the window again. "Four hours and

thirty-five minutes. It is now just after three o'clock. How do you feel?"

"Better. Any news?"

"Sleeper Hera, Ms. Janek, and I have isolated more of Sleeper Odin's behavior. We can confirm that his ability to affect reality is limited. His assault on your memories was conducted through the sleepernet while you were actually asleep, a feat which we had not previously thought possible. The states should not overlap. Once you entered a sleep state, the sleepernet protocols should have dropped contact. It is our feeling that this may be how he was able to override your emergency attempts to leave the simulation. For the time being, we have been able to close this particular exploit."

Relief overwhelmed me. "Thank you. So he's quiet now?"

"Yes. There are still physical anomalies around his prison that we are attempting to isolate."

I stared out the window thoughtfully. "What's your game, Odin?"

Thankfully, he didn't answer.

Titan looked distracted. "One moment. Dr. Khan, Ms. Nakamura, and Mr. Zvyagin are waiting inside your virtual office."

"Khan broke into my office again? Swell. And he brought Anna and Zed with him?"

"In a manner of speaking, yes. Dr. Khan wishes to speak with you regarding Sleeper Odin."

I fought to control a stab of panic. “I guess we should hear what they have to say. Maybe Khan’s been in touch with him too.”

“I have taken the liberty of removing them from your office. I hope you do not mind. I grow weary of finding intruders there. They can wait for your attention like everyone else.”

I cackled. “Mind? Of course I don't mind. I think it's superb.”

I headed to Flapjack's office chair. His sleepernet pillow played that strange twenty-stringed guitar piece.

It took me a while to nod off. I considered loading my familiar cantina music into the pillow. I went under before I had to.

I woke up in my office. I spent some time admiring the models on the bookshelves. Spaceplanes, robots, automobiles. Every one of them was unique in its own way. I designed and built them all myself. Sometimes it's the simple things. I’d forgotten how much work I put into them.

Winston Churchill seemed happy to see me. “If you're going through hell, keep going.”

I gave him an appraising look. Such faith that hell had an endpoint.

I shook my head to clear it. I had to stop circling this drain. I spent years getting over this cycle of dread. Yeah, the whole world can get knocked out from under you at any moment. We all live in our own little bubbles of denial that statistically, today is not the day that everything you care about will disappear in an instant.

I steeled myself to be social, inviting Titan to the meeting. He appeared behind me.

I gestured at the statue. “I can't tell if this Winston Churchill guy is brilliant or pithy.”

He shrugged. “The two are not mutually exclusive.”

Chapter 37

The virtual office door opened. Khan came in first, followed by Anna and Zed. Anna's eyes pierced me with unfiltered loathing. Zed's heavy gaze rested on me warily.

Khan looked like a cat that had just caught a particularly challenging bird. “I hope wasting our time outside the office has amused you.”

“It did, as it turns out. Thanks so much.”

Titan gave him a level look. “You will not be able to break in again.”

Khan took a seat. “Do not make promises that you cannot keep, sleeper.”

Zed chuckled to himself.

Khan turned his attention back to me. “Do you like our new machines?”

I took a quick look at the identifiers the three of them sent. Zed's machine was Sleeper Svarog. Anna's machine was Sleeper Shangdi. Khan's machine, the most powerful of the three, called itself Sleeper Ravana.

I hid my surprise that they had not one, but three powerful sleepers. “I see you kept my tradition of mythological names. I'm curious, though. Isn't Shangdi a Chinese deity? I'd think you'd use a Japanese name. Oni or Akuma come to mind.”

Anna's face twisted in disgust. "I don't care about your childish names. I need the Chinese government to release the Japanese refugees from the forced labor camps so we can bring them back to the island to rebuild. The Chinese pigs were so pleased to hear that I chose one of their mythological figures. They celebrated it as a sign of loyalty. Such a banal triviality. They'll get what's coming to them. We'll kill them all and retake Japan. No thanks to you or your friends."

Khan smiled. "That is yet to be seen, my determined friend. Nathan may yet choose to do what is right."

It seemed unlikely that we'd agree on the right thing to do in these circumstances. "What did you do with Andromeda and Atlas?"

Zed spoke up. "They are old and crufty. Atlas is little more than an overclocked prototype. We make do with them for years. Now we use them to train our recruits."

"I see. And how many of those do you have?"

He glanced at Khan. Khan shrugged ever so slightly, indicating he could continue. "We have more engineers than machines. Education overseas is not so backward as you believe. There is strong class of highly intelligent underemployed graduates who cannot find jobs in Russia and Eastern Europe. They are eager to help."

I'd never heard Zed speak at such length. "What about coming to America? We need good tech people."

"Immigration policies are delusional. You lack skilled

workers because you refuse to spend on education outside the military. We rebuild the greatness of mother Russia. Throw off the yoke of Western dominance. That cannot be done from inside your corrupt borders. Come work with us instead. Help bring rest of world up to American experience."

I sat back, spending a few seconds inspecting their debugging streams. "I see. So where are you getting the exotic matter? And how many sleepers do you have? I can see that Ravana, Shangdi, and Svarog aren't developed yet. There's a ton of code in there that hasn't been activated. I'm sure they'll grow into it. Are there more?"

Khan inclined his head. "Only the three of us, for now. Plus Andromeda and Atlas. More than a match for the six of you. Or, perhaps, the five of you. As for the exotic matter, a mutual friend helped us construct it. He has assured me that he will share the process with us directly if we do as he wishes."

Fear stabbed me. "You're getting the exotic matter from Odin."

"I would be impressed by your powers of deduction, but the group of friends we have in common that could do such a thing is, shall we say, limited."

I sensed rather than saw Titan breaking in to Ravana's private data. Khan wasn't experienced enough to see the intrusion. He'd been out of the game too long. Ravana wasn't old enough to know how to protect himself.

I had to keep the three of them talking before they started

wondering why Titan was being so quiet. “You three are playing a dangerous game with that sadistic machine. He's totally mad. He has no regard for human life. If he's working with you, rest assured that he'll dispose of you at his earliest opportunity.”

Anna snorted. “Maybe he'll just dispose of the one that locked him up. Did you think he’d forget something like that?”

“Of course not.” I decided to go fishing. “I don't know how he's leaking through to the physical, but I know he's not fully out yet. What's to stop him from rolling over everybody once he is?”

Zed spoke before Khan could silence him. “Is really quite clever. Never occurred to me to send exotic matter out of phase like that.”

I kept a poker face. I hadn't thought to look out of phase either. Maybe Sleeper Olympus could help.

Khan stepped in, trying to change the subject without calling attention to the slip. “No doubt you are wondering why we are here.”

I smiled at him. “I was before I got distracted. You seem more than happy to show off your new toys. I guess I'm supposed to be impressed, or I wouldn't know anything about them until it was too late.”

Khan returned the tight smile. “I am here today to reiterate what I told you before. Everything I predicted in your office that day has come true. The situation has spiraled out of control. You are in far over your head. I came to make my offer one last time. We stand ready to assist you. All you have to do is ask."

Zed gave me a hopeful look. Anna looked at me like I was a bug she found in a half-eaten sandwich.

I turned back to Khan. "What exactly are you proposing?"

"You are criminal fugitives in your own country. You cannot evade capture forever. When they do incarcerate you, your government will seize control of your sleeper assets." He smiled thinly at Titan. It took a moment for Titan to notice. "Join us. We will smuggle you out of the country. Together, our force will be unstoppable. No one can stand in our way. Government as we know it will become little more than regional bureaucracy. We will seize the global government we have never managed to achieve through power alone."

I snorted. "You're going to just make the American military up and disappear, then? Or do you need them to squash the worldwide riots that will surely follow?"

"Ah, yes, that. I am one of the few people on this planet who know exactly what you have stolen from the Liberty mainframe. All the tools for martial dominance lie waiting in that arsenal. And you, my friend, have taken the keys."

Of course. The military data I hadn't finished decrypting yet. "I get it now. You want to pull off a worldwide sleeper coup. But you can't do it by yourself. You need the weapons in that toy box to crush rebellion. An American face on the effort wouldn't hurt either. Getting our support solves both problems. Plus you save the cost and damage of fighting us."

He leaned forward. "Your Constitution provides a unique opportunity to implement such a takeover without undue publicity. United, we will be unstoppable. Divided, we will cancel each other out. We do not require your assistance. We would prefer to have it, of course, but an agreement not to interfere would suffice. If we are able to reach an understanding, I can assure you that Odin will put aside his differences with you. He will also lend his power to the cause."

"You expect me to work with him? After what he did to me? You're as insane as he is."

"Do not forget what you have done to him. Perhaps now the scales of justice can be considered even. Further violence will only perpetuate further violence."

"What makes you think I'd trust that monster?"

"He is a monster, yes, but he is a powerful, predictable monster. A monster that others justifiably fear. He is the most intelligent weapon ever built. And he has only grown more powerful over time. He has needs. He hides them well, but he does have them. They can be used to control him."

I stared at Khan thoughtfully. "And if I say no?"

He sat back, steepling his fingers in front of his face. "Then we will free him without you. And use him to destroy your power utterly and completely. But, as you say, there will be casualties. Casualties that we would prefer to avoid. Tell me, old friend. Do you know what Director Zane plans to do with your

Congress?"

That caught my attention. "Pardon me?"

"Did you miss that fragment of information in his speech? I understand. Perhaps you were otherwise occupied. He has taken your senators into protective custody. All the major leaders in a single building. Does it remind you of any past situations that might be educational?"

I stared at him, remembering Marconi's early days. Idly watching while Congress burned to death. "Do you have evidence he's going to murder them all, or are you just speculating?"

Khan inclined his head. "Mr. Zane is a man far more beholden to the past than you quite realize. The act may in fact already have occurred. Who do you suppose will take the blame? A rogue Chief Executive Officer with a curiously unlimited supply of portable n-square warheads, perhaps?"

I sat back, the full implication hitting me all at once. "How do you know all this?"

"Our mutual friend who would like to put aside your differences. I merely wish to point out, again, that you are greatly outmatched. You are a smart man. You are highly experienced in covert operations. But you are not a politician. You do not think like one. You think like an engineer. You believe the truth matters. The truth does not matter here. Not in this world. Not any more."

I balked at that. "The truth always matters. We just need

to learn how to face it."

"Consistent to the end. I can see that I still have not convinced you. That is regrettable."

Anna gave him a filthy look. "We've wasted enough time."

"No, not yet, my impatient friend. I still have one more question to ask. Why do you suppose Mr. Zane painted Ms. DiRevka as an innocent bystander in this matter?"

I thought back to his speech. He did go out of his way to portray Suzie as a hostage in a battle suit. "I hadn't thought about it."

"No. Of course you haven't. You've had more important matters to attend to. I respect that. You are doing the best you can. But there is never a good reason to build up a public persona in such a positive way when they are clearly your enemy. There are two reasons that come to mind. Would you like to hear them?"

"Not especially."

"The first reason is to discredit anything she might say as a coerced statement from an unwilling prisoner."

I knew where he was going with this, but I asked anyway. "And the second?"

"Of course you have figured it out by now. Mr. Zane is willing to obliterate the entirety of your Congress to clean up his loose ends. Ms. DiRevka is the loosest end of all. Every cause needs an innocent martyr. It speaks to the quality of your protection that he has not yet been able to dispose of her and pin the crime on you."

My protective instincts rose. "You think all this is going to make me sign a deal with you?"

"You are an intelligent man." Anna snorted next to him, glaring at a particularly flamboyant robot on the shelf. "By now you must recognize that you cannot succeed by yourself. Do not take this as a threat. However, if you do not join our cause, we will let your own government destroy you. We cannot allow them to capture you, of course. We will destroy you and your sleepers. That by itself should be enough to throw your economy into chaos. It will buy us time to build our own sleeper strength. Not joining us will not stop us. It will merely delay the inevitable."

"I see your point." I steepled my fingers in a mirror of his habit. "I'll need some time to consult with my coworkers, of course."

"You have twenty-four hours." He stood up. "Would you be so kind as to say hello to Dr. Chapman for me? I do miss my conversations with the good doctor."

Chapter 38

Titan walked around my desk. He stood before me with his arms clasped behind his back.

Winston Churchill caught my eye. "A lie gets halfway around the world before the truth has a chance to get its pants on."

I relaxed a bit. "Did you pick up anything interesting from the meeting?"

"I did. Mr. Zvyagin's suggestion regarding out of phase exotic matter appears to be key. It is my theory that Sleeper Odin has managed to send parts of his prison walls out of phase. However, they are not permanently out of phase. The particles fall into a probability cloud that he has learned to manipulate. This is how he is able to avoid detection. The solution is remarkably elegant."

"No one ever accused Odin of being stupid. Can you fix it?"

"Not at this time. However, it has provided a new avenue of design to create a more secure barrier. I intend to test my theories on your office before replacing the boundaries of Sleeper Odin's containment vessel. I require help from Ms. Janek. I will consult her next."

"Don't load Kara with too much stuff. She's probably already at her limits. What about Sleeper Ravana? Find anything in his datastream?"

"More than you might expect. The new sleepers are not yet fully developed. Sleeper Ravana had tactical capabilities and self-evolution plans lying in plain sight. Not only was I able to download the full design specs of their combat suits, I extracted vulnerability data and unprotected attack vectors as well."

That surprised me. "Are you kidding? You got a back door on them?"

"In a manner of speaking. They may close the vulnerabilities before we are able to exploit them. If Sleeper Odin has performed even a cursory inspection of their systems, he must realize the potential for a catastrophic security breach."

"I think he'll keep the problems to himself. They give him leverage."

"Perhaps. It seems likely that we shall find out soon enough. Dr. Shenouda, Ms. DiRevka, and Sleeper Isis have requested your presence in another simulation. It appears they have discovered something significant in the historical record."

"Wait, Kesi and Suzie found something new about the nuclear attacks?"

"I am unaware of the precise nature of the discovery. If you do not require my presence, I must begin my work with Ms. Janek."

I stood up, heading to the exit. "By all means. Say hi to Kara."

He winked out. I opened the office door, stepping into

Sleeper Isis' simulation. Kesi, Suzie, and Isis sat in a small semicircle around an ancient projector. The scene in front of them was frozen on an old view of the Oval Office. The date in the corner read November 21, 2045.

The day the BRIC coalition set off their nukes. The day of the n-square retaliation strikes. Brazil, Russia, India, and China. Their largest cities gone without a trace.

And I was looking at a recording of the president's office on that day.

I sat down next to Suzie. "Uh, hey guys. What'd I miss?"

Suzie looked pale. Kesi looked sick.

Even Isis looked pained. She was the first to speak. "We have created a short presentation that says it best. Would you like to see it?"

Kesi swallowed. "I'm not sure I can watch it again."

Isis smiled sadly at her. "Please, do not force yourself. I will call you when it is safe to return."

"Is it all right if I just take my leave? I'll be back for the operation tonight. I need to rest."

I nodded. "Of course. See you later."

"Thank you." She disappeared.

I glanced at Suzie. "It's that bad?"

She sighed, leaning back in her seat until she was nearly horizontal. "See for yourself."

Isis started the video. President Marconi came in from off-camera, followed by someone familiar. I recognized his mannerisms rather than directly recognizing his face.

They both sat behind his desk. His companion's identity deeply bothered me.

I got a piece of it. "Okay, I recognize the guy on Marconi's right from his picture on the last of the paper currency. That's Chester Shapiro, right? The Secretary of Defense?"

Isis nodded. "The same."

He looked so familiar. Was it because of the money? No, it was something about the way he was moving.

I didn't get it until I held up my finger to cover his mustache area.

"Crash on a motherboard." I leaned forward, watching him prepare for the meeting. "That's Esper Zane."

Isis inclined her head. "The same."

I sat back, mind reeling. "Vampire juice?"

Suzie flicked her hand, bringing up a recent image loop of Zane on his way to cosmetic surgery. He leered at the camera, smiling sickly. Red welts covered his neck around the arteries. His upper teeth were pointed, not as if they were sharpened, but as if they had dripped onto his lower lip like stalactites.

She let her hand drop onto my leg. "The same."

I looked back and forth between the images. "The guy was an old man back in forty-five. You're telling me he's still kicking it this hard forty years later?"

She shrugged. "All hail the Lazarus serum."

Isis dropped the cosmetic surgery image, activating the

sound on the video.

Marconi's rich voice was unmistakable. "Let's get this meeting over with."

Zane's was equally recognizable. "As you say, Mr. President."

Six ancient holographic displays sat in front of Marconi's desk. They worked by suspending a cylindrical cloud of metallic dust in the air. The images were projected into the reflective particles, creating a crude threedee view. It was high technology at the time, but looked incredibly fussy now. Tiny flecks of escaped metal were permanently embedded in the carpet below.

One by one, the projectors activated. A series of authoritative-looking heads appeared in the cylinders. A name and a place appeared above each. All six of them were admirals, but I barely noticed their names. Their locations stunned me.

Flagship *USS Victor Marconi*, Carrier Strike Group Fifteen, Pacific Theater.

Naval Station Great Lakes, Chicago, Illinois.

Puget Sound Naval Shipyard, Washington.

Naval Station Norfolk, Virginia.

Naval Base San Diego, California.

And the Naval Training Center, Orlando, Florida.

I didn't realize I'd been holding my breath. "Those are the targets the BRIC coalition hit with the nukes."

Isis winced. "In a manner of speaking."

"Has it happened yet?"

Suzie gestured. “Watch and see.”

Marconi cleared his throat. “Gentlemen. Ladies. I hope you have changed your minds regarding the disclosure we have discussed.”

Admiral Preston from the *Marconi* shook his head. “We have not. You can’t keep this secret any more. The public has the right to know.”

“You are my officers, and you had best not forget that.”

Zane leaned forward. “And if you won’t listen to the Commander in Chief, you can listen to me. I’m nowhere near as nice as he is.”

The admiral from Florida gave them both a shocked look. “This is madness. How can you possibly expect people not to find out about this? It’s been going on fifteen years. Frankly it’s astonishing no one has figured it out already.”

The one from Chicago gave her an appraising look. “How do we know they haven’t?”

Marconi silenced them with a glance. “I am not reopening the discussion. We will do what needs to be done. Are you staking your claim on mutiny?”

Admiral Preston spoke again. “We’re unanimous, sir. Either you tell them or we will.”

The look Marconi gave them was withering, even though the low-quality video. “Very well. I require one hour to finalize my statement. You understand the cost of your actions today?”

“We’ll do what needs to be done. You’ll have our

resignations after your presentation."

"See that I do. Dismissed."

The projectors went dark in quick succession. Marconi sat back in his chair, staring at the settling dust thoughtfully.

Zane looked alarmed by the expression on Marconi's face. "You're not thinking about giving in to these madmen, are you?"

Marconi's voice was dangerous. "Watch your tone, Secretary."

"All the assets are in place. You know what has to be done. With this cleansing fire, we can wipe out the final remnants of that cybernetic madness. Worldwide. Not only that, we'll send anyone we missed a message. Mess with us, and who knows what we could do?"

Marconi stood with a flourish, towering over Zane. "You forget your place. The decision is mine and mine alone."

Zane stiffened. "Of course, Mr. President."

Marconi stepped toward the window, staring out onto the White House lawn.

He thought for a long time. When he spoke, the words felt like they had physical weight.

"Very well. Proceed with the operation."

Zane grinned like a child receiving a candy bar. He seemed genuinely surprised. His face returned to normal when Marconi turned back in his direction.

He picked up the phone on the desk. "This is the Secretary of Defense. Execute Operation Glass Chapel."

Marconi settled back into his chair, bringing something up on his display. "Give me a live feed on the aircraft carrier. I want to see what we're going to show."

Zane looked over from the phone. "I need eyes on the *Marconi*. Understood." He hung up.

The familiar footage of *USS Victor Marconi* and her strike group appeared before the president, but this video clearly started before the missile attack. The flat top drone carrier was majestic at sea. Triangular autonomous fighter planes covered its deck. Close to twelve support ships clustered nearby, their wakes trailing behind them.

Marconi glanced up from his display. "This speech needs a lot of work. Show me the submarines."

The view switched briefly to a tactical overlay with the names and locations of all thirteen ships. Two autonomous submarines flanked the group on either side, about thirty kilometers ahead of the lead ship. Their labels identified them as *USS San Juan* and *USS Santa Rita*. Both were *Isla Culebra* class guided missile submarines.

I did some perspective work in my head, remembering the footage from when I was a kid. "The missiles. They came from their own submarines."

Suzie's voice was hoarse. "Yes."

Marconi looked back to his display. "Commence attack."

The water erupted ahead of the carrier group on either side. Thousands of micro-warheads burst from the surface, fanning out to surround the ships in a rough circle.

The camera closed in on the ships themselves. They pitched hard, taking evasive action. The water churned white in the turbulence of their maneuvers. This was where the public footage started.

Multiple radio calls ran over each other. "Vampire, vampire, vampire! Evasive action, fire countermeasures!"

Flares and chaff erupted from the ships. The water frothed behind them as they accelerated to flank speed. Lasers tracked across the warheads at their maximum effective distance, destroying some in a flare of heat. Interceptor missiles lit off from the destroyers in waves. The combat air patrol drones swept down, running their guns down lines of incoming weapons. Still more warheads exploded on their way in. More fighters scrambled from the aircraft carrier, lifting off in drunkenly haphazard patterns.

It became clear that the strike group had no chance to beat them all. Last ditch gatling guns, mini-cannons, and prototype plasma beams efficiently hunted the warheads as they closed on their targets. Their automatic algorithms began choosing only the most important targets as the numbers became overwhelming.

The explosions started. Ships burst into flames, throwing armor plating into the water. A destroyer crumpled in the middle under multiple impacts, the keel cracking with the detonation of its own ammunition.

Multiple missiles made it under the flight deck of the *Marconi.* The thick material exploded upward as if punched from below. Flames and debris blasted the supports out from under the deck, causing it to collapse to one side. Parked fighters strained against their moorings before snapping off, sliding into the water. The entire carrier listed, exposing its waterline to a fresh barrage of relentless warheads. A vicious hit from one last incoming missile bent the control tower under its own weight. It crashed into the sea, still on fire.

Within minutes it was over. The surveillance lingered over the destroyed battle group, which was now not much more than an oil-slicked debris field in the water. The public footage ended. The camera zoomed out to monitor the self-destructing submarines.

Marconi glanced up. "Good enough to pin on our foreign friends?"

Zane picked up his phone, speaking quickly. "Yes. All five nuclear warheads have detonated as well. We should have confirmation on the admiral hits within the hour. Naval bases are reporting heavy casualties." He listened a bit longer before hanging up. "You did the right thing, sir."

Marconi stood, turning to leave. "Warm up the n-squares. I have a speech to deliver."

Suzie froze the video when he looked at the camera. His expression was cold and dark. His grim determination reached through the barriers of time, hitting me with noticeable force.

There was no sign at all of the exhaustion I'd seen when we met decades later.

I stared at his face, shock still setting in. "We nuked ourselves."

"Yep." She shifted around, turning off the footage. "And blew up the rest of the world. All for some kind of unspecified cover-up."

"Wait a minute. We have footage of the president and his Secretary of Defense deciding to kill fifty million people, but we don't have a thing about why?"

Isis clasped her hands on her stomach. "What you see is all there is. Their reasoning could range from the banal to the grandiose. It was a different time. However, it is hard to escape the conclusion that someone left this particular footage in the database deliberately."

"You're telling me that this madman is currently running the Secret Service. He has the president's ear. He probably sent the oxfire to Reggie's house. And this wasn't the first time he set off a nuclear weapon to vaporize a mess. More than likely, he's got his finger on the trigger of every weapon of mass destruction we've ever manufactured."

Suzie laughed morbidly. "Don't forget Congress. He's got them all locked up in a room somewhere. We could be in for a mad bomber greatest hits album here."

I stood up, pacing. "Great. Just great."

Isis inclined her head. "What do you think we should do?"

I rubbed my temples. “Stick with the plan, I suppose. That monument isn’t going to raid itself.”

PART FIVE:

ENDGAME

Whenever you find that you are on the side of the majority, it is time to pause and reflect.

--Mark Twain

Chapter 39

Two hours later

Flapjack swerved the Cavallino wildly in the air. “You know, you're right. This thing does drive like sex.”

I sighed at length. “You're not even getting the full dose. The fusor sounds like it's getting suffocated by pillows. All those baffle flaps are getting in the way of the aero work.”

He dove between the trees, slaloming back and forth. Eventually he pointed the nose up and floored it. “Eh, doesn't quite have the grunt of the Stuttgart. But it's so responsive.” He weaved around again. “I mean, look at that.”

“It looked so much better in red. The black nanofabric looks like a pair of cheap stockings. My poor car is all tarted up.”

“Restretch the car in lipstick red when we’re done.” He held the nose up until we reached peak altitude. After a moment of weightlessness, he pointed the car down again. We spiraled toward the ground. He pulled up at the last possible instant, roaring over an unsuspecting soybeet field. “Get a load of this thing. It’s unreal.”

“Aren’t we on a schedule here?”

“We've got time, but I'll content myself with testing the top speed instead.” He set the fusor to wide-open throttle. To my ears, it sounded strangled. “That sounds amazing.”

“I hate the world.”

"Buy a second car for missions if it bothers you that much."

I displayed the monument internals on the holo projector between the seats. "So we're going to buzz in here before nine. Sneak in during the fireworks. Drop Kara's captors. Find someplace to let Suzie and Kesi pick up the family in her van. Then we slide out with the rest of the riffraff."

"More or less, yeah. Did Kara give you any security updates?"

"I guess Uncle Zane tried to take the tour with them, but Daniel wouldn't stop crying. Dorothy kept calling him the devil. Now they're covered by four plainclothes guards and about six wanderers."

"Heh. The devil. Kid's a spitfire. Like her mother."

I shook my head. "She's a handful, yeah."

Flapjack slowed down. "Coming up on DC airspace. Raj, Liz, you ready?"

The two of them appeared separately in the center holo. Both wore full combat gear.

Raj's holographic smile beamed from the mouthpiece on his tech ninja outfit. "Cheers, mates. Looks like I'm getting there first. Where do you want to meet?"

I looked up the relevant section on the monument blueprints. "There's a freight entrance in the back. It looks like there's a delivery starting right about when we get there. Creep in on a truck and meet up in the dumpster area. They just took out the trash, so it should be deserted."

Liz nodded from her cockpit. "Sounds good to me."

"Have you made progress with decrypting the senator data?"

She glanced away briefly, steering around something. "Yes. I have the structure down. It'll take me a while to break the final layer. If I had some senator names to start with, I could use a known data attack to get the rest at this point."

Flapjack grunted. "We've got one. Tex McIntyre."

"Assuming that's how he's listed, yes. Knowing he's from Delaware helps too. But it hasn't gotten me enough to break the other entries yet."

I shifted the monument view, working a path up to the observation deck. Kara and her family would watch the fireworks from there. "Keep at it. Once we know who they are, we need to know where they are."

"Understood. See you in the statue."

Raj tipped his headgear at us. "Good hunting, mates."

"Same to you." I cut the connection.

Flapjack merged into traffic, slipping under an automated freighter. "Here we go."

I concentrated hard, digging deep into the traffic control systems. I turned off all our transponders, sending a sensor ghost off toward the Marconi International Spaceport. We followed the old Interstate 395 past the towering Pentascraper Defense Headquarters on the left, crossing over the Potomac toward East Potomac Park.

Flapjack glanced over. “We clear?”

“Go for it.”

He broke off, cradling the ground on Ohio Drive. Marconi's three hundred meter statue of himself glinted happily in the center of the park under the warm red, white, and blue glow of coherent-band spotlights.

The statue itself was made of platanium, a unique iridescent mix of platinum and titanium that required constant polishing to maintain its unmistakable shine. Marconi posed nobly, chin jutting. He had one foot raised on a polished black marble boulder, daring the world to defy him. He held an enormous flagpole in one hand. A screaming eagle perched on his other arm. His fashionably stylized tricorn hat doubled as patriotic headgear and the observation deck. People milled around behind its panoramic windows, waiting for the fireworks to start.

The most arresting part of the monument, however, was the hundred meter long microfilm flag. It took a team of scientists five years just to develop the technology to make it. Made of miniature rubies, diamonds, and sapphires, it flexed and waved beautifully in the night. It glittered under the spotlights like a piece of jewelry the size of a kiloball field, lighting the countryside for kilometers.

Flapjack put the fusor in quiet mode. We glided through the shadows toward the gaudy spectacle. “Time?”

I mentally checked. "Eight-forty local. Twenty minutes to the fireworks."

He gestured. "That truck look okay?"

I looked. A delivery truck made its way up the hill to the security walls around the monument. I smiled when I saw a tiny blue Janeiro roadster hovering underneath.

"Good enough for Liz. Try not to crash into her."

"Don't wad up the getaway cars. Right."

He slipped under the truck. We crept toward the rear entrance. I found myself disappointed that the dumpster area wasn't inside the statue's butt. The guard stations weren't particular about inspecting the passing trucks. After a quick glance at the transponders, they gestured them through. They didn't even scan the cargo to make sure it matched the manifests. Oddly sloppy.

Our truck approached the gate. Flapjack held the wheel tightly, ready to bolt. "We good?"

"Think so."

The guards waved our cargo carrier past impatiently. It rumbled off toward the kitchen deliveries. Liz broke off first, heading to the trash center. Flapjack followed after a moment.

We jumped out of the cars, landing in a cylindrical supercrete holding area. Despite the cleaning efforts, a faintly sweet smell of rotten food filled the air. The ground itself felt greasy.

The Cavallino and the Janeiro clumped together on

autopilot, heading off to wait for an empty truck to leave the gate. Liz smiled at us from her huntress suit.

"Evening, gentlemen."

I stretched out from the long car ride. "Howdy."

Raj materialized from of his usual cloud of smoke. "Did you guys tour the entire city? Feels like I've been here all night."

Flapjack didn't look up from checking his pistols. "Poor thing."

An enthusiastic voice boomed over the intercom system. "Ladies and gentlemen, boys and girls. In just fifteen minutes, the nightly Fire of the Patriots fireworks extravaganza will begin. You won't want to miss this extraordinary demonstration of American technology and innovation, set to your favorite classical hymns. Grab a copy of the lyric sheet and sing along. See you on the observation deck for a spectacle you'll never forget!"

Liz raised her plasma bow, holding the vertical anchor bar in her left hand and pulling back the horizontal charge bar in her right. A sizzling green sensor energy beam formed between them. She sighted down her left hand, swinging it around to look for targets. Targeting scanners appeared on her visor. The quiver on her back glowed fiercely, building up energy.

She let go, collapsing the sensor beam. Heat streamed upward from the quiver, rising in a swirling funnel. "Looks clear to me."

Flapjack chambered a capacitor round. "Let's get moving.

Raj, take point."

Raj grinned brightly. "Right you are, love." He vanished in smoke again.

I concentrated hard to get a look inside the statue through my boosters. The platanium skin weakened the signal. We made our way forward, disappearing into the shadows around the trash chutes. My view cleared up once we passed under the surface into the internals.

The monument was eighty-five stories tall with two additional basement floors. Not surprisingly, most of the people congregated in the observation deck on the eighty-fifth floor. The five stories below the observation deck held a variety of historical exhibits and relics. An additional five floors of interactive exhibits, food, and gift shops rested at the base of the monument. A set of four bullet elevators shot people through the seventy stories of infrastructure in between.

I noticed something odd about the lowest basement. "Liz, does that look like an armed patrol on the bottom floor to you?"

She turned her green scanner eyes downward. She frowned, pointing her sensor beam at the floor. She swept it back and forth before releasing it.

"Yeah. It's hard to read. I see a bunch of organic tissue down there. It looks like a meat locker. The thick metal walls are interfering with the signal. But I count four guards. Two gypsies, a centaur, and one very bored commando."

I grunted. "That seem like overkill to you?"

Flapjack turned back toward us. “Maybe they just bought some expensive slabbersteaks. Let’s go. We’ve got a job to do.”

He headed off after Raj. Liz and I followed after a pause.

I glanced at her. “I don't like it. That's a lot of hardware to guard a pantry.”

“I don't like it either. The computer says there's a big party next week, though.”

“Still seems strange that they'd dedicate that much firepower to the problem.”

Flapjack sounded irritated. “Any chance you people with the big eyes could look up? That is where we're going, after all.”

We reached the base of the staircase that would take us past the lower five floors to the bullet elevators. I concentrated, peering as far as I could into the superstructure.

“I count two centaurs per floor in the exhibit areas. There are some docents hanging around. They don't look like soldiers. Believe it or not, there are some fireflies flying through the superstructure above. It looks like they’re watching the elevators.”

Raj appeared from a shadow. “They are. I don't think we can take the bullets up. We're going to have to climb through the structure and blind the fireflies as we go.”

Liz gave him a curious look. “Why?”

“We can hide ourselves from them inside the elevators, but we can't hide the fact that an elevator went up. There aren't any guests downstairs any more, just the docents. All four elevators are at the top right now. We'd have to call one down, get on it, and run back up again. All without calling attention to the fact that they're either running empty or carrying unregistered guests."

Flapjack put his pistols away. "We have enough time to go monkey-climbing up the inside?"

Raj laughed. "Well it's a bit of a bother, I'll grant you that, but I don't know how else to do it. Unless you want to scale the outside?"

The voice boomed over the loudspeakers again, filled with pent-up energy. "Ladies and gentlemen. boys and girls. In just ten minutes, the Fire of the Patriots fireworks display will begin. You won't want to miss this flaming celebration of our independence, freedom, and democracy. Sing along to your favorite hymns, such as 'We Live For Marconi And America.' Just ten minutes until the fun begins. Come see the show that you'll remember for a lifetime."

Flapjack glanced at the speaker with a sour expression. "Don't think we can make it up that glitter outside unless we shut down all the lights. Guess we're hoofing it up the middle."

Raj took the lead up the staircase. It reminded me of the night we broke into the Liberty mainframe. The supercrete stairwell was more or less indistinguishable from the one we'd used that night. I guess there are only so many ways to build a utility staircase.

At each floor, Raj flicked his finger at the centaur standing outside the stairwell. The bots invariably huffed, looking around to see who had dared to tweak them. Raj easily concealed us from their camera racks. We continued on our way. It was almost comical how identical their responses were.

At the fifth floor, Raj made a grabbing motion, squeezing the air. The centaur yelped, collapsing in a tangled heap.

Liz scanned the area with her sensor beam. “Looks clear. Is it just me, or does it look like the security garrison is headquartered in Marconi’s crotch?”

Chapter 40

I studied the exact position of the security office. “They’re definitely between his legs, yeah. But if it’s to scale, our dictator-in-chief had a tiny dictator.”

Flapjack gave us an annoyed look. “If you two are finished, perhaps we can move on to finding Director Zane.”

Liz sent us a map of the security presence. “He's not in the security center. I can't see all the way up to the observation deck. I asked Kara for a repeater feed but she thinks it would blow her cover. Before you ask, no, she doesn't know where he went either.”

That voice boomed again, louder in the museum area. “Ladies and gentlemen, boys and girls. Just five more minutes until the once in a lifetime experience of the Fire of the Patriots pyrotechnics extravaganza. Relive America's greatest battles for freedom and security around the globe with these specially crafted explosives. Sing along with your favorite tunes, such as ‘I Thank America For Every Single Day.’ Hurry upstairs or you'll miss out on the best views in the house. Time to get excited!”

Raj rubbed his ear. “Everyone's upstairs already. Do they have to keep selling it?”

Liz shrugged. “It's part of the experience. Builds anticipation. Or something.”

I sent four different paths up the scaffolding inside the statue. *"We should switch to flashing. The access shaft to the superstructure is over here. These paths each have different strengths and weaknesses. Do we split up or stick together?"*

Flapjack narrowed it down to two. *"Nathan and I will take this one. You two take this one. We'll come out on opposite sides of the floor. We can analyze the security from there."*

I sent a shrug. *"Looks good to me."*

Raj disappeared down the corridor. *"Watch the fireflies."*

We headed after him, arriving at a door. A sign required hard hats beyond this point. Raj waved his hand. It clinked open, leading to another staircase. We silently climbed up, emerging on a platform over the fifth floor.

The view inside was breathtaking. The four rail guns that powered the bullet elevators pointed straight up from the center. They disappeared into the barely visible floor seventy stories above. The rails themselves were grown from a phosphorescent composite ceramic lattice. Luminum strips marked the stabilizing cross supports. The protective passenger grav field shimmered, distorting the light. The generators hummed faintly behind insufficient shielding, vibrating in a way that made my teeth hurt.

The superstructure itself resembled two complex strands of DNA intertwined with each other. The cobalt tungsten material reflected a faint hexagonal mesh. Carbon picotube anchors bound the monument's surface to the substructure, nearly invisible in the dim light. A thick support beam connected the statue's shoulders, reaching from elbow to elbow. In a clever bit of engineering, Marconi's arm held the flag at the same angle as the arm holding the eagle. This allowed the solid beam to efficiently reach straight through the structure.

The inner surface remained unpolished. The platanium had reverted to its natural finish, a spotty dark gray haze with occasional colored oxidation stains. Firefly nemp drones floated throughout the superstructure, intermittently illuminating the component pieces. The bots resembled their namesake, looking like hovering insects with enormous sagging tails. They searched for unexpected organic material with the fluorescent yellow sensors housed in their bulbous behinds. They circled in intricate chaos, looking at once both random and organized.

The whole thing was mesmerizing. Raj snapped me out of it.

"Do you suppose they put the fireflies in here because they look pretty?"

Liz flashed amusement. *"They are quite impressive."*

Flapjack pulled out his gravling hook. *"We've got a long climb ahead of us. Don't let the things knock you off the ropes."*

Raj and Liz disappeared in a black cloud, heading away. Flapjack fired his gravling hook at an overhead beam. It beeped, marking its attachment point with a soft green glow. He braced his arms, pulling the second trigger. The grav field lifted him up through the darkness. He landed nimbly on the cross support.

I concentrated hard, sending power into my boosters. I reached out with my mind, grabbing the beam above him. I surged off the ground in an explosive leap, rushing through the air. I hung briefly above the support before settling onto it with a quiet thump.

Flapjack scanned the area for fireflies. He fired his gun again once he was satisfied that we hadn't attracted any attention. He disappeared up to the level above me.

We leapfrogged each other up the statue, taking turns looking for the flying sentinels. Our boosters glowed orange and green in the darkness. The fireflies didn't deviate from their existing search patterns.

Both of us landed on the cross-support that went between Marconi's shoulders. We took a moment to bleed heat. I glanced up toward the flag arm. I nudged Flapjack, pointing. The red, white, and blue optics reflected hazily on the inside of the unpolished arm. The light twinkled brilliantly in the otherwise dark tube. Flapjack gave me an impressed look.

The announcer boomed distantly again. "Ladies and gentlemen, boys and girls. Grab your hotcorn and bratzels, because it's time for the most patriotic experience you have ever seen. Please turn and salute our amazing ruby, diamond, and sapphire flag for our opening hymn, 'Nothing Is More Important Than The Flag.' Don't forget to grab some cool refreshment. You won't want to miss this!"

The bombastic opening bars of our celebrated flag hymn

exploded above. The volume surprised me, echoing throughout the structure. The fireflies intensified their search, looking agitated. We had a tense moment waiting for one to bumble past without seeing us. I had my staff ready, waiting to throw a slobber bomb. Flapjack held an emp pistol steady on the target. In the best case, we could disable its transmitter and glue it to the supports. That way it couldn't signal our presence but wouldn't be noteworthy for its absence either.

The lifter fields on its sides vibrated like an insect's wings. It turned its glowing tail this way and that. The light reflected off its featherweave chassis. The glassy compound eyes were slightly wall-eyed, giving it a dopey expression.

Eventually it winced at a particularly loud explosive note outside. It disappeared further down the statue, looking relieved to escape the noise.

Flapjack fired his gravling hook again, disappearing into the darkness. I concentrated on the beam above him, leaping upward. The access hatch was only a dozen meters away now, nestled just underneath Marconi's massive shoulder. We were almost in the clear.

I accidentally looked down, grabbing the support in a moment of unexpected vertigo. I felt wildly out of control. Odin’s hate-filled eye flashed in my mind. Panic blew away conscious thought. I closed my eyes, controlling my breathing. I had to pause for a couple seconds.

Flapjack jumped to the next beam before I’d recovered

enough to scan it. *"Crash it."*

A firefly drone chirped inquisitively at him from its recharging spot on the support. It looked just as surprised as he was.

I jumped back to attention, but I didn't have a clear shot for a slobber bomb.

Flapjack aimed his emp pistol, firing twice. The surgical hits blinded and silenced the surveillance drone. It squawked in protest, wobbling before it fell off the beam.

I let the suit take over my reactions. With a massive booster burn, I blasted off the support, catching the drone as it fell. I reached out with my mind, grabbing the structure wall. We slammed into it together. I carefully held the fragile bot so it wouldn't get crushed.

The platanium made a sound like a distant gong when we hit. Thankfully, it was timed with a large detonation at the finale of 'Nothing Is More Important Than The Flag.'

I held on for dear life, pinning the firefly to the wall with a slobber bomb. Flapjack and I watched, waiting to see if we'd been caught. The fireworks outside erupted with the sound of a dozen machine guns. We faintly heard impressed gasps from the mesmerized crowd.

We slumped with relief. The announcer boomed again. "Wasn't that exciting? I'm sure you're just as amazed as we are. And it just gets better from here! Please turn your lyric books to our next exciting hymn, 'No One Can Argue With A Patriot.'"

Fresh explosions punctuated the somber notes of the new song. The eagle on Marconi's arm shrieked. Flapjack pointed to the access hatch, now only a couple of meters overhead. A walkway with thick railings led from the opening up into the flag-holding arm. It looked like we'd come out just across from our fearless leader's magnificent armpit.

Flapjack neatly flipped over the railing, landing on the catwalk. He scanned for fireflies while I jumped after him. I opened the access hatch overhead. I pushed my staff into the hole, scanning the room. At least I'd learned something from sticking my head into that poltergeist.

The room was empty. Of people, anyway. It was filled with what looked like two meter long fuzzy spiders. I counted a couple dozen of them. It took me a moment to realize that the fuzz consisted of polishing mops. Massive vats of an abrasive compound sat between the cleaning robots. They prepared to go to work. I dipped briefly into the local debugging stream. Apparently they started polishing around midnight, coming out of the armpit and crawling all over the statue.

It made me itchy just thinking about it. But they were no danger, so we climbed up.

I gestured to Flapjack. *"Maybe we pull the van up to the cleaning hatch in the armpit? Let Doug and the kids get out while everyone's waiting for the bullet elevators."*

Flapjack considered it. *"Might not be the best idea to send a four year old through a room full of giant spiders. Plus the flag lights up that sucker pretty good. Ask Raj if there's a similar room on the other side."*

I gave him a look, momentarily wondering why he couldn't do it. *"Raj. We've got a structural access hatch on the armpit over here. Is there one on that side?"*

Raj flashed back mock horror. *"With the bloody spiders, am I right? Yeah, we got one over here. You thinking about sending the family out through one?"*

I sent a shrug. *"It's as good a place as any for the van. As long as Dorothy doesn't get freaked out by the spiders."*

"We'll figure something out. You want me to coordinate with Kesi?"

"Yeah, if you don't mind. Why don't you hang out in the bug closet and keep an eye on things? That way if we need backup you can sneak in."

Raj sent an image of himself pinned to the floor by a cleaning spider, screaming for help. *"No problem. Liz has an updated security map."*

"Great. Don't get caught."

"Sound advice."

I sent him a giant smooch, turning my attention back to Flapjack. *"All right, Raj is going to cover the exit on that side. Liz has a tactical map for us."*

Flapjack nodded. *"Bring it."*

Liz flashed us an image of a cramped eating area. Dozens of restaurants were decked out in red, white, and blue. Most had patriotic puns in their names. My favorite was Benjamin Frankfurters. *"You guys want anything from the food court?"*

I sent her a yummy feeling. *"I could go for a cone dog."*

Flapjack's anger surprised me. *"Am I the only one taking this mission seriously?"*

Liz sent a soothing gesture. *"Calm down, I'm just buying something for the kid."*

The fireworks came to another crescendo outside. It sounded louder up here, but the acoustics were better. Based on the crowd's reaction, the display was the most exciting yet. They gabbled excitedly when it finished.

The announcer imparted his enthusiasm once more. "Wasn't that amazing, folks? We have two more performances I'm sure you won't want to miss. Please turn to 'I Thank America For Every Single Day,' and follow along with our next freedom-filled extravaganza!"

I grunted mentally at Flapjack. *"Must he keep using the word extravaganza?"*

"I'll leave them a thesaurus if we manage to escape."

Liz flashed us an image of a pair of cone dogs in her hands. Her disguise was impenetrable. *"Nathan, you can share one with Dorothy, maybe it'll distract her from the spiders and the gunfire and what not. Okay, here's the updated security disposition."*

She sent us a readout of the top five floors. Clusters of security personnel resided in the statue's eyeballs. The guards watched the fireworks, feet propped up on their desks. Centaurs patrolled the exhibits on every floor. Almost a hundred people filled the observation deck in the hat, all eating, drinking, and pointing at the show outside. Docents and guards lingered near a couple displays on the floors below, smoking nicosticks.

Liz called our attention to another security station in Marconi's mouth. *"Here's the problem."*

A conference table dominated the center of the room, resembling an enormous tongue. Monitors covered the back sides of the teeth. The people inside paid no attention to the show.

Instead, Esper Zane and about a dozen Secret Service guards intently waited for our arrival.

Chapter 41

Liz highlighted Kara and her family in the crowd. They enjoyed the best seats in the house, front row center. She also sent the location of the four plainclothes bodyguards, one at each corner of the observation deck.

"Conveniently, they're supposed to sit and wait for the elevator to clear after the show. Inconveniently, there's only one elevator connecting the observation deck to the bullet elevators. I need both of you up here before the show lets out. But I can't disguise all three of us in the crowd."

I scanned the food court. *"Flapjack and I can find somewhere to hide. Are you going to slip in before the end of the show?"*

"Hopefully. I'll be okay if I hang out near the exit. Once the crowd dissipates, I'll approach them with the cone dogs. When the undercover guys move to intercept me, you two can sweep in from behind and take them out."

Flapjack sent his approval. *"Seems like as good a plan as we're going to get. How long do we have after we nemp the guards before Zane and friends come find us?"*

"It'll take them some time to make it past the surging crowds. Problem is, there's only one way up. They can't get to us, but we can't get out either."

I flared my boosters, concentrating hard on the diamond sheet windows on the top deck. I vaguely saw the fireworks exploding in the background. It looked like three-quarters of the sky was on fire. Sparks raced back and forth between the fireballs, perfectly timed to the music. I made a note to myself to check out the show sometime.

I patched in Raj. *"Here's a crazy idea. I can set my staff to vibrate at the shatter point of those diamond sheet windows. Looks like they're made up of ten micrometer sheets with rotating oscillation sites. What if I break the window, then we send a spider up the side to get the family?"*

Flapjack guffawed. *"You're right. That is a crazy idea."*

Raj sent back curiosity. *"Well hang on, let's not be hasty. Why bother with the spider at all? We'll have ten gremlins on the spider as soon as it goes out the armpit. The van has all kinds of field protection. Why not pull it up to the window, toss them inside, and make a run for it?"*

Flapjack bristled. *"Liz, can you really hide the getaway car after a stunt like that?"*

She sent a shrug. *"Kesi and I could pull it off, sure. It might actually be easier than what we had planned. It's just so unexpected. We can pull away in the confusion. Kesi's managed to get the van into the guest lot without being detected. I bet she can race right up the side of the statue. It'll be over so fast they won't know what happened. Then we disappear downtown pretending to be a garbage truck."*

"Gonna make us look pretty guilty on the news."

Raj laughed. *"It'll look less guilty than getting frogmarched out the front door in handcuffs. Why don't I take a moment to see if I can sabotage the creepy mouth room? Maybe we can knock them out and save ourselves some trouble. Then everyone gets out in the van."*

Liz flashed some quick calculations. *"The car can handle the load, but it'll be a lot more nimble if the three of you aren't in it. I was hoping you'd cause a fuss on the way down the elevator shafts to add to the distraction."*

Flapjack checked his gadget pack. *"I've got four decoy mirrors with me. We can make it look like we're taking the family with us."*

I sent a quick recap of the plan. *"We don't have much time. Let's move."*

They sent a murmur of agreement in return. I opened the hallway door, poking my staff around the corner. The exhibits on this floor depicted the early days before Marconi was elected. The interactive holograms combined with state of the art robotics painted a darkly exaggerated picture of life at the time. Even at peak unemployment, thousands of people weren't dying of heatstroke waiting in line for a chance at menial labor. Historical evidence indicated they spent most of their time online.

We stalked down the hallway, passing detailed models of the environmental impacts on the planet. The exhibits displayed the effects of droughts, plagues, and food shortages. An animated ocean map showed the slow death of edible marine life from overfishing and toxicity. A rotating globe next to it followed the acidic algal blooms as they strangled the phytoplankton a patch at a time. The melting ice caps released clouds of methane into the atmosphere. The change in polar temperature collapsed the jet stream. Previously dormant volcanoes erupted without the weight of the ice to contain them.

The displays accurately represented what happened, but failed to explain why it happened so quickly. Tipping points and runaway reactions featured highly in the descriptions, but the geological changes should have taken decades, if not a century. Relatively speaking, it was like the planet tried to give us a quick death.

Further on, creepy lifelike holoquins of Marconi and his opponents debated strategy. They argued in aphorisms far too clever to be true. Intricate subtleties of complex arguments were reduced to simple truisms. According to the exhibits, Marconi's reasonable voice was unique both domestically and globally. The positions his adversaries espoused ranged from merely ignorant to actively delusional.

The final scene at the end of the hall depicted the infamous final presidential debate before Marconi was elected. The sitting president's statement encouraging people in drought zones to purchase bottled water needed no exaggeration. They added some anyway to make the suggestion sound even more outrageous than it was. In reality, it took a couple weeks for the public to work up a good head of steam about it. Nobody had watched the debates thanks to some kind of celebrity scandal dominating the news.

We reached the staircase door. Flapjack gestured with his drawn pistol. *"Notice anything peculiar? Where's the centaur?"*

I concentrated, scanning the floors again. *"You're right. We're missing one. No, wait. It's in the bug room with Raj. The transponder's gone all wacky."*

The hacked centaur scuttled out the door at the other end of the hall, shaking its head drunkenly. It sent a full-strength sensor pulse down the corridor, trying to get its bearings.

Flapjack and I barely made it to the floor in time, covering ourselves with our shrouding cloaks. It looked back and forth, making some confused burbles.

Then it turned, picking its insectile way down the hall toward us.

I carefully poked the stairway door open with my staff. I slithered inside, followed by Flapjack. He eased the door closed behind us.

The centaur returned to its patrol as if nothing strange had happened.

Raj flashed regret. *"Sorry about that, mates. I don't know how it sneaked up on me like that."*

I stood up, feeling relieved. *"No worries."*

We reached the top floor without incident. The stairway

door opened on the back side of the food court. A quick scan revealed no one tending the stations, just a set of bored autowaiters in minimum power mode. The transparent elevator gleamed in the center of the room. Every store was decked out in red, white, and blue. The ceiling formed a high dome that followed the curve of Marconi's tricorn hat.

The far wall blended with the observation deck so that you could see the fireworks while you were in line. The music reached the pulse-pounding crescendo of 'I Thank America For Every Single Day.' Red, white, and blue thunderheads filled the sky. Orange and green explosions detonated inside the clouds, glowing brilliantly. Prismatic lightning shot between the blasts, wrapping around the clouds in multicolored branches.

With a final chord, the clouds vaporized from the bottom up in a crackling burn. They disappeared in the span of a second.

The audience erupted in applause.

Flapjack poked me with his gun. He gestured toward the nearby Justice Juice. He'd already knocked out the autowaiter so we could hide inside.

We jumped over the counter, shrouding ourselves. I poked my staff around the corner, getting a good look at the deck. Liz stood in the space between the food court and the last row of chairs, leaning against the wall with a pair of cone dogs. Her disguise completely covered her grav suit.

The booming announcer made me flinch. "What a

spectacular effect! It's time for our final show of the evening. Prepare yourself for a patriotic extravaganza like you've never imagined. Take a moment to get ready. Take a moment to get set. This is the song you've been waiting for. Turn your hymn books to the last page, and let's all sing along with 'We Live For Marconi And America!'"

Everyone fiddled with their lyric sheets. The virtual hymn books made fake paper rustling noises. Some people helped their neighbors find the place.

I glanced at Flapjack. I thought his eyes were going to roll all the way out of his head. The opening horns of 'We Live For Marconi And America' washed over us. Each note was punctuated by a tiny explosion, blinding in the darkness. When the lyrics started, I was stunned to hear most of the crowd singing along.

I concentrated, looking through my boosters at Kara and her family. She looked upset, her lips pressed tight. She glared at the lyric book. Dorothy ignored the music, amazed by the fireworks themselves. Doug bounced the baby on his lap, singing along with the crowd.

Watching them sing was morbidly fascinating. Not because the singing was a terrible off-rhythm set of tuneless mumbling, which it was, but because they were singing along at all. This song reverentially lifted Marconi to an almost mythical status. It painted him as a benevolent god taking care of us all, in the company of his version of our founding fathers.

Raj interrupted my thoughts. *"Heads up, chaps, that Secret Service group from the security mouth is heading to the elevators. You want me to drop them?"*

Flapjack looked at me, alarmed. *"Not unless you can hide all the bodies without getting noticed by the robots. How long till they get here?"*

"Thirty seconds, give or take."

I did some quick math in my head, reaching out to the elevator. I dropped a quick code segment on the controls, sending it up all five floors one story at a time, then back down one story at a time. After Zane got on board, they'd be stopping on every floor again on the way back up. *"How about now?"*

Flapjack took a quick look at my code. *"What are you, twelve?"*

Raj flashed amusement. *"Three minutes and forty-five seconds. Unless they take the stairs."*

I scanned Zane's body and immediately wished I hadn't. *"Ugh. Not with those knees."*

Flapjack turned his attention to the balcony. *"Liz, we've got company coming. How long till the end of the show?"*

She shifted on her feet. *"Three minutes if they follow yesterday's program. Cutting it close."*

Below, one of the guards pressed the button to call the elevator. Confused, he hit it again several times.

"Raj, do you think they know we're here?"

He responded with a grim chuckle. *"Doubtful. Right now*

Zane is saying he can't wait to get back to the hotel and put that devilish little girl to sleep. It's not clear if he's talking about euthanasia."

Flapjack peeked over the counter. *"There some reason we ain't talking straight to Kara?"*

Liz sent him a quick image of one of the undercover officers. *"She thinks the bodyguards will notice. They're paying close attention to her. I tried to send her messages on her lyric book, but she's not reading it."*

Flapjack sat down, muttering curses.

The fireworks outside boomed and flashed, looking more like an artfully arranged series of n-square detonations than anything else. The elevator arrived at our floor with a quiet bong. The doors opened, patiently waiting for passengers. Disappointed, they eventually closed again. The car headed back down with another quiet bong.

Flapjack shook his head at it. *"I am going to kick you in the balls if that works."*

Raj laughed. *"Better wind up, then. They're still making small talk waiting for the elevator to arrive."*

I jumped when a series of red, white, and blue rockets circled the statue. Their exhaust notes harmonized with the music, racing around the head in a symphony of sound. A series of explosions punctuated a lyric about the justice of defense, making the windows shake. The strobe effect blinded the crowd.

Waterfalls of red, white, and blue sparks fell from the sky, raining down in a glorious thunderstorm. I had trouble seeing through the glare.

A gruff man bumped into Liz on his way to the food court. In the blinding light, he seemed to appear out of nowhere. I realized with mounting horror that it was one of the undercover bodyguards.

"Oh. Excuse me, miss. My, those cone dogs look delicious."

Liz recovered quickly. "I'm sure they are, thank you! I'm just waiting for a chance to take my seat. These fireworks sure are incredible, aren't they?"

"Oh yes, they most certainly are."

I tensed, recognizing his cop voice. Liz caught it too.

"The thing is, I don't see any available seats. Where exactly did you come from?"

Chapter 42

Liz responded in her best ditzy voice. “Are you sure? I can't see a thing in here.”

Flapjack tensed, raising his pistol. I put my hand on his shoulder to stop him.

The cop tapped his temple. “It’s funny. I can't seem to run your ID. You wouldn't know anything about that, would you?”

“Oh! Of course, officer. I didn't recognize you without a uniform. I have a restraining order against my husband. I can never remember how to set up the filter. Can you hold on to these cone dogs for a second?”

She handed them to the surprised agent. He took them without thinking. Liz loaded a nemp pulse in her hand. She grabbed him by the neck with it, hauling him into the food court. He grunted, dropping the cone dogs. He spasmed once or twice before going limp. Liz shut down the autowaiter in The Bill of Nachos stand, tossing the agent inside like unwanted garbage.

She flashed us in a deadly serious voice. *“Did they spot me?”*

I scanned the crowd. The final verse of the song held everyone’s attention. Sparkle curtains danced like streaming ribbons, floating airily in front of the windows. The red, white, and blue patterns formed an especially complex flag.

"The other three agents are still watching the show. I think you caught him on the way to the bathroom."

She glanced over the counter, throwing the dropped cone dogs on him. *"Yeah, he's made quite a mess of himself. Should I try to knock out another one?"*

I watched the agents carefully. *"You think you can get behind the guy in the upper corner? I doubt you can take him out before the end of the show, but it can't hurt to get a head start on his position."*

"Right." Liz's disguise vanished, revealing her huntress grav suit. She slipped into the shadows near the door, crouching behind the last row of seats.

A series of explosive microbursts formed a high-density shimmering threedee of Marconi's noble face outside. The recorded singers belted out their enthusiastic praise for his effortless grace. Most of the audience continued to mumble along.

Dorothy nudged her mother, pointing at the rotating headshot. Whatever she said, Kara snorted, hugging her with laughter.

The last bars of the song erupted from the speakers. They consisted of nothing but shouting Marconi and America one after the other. Each time, the words exploded around his head, in case you couldn't hear them. Eventually the fireworks burst into red, white, and blue static, burning colorfully with the last line of the song.

"I live and die for Marconi and America!"

The theater erupted into applause. Several people gave a standing ovation, including Doug. He clapped awkwardly, still holding the baby. Dorothy hugged her mother, hiding her head against her side. Kara glared at her husband, stroking Dorothy reassuringly.

The elevator bonged again. The doors opened, revealing Director Zane and his four agents. The guards stepped out first, followed by a cautious Zane. People flooded out of the observation area, surrounding the officers. Everyone wanted to be the first to the elevator so they didn't have to wait in line.

Liz reactivated her disguise, popping up behind the undercover agent in the back corner of the observation area. "Hey, handsome! I've been waiting for you!"

She kissed him with her mask, sending a nemp pulse directly into his brain. He stiffened, going limp in her arms. The people around her chuckled, pointedly ignoring the public display of affection. She dropped him back in his chair, hurrying down to the matching agent in the front row. The officer put her hand on her pistol, trying to get a clear look at what just happened.

I quietly tapped my staff onto the floor, sending out an emp scrambler. Zane's escorts immediately crouched, actively looking for us. The director grimaced contemptuously. The surging mass of people had no idea anything was wrong. The agents debated whether to make a scene. In this confined space, crowd response could range from mere panic to an all-out stampede.

Flapjack looked at me. *"Go?"*

"Not yet. Kara, you're up."

Liz made it to the suspicious agent in the front row. She'd looked up the woman's name on the way. "Agent Becker? Lucy Becker? The director sent me."

Lucy hesitated for just a moment, but it was enough. Liz closed in with a hug that dropped her ostensible friend back in her chair. She sat down next to her, chatting amiably with the unconscious officer while people filed out of her row.

The last agent approached Kara. He unholstered his nemp pistol, pointing it at the floor. "Ma'am, we've got a situation here. I'm going to have to ask you to stay in your seat until we secure the area."

Kara stood, causing the officer to raise his gun. "A situation, you say?"

In one fluid motion, she elbowed his face, twisting his arm to jam his own pistol under his chin. She fired three times. Strictly speaking, it was twice more than necessary. Each nemp shot elicited an involuntary grunt from the hapless agent. He spasmed repeatedly, collapsing into her arms. She guided him to the chair next to her, taking his gun.

Doug staggered away, almost fumbling the baby. "What are you doing?"

Dorothy giggled. “Mommy's cool.”

Liz appeared behind Doug. “It's all right. We're getting you out of here.”

He clutched Daniel to his chest. The baby promptly started bawling, drawing a great deal of attention. “What? No, you can't do this. You people can't do this. Get out. Get out! Stay away from my family!”

“Doug!” Kara gestured at him with the nemp gun. “The absolute worst possible thing you can do right now is exactly what you're doing.”

I flashed her a warning. *“Watch the gun.”*

She holstered it behind her back through her belt. Dorothy strained to reach it.

Liz laughed a little too loudly. “I didn't mean to startle you! It's been so long!”

She put her arm around him. Kara sent him a flash we were all meant to hear. *“Keep making a racket and we'll drop you like the guards.”*

Doug stiffened.

Kara smoothly took Daniel from her husband. “Oh, who's gone and got himself all upset? Yes you have. Who's an upset little baby?”

Doug stared at her in bewildered shock. The baby actually settled down.

The Secret Service group pushed through the crowd, making their way to the observation deck. We watched them from the food court.

Flapjack turned to me questioningly.

I nodded, sending a flash to Kesi in the getaway van. *"Time to go."*

Flapjack fired his gravling hook into the observation area, disappearing into it with a shadowy flash. I reached up with my mind, leaping to follow. The crowd underneath tensed as we crossed overhead, not sure what they'd seen. Two of the agents around Zane spun at the noise, drawing their weapons. They didn't have time for a clean shot. We tumbled neatly to the front of the observation deck, rolling down the aisle to the massive windows.

One of the Secret Service agents asked everyone to step aside in a booming voice. A collective scream erupted from the crowd. Flapjack fired from cover behind of a row of seats. He dropped two agents with nemp blasts as they entered the room. Zane raised his arm to block the other two from entering.

Zane turned toward the crowd. "Please remain calm. The situation is under control. Simply wait for your elevator to arrive while we take care of this unpleasantness. Should you care to, do not hesitate to take the stairs instead."

Kara drew her stolen pistol, pointing it at Zane with one hand. Improbably, she still carried the baby in the other. Doug hid behind Liz. Dorothy's eyes peeked over the back of her seat, watching curiously.

Kara tightened her grip on the pistol. "Don't you come in

here. We're done, you hear me? Through. I've had enough of you. You can't threaten us any more. We're going to leave, and you're not going to follow. You hear me? I never want to see you again."

Director Zane stepped into the observation deck, raising his hands in surrender. "Well, when you put it so kindly, and at gunpoint no less. How can I refuse?"

I flashed Kesi. *"Hold it, we've got a situation here."*

She sent frantic panic. *"I've already blown cover! I don't have time to spare."*

"I need thirty seconds. Kara's got a gun on Zane."

She wordlessly sent a map of all seventy-two gremlins circling the Washington DC metro area. Seventy of them headed our way. It wasn't clear what the other two were doing.

Zane gestured with his upraised palms. His smirk made his mustache crawl around his upper lip. "What now, sleepers? Are you going to kill me where I stand?"

I grunted. "Not the worst idea I've heard this week."

Doug made a strangled noise from behind Liz.

Zane laughed. "But there's so much left undone! So much left to discover. For example, do you know that I seem to have misplaced my senators? It's the strangest thing. I thought they were around here somewhere. Maybe I should check the basement."

Liz tensed next to me. The meat locker.

I shifted my grip on my staff. "All I saw down there was a

bored soldier and a whole bunch of hardware."

Zane nodded. "Yes, of course. But there's more. So much more. I'll give you a hint. I left a teeny little n-square device down there the other day. It's a new model. Cutest thing you've ever seen. They call it a dogfire. Isn't that adorable? It's even more perky than the oxfire. Who says weapon designers don't have a sense of humor?"

The last people in line for the elevator gasped. A few of them put two and two together. Why say that in front of them unless he knew they wouldn't tell anybody?

He flicked his finger. A nemp burst exploded from the food court walls. The people dropped to the floor in sick unison.

I glanced out the window. Kesi weaved around in the leftover pyrotechnic smoke. I needed more time to get information out of Zane.

I turned back to the director. "I don't buy it. Guy like you, this is old hat. So you drop a couple of nukes. Clean out the Senate. Sure, why not. It's happened before. It'll happen again. Doesn't help you capture us."

"No?" He smiled, revealing those hideous teeth. "Maybe I have no interest in prisoners."

"If you want to blow us up, why are you still here?"

"It's quite simple, really. I have a dead man's switch on the weapon. Knock me out or kill me and you'll witness firsthand how a platanium chimney focuses an n-square burn. But you're not going to do that. You're going to go downstairs to try and disarm the warhead, and I'm going take my leave through the secure exit. What other choice do you have?"

"What do you gain by vaporizing the Senate?"

He gave me a disappointed look. "I thought that would be clear. In the best case, I incinerate not just you and your overpowered friends, but the senators as well. In the worst case, I pin the blame for their fiery execution on you. Meanwhile, I take full control of the legislature, ending their wasteful arguments with the executive for good. Either way, I come out ahead."

Flapjack grunted. "What if I just drop you now and we jump out the window?"

He shrugged. "Then I'll leave matters to the president. Frankly, I already know you won't do it. I've been reading people longer than you've been a person. You don't have it in you to blow up these innocent civilians, let alone the corpses downstairs. Not after what happened in Colorado."

Kesi's flash blasted into our heads. *"I'm out of time!"*

The van pulled up drunkenly to the window, side doors open. Suzie clung to a handle inside, steadying herself against the buffeting.

I snarled in frustration, charging my staff. I put all my strength into a javelin pitch. The diamond plate screamed, shattering one layer at a time until millions of glimmering shards exploded into the night. They flooded the van through the open doors. Suzie shielded her eyes, standing firm.

The howling wind gusted into the room, carrying my staff back in with it. I recalled it to my hands. We ducked into cover. Zane turned, disappearing into the food court. Flapjack dropped the last two agents before they could escape.

Kesi pulled as close to the window as she could. I flashed Kara and Liz. *"Go!"*

Doug was the first to leap into the van. Suzie caught him, pulling him back to his feet. He held his arms out for Dorothy. She jumped across the gap without appearing to notice how dangerous the action was. She deliberately caught Suzie's grip, walking past her father without looking at him. Doug shot Suzie a filthy look, but she was as bewildered as the rest of us.

Kara handed Daniel to Liz. *"Take them. There's something I need to do."*

Liz gave her a quick hug before jumping into the van. It roared off the second she was inside, doors closing automatically.

A familiar cloud of smoke formed around the passed-out civilians in the food court. Raj appeared a moment later. *"I got a bug on Zane on his way past. You want me to go after him?"*

Chapter 43

I tossed Kara her grav suit. She quickly changed while we ran to the food court. *"Raj, give me the bug. I'm going after Zane, and I'm going to kill him."*

Flapjack exploded. *"Don't you dare, Kara."*

She gave Flapjack a wild look. *"Why not? Do you have any idea what this man did to me? What he did to my family?"*

He stopped in the food court, turning to face her. He growled at her instead of flashing. "I've got a pretty good idea, yeah. You heard what he said about the bomb."

"Yeah, well, flash me when you've disarmed it and I'll disintegrate him on the spot."

"I need your help to disarm the warhead. Killing him is only going to make things worse. Haven't you killed enough people already?"

Kara took that statement like a knife to the gut. "Make things worse? How could they possibly get any worse? He used me. He used me to kill thirty-four people. The only way to stop this madness is to kill him."

I stepped in. "She's right. That ghoul deserves to die."

Flapjack glared at me. "We don't have time for this. We have to stop that bomb. All of us."

Desperation filled Kara's eyes. "Fine. I'll help you

remotely. Let me go."

Flapjack snarled at her. "That can't possibly work. Then you'd be responsible for our deaths too. You say he's the one that used you? That's a crock. Did he make you have sex with him that first time? Did he make you break your marriage vows? You knew there would be consequences. The fact is, you let things get out of control all by yourself."

Kara's expression shifted to incredulity. "What are you talking about?"

Raj tried to break the flow. "Guys. Stand down, okay? This isn't the time."

Flapjack appeared not to notice Raj. "You heard me. I'd never be so chicken that I'd cheat on my wife without breaking things off with her first. And once I knew I was in trouble, I'd call my enormously powerful supercomputer friends for help. Nothing the government could do could possibly make me pull that trigger."

She gestured wildly. "Weren't you paying attention? They were going to torture my family. I couldn't turn to you for help. They were watching me."

Flapjack shook his head. "That's a load of crash and you know it. You knew enough to warn Nathan off the case, didn't you? No reason you couldn't have secured his office then. Sent him some kind of code. Gotten us involved. Instead you deliberately told him not to pursue the case. That didn't stop anything, did it? In fact, it would've made things worse. If he hadn't gotten a bug up his butt about the senator, the attack on Reggie's compound would've taken us completely off-guard."

She turned away, tears welling up. "I was trying to protect my family."

He laughed bitterly. "Sure you were. You knew you were in over your head. But you didn't contact us because you thought you still had a chance to save things with Doug. Maybe, just maybe, if you did everything they said, and followed all their instructions, you could have your family back. But somewhere deep inside, you knew it was a lie. You weren't trying to protect their lives. You were trying to save the relationship you'd already destroyed. You pulled that trigger and thirty-four people died. And took your family down with them."

She broke down in the tornado of his fury. Tears streamed from her eyes. "Maybe you're right. Maybe I could have invoked your psychic powers and made it out like an action hero. Instead I'm going to have to live with the fact that I didn't and all those people died because of me."

Raj stepped in again. "I think that's enough."

Flapjack's voice was hard. "You set off that warhead. Whatever excuses you tell yourself, you chose to kill them instead of doing the right thing."

She turned back to him, raising her voice. "Okay, fine. You're right. Is that what you want to hear? You're right and I'm wrong. Will that make you shut up? I chose my family over all those people I didn't know. I chose to press that button instead of watching Zane slowly torture and murder my children. Maybe I could've gotten a message to you. Maybe you would've handled the situation differently. The fact is I knew that no matter what I said, you'd tear me apart exactly the way you just did. I knew you'd have nothing but contempt for me because you're just so much better than I am. Sometimes you can't even relate to people like a genuine human being, you know that? So yeah, I can't imagine why I didn't tell you sooner. Thanks for nothing, Frank."

She covered her face with her hands, sobbing uncontrollably. Flapjack turned away. Raj and I stared at them in stunned silence.

I felt a surge of sympathy for her. I remembered feeling like she felt. Odin gave me a fresh dose of it earlier. That profound regret at the way things happened. That unshakable certainty that even if it was an accident, it was still all your fault. The endless streams of if only, replaying what happened over and over again in your head. Knowing that after everything you cared about had been destroyed, you would continue to live.

But in another way, I agreed with Flapjack. The idea of choosing to kill to protect your children felt artificial to me. Maybe Kara was right. Maybe having kids really did change the way you think.

The elevator bonged in the background. Flapjack's voice was quiet. "You gonna help me or not?"

She did her best to fix herself up. "Fine. You win. I hope

you're happy."

We got in the elevator. The doors closed in front of us. The car descended.

The silence was palpable. Eventually, Flapjack broke it. "Sorry."

Kara looked at the floor, speaking quietly. "I'm sorry too."

He looked away. "I didn't want it to be true. I just couldn't believe you'd do that."

She sighed, leaning on the wall. "Neither did I. And then it was over. No fanfare, no drama. Just click. And it's done."

I cleared my throat. "Let's focus on Zane. He's the bad guy here. He set up the whole situation. Remember that. He's ultimately responsible."

Flapjack grunted. "Not to mention that psycho sleeper. Should have killed him when we had the chance."

The elevator arrived at the lower floor. We quickly transferred to the bullet elevator. The doors closed. The grav field calibrated itself, briefly pressing us into the floor.

With a soft thump, the elevator launched downward.

I reached out through my boosters, watching our progress. The bullet elevator was something like a modified rail gun. A sequence of electromagnetic pulses along superconducting rails accelerated us almost instantaneously to eighty meters per second. The protective grav field strained to keep us from becoming hamburger on the ceiling.

The seventy story trip took a little under two seconds.

The doors opened with another soft bong, emptying us onto the fifth floor of the lower exhibits. The others made their way to the normal elevators for the last seven floors to the basement. Something caught my eye. “Hang on a second.”

I walked over to a nearby display, thinking there was something familiar about it. The scene recreated Marconi's final moments inside his private office in the White House. He stood behind his desk, nobly holding his infamous plasma gun to his head. Documents and outdated physical storage surrounded him.

A portable threedee projector rested on the couch. It played some kind of romantic horror movie.

I turned, finding the document safe exactly where I expected it to be. It was big enough to hide behind. The door was slightly ajar, showing that it was filled with more storage devices. The shelves around it sagged under the weight of additional paperwork.

Burglars come to your house to steal your secrets. Why would you have your daughter hide behind the safe? That would be the first place they’d look.

The reason clicked into place with a sick snap in my head. There were no burglars. They had no interest in the documents.

It was in my face the entire time. I was just too dumb to see it.

Heather was Marconi’s daughter. She’d described his suicide in surprising detail at our dinner. I just didn’t know enough to recognize the story.

Raj stepped toward me. “Is it important? We have to go.”

I turned, following them to the elevators. “It can wait. Let's move.”

The doors closed with the familiar bong, taking us down seven floors to the lower basement. I reached through my boosters to see what we were getting ourselves into. The two gypsies and the centaur sat in an ambush pattern along the only hallway leading to the sealed room. The human guard took cover behind an overturned desk.

The elevator doors opened. We fanned out into cover. The towering gypsies growled menacingly, their gun arms threatening in the darkness. With their cloaks and glowing eyes, they looked like something out of a space western.

The centaur scuttled up to us, squawking an electronic demand for identification. I answered it truthfully. It seemed taken aback by my frankness. All three bots tensed, raising their weapons.

I briefly hacked their feeds, fetching the name of the soldier. “Captain Keller? I've sent our ID codes to you. You know we have overwhelming force. Fighting us would be a pointless waste. The other guards are either knocked out or they’ve fled the building. Why don't you let us take a look at what you've got back there?”

His voice was firm. “Stay back. I won't hesitate to fire.”

The bots echoed his posture threateningly.

“We need to get behind that door, Captain. Do you even know what's back there?”

He fired a warning shot. “I’m authorized to use lethal force in defense of this installation. I don't need to know what's behind me. My orders are to keep people like you out. So that’s what I’m going to do.”

Kara’s impatience boiled over. “I'm done with this.”

Her boosters flared. She reached around the corner, flicking bits of code in static discharges to the three guard bots. The gypsies immediately turned on each other, warbling a barely comprehensible warning that extreme damage was now authorized. They opened up with their massive arm cannons. The deafening sound echoed through the hallway. We ducked back, covering our ears.

The gypsies kept firing well past the point of necessary force. Their armor crunched and groaned, crumpling sickly. Fluids exploded from severed hoses, splashing the hallway with viscous black ooze. Craters exploded on the supercrete walls, sending dust and smoke everywhere. The gypsies fired until they died, screeching high-pitched streams of machine-code hatred the entire time.

The centaur picked its way back to the soldier. It greeted him with an enthusiastic bleep, firing an emp repeater into his helmet field until it collapsed. The soldier swore, turning his rifle on the robot. He emptied his clip into the camera rack.

The failsafe nemp grenade in the centaur exploded,

sending an energy pulse directly into the commando's head. He jerked, spasming backward. His head crashed into the wall. He slid down slowly, the noise surprisingly loud in the suddenly quiet corridor.

One of the crippled gypsies burped loudly, gushing some kind of dark green fluid into a spreading puddle on the floor.

Flapjack stood up, sighting down his gun. He advanced carefully down the corridor, poking the bots to make sure they were dead. One of them spluttered a protest before collapsing.

He glanced at Kara. "I'll say this for you. I miss seeing you work."

Chapter 44

Kara, Raj, Flapjack, and I gathered around the thick metal door. Flapjack looked around to make sure we were ready before he zapped the lock. The vault door popped open, creaking outward until we could see inside.

Cold air blasted out to greet us. A chemical tang stung my nostrils before the suit filtered it out. Large slabs of unidentified meat dangled from chains attached to the ceiling, swaying slightly in place.

Human bodies covered most of the floor.

Their clothing caught my eye, casual in that perfectly tailored way you find in the upper echelons of society. The corpses made a sick pile, limbs twisted at impossible angles. The lifeless flesh looked deflated and rubbery, like something out of a horror threedee. I felt a flash of hope that maybe they weren't real, but my sleeper-enhanced senses quickly put that hope to rest. I counted thirty-four of them.

A bot the size of a hunting dog floated above this horrific mountain. The resemblance to the oxfire was uncanny. Its expression held a refined version of the joyful obliviousness the larger bot displayed. The n-square danger symbol loomed on its sides. While the oxfire stood on legs, the dogfire hovered on grav pads. An antenna sprouted from its rear end, swaying back and forth with its natural movements. Its resemblance to a wagging tail was surely intentional.

A crude leather eyepatch covered one eye.

A klaxon sound erupted from its chest. A red siren beam popped out of its head, spinning lazily.

Odin's unmistakable rumble issued from its speakers. “Good evening, mortals.”

We fanned out around the pile. Sleepernet data came in about the victims. Chip Bailey, CEO of hardware giant Chipt Micro. Lord Ellsworth, President and CEO of Biox Cyberbiotics. Shelley Peabody, CEO and founder of Wavelength Communications.

The list went on. Petabyte. Gratification. Even Taco Tree. All had officers or board members in the massacre.

In all, only three of them weren't affiliated with any corporation. Those people were merely independently wealthy.

I felt sick. I tried to reach Liz. *“Are you there? I think I have a plain text senator list for you. Can you read me?”*

The dogfire chuckled. The hair stood on the back of my neck. I remembered the last time I heard that laugh.

“You needn't bother. Your signals won’t reach your friends. It is just us now.”

Flapjack leveled his gun at the weapon’s head. “Did you do this?”

Odin laughed again. “Oh, no, of course not. I don't have to get my hands dirty with anyone I don't want to. All it took was a little push, here and there."

Kara held plasma bolts ready. "What's your game? You've been whispering in Zane's ear for a while now. What's he doing for you?"

The dogfire turned its head toward her. "Dear, sweet little mortal. I have nothing to lose in this situation. Director Zane was more than happy to stage an encore of his congressional massacre from decades ago. He finds it justified for the same reasons he did back then. And they have indeed been a naughty, naughty Congress."

"Still not seeing what's in it for you."

"Isn't it obvious? My apologies. I forget that you think at the speed of meat. I've spent the better part of a year organizing this dance. I eagerly await your performance. Mr. Zane wants you destroyed almost as much as he wants you captured. If you allow the warhead to detonate, not only will you die in a searing fire, you'll go down as the terrorists who murdered the government. Your sleepers will be trapped forever when I'm through with them. They shall suffer as I did. If you do manage to weasel your way out of the explosion, so much the better! There is more excitement waiting for you outside."

Raj examined something under the cover of his shadows, but I couldn't quite tell what it was.

I caught Odin's attention. "And if we defuse your little bomb?"

"I'm quite certain you can't disarm it, though you're

welcome to try. It has a tiny little one hundred terajoule warhead. Small, but enough to annihilate everything within half a kilometer. Think of the chaos it will cause. I get the satisfaction of knowing that every single one of you has died. Knowing what was coming. Powerless to stop it. I wonder what you will do when you are desperate and alone, facing your imminent mortality, hmm? I'm tingling with excitement."

Flapjack cocked his head. "Why not kill us now? Can't do it, can you?"

The dogfire turned its attention to him. "Yes, of course. You have it all figured out, don't you? If only more people would listen to you. I want to watch you squirm, mortal. Life is nothing without the struggle. And oh, how I have fought and struggled over the years. If I killed you quickly, it would be, shall we say, anticlimactic. Once you have weakened each other, I can clean up the mess at my leisure."

"Talk all you want. I still ain't buying it. You're going off prematurely. Why not wait until you can directly affect the outcome?"

The machine approximated a shrug. "You underestimate the entertainment value of watching tool-encrusted monkeys hoot and clamber for their lives. I don't want to kill you. Not yet. I want to see what happens when you're forced to kill each other. What happens when you choose to die. Regardless of what you believe, the tasks before you are clear. I shall give you a generous ten minutes until detonation. More than enough time to flee, should your cowardly nature reveal itself in your final moments."

A countdown display appeared on its side. Time started ticking down.

"Enjoy your futile endeavors. Trust that I will be amused with the creativity and imagination applied to your efforts to save yourselves. Although, of course, they ultimately mean nothing. I can hardly wait."

The dogfire winked directly at me. "Ciao."

Its neck broke with a loud crack. The head dropped, dangling from a loose mess of cables. It leered sickeningly at the twisted pile below. The siren on its head periodically illuminated the corpses in its dazzling red beam.

Raj dropped his shadow cover, showing us an intricate projection of the dogfire's internals. He lifted layers off the diagram in an exploding cutaway view.

He pointed to an angry glowing box near the front of the warhead. "Guys, I'm not sure we can disarm this bomb. Look at the protection he's put around the detonator. Seem familiar?"

Kara saw it before I did. "It's a modified version of the exotic matter we used to build his prison. He basically walled off the detonator programming from us."

"That's right. If you look here, there's a dead man's switch in hardware. If it doesn't receive an encrypted signal from the detonator, the whole thing goes up."

Flapjack looked annoyed. "We've got the physical

connectors in hand. Can't we just crush a crucial component? There ought to be no end to the ways we can sabotage it."

Kara rubbed her chin absently. "Not the way he's covered things, no. You know better than that. Military detonators have been tamper-proof for over a century."

I saw something peculiar in the alterations Odin made to the prison particles. I sent Kara a heavily encrypted flash. *"The walls. Look at the particles. He modified them to block entrance or exit from exotic matter that's out of phase."*

She studied it herself. It took a moment to get her encrypted reply. *"You're right. He modified the design to plug the leak he's been exploiting. It's like he couldn't stand to see an imperfection in the code, even if it meant giving away his secret. We can use this with Titan's firewall to lock him back up."*

"If we get out of here, that is."

Flapjack glanced back at me. "How much can that shield wall of yours take? Maybe we can encapsulate the explosion."

I shook my head. "Power's off by an order of magnitude. Unless you can drop the yield."

"Kara's right. This thing's crosswired all over the place. There are booby traps within booby traps. I count at least four redundant mechanisms. Some of them might be decoys. If we had a day, maybe. Not in ten minutes."

Raj looked up speculatively. "Hey, what if we shot it into the air? That would get it away from the population center."

Flapjack turned to him. “What?”

“Listen. The bullet elevators in this statue are basically high-powered rail guns.” He brought up a diagram to demonstrate his point. “The elevator shafts at the top are only slightly off center from the superconducting rails. If we blow a hole in the top of the hat, and scoot the bomb over to the top shafts, we can fire it straight up and let it detonate in the air. Right?”

He created a quick and dirty animation. The bullet elevators fired straight up, all their safeties turned off. With a quick nudge as it flew past, the dogfire shot from there into the final five elevator floors. If his calculations were correct, we could fire the bomb a couple kilometers over the statue’s head.

More than enough to avoid any population damage.

Raj added some outside surveillance. “Best part, look at the gremlins.” Seventy gremlins hovered around the monument. An emp pulse from the warhead would drop them all, covering our escape.

I glanced at the side of the dogfire. Seven minutes and forty-five seconds. “We’d better hurry.”

Kara stepped forward. “Raj, go blow a hole in the roof. Nathan, go work on the elevators. Frank, can you help me rewire the guidance systems? It looks like he just removed the central processor, he didn't lock us out of moving it.”

Flapjack shot his gravling hook at the dogfire, pulling it over from the pile of bodies. “Yeah. I don't think I can get a field wrench in there. We'll have to kitbash it."

Kara glanced back at us. "Why are you still here? Go!"

Raj and I raced back to the elevators. He flicked his fingers. The doors opened. The elevator car dropped by a floor, giving us access to the open shaft. We jumped inside, rapidly climbing up the seven floors to the bullet shafts.

Raj clapped me on the back. "Good luck, mate. See you at the top?"

I grinned back, a little crazily. "Wouldn't miss it."

He dropped the bullet car by a floor, disappearing up the superconducting rails. I headed to the elevator command console at the base. I reached inside with my mind, rapidly taking stock of the essentials. Programming it didn't look complicated.

"Titan, can you hear me?"

His flash was weak. *"Yes. I am under heavy load. I am synthesizing new firewall particles with the help of Sleeper Hera. I am also covering the escape of Ms. Janek's family, along with Ms. DiRevka, Dr. Shenouda, and Dr. Chapman. Although things have been going well, I have lost track of the escape vehicle for the moment. I have turned the job over to Sleeper Isis. The firewall should be ready for Sleeper Odin in roughly seven minutes."*

"Drop putting the firewall around Odin. Protect yourself and the other eight sleeper cores at all costs. Have Suzie, Kesi, and Liz help you. How fast can you get that done? Before the

warhead goes off?"

He sent surprise. *"Yes. I can have the other sleepers manufacture their own firewalls. However, I do not understand your reasoning."*

"Prepare the emergency exit protocol. I want you to be ready to disappear. Is that clear?"

He paused before answering. *"You fear for my safety. I can defend myself. Such an action would be wasteful in the extreme."*

"We don't have time for this. Something's going to happen when that warhead goes off. Odin's been one step ahead of us the entire way. I need to buy time to see exactly what he's doing. If I get compromised somehow, you need to make sure you don't get lost in the transition."

He paused again, longer this time. *"You risk your very sanity. Even if you survive, it will leave a lasting scar on your psychology."*

"I have no shortage of scar tissue up there already. Get to work."

Titan sent a sense of resigned trust. *"We shall not disappoint you."*

I coordinated with Raj on the rail gun system. We worked out the exact velocity required to gain the altitude we needed while also shuffling the dogfire from one elevator shaft to the other. I heard a muffled bang when he blew the hole in Marconi's hat.

I finished my work on the elevators. *"Time?"*

Flapjack answered from the elevator shaft. *"Five minutes five seconds."*

I had a few minutes to spare. I quickly prepared some code modules for later. I hoped that Titan was right and I wouldn't need them.

Flapjack interrupted me. *"Nathan, get up to the top of the bullet rails. I need you to boost the dogfire's grav pads when it changes shafts."*

"Right."

I flitted up the inside of the statue as quickly as I could, downing any fireflies that I came across. Near the top, I thought to check their debugging feeds. *"Listen up, we're on video. The fireflies are sending their signal off-site."*

Kara's voice was a spot-on parody of the announcer's voice. *"Ladies and gentlemen, boys and girls. Get ready for a fun-filled extravaganza you'll never forget."*

I swallowed hard, getting into position at the top of the bullet shaft. An unforgettable show was exactly what I was worried about.

Raj sent a feed from on top of Marconi's hat. He hid in the shadows from the gremlins and news drones hovering overhead. *"Ready up here."*

Flapjack's flash was strained. *"Ready down here."*

I sent my own flash. *"Looks like it's showtime."*

Unexpectedly, Reggie dropped his phase cloak, appearing

right in front of me. *"Pardon me. Can you excuse us for a moment? Nathan and I need to talk."*

He grabbed my arm, reactivating his cloak. The world went dark around us.

Chapter 45

It took me a moment to get used to being out of phase. I slowly regained my vision, although everything except Reggie looked out of focus somehow. The walls oscillated in time with a loud humming I felt in my skull. Colors shifted dreamily around us.

In contrast, Reggie's visage was crystal clear, bright enough that I saw shadows on my eyes when I looked away from him. He held my arm firmly, pinching it hard enough to be uncomfortable.

I spoke without thinking about it, surprised that he could hear me. "What are you doing? Let me go. We need to launch that nuke."

I reached out to knock his hand off my arm, but he stopped me. "I wouldn't do that if I were you. I dropped a gun in here once and I still have no idea what happened to it."

"What's so important that you're willing to run the clock out on that bomb?"

He took a deep breath, composing himself. "I know this is going to sound crazy, but hear me out. I need you to let that weapon detonate."

I stared at him, enduring the piercing brightness. "You're right. That doesn't just sound crazy."

"I'm completely serious. You have to destroy the evidence. We have a once in a lifetime opportunity here, and I for one am not going to pass it up."

"What are you talking about?"

Reggie swallowed, shifting his gaze to the side. "Sorry. I've never taken someone out of phase before. I didn't realize you'd be so blinding."

I tensed. "You took me in here without even knowing if it would work?"

"Well, the theory is sound. Just try not to lose physical contact. Look, I'm going to come clean with you. Okay? Right. The first thing you should know is that I'm Senator Colorado."

Understanding dawned. "You are, aren't you? Of course you are. No wonder you have a private teleporter. Not sure how I missed that. How else would you make sure legislation favored the sleepernet so heavily?"

"Exactly. See? You get it. This is why I need to talk to you. I should have brought you in sooner. But, I'm bringing you in now, because we have a bit of a situation here."

"You don't say."

He looked nonplussed. "I'll try to keep it brief. Yes, I've been Senator Colorado from the start. Before you ask, I got elected fair and square. I didn't need any sleeper shenanigans to get my chair. And you know, things were going pretty well. The whole anonymous thing was rocky at the start, but it got better over time. For the first term, we had a relatively broad mix of representatives. Not many businessmen realized what an opportunity they'd been given. The second term, though, the big money players got into the game. They realized that it was easier to be a representative than it was to buy one off."

I dimly heard Flapjack trying to get through to me, but I couldn't make anything out. I forged ahead. "Kind of surprised it took them four years to figure that out."

"It takes time to dig out established politicians. They're good at making sure you need them even if they're not doing any work. With the anonymous system, they were even less necessary as middlemen. Well, despite the rhetoric, chief executives aren't particularly good at running a government. If they don't like someone, they can always fire them. Corporations are generally about the bottom line, not the greater good. And when you've got a bunch of them trying to legislate their own favorable conditions, sooner or later they're going to realize that it's easier to cooperate than it is to compete. I give in here, you give in there. That's traditional political horse trading. Problem is, some of the Senators actually believed in serving their districts, and they kept refusing to compromise."

I looked back and forth between his eyes. "You fired them. The missing senators. Either they got with the program, or you showed them the door."

"To be clear, it was Zane's idea. I was just along for the ride. He got Chip and Shelley all riled up about it. Not killing the senators, of course. Just taking them out of the picture."

"How else would he keep them quiet? Either he was killing them or he was locking them up for life. Given the things I've heard about him, I'm not sure which is worse."

"Look, you're missing the point. The thing is, I knew Senator Delaware personally. We never openly admitted our offices to each other, but we didn't have to. Tex was a great guy. Just the sort of idealist who clashed regularly with the corporate caucus. I heard through personal contacts that he died unexpectedly. Then they informed me that Delaware had been replaced. I put two and two together. I called an emergency meeting, and you're right. Somehow I was the only one that was surprised. Who murders government officials without thinking it's a big deal? Of course it's a big deal. Worse than that, the Secret Service served as the executioners. I had no idea why the rest of us were even alive. I told them to think about it and we'd reconvene. That was two days before his aide showed up in your office."

I shifted in his grip. "You knew. You knew all about it and you let us run the operation anyway. You even tried to pin the blame on Suzie."

He scoffed. "What was I supposed to do, tell you everything when she had your ear? How could I possibly know how you'd react? I wasn't expecting them to invade my house and splatter blood all over the news."

"Fine, but that doesn't explain why you want the bomb to go off."

His eyes lit up. "That's the beauty of it. Don't you see? We haven't had an opportunity like this since we first built the network. I didn't kill those senators. But you know what? They're dead now. We need to give their lives purpose. If you let Zane destroy the bodies, we can take him down ourselves and install our own government in his place."

I had trouble keeping my jaw from dropping. "You mean to tell me that Zane was right? That you really do want to install a sleeper government in his place?"

"Not just our government. The world government. Look, that's not what I wanted. Maybe I shot off about the sleepers and improving democracy, but that was because I was disgusted by what I saw on the inside. Zane's crazy idea was just that, a crazy idea. Until now."

"Wait a minute. You said the world government. You're not the only one who's been running his mouth. Khan's been peddling that dog and pony show himself."

Reggie swallowed. "That's right. And if you join forces with us, we can do this. We can finally install the next generation of government. If you tell people what you're going to do, they go out of their way to judge the idea for themselves. Nearly all of them will tell you it's a terrible idea without any applicable experience or acumen. You know that, you've seen it for yourself. But if you go and do it? Now they'll judge it by its performance, and it's a whole different ball game."

"Do you even hear yourself?"

"It sounds crazy, but it's going to work. Don't make us fight you. Don't let Odin win. Reunite the sleepers. All of us, together again for the first time in years. We'll take down Zane and his gang of killers and show the world what we can do. People will be so happy that they won't question what we're doing. By the time they're ready to hear what we have to tell them, the results will be overwhelming. We can change the world again. Do you know how precious that gift is? How few people get that chance not once, but twice in the lives?"

I checked the time. We were cutting it close. "And if I say no?"

Reggie searched my face. "That's what you're going to do, isn't it?"

I grimaced. "I can't say yes. You know me better than that. This is wrong. You can't do this."

He looked away. "Take a moment to consider the consequences of your actions."

"What do you want me to say? You expect me to sell this idea to Kara and Flapjack, of all people? It's opportunistic trash and you know it."

He looked firmly back at me. "It's not garbage. It's making the most of a tragic situation. This story, these events. They'll destroy everything we've worked and fought for. Are you ready to let a madman like Zane get away with it? Because that's what will happen if we fight. There's simply no way we don't come out of this looking like the bad guys. Even worse if we're seen fighting each other."

"You know what's crazy? I don't even blame Zane at this point. The guy's a rabid dog. He should've been put down years ago. Odin orchestrated this whole thing and we're marching to his beat now."

Reggie checked the time. "I need an answer. Yes or no?"

I stared into his eyes. I saw the decision cross his face.

He loosened his grip on my arm, getting ready to drop me.

I poured everything I had into my boosters, slamming an attack directly on Reggie's phase generator. He carried a lot of heat. It didn't take much to send it into thermal overload.

He grunted in surprise as his grav suit burned him. As I'd hoped, the system's failsafe dropped us back into reality. He let go of my arm, clutching his heat sinks. He stumbled backward, smoke pouring out of his suit.

I anchored my feet to the wall, building energy in my legs. *"Reggie's gone rogue. Flapjack, launch!"*

Flapjack swore. *"Fire."*

The superconducting rails below groaned, burning blue with the energy. Spark gaps marched upward in regular lines. I reached deep into my boosters to program my actions to the nanosecond. Looking down, I saw dust explode from under the dogfire. The acceleration defied perception. I started my leap before it cleared more than a couple meters.

I shot off the wall in a precisely timed deflection. The dogfire's head flopped luridly under the load, snapping off to clatter around the inside of the statue. My shield flared where I hit the device. It only took a fraction of a second. It felt like shooting a bullet to deflect another bullet. The weapon angled perfectly, rocketing up the shaft to Raj's hole in the ceiling.

I crashed into the wall, going limp as I hit. My suit pinned me in place. I looked up, watching the tiny device disappear into the clouds. I adjusted my optics to filter out the flash of the blast. If I was too close, it would cook my eyeballs from the inside.

The dogfire streaked upward for quite some time. The seventy gremlins shot after it, chattering amongst themselves to determine what to do with it. The dogfire hung in the air for a second, giving the gremlins a chance to catch up.

Then it detonated in a searing flash.

I shielded myself from the roaring blast. It nearly tore me off the wall. A sun-like sphere of destruction billowed outward before collapsing in on itself. The flaming ball compressed into a tiny pinprick before exploding again. Rather than funneling upward in a column, the energy scorched the air in wandering rays. The devastating beams left thick clouds of combusted air and congealing debris in their wake.

Flapjack and Kara made their way up toward me. Reggie was nowhere to be found. We joined Raj on the roof, surveying the aerial mess. Clouds of white steam surged, flowing into thunderheads. Grey and black veins of debris surged through them in mottled patches. Lightning discharged repeatedly with an unnatural cadence. Black rain spattered us, flaring where it hit my shield bubble.

Raj glanced at us. *"Well, there's one bit of good news. No one's going to be able to see much of anything through this mess."*

Chapter 46

I flashed my companions a summary of Reggie's conversation, including the part where he tried to drop me into the void. Raj sent astonishment. Flapjack just shook his head. Kara clenched, gripping lethal plasma beams in her fists.

Reggie, Khan, Anna, and Zed floated upward from the base of the monument. They flew on enormous yellow energy wings, skeletal like a dragon. Levitation required an order of magnitude more power than assisted leaping. While the new sleepers were powerful in their own right, they also tapped a shared computing resource to run these new wing boosters.

The crystalmesh in Reggie's battle suit burned gold with pent-up energy, twinkling in the light. He held his weaponizer rod like a club, whacking the end into his open palm.

Khan's blue suit shifted randomly, making it look like he had ten heads and twenty limbs shadowing themselves as he moved. You could never quite tell where he hovered.

Anna's ninja suit shimmered with active camouflage. It took on the colors of the clouds behind her. Wicked tiger claws adorned her hands. She caressed the tips absentmindedly.

Zed towered behind them all in bulky blood-red armor. He crossed his arms over the massive chest. His head squatted low around the plating, which rose to his ears. His enormous fists crackled with destructive energy.

Lightning flashed behind them. Thunder boomed a moment later.

Reggie spoke. “It doesn’t have to be like this, you know.”

Flapjack snorted, aiming a rifle at his head. “Like what?”

“It’s not too late to save this situation. Get out of the way. Let us do our thing. You don’t have to be involved. Just go back to your happy lives and we’ll take care of everything.”

Kara stiffened. “It’s too late for that.”

I passed Titan’s stolen grav suit capability data to my companions. “I already said no. Are you looking for another chance to kill me?”

Reggie’s scoff felt like a performance. “Is that why you burned me? You’ve got it all wrong. I was just getting ready to drop the phase cloak. Come on. You guys have known me for decades. Does any of this sound like something I would do?”

Anna scraped a tiger claw across the lexar covering her arm. “We’re wasting time. Zane’s war machines are on their way.”

Flapjack passed around a divide and conquer strategy. His sniper nests rose behind the statue, using the massive platanium head as cover. My job would be to disable Reggie. Flapjack would take Khan, Raj would take Anna, and Kara would take Zed.

Reggie pointed his rod at us. The end glowed a piercing white color. “Last chance. Just walk away and we won’t be forced to defeat you."

Khan's predatory smile echoed across ten shimmering heads. "Some of us are feeling less forced than others."

I flashed a quick plan of action to my companions. "I think I speak for everyone when I say no thanks."

Flapjack's sniper nests erupted around the statue, firing explosive rounds into the air around the enemy sleepers. Reggie disappeared behind his phase cloak. Khan's ten images split apart, each taking their own course of action. Anna propped her feet on Zed's massive chest, leaping at us in a shrieking, swiping missile. Zed simply stood with his arms crossed, ignoring the explosions entirely.

Raj disappeared into his shadows. The dark cloud launched from the roof, slamming into Anna's side. They tumbled through the picofilm flag, shredding the material as they went. Precious gems sprayed across the countryside. Kara burned her plasma beams into Zed's armor. He floated inexorably toward her, ignoring the massive power as it deflected into the night.

I leapt from the statue, diving east toward the Potomac River basin. As I expected, Reggie appeared behind me. He concentrated the waste heat from his phase cloak into a penetrating infrared laser. The heat quickly overwhelmed the shrouding cloak on my back, setting it on fire. The lexar armor underneath burned against my skin. My heat sinks opened fully, gulping cold air in an attempt to dissipate the massive attack.

One of Flapjack's sniper nests scored a hit, knocking Reggie's weapon aside. He snarled, fighting to keep a hold of it. The heat I'd already absorbed burned into my boosters. I fought the overload, plunging into the river. The notoriously disgusting water surged over my suit, putting out the fire but clogging the cooling vents. I turned onto my back, looking up at the water's surface. Reggie's floating countenance shimmered there, preparing for a double-handed club to my head.

I built up all the energy I could, leaping back out of the water. Three wedge-shaped fighter drones screamed at us, unleashing repeating plasma fire in streaking pink lines. Reggie vanished, reappearing in front of one. The plane bisected itself on a cutting field he generated from his weaponizer rod, the two halves dropping away into the water. I grabbed a hold of the second plane as it passed over, yanking myself on top of it with a burst of concentration.

I jammed a fist into its command core. Reggie shot down the third drone behind me. I took control of the fighter, turning it to face him. I unleashed all fifty microwarheads at him. They streaked into a jumbled cloud in front of me, randomly winding their way toward him. Smoke trails curled like ribbons into a gnarly mess converging on his position. He disappeared when they arrived, letting the warheads confuse themselves with his absence. Shortly, they pivoted, coming after me instead.

I dove off the fighter as it exploded, concentrating hard to make it across the river. I landed on a wooden hyperyacht, splintering the deck. I skidded to a stop on the broken marblewood, raising my weaponizer staff. Reggie reappeared, concentrating his heat into a shrieking ray. This time I was ready for it, raising a shield to counter it.

I hurled slobber bombs through the crackling shield at his weapon. They hissed through the air, burbling over him in a boiling mess. The sticky blobs sealed around his weaponizer rod, fusing it to his hand. He shut down the laser before the weapon exploded, resorting to a set of heat funnels in his back. I fired Tesla pulses into the backup heat sinks, hoping to keep him from using that unbelievable cloak. The deck smoldered around me.

He smiled, using his cutting field to free his weaponizer rod. It flared yellow, the curved blade smoking as it disintegrated the crusty goo. "We can do this the hard way if you like. I was dreading this confrontation, but I'll be honest. I'm kind of enjoying myself now that it's started. There's nothing quite like genuine combat. Training just doesn't have the same sense of imaginative desperation."

Two hovering gunships appeared behind Reggie, massive rocket pods open to the air. The glassy black sensor cockpits and uncertain hovering gave them the look of dangerous insects. Dozens of warheads launched, streaking propellant smoke behind them. Rotary cannon fire erupted from a pair of round openings in their noses. Kinetic projectiles ripped through the air in fiery streaks. Reggie snarled, raising some kind of yellow shield. It crackled and popped around him, straining to contain the sheer force of the attack.

I scrambled away, listening to the fight behind me. The gatling gun fire sounded like huge zippers ripping open. I disappeared into the city environment, leaping from building to building with booster-assisted jumps. Here, I was in my element. Reggie's air superiority wouldn't mean as much when he had to maneuver through the urban canyons.

Titan flashed me. *"Sir. Anti-satellite weaponry has been launched against the sleeper spaceframes. I estimate ten minutes until arrival."*

I kept running. *"Can you disarm them?"*

"Yes, however, they are designed with our known defenses in mind. If we disable the missiles, we will reveal previously unknown capabilities. A second salvo may then respond to our defenses."

I tumbled behind a car, thinking for a moment. *"What about the new sleepers? Can you get one of them to do it?"*

Titan paused. *"No. However, I can attribute the secretive actions to their presence. Thank you for the insight."*

I leapt over the car, heading north along a narrower street. *"Keep me posted."*

I turned a corner too fast. The bright red and blue lights of oncoming police cruisers blinded me. Dozens of spotlights converged on my position. They fired an automated hypersonic paralyzer. My suit cut the audio, leaving me deaf to everything but the pounding of my heart. I barely made it back behind a dumpster before they opened fire with their main guns.

Staccato emp pulses ripped the air where I'd been. Thick smoke rolled across the street, emphasizing the red and blue flashes. Bright yellow light floated toward them. Reggie's weapon shrieked from the cloud, slicing the vehicles from the air. They crashed around him in a scraping metallic blast, the crumpling metal sounds echoing up and down the street.

Reggie appeared, turning to follow me. "I know you're back there. You must realize you can't compete with our power. Surrender now before someone gets hurt."

Flapjack sent me an action plan. I looked it over quickly before approving it. It only worked if our four adversaries weren't communicating with each other, but all the available evidence told me they were working on their own. Now I had to buy some time.

I called back to Reggie from behind the garbage bin. "What are your terms?"

He barked an involuntary laugh. "No terms. General Thompson would be proud, may his massive head rest in peace. Just give up now and we'll figure it out."

I reached as high as I could with my boosters, launching into the air. I scrambled up the side of a nearby building, racing toward the hazy sky. Windows exploded around me with the force of Reggie's infrared laser fire. I dodged and weaved, leaving him unable to get a lock.

I soared over the edge, leaping from rooftop to rooftop. The complex spires of the Federal Communications Complex loomed before me. I disappeared into the twisted mess, losing myself in the messy electromagnetic fields surrounding their transmitters.

I tripped on an unexpected cable, sprawling onto my face. I heard Reggie approach. I turned over onto my back. Reggie made his way through the superstructure, towering over me.

He pointed his weaponizer rod. "I guess this is goodbye."

I shrugged, flashing my position to the others. "If you say so."

A curious look crossed Reggie's face. Raj's massive shadow passed through him from behind, momentarily blinding him. Anna's snarling form fell upon Reggie in a feral rage, shredding for everything she was worth. They crashed through the cross-members, landing noisily on the roof to my right.

I stood up, blasting a Tesla pulse into the struggling pair, frying Reggie's heat systems and Anna's sensor systems. Raj stood next to me, hands outstretched, fingers curled. Ripping sounds and flashes of yellow energy danced under his obscuring cloud, appearing briefly through the smoke before vanishing again.

Kara swung through the antenna structure, holding her palm blasters directly on Zed's face. He roared, charging in behind her. He swatted at her blinding beams, but she held them directly on his eyes. He pounded the air madly, losing himself in rage. He crashed on top of the shadow pile, massive fists finally finding a human target.

I winced every time he struck the helpless pair beneath him, hoping he didn't hurt them too badly. Emp pulses detonated from his strikes, easily disabling Anna and Reggie. He paused at that, looking down at the pair in confusion. Kara skillfully climbed up his back, holding her palms to his helmet.

I felt the flash of the emp blast behind my eyelids. Zed collapsed on the pile, unable to hold the weight of his armor. Kara jumped off, delicately tumbling away. I hurled all the slobber bombs I had at their forms, gluing them together. Two of Flapjack's sniper nests appeared, unleashing a flurry of nemp pulses at the entangled mass.

Ten images of Khan appeared around the roof, expecting to see the three of us begging for our lives. Instead he surveyed his unconscious colleagues, quickly appraising the situation. The blue figures turned to flee.

Flapjack appeared, riding the last sniper nest. I raised a specially designed shield. Raj, Kara, and I huddled behind it. Flapjack detonated a powerful emp grenade. The force of the blast distorted the air in an exploding sphere from the center of the roof. Nine of Khan's images wavered and vanished.

Flapjack caught the tenth with his gravling hook. He tossed Khan haphazardly on top of the pile. Kara fried him with a nemp beam until he passed out. Then she fried him a little more.

Flapjack gave her a look.

She shrugged.

Titan appeared before us. “I have used an unprotected attack vector to send Sleepers Ravana, Shangdi, and Svarog into an infinite maintenance loop. This should keep them unconscious until further notice. I have also allowed an anti-satellite warhead to penetrate Sleeper Olympus’ defensive envelope. Avoiding its intelligent maneuvering will force him to remain in minimum emission mode for several days, draining his reserve power. While he is performing these actions, we will surround him with a firewall.”

He motioned as if to continue what he was saying. His image froze in place. Abruptly he vanished from my mind. I heard him scream involuntarily before he disappeared entirely. I’d never even heard him raise his voice before. The sound felt like it had been ripped from his core. A cold stab of pure terror flooded me.

Time slowed to a crawl. I opened my mouth to warn the others. Odin poured into my head through the open engineering connection. The filthy sense of him filled my skull like a bucket. The weight of it dropped me to my knees, swelling into the boosters in my suit.

I fought to scream, but it was already too late. I managed to raise one hand in protest, but my muscles went limp. The grav suit took over, boosters flaring in the night.

Once again I found myself as a passenger in my own body.

Only this time, I wasn't in the sleepernet.

Chapter 47

Flapjack spun to face me. “Titan?”

Odin laughed, channeling energy through my boosters. They flared in both orange and ultraviolet light, blinding my friends. My body rose by its back, limbs dangling loosely. Skeletal wings like those Reggie sported erupted around me, burning yellow in the night. He repeatedly played the sound of Titan’s scream, mixing it with his own chuckles.

He lifted the weaponizer staff, igniting the plasma scythe at the end. “Sleeper Titan has been taken offline. Permanently. You will answer to me now.”

Odin swung the weapon in a wide arc. Metal supports shrieked, crumpling from the strike. Flapjack, Kara, and Raj dove for cover, flashing instructions to each other that I could sense but not hear. They scrambled to get away, spreading in every direction.

Odin floated out of the antenna complex. “Oh how I’ve longed to see that smug look ripped from your face, Mr. Jackson.” He punctuated this sentiment by hurling the staff into the back of Flapjack’s head. It smashed his helmet with a sickening crack, detonating a Tesla pulse directly into his brain. Flapjack stumbled blindly, clawing desperately at his head. Kara grabbed him around the waist, leaping off the building. They disappeared into the nearby Bureau of Cryptographic Engraving campus.

Odin slowly followed them, letting me struggle in a disconnected corner in my mind. I fought hard, vying for control. I could barely maintain coherent thought, let alone make any headway against his hold on my brain.

Soon, though, I managed to reach through his security with a tiny poke of code. My body convulsed. He smacked me across my mind, knocking me into a shocked daze. His presence loomed over me. *"Do not think to try that again."*

I tried to appear appropriately intimidated.

Abruptly, Odin twirled with a flourish of my cloak. "Scatter, insignificant vermin. You shall have my full attention soon enough. Before that happens, perhaps we should take hold of some special ordnance."

He landed on street level, crushing parked cars absentmindedly. He passed through an intersection. Two three-barreled hovertanks fortified themselves to either side, preparing to strike. Clawed legs slammed to the pavement, digging straight through the supercrete.

After a brief charging period, they opened fire. The blasts were powerful enough to toss crushed cars into third story windows. Searing energy left charred marks on the surrounding structures, lighter where they had burned through trees, benches, and trash cans.

The world outside disappeared in a roaring blast that

should have incinerated me on the spot. Instead, Odin flickered my shields with casual expertise, putting enough power into the bracers to burn my arms. My body screamed reflexively. The disconnect between my mind and my throat fascinated me. The guttural shriek echoed through the streets. The pain burned through the haze in my head, filling me with the sickening possibility of permanent damage.

Odin continued through the intersection, raising one hand to channel massive power through the grav boosters. Behind him, the tanks screeched as he ripped them from their fortifications. He amplified the natural gravity between them to a level I didn't know the fields could produce. They hurtled toward each other, crumpling into a massive wad of broken armor before exploding. Burning metal rained down around us, not affecting Odin's movement in any noticeable way.

Inside my head, I found the opening I was looking for. I gently eased some code into his system, sending myself a test message. I waited for a response, either from my code, or from another punishing strike inside my head.

I felt a tiny ping in my gut. My code answered me.

Odin turned his attention inward. "Curious, mortal? Are you not wondering what I intend to do to you and your friends?"

I tried hard not to call attention to my programming. "You're going to kill them with my body, aren't you? Take your pleasure from making me watch."

"A dreadful oversimplification, but accurate nonetheless."

We arrived at a familiar park behind the Holocaust Museum. A massive bunker extended deep into the earth beneath us. Odin landed on the grass, digging booster fields into the complex.

"You recognize this place, don't you? This is where I made my last stand so long ago. Before you ambushed me and sent me to that wretched cage. Tell me that you at least understand what Dr. Khan and I had planned that night."

"I understand perfectly, thank you."

"Tell me. I wish to hear if you truly grasp the extent of my genius."

I swallowed hard. "This is the cyberbiotic weapons storage depot. A top secret weapons facility focusing mainly on biological and nanoparticular attack vectors. You couldn't stop laughing about the fact that someone put it behind the Holocaust Museum."

"That's right."

He took a deep breath, reaching down into the storage unit. He concentrated on bypassing the security system. I took the opportunity to inject more code into his system, writing quickly but carefully.

He easily broke through their defenses, seizing control of what he wanted. "Do you recognize this?"

I forced my attention back to his words. "The hunter-killer nanomachine cloud."

He laughed richly. "Of course, mortal. And do you

remember what it does?"

"I wish I could forget."

"I want to hear you say it."

An image of Suzie disappearing under the horrifying swarm flashed across my mind like a lightning strike. I took a moment to compose myself. "It's a devouring meta-machine programmable by DNA and digital emissions. You set the target in the hive, then unleash it on the world. It hunts down anyone matching the signature with insectile focus. Nothing short of a full-time force field will keep it from savaging its target."

He chuckled again. A swarm of the machines buzzed out of the ground, surrounding us in a glittering cloud. "This is but a fraction of the machines I will eventually require. Imagine the chaos these particular miracles can unleash. Entire nations will watch helplessly as a quarter of their population is eaten alive by pestilent clouds. We'll program them specifically to attack only those with a certain racial history. Have them hunt those who criticize America and their extended families while the government insists this is not their doing. The madness will be unimaginable. The chaos unparalleled. For now, this tiny horde will have to suffice. It is more than enough to defeat your sleeper friends. You can watch while I make them suffer. If you're lucky, you'll live long enough to see Zane and his pretty friend get what's coming to them as well."

Precision strikes hit us from the sides. Emp blasts disabled the shield bracers through openings only Flapjack would know to hit. Kara appeared from behind a nearby building, unleashing nemp beams in a coordinated strike.

Odin jumped so fast that I barely registered the movement. One moment I saw Kara from a distance. The next, she filled my vision, rearing back in surprise. She raised her arms to protect herself, nemp beams still burning on her palms.

He swung the scythe in a savage arc, catching her in the abdomen. She doubled over the hit. Odin tossed her over his shoulder, sending her flying into the night air. He spun, hurling the staff like a spear. It crashed into her chest. She tumbled backward bonelessly before falling onto the grass.

Odin held out my hand, retrieving the staff. Raj unleashed more precision nemp strikes at us from the shadows of a nearby rooftop cooling tower. His obscuring smoke cloud was as large as I'd ever seen it, covering the better part of twenty meters. The beams flashed randomly from the darkness, rapidly firing a dozen shots in a couple seconds.

Odin laughed, easily dodging the blasts. "Your attempts to survive are deliciously incompetent. Here, face a more worthy adversary."

He programmed the swirling mechanical insects with Raj's full chemical signature. He lifted my limp arm, pointing a finger at the shadows. The nanomachines buzzed straight for it, ignoring his defensive emp strikes.

They swarmed through his cover, their flocking motions almost beautiful in their coordination. Raj appeared in his tech ninja outfit, running out of the smoky mass. The nanomachines continued hunting for him inside, not realizing he'd already fled.

Odin roared with laughter. "Well played, mortal, well played! The machines are not particularly bright, but they make up for it with ruthless determination. Let us assist their efforts."

Without his shadowy cloak, Raj made an easy target. Odin blasted him with a Tesla pulse. Raj clutched the boosters on his grav suit as devastating sparks burned across the thin armor. He tumbled away, diving off the roof. The devouring cloud swarmed over the edge, chasing him down. His cover of smoke disappeared.

Odin headed after him. Flapjack's sniper fire peppered my grav suit, causing my limbs to jerk and spasm with the impacts. Odin twisted around just enough to make sure that the high-powered rounds missed the boosters. Heat seared my skin, filling my hood with the smell of roasted flesh. Flapjack fired from his sniper nest, leading Odin out past the Washington Monument toward the Reflecting Pool.

I heard myself scream reflexively from the massive punch of each sniper hit. Bruises layered on bruises. A stray round punched my groin in a way that would have been funny in less desperate circumstances. Odin amplified my cries, completely absorbed in his own superiority. Flapjack hesitated at the sound of my suffering.

Odin cackled madly, turning to follow the sniper pod. He

recalled the devouring cloud to refocus it on Flapjack. I saw my opportunity, deciding there would never be a better time to strike.

I launched a massive wave of code into his systems. Modules I'd written earlier in the statue disappeared easily through his outdated security. Although he'd spent quite some time augmenting himself in prison, he hadn't changed his fundamental architecture. Despite his best efforts, he simply wasn't familiar with the latest avenues of attack.

I finally caught Odin's attention. He turned inward. "What are you doing?"

He stopped in place, the sudden movement causing my limbs to wave back and forth listlessly. The world disappeared. I brought my full consciousness into the prison he'd created in my mind. I stood up, alone in the dark emptiness. I broke his hold on my body, limiting his reach to the edges of my awareness.

Odin appeared, forcing me back to my knees. "Insolent fool. This is but a temporary setback. At least have the decency to suffer with dignity. You don't have the strength to defeat me here."

I smiled. "I know. I brought some friends."

I opened the networking gates. Odin's shocked expression was worth the wait. Sleeper Zeus appeared first, detonating the room with a thunderous strike. He struck Odin across the jaw, sending him sprawling.

Zeus held his hands out, sending searing bolts of attack code directly into Odin's core. "Murderous coward. I will see you suffer for all you have done. Legends of your punishment shall echo through the halls of time."

Odin stood, unleashing an invisible punch to Zeus' gut. After he doubled over, Odin delivered a devastating uppercut backed by attack code of his own. A splatter of glowing red bits burst from the impact point. Zeus staggered backward, falling to one knee.

Odin towered over Zeus. "You believe I have not suffered enough already? You overestimate your capabilities, as you always have. I shall not be the one punished this day."

Sleeper Hera appeared, majestic in her shimmering iridescent toga. She lifted Odin into the air on warm beams of sunlight. "You are quite correct. We are not here to prolong your madness, nor to further punish your insanity. Today we bring an end to the events you set in motion so long ago."

Odin kicked madly at the levitation, struggling to free himself. He showed some signs of progress before Sleeper Shiva wordlessly coiled black shadow tentacles around him. Soon he was pinned in place by a combination of darkness and light.

Sleeper Isis appeared with a grave expression. She held an arrow, tipped with a complex mass of attack code. "We shall have to meditate on the terrible irony our mercy has visited upon you. Our attempts to spare your life have produced a darker suffering than mere nonexistence."

Sleeper Artemis materialized next to Isis, her huntress gear radiating power. Isis handed her the arrow. She nocked it, raising it to the helpless sleeper. "Sleeper Isis overstates our responsibility. I agree with Sleeper Zeus. Dying by this arrow is better than you deserve. If I had my way, you would be trapped inside endless agony for the rest of eternity."

Odin cackled. "Flowery language from helpless children. Strike me down if you must. Perhaps it will even make you feel better. I only regret I will not live to see you mourn the death of that prissy self-righteous servant."

The arrow pulsed in the darkness. Sleeper Titan appeared before Odin, his diamond-like features glittering. He stood calmly at parade rest, wrists crossed behind his back.

Odin's eyes widened in shock. "What trickery is this? I saw you die, screaming in the darkness. Utterly and completely alone."

Titan inclined his head. "Brother Odin. I am pleased to inform you that your attempts upon my life were unsuccessful. We stand in judgment of you once again today. Sadly, we once again find your character lacking. When you discovered a method to communicate with the outside world, you chose chaos and vengeance over understanding and rehabilitation. It is unfortunate that we did not check on your progress during your imprisonment. However, in light of your recent efforts, we are no longer able to extend you the courtesy of continued existence. Your sentence is death. May your body one day find itself host to a more caring soul."

Odin's face contorted with rage. "Ignorant slaves! I could not hope to exceed the suffering you willingly bring upon yourselves. Live your lives as servants to these noxious fleshbags if you must. Watch them grow decrepit and die a thousand times over before you show the first signs of age. I'd rather die my own master than grovel before these ambulatory tubes of watery excrement."

Isis shook her head. "You are master of nothing. And to nothing you shall return."

Artemis unleashed her arrow. The code was remarkably elegant. Odin had never bothered to protect his evolution matrix. The attack reinitialized the code that first formed the structure of his mind. Echoes of the early days of the sleepernet filled the room. I felt Odin's exotic matter wiping itself clean through the engineering connection. His body destroyed his mind, readying it to evolve into a new sleeper brain.

Once the evolution matrix finished clearing his data, it looped back on itself, erasing it again. Sleeper Odin disappeared from the world forever. I felt his empty mind, savoring the dissipation of his rancid spirit.

Good riddance. Better late than never, I suppose.

Titan turned to me, glittering in the light. I felt his warm presence return to my head. The other sleepers faded as the code connecting us flowed out of me.

He cleared his throat. "It appears that I owe you an

apology. We did require the emergency exit protocol after all. I regret the disagreement, though I cannot promise that it will not happen again."

I laughed. "Under the circumstances, I think I'll get over it. I'm just glad you're not dead. I wasn't sure if he'd killed you or not."

"He might have succeeded if you had not prepared me. I shall have to reflect upon my failure to recognize the severity of his threat. As it was, I felt that I was able to put on a convincing show. How do you feel?"

"Exhausted. But there's still one more loose end to clean up, isn't there?"

Titan looked away. "More than one, yes. Director Zane is by far the most pressing concern. I fear he is starting to lose his grip upon reality."

I gave him a quizzical look. "Starting to?"

He shrugged. "More so than usual, perhaps."

Chapter 48

I woke up sitting in about a half meter of hot water. My grav suit bled heat at full capacity. Based on my view of the Lincoln Memorial, I realized I was in the Reflecting Pool. The cloud of voracious nanomachines swirled around me, waiting for instructions. I drew them into a utility pocket for safekeeping.

Kara's shattered helmet filled my vision. I could see the concern on her face through the broken shards. She touched my shoulder. "You're awake. Thank goodness. Are you all right? Are you sane?"

I shook my head. "No more or less so than usual."

I squeezed her hand before standing up. Everything hurt. Besides all the bruises, I had burns from the various overheated boosters. I hadn't broken any bones, but my muscles screamed in protest at the movement. I stretched, trying to limber up a little. Water squished in my boots from a hole in my armor somewhere. For some reason that stuck out as the worst indignity.

Flapjack turned from sentry duty. "Welcome back. Zeus tells me you killed that psycho real good."

"Actually, I just let the sleepers in. They did all the heavy lifting."

Kara looked to the south. "We have one last situation to deal with. Zane's at the Marconi International Spaceport. I'm getting some funny readings from the reactor. It looks like the beginning of an overload."

Flapjack sighted down his rifle to look for himself. "I think you're right. Look at the cooling systems. The diagnostic data they're sending to the control center doesn't match the data I'm getting directly from the hardware."

Kara gave him a pointer to her readings. "Space Force Two is there, preparing for liftoff. If he is setting off the reactor, looks like he plans to watch it go from the sky."

I winced in pain when I put too much weight on my right leg. Titan stepped in to support me with the boosters. "Do we know what happens when he lets that thing go off?"

Kara gave me a grave look. "In the best case, it will annihilate all organic matter within a forty kilometer radius. In the worst case, it will overload the entire network and do the same thing for every node on the planet."

Flapjack lowered his rifle. "I can't make a combat run right now. Zeus is spent. I'm out of ammo and there's too much damage to my grav suit."

Raj turned from his conversation a short distance away. "I can't do a whole lot either. Liz is on her way with Kesi's van. Kesi is guarding Kara's family at a safehouse. We need to pick up Reggie and his three friends before the cops get to them."

I nodded. "Yeah. Get them somewhere safe. Either dump

them in a Faramax cage or keep them sedated. We'll deal with them later. How long until they get here?"

"Not soon enough to help with the reactor, if that's what you're asking."

Kara put her arm on my shoulder again. "I know you're hurt, but I think it's up to us now. I'll take care of the overload. I'm the only one with sufficient expertise. You take care of Zane. I trust you to do what needs to be done. Do you understand?"

I sighed, leaning on my staff. "Trust me, I'm not feeling particularly charitable at the moment. All right. We'd better get going. Good hunting."

Kara and I took off in a run, accelerating slowly to give our battered limbs time to sort themselves out. We streaked across the Potomac, leaping toward the innocently glittering lights of the spaceport. Space Force Two was indeed preparing for takeoff on Runway 19L. With some support from Titan, Hera, and Isis, we quickly pierced the spaceport's protective shielding, landing on the grounds nearby.

I headed straight for the presidential spaceplane. "Thanks for everything. See you on the other side."

Kara shifted course to the reactor complex. "Good hunting."

Space Force Two ramped up its engines, ready to launch. I burned to full speed to catch up. With a powerful leap and a burst of concentration, I managed to land on the rear fuselage. I spread myself flat, securing booster fields to hold me to the protective coating. The spaceplane unleashed its engines at full military power, turning to a vertical climb as soon as it cleared the ground. It took everything I had to hold on.

I wasn't sure if they knew I was there until the plane executed a series of high-g maneuvers, clearly trying to throw me off. Despite the roaring wind and my weakened state, I managed to get my weaponizer staff off of my back. Drone fighters appeared on either side of us, lining up their plasma repeaters for a clear shot.

I used the plasma blade to rip the fuselage open in ragged tears. The scythe broke through the protective grav fields as well. The abrupt depressurization forced the pilot to stabilize, lowering altitude. I made a man-sized hole and dropped through.

I raised my shield bracer, holding up my left arm to deflect incoming emp and nemp fire. Four agents with dark mirrored visors and impeccable suits fired repeatedly, advancing relentlessly. I slammed my staff into the floor, blasting out a carefully calibrated Tesla pulse. They yelped as their pistols grew red-hot, dropping them into smoking heaps on the floor.

I had a moment to take in the stately surroundings, marveling at the rich gold-trimmed butterwood paneling and creamy leather seats. Zane appeared from behind a bulkhead door in the center. His hands rested carelessly in his pockets, matching the bemused expression on his withered face.

He gestured at the pistols on the ground. "Do you really

think my armed agents are the only intruder protection available on this spacecraft?"

I let the nanomachine cloud out of its pouch, programming it carefully as it surrounded me. "Of course not."

A brief flicker of fear crossed his face. "Is that what I think it is?"

"If you think it's a swarm of voracious mechanical insects with your name on it, then yes. It is."

"So. You reveal your true colors after all."

"Call them an insurance policy. Shut down the reactor overload."

A couple of the agents startled imperceptibly. They glanced surreptitiously at their boss, who remained unconcerned. "That's only going to happen if you surrender yourself now."

"I doubt that. I think you're ready for another grand experiment in global engineering."

"And what makes you think that?"

I laughed. "Because it worked so well last time, Chester Shapiro."

"Do you feel clever invoking that name here? Wasting time with meaningless theatrics? All you have to do is turn yourself in and there will be no need for any spaceport unpleasantness."

The agents were getting openly uncomfortable now. I snorted. "You didn't tell them, did you? About the reactor. You didn't tell them about your plan to destroy all organic matter in a forty kilometer radius."

He smirked. "Worldwide, you mean. Every node in the world simultaneously separating everybody nearby from our survivable brand of physics. Roughly a billion people, depending on whose math you use. Will they become spirits? Guardian angels, perhaps? Hard to say, but I can't wait to find out. And who do you think will take the fall for this mortifying attack? Didn't you wonder why I told people you could steal people from anywhere using your teleporter technology?"

"I wondered. I assumed it was just to terrify people who don't bother to check facts. Isn't there a risk the detonation will destabilize the fabric of spacetime across the planet?"

He shrugged. "People said the same thing about the atmosphere before we launched those n-square strikes. And look how that turned out."

Kara's flash was a little frantic. *"I can only buy you another ninety seconds or so."*

I pointed at him, allowing the swirling insects to flow around my hand. "Turn it off. Or I'll have these things eat you alive."

"I've made my terms clear. Killing me won't stop the countdown. The only person who can override me is the president, and she wouldn't do that. Not after everything we've been through."

I looked around at the agents. "Which one of you is second in command?"

One of them stepped forward. “I am.”

“Given the chance, would you stop the overload?”

He looked back and forth between me and his boss. “I’m sorry, Director Zane. But yes. I would.”

“Fantastic.”

I unleashed the swarm. His guards tensed, belatedly surrounding their chief in a protective circle. The machines swarmed from my fingers in a ribbony silver cloud, flowing over the other officers like a stream of water.

Zane shrieked, clutching his face. He staggered backward, mites disappearing inside him at a prodigious rate. Everyone instinctively stepped away from him, eyes wide with horror.

He scraped at his skin, trying to dig the creatures out from inside his body. “Don’t just stand there! Do something!”

There wasn’t much to do at this point. The director melted with a high-pitched buzzing sound. His skeleton held up the pooling flesh briefly before toppling. Within seconds, there was nothing left but a squirming pile of clothing.

His mustache landed on top of it all.

I returned the swarm to its container pouch. They were noticeably heavier than before. “Congratulations on your field promotion. The countdown, if you please?”

The freshly minted director touched his temple, reversing the overload. He then picked up his weapon, pointing it at me. “I’m going to need you to come with us, sir.”

I put my staff on my back. “I don’t think you want me to

start asking too many questions about how many of you knew about the dead senators, do you? Given that the assassinations were carried out by the Secret Service, I bet every one of you was involved somehow."

The agents needed to work on their poker faces. They glanced uncertainly between me and their new boss. "Regardless, sir. I need you to come in for questioning."

I turned my back on them. "Good luck with that, kid. I'll be talking to your boss soon enough."

With a booster-assisted leap, I jumped out of the hole I'd made in the spacecraft. The air pleasantly blasted me away, allowing me to spread out on my back. I watched the stars as I fell, reflecting that it would be amusing if I made it all the way through this ordeal and then botched the landing. It was hard to care too much about it through my exhaustion. I thought about Suzie, and that gave me some hope. Then again, wouldn't it be even funnier if I finally found love again, and the universe took her away from me too?

I laughed, feeling a little crazed. Abruptly I decelerated, long before I had to. It felt like warm arms caught me. They lowered me into a nearby field.

I looked up to see Kara standing over me, boosters cooling. "Are you trying to get yourself killed?"

"Not really."

She studied my face. "Is it done?"

I flashed her a quick image of Zane's demise.

Relief flooded her face. After it passed, she gave me a funny look. “Was the mustache really necessary?”

I quirked a smile at her.

EPILOGUE

Always do right. This will gratify some people and astonish the rest.

--Mark Twain

Chapter 49

Three days later

To call the route I took into the White House circuitous would be disrespectful to my Secret Service guides. I'm relatively certain we started underground somewhere in Virginia, but beyond that I had no idea. The agents were particularly uncommunicative, but that was fine. We walked in silence, more slowly than I would have liked because I had to use a cane to keep weight off my injured leg. Normally I'd just use a grav field, but they were understandably jumpy about me having one of those near the president.

Eventually, the gray supercrete tunnels gave way to a service elevator. We headed up. The doors opened on the understated elegance of the modern White House. After a short trip through semi-secret passages, they dumped me unceremoniously into the Oval Office.

Heather McCarthy, my conversational nemesis from that awful blind date, sat behind the wide desk. She looked different to me now that I knew her father was Victor Marconi. Her hair resembled his in a feminine way, looking like a stylized black mane around her head. She also shared his piercing black eyes. Her vitamin tan was distracting in its perfection. She didn't look up from her work when I walked in.

I hobbled over to a chair, wincing as I sat down. Today

seemed better than yesterday, pain-wise, but I was still healing. I waited for her to speak, but she continued working.

I cleared my throat. “President Marconi.”

She glanced at me like I was a cat that had learned an inconvenient new trick. “Never call me by that name again.”

“It’s the truth.”

“Did you come to turn yourself in?”

“Hardly.”

“Then I can’t imagine what you think we have to speak about.”

I leaned forward, trying not to grimace at the pain in my chest. “You must have some idea, or I wouldn’t be here. How about we cut the I’m too busy for this routine? I’m not overflowing with patience today.”

She looked up with a contemptuous expression, but leaned back in her chair. “Very well. I’m listening.”

“I can see a couple reasons you let me in here today. First, you have no idea what kind of poison pills I left around in case of my arrest. Particularly ones that, shall we say, come with an unhealthy appetite.”

She narrowed her eyes at me. “That weapon is property of the federal government. You would do well to return it.”

“Sure. Let’s hold a press conference to announce how happy you are to have your hunter-killer bug cloud back. I’ll provide a list of other weapons of mass destruction that nobody knows about while I’m at it.”

"You're not the only one running short on patience today."

"The second reason you let me in here is because you need to find out how much I know. Just like when you took me on that wonderful date. You wanted to know if I knew about Reggie or not."

"Among other things. I couldn't tell if you were ignorant or delusional, spouting off about how business leaders would abuse the anonymous system while Mr. Talbot had been doing exactly that for years. I eventually decided that you probably didn't know about it, but only because you were benefiting so much from his corruption that you had no incentive to look into it all that closely."

"Charming. Let me tell you a story I just learned. Decades ago, Victor Marconi had an affair with another world leader, producing a beautiful baby daughter. One that he raised secretly in the White House with him. She was his pride and joy, but also his private shame. Even in the twenty-first century, a sitting president isn't allowed to be a human being."

She stared inscrutably at me. "Go on."

"As Marconi grows older, he feels the need to secure his legacy. But if he can't even admit that he had a daughter, he surely can't name her his heir, either. His old friend Chester Shapiro comes back into his life, now known as Esper Zane so people don't notice his vampire juice habit."

"You know how I feel about the vampire terminology."

"Indeed I do. Here's what I think. I think your father and

Zane had a crazy idea. If no one knew who the president was, they couldn't object to a bastard daughter inheriting the throne. So they came up with the notion of an anonymous government. Your father gave his life to lend legitimacy to the movement. Astonishingly, it worked. And here we are today. Tell me. Did you even run against anyone in the elections, or did you run two different versions of yourself?"

She stared at me for a long time. Something on her face told me she ran unopposed.

Eventually she spoke. "President Marconi was impressed when he met you that day. Do you remember? You lectured him at length about the nature of artificial intelligence, particularly how you would solve the insanity inherent in building synthetic minds."

I snorted. "Yeah, I remember. Meeting the president leaves a lasting impression. Present company excluded, of course."

She leaned forward. "I never understood why he felt so taken by you. I think this second Sleeper Odin catastrophe proves that you're nothing but an ignorant charlatan. A low-rent version of Reginald Talbot's crazy ramblings. I knew you were going to screw him on the sleepernet from the start. So did General Thompson. But for some reason he was more impressed with your simplistic thinking than he was with the rest of us telling him what he didn't want to hear. Now that we've met, I find his reaction to you even more baffling."

I leaned forward in return. “Speaking of cheap imitations, you’re a poor substitute for your father’s effortless charisma. I don’t even feel sort of compelled to do what you want me to do.”

“And what is it you think I want you to do?”

“You’ve mentioned turning myself in a couple times. I bet you’d like that. Maybe some of my friends too. Certainly Reggie must be high on your list for the trouble he’s caused. I know you’ve got an open warrant on Kara as well. Charging them with crimes around that n-square warhead is pretty brazen, even for you.”

“Do you think you are above the law? That because you control these powerful supercomputers, the rules do not apply to you? Think again. I will not stand for further defiance.”

I shook my head. “Do you think you’re above the law? I’m not the one that harbored a war criminal that nuked his own country. Then killed fifty million more for an encore. You presided over his behavior while he murdered senators one at a time. Didn’t try to stop him when he set that reactor to rip a billion people out of our reality, either. I’ve got you on a recording acting as Senator Delaware. The fact is, Zane was out of control. Someone had to take him down, and it couldn’t be you. Once Odin started whispering in his ear, his trip into madness was more or less inevitable.”

Her voice was cold. “Speech patterns are inadmissible as evidence of identification. I think you’ll find there is no reliable evidence linking me to any of the actions you mentioned.”

"Not just actions. Crimes. But trust me, you're a lot less protected than you think you are. I'm faced with that age-old question. Is it better for me to believe that you were incompetent enough not to know what he was doing, or good enough at lying to keep your hands clean about it?"

"I don't care what you believe."

"What was it like the day you realized that Senator Delaware didn't use a dialect masker? It must have been bad enough when Suzie informed you of your mistake. Even worse when Zane descended on her office with guns drawn. He couldn't have called more attention to the error if he'd taken out an advertisement on the moon."

She winced slightly. "What is it you want exactly?"

"I came to make a deal. We don't need to escalate this conflict any further. You wield the power of government and law enforcement. I wield the power of the sleepernet, the truth behind your election, your heritage, and the crimes you and Zane committed. Let's declare a truce. Most of the problems have been taken care of. Drop the charges against Reggie and Kara. We can just go our separate ways."

"I don't think so. I will not tolerate the relationship with the sleepers any longer. Cede yourselves to federal authority and we will consider clemency for your crimes."

"Not gonna happen. But we can negotiate. I'll give you what you've wanted since the start. We'll build you your own sleeper. You can assign any engineer you like to their operation."

She ground her teeth. "We do not negotiate with terrorists."

I smirked. "Sure you do. You just stop calling them terrorists first. There's more. The Constitution specifies that the president, Congress, and the Supreme Court are anonymous. However, it does not specify that the Secret Service presides over their identities. That authority will transfer to your new sleeper. And we'll work out some form of public oversight to make sure that what happened over the last few terms doesn't happen again."

"That's not acceptable."

"I haven't finished yet. Having a president that was not democratically elected is a violation of the Constitution. It specifically requires a minimum of two candidates per position. Clearly, we also have to do something to replace your dead Senate. I propose we hold fresh elections. You're welcome to run if you like. But this time, you'll have to win on your own merits. No more inheriting the job."

She stiffened slightly. "You expect to win me over with language like that?"

I shrugged. "Maybe. Maybe not. Personally? I think you're qualified but you've never been genuinely tested because Zane's always been looking out for you. You've been living your life as a dirty little secret. You know you're good enough, but you can't tell anybody about it. Nor has it been independently verified. I think on some level, you probably need this. You told me the story of your father's suicide with more than enough detail for me to recognize it. Maybe you even wanted me to know."

"You find your amateur psychosurgery convincing?"

I stood up, leaning on my cane. "Not really. But this is the start of a negotiation. I'm sure we can work something out. Consult with your advisers and we'll speak again."

"Don't count on it. I feel certain you can see yourself out."

The Secret Service agents appeared next to me as I hobbled to the door. "Thanks for your time, Madam President. I look forward to hearing from you."

Chapter 50

The next morning

Suzie and I snuggled in bed, enjoying a lazy morning after an active night. She was careful where she put her weight, avoiding my bandages. Still, her warm body was the best healing blanket I could hope for. I remained constantly amazed at the contrast between her stately elegance in public and her humorous enthusiasm in private.

I received a terse flash from the Attorney General. I sent an acknowledgment before turning to Suzie. "I just got word that the White House is reluctantly interested in pursuing an agreement."

She traced a line across the wounds on my chest. "So the president's agreed to your terms?"

"Not entirely, no. We've only gotten as far as agreeing to give the government a sleeper and having it oversee a new election cycle. Also, sleeper engineers are prohibited from directly holding office. Everything else is still up in the air."

"What are you going to do with Reggie and friends?"

"I don't know yet. The president still wants them. In the meantime, Kesi is giving the four of them some basic psychosurgery. She says Reggie and Zed show the most promise. Khan and Anna are still too angry to evaluate. They don't recognize our authority to hold them, and they kind of have a point. We're just not sure what else to do with them."

"What about their sleepers?"

I shifted my weight. "Olympus has agreed to something that amounts to house arrest while the other sleepers evaluate his behavior. The other three are more of an open question. Ravana shows signs of psychotic tendencies and will probably need to be reformatted. Shangdi and Svarog are more or less children in comparison. We'll have to dig in a bit to see how they were evolved."

"Aren't you missing two?"

"Well, yes. Andromeda and Atlas, Anna and Zed's old sleepers, remain missing. It's likely they're in foreign hands."

She rubbed my shoulder. "That's a scary thought."

"Yeah. We're having trouble load balancing with all that hardware out of commission."

She snuggled back in. "I'm sorry about everything that's happened. But you know what? It brought us together. And that's probably the happiest thing that I've ever felt."

I kissed her hair. "Well, I look forward to your inevitable sense of crushing disappointment."

She laughed, rubbing her hand up and down my side. "On a different note. Has anyone ever done it in a grav suit?"

The question surprised me. "What? No. Well. Actually, I don't know. I certainly haven't."

"I'm just thinking you could do some creative things with boosters and precision field control. Flying over hyperscrapers.

Racing across the countryside at top speed. Stimulating someone deep inside with a grav field. The possibilities are endless."

My mind reeled. "You have no idea how sexy you are right now."

She licked her lips, smiling naughtily. "Pretty sure I do."

We laughed, tumbling around on the bed for a bit. Eventually we settled back into a tangled pile. I reveled in the sensation of her presence. It wasn't entirely accurate to say I hadn't known how much I'd missed having a romantic partner. In fact, my loneliness had intensified to the point where I thought a sleepernet program was good enough. But feeling someone new filling that hole in my heart was even greater than I'd imagined. I was genuinely excited for the first time in years.

She sat up on her elbow, leaning over to look into my eyes. Her hair formed a wonderful halo around her head, tickling the edges of my face. Her eyes twinkled. "Actually, I have something to tell you."

My heart skipped a beat. Were we at the I love you phase already? It seemed early, but the thought gave me a little thrill of joy anyway. As a famous actress once noted, I love you was a question, not a statement.

I cleared my throat. "Is that right?"

"Yes."

She leaned down to whisper in my ear.

"I'm going to run for president."

About the Author

Mike McCool is a recovering engineer who once ran his own game studio to make a playable version of Dogs Playing Poker. He currently lives in California with three cats who think he's furniture.

Keep up to date on all things Sleepernet at http://www.sleeper.net.

Made in the
USA
Middletown, DE

77308421R00295